A Young Princess

Steve A. Hall

ISBN: 978-0-6151-7107-4

Contents

For all those who don't believe that a single moment in time can change your life forever.

Section 1

One Majestic Night

Two people so special in so many ways
A princess to be and a peasant who slaved
Two people so different in so many ways
Their lives crossed paths at this majestic place

Chapter One:

There Was a Poor Family

There was a poor family who lived in a village, surviving each day on food scraps they salvaged. Those words summarize all too well the everyday life of Martin and Shaylene, parents of two young sons, Stefan and Lolek. The family was as poor as could be, but it mattered not, because they were wealthy in love and rich in compassion. They lived in a shabbily built mud flat home, on one of the outlying streets of the village of Norwalk, located in the heart of the land called Astoria. Although he never voiced it, Martin appreciated the fact that he lived on an outlying street, instead of living closer to the village center. Sure, Martin had to walk farther in the cold mornings to get to the landowner's estate where he worked. But living here at the outskirts of the village, Martin felt a measure of safety for his family, and particularly, for his two young boys. Especially in view of the recent reports of kidnapping which were circulating throughout the land. As he sat next to his beloved wife Shaylene on one of the simple benches inside their home this evening, Martin reflected back on the whirlwind of the past two years.

It was about that long ago when their firstborn son Stefan came into the world. And now that blond haired boy was walking, saying a few words, and even pretending to be a worker like his father. It seemed like Stefan could never get enough of playing with his digging tools, which were actually a couple of small sticks that Martin carved to look like the real thing. Martin was sure his oldest son would grow up and work for one of the local landowners, working long days under the sun cultivating ground, just as Martin did. And then there was Martin's youngest son Lolek, who turned a year old only a few days ago. Despite Lolek's very young age, Martin thought he could see right into the boy's heart and mind, as he displayed such a playful personality. Lolek seemed to especially gravitate towards music and sounds, because whenever his mother played her wooden flute at night, the boy was mesmerized. As he did regularly, on this night Lolek fell asleep listening to the soft sounds of the flute. And now he was lost in his dreams, resting peacefully in the basket on a table near where Martin and Shaylene were sitting. Lolek was sick recently with Arrowweed Fever, but seemed to be getting better by the day.

The older boy turned out to be a light sleeper, so his basket was located in the back room of the mud flat home where it was quieter. That was really important in the early morning when Martin would get up and leave for work before the crack of dawn, to make sure Stefan did not wake up at the same time. Both boys wore special hand made necklaces holding pendants cut out of brasta wood, which was imported from lands far away. The necklaces were very rare, extraordinary presents from the landowner Martin worked for, one of the few kind things which happened to him over the years. As Martin was thinking about these things and with Shaylene resting her head of long black hair on his right shoulder, Martin began to drift off to sleep.

Suddenly there was a pounding at the front door and Martin awoke with a startle. "Open up in there! Open up in there!" a growling voice shouted from outside of their home. Martin glanced from the door back to Shaylene. He saw her instinctively leap up, hurrying off into the back room where Stefan was sleeping. The pounding and shouting started once again, but this time there were several voices. Martin looked at the door once again, and he observed what appeared to be the reflected light of torches coming through the bottom crack of the wooden door frame. "This is your last chance. Either open up or suffer the consequences!" the voice outside demanded. Martin stood up and it dawned on him that he didn't have any weapons in the house with which he could defend himself or his family. Martin was a man of peace, not of fighting. Slowly fear gripped him by the throat.

He was shaking so much he could barely get the words out of his mouth, "What do you want with us? Leave us alone." At that exact moment the door came crashing in from the top and slammed onto the mud floor with a thump. Three large men entered the home, two of them with torches and all three of them with swords. The commotion woke up the youngest boy Lolek and caused dust and debris to fly into Martin's face as he fell backwards onto the ground. With the sound of Lolek's crying coming from behind him, Martin looked up at the three men who had come into his house. They were wearing dark clothing and their faces appeared to be covered with some type of mud or charcoal coating. The largest man, who was holding only a torch, moved forward a couple of steps in front of the other two. He walked with a noticeable limp and was the one who spoke.

"You know why we are here. You didn't pay your dues last month to the Order of Rebels. Every citizen in this disputed territory is required to pay two silver coins per month to receive our protection. Those who don't pay up suffer the gravest of consequences, as you are about to."

"Please give me a chance to explain," pleaded a clearly frightened and intimidated Martin. "I needed to use the money to buy some medicine because my youngest boy came down with a serious case of Arrowweed Fever. If I hadn't bought the medicine, his life could have been in danger. And the illness could have easily spread to his older brother."

"We don't want to hear your sob stories," responded the largest intruder, "but I tell you what. Since you're so concerned with the health of your two sons, we are going to do something nice to help care for them tonight. We are going to take them with us and raise them to be a part of our rebel army." The intruder motioned his arm towards the crying child in the basket and ordered, "Soldiers! Take this baby into custody and search the house for the other child."

Martin was now sitting up on the ground, but found himself paralyzed with fear. Summoning every last ounce of strength and willpower, Martin shouted, "Shaylene, run for it!" But it was too late.

5

Not too late because the two rebel soldiers were able to stop her, but too late because she was already gone. The moment Shaylene heard the pounding at the door, her instinct caused her to rush into the back room. She wasted no time in taking Stefan out of his woven basket and climbing out the back window into the dirt alleyway behind their home. She paused only long enough to grab a sheepskin blanket to wrap around Stefan later. Running out into the night, she knew there would be no safe haven. There would be no place she could run to, no place she could hide. Nobody in Norwalk ever dared to venture out into the streets after dark, for the rebels had spread fear throughout the land.

Martin finally came out of his temporary paralysis. He almost jumped halfway across the room as he tackled the soldier reaching for Lolek. Martin and the soldier fell down hard onto the dirt floor, with Martin landing squarely on top of him. Seeing this, the other soldier diverted from his planned route into the back room. Martin was completely overmatched as he faced two highly trained rebel soldiers. But his plan wasn't to defeat them, his plan was to delay them, so Shaylene would have more time to get as far away from here as possible. And it worked, as he was able to struggle with them for nearly a minute before being subdued once and for all.

"You fools!" shouted the largest rebel, obviously the leader of the group. "The wife and other child are escaping. Quit wasting precious time on this worthless peasant and get after them! Prince Agis will be very upset if we don't return with two children tonight. And if he's upset, then I will be upset. And I'll make sure you both understand that very well." Leaving the lead rebel, an injured Martin, and one hysterically crying baby behind, the two soldiers hurried into the back room. The dark room was instantly brightened by the torches they carried with them. The soldiers slowed down and moved cautiously toward the open window, exiting it one by one.

"Which way do you think she went?" one soldier asked the other once they were both outside.

"That way," the other soldier answered as he pointed to something on the ground. It was the blanket Shaylene brought with her at the last second. When it dropped to the ground as she started running, she decided she could spare no more time and kept going. The guards withdrew their swords and headed off in the same direction, toward the village cemetery.

Shaylene continued down the dark alleyway holding onto Stefan as tightly as she possibly could. She didn't see any candle lights burning in any of the other windows of her neighbors' mud flat homes. As she was looking desperately into the last window at the end of the alley, she turned her head back in time to see something lunge toward her out of nowhere. Fortunately, it was only a white cat she spooked with her fast approaching footsteps. At the end of the alleyway she found herself at the main dirt road leading into town. She had two choices at this point. She could turn south and head further away from the village into a maze of mud flat homes. Or she could turn north and go directly into the village center where she could hope to run into the two royal guards who were posted in Norwalk. Of course, Norwalk was a sizable village, and who knew where the royal guards would be at this time, or even if they would be awake and fulfilling their duties. With sweat now dropping from her face despite the freezing cold temperature, Shaylene made her decision. She went with the unthinkable, which was choice number three. Directly in front of her was a small hillside which led up into the village cemetery, which was surrounded by oak trees, but no fences. Surely somewhere in the large cemetery filled with tombstones, Memory Gardens, and plants, she would be able to find a place where she could hide from the rebels, should any of them decide to come after her. Besides, this was a bold move on her part. If anything, the rebels would expect her to turn north, heading back into town, hoping to find help. The crescent moon above provided enough light for her to make her way up the hillside into the midst of the cemetery. Meanwhile, Stefan had literally been shaken awake with all of the running, but he stayed quiet as a tomb.

About two minutes later the two soldiers emerged from the dark alleyway at the same junction. And like Shaylene, they too paused to debate their next course of action. "We better get this right. You heard what the boss said back there," one soldier muttered to the other.

The other soldier, who was named Owen, responded with logical thinking. He said, "Look, Trent, there is nothing to discuss. She is going to try to head towards the village center to look for the royal guards. Our surveillance puts them near the King's Fountain usually at this time of night, but I highly doubt the peasant's wife knows that. It will literally take her hours to find them, and by then we will have taken her and the other child into custody. Let's get a move on it!" With that, they turned north towards the village center, unaware they were being watched by a middle aged peasant woman who was holding her two-year-old son at the top of a hill behind an oak tree, not more than one hundred yards from them.

As she watched them head away from her around a bend, Shaylene finally breathed a sigh of relief. "That was so close," she whispered to her oldest son. He looked back at her and smiled, not understanding what she was saying but evidently aware there was some kind of danger which had now passed. He was still looking in her eyes when she continued talking, "You must be so cold, my dear boy. I'm sorry for dropping your blanket back there. But mommy needs to make sure you are safe first and then I'll take you back home to get another one, okay? Now let's go see if we can find a warm hiding place where we can stay tonight." By her estimates, Shaylene knew there were still about five hours until the first visible light would appear on the horizon. Her plan was to search through the overgrown smaller trees and dense shrubs which grew in the Memory Gardens of the cemetery, until she found a perfect place for them to hide in until daybreak.

As she passed by the tombstones, Shaylene inadvertently zigzagged through them taking a familiar route. It was only a few months ago she had been here in this exact cemetery burying her parents. They had lived a happy, fulfilling life in Norwalk, despite being poor peasants until the day of their death. They taught Shaylene from an early age that happiness comes from appreciating what you have, not longing for what you do not have. As she passed their grave markers, Shaylene thought about the lesson and realized it was something that could help her survive this night. She had already likely lost Lolek and possibly even her husband Martin to the rebels. But no matter what, she could still save Stefan. She needed to stay alive and keep him safe, so she could raise him to have a good life. As she came to the edge of the grassy area of the cemetery, she heard the faint sound of thunder rumbling in the distance. It caused her to hurry a little bit quicker, as she turned to the north, taking a dirt path into the Memory Gardens.

Meanwhile, the two soldiers jogged nearly a half mile towards the main part of the village. The dirt road they were on began to abruptly break away from the hillside it was following. Also, a river came in from the west and turned north, flowing parallel to the main road into the village center. Noticing this, the rebel soldier Owen said, "Hold on a minute. I have an idea."

"All right," the rebel Trent responded, "what is it?"

Owen quickly explained, "Think about it for a minute. We've been pushing hard for nearly five minutes and the woman and child are nowhere in sight. We're about to lose our only advantage because the road is turning away from this hill. Our best bet is to go to the top of the hill where we can get a clear view of the village. There's nobody else out in the village at this hour, so we will be able to clearly see if there is any movement on any of the roads. I say once we are up there, we will spot her in a matter of seconds, not minutes."

"All right, but if you're wrong, you're taking the fall for this one," Trent barked back. The two rebel soldiers threw their torches into the river as they turned off of the road and began climbing up through the grassy brush. The iron handled torches slowly sank to the bottom after hissing upon contact with the water and letting out a small cloud of steam. Though they didn't realize it, the two rebel soldiers were now climbing up the same hillside Shaylene went up, although they were further down from her.

Back at Martin's mud flat home, quiet prevailed for the time being. But it was only because the largest rebel, the one leading the small group that had broken into Martin's home, knocked Martin unconscious when he would not stop yelling for help. The largest rebel's name was Robbins and he was really focused on fulfilling his mission. When Martin and his family did not pay the two silver coins required of all peasants in the area, they were targeted by Prince Agis, the leader of all rebels, to lose their children. Robbins didn't feel bad about kidnapping, because he himself helped raise some of those who were taken. Prince Agis had instituted this new campaign with a twofold purpose. First of all, to strike fear into the hearts of families throughout Astoria, making them think the royal guards couldn't protect anybody from the rebels. And second, to provide the next generation of rebels, ones who would be ready to take up the cause and fight in ten to fifteen years, depending on their age. Robbins thought of it as a foolproof plan, one showing the brilliant mind of Prince Agis. 'That's why I signed up for this cause,' he thought, 'because Prince Agis will someday restore this land to its former glory.' Robbins even thought about the possibility that if he completed this mission successfully and brought back both boys, he could be promoted and become one of the few people who has actually seen the face of Prince Agis. The thought of that compelled him to work a little faster, as he tied Martin's hands behind his back with some strong rope.

In the Memory Gardens of the cemetery, Shaylene found what appeared to be the perfect hiding spot in the midst of some thick overgrown brush and small trees. The only thing that made hiding inside of it difficult was the light drizzle which started to come down a few minutes ago. The clouds continued to cover up more and more of the sky by the minute and the sound of thunder grew ever closer. If the rain became much worse, Shaylene was going to have to move, or she would risk allowing herself and Stefan to get drenched and potentially sick. That was the last thing she wanted for Stefan, after the harrowing experience she went through recently with Lolek's sickness. Lolek somehow caught Arrowweed Fever, which proved to be one of the deadliest sicknesses in the region during the past decade. It seemed that mostly children under five years of age were susceptible to catching it, particularly among the peasants. Shaylene knew of three children in Norwalk besides Lolek who came down with the fever during the past few years. One of those children, a four-year-old girl, tragically died because of it. The girl's family was unable to come up with the necessary money to purchase the medicine needed to cure her.

Eventually, they appealed to both the village statesman and the royal family for help. One of the local landowners finally donated the funds, but by then it was too late. The girl was too far gone and could not recover. Being at the cemetery reminded Shaylene of that whole situation, knowing the girl's grave marker was somewhere in the midst of the rows and rows of tombstones. Shaylene and Martin were determined not to let their own son end up with the same fate. Thus, they took the risk of using the two silver coins which were supposed to be given to the rebels, to buy medicine for Lolek. Shaylene and Martin were hoping the rebels would either not have noticed the missing funds (which were supposed to be left in a bag tacked onto the front door on the first of every month,) or they would have been understanding when they learned of the reasons for not being paid. After all, the tax the rebels demanded of the people was unlawful. The royal family had assigned two royal guards to the village in the hope of clamping down on the illegal activities there. But the end result was it appeared to be a token gesture, because nothing much changed. Abruptly, Shaylene's thought pattern was shattered as a lightning bolt struck the ground about fifty feet from the place where she and the baby were hiding. It was followed instantaneously with a large boom of thunder and shrieking cries of fear from Stefan.

The two rebel soldiers had been standing at the top of the ridge for a few minutes now, muttering complaints about the weather and surveying the town below for any signs of life. "Well, you've done it now," Trent started to say. "Robbins is going to put us both in stocks for a week after th..." The soldier's words were cut off by a flash of lightning which lit up the whole sky. Both soldiers turned to see the last remnants of the lightning strike behind them. It was followed by some loud thunder and something else, almost like a shriek, or perhaps a scream. "Did you hear that?" the rebel soldier Trent asked. "What was that?"

"That, my friend, is our second chance," responded Owen. Both of them took off running slightly downhill in the direction of the lightning bolt and Shaylene's hiding spot.

Shaylene tried to calm the child down quickly, but a few of his screams carried on past the end of the thunder. The rain was getting more steady now and Shaylene was really worried about being caught. If the rebels were down on the road below the cemetery, she knew it was likely they heard Stefan's screams. Or worse yet, if they were searching some part of the cemetery, they would be able to quickly narrow down the search area and find her now. Sound carried really well at night, particularly in a village where nobody goes out after dark. She debated the decision briefly, but decided to stay put for a little while longer. She couldn't risk going back down to the main road. And she couldn't risk leaving her hiding place to try to find a new one yet. The only other thing she could do was exit the cemetery on the other side, opposite of the direction she first came in. She knew the hill crested after a short distance and went back down towards a river, which followed the hillside for a while and then made an abrupt turn into town.

Through the sound of the rain, Shaylene thought she heard voices and footsteps, not close, but some distance away. She shifted her weight onto her knees and tried to peer through the dense brush she was hiding in. As she was trying to look, she didn't realize that more rain was getting on Stefan. He made a few sounds as if he was about to cry. Hearing this, Shaylene quickly pulled back to the relative shelter of the thick brush and sat back down to try to soothe Stefan. She knew that one scream or bout of crying from Stefan would mean they would be caught and she would lose Stefan, possibly forever. She refocused all of her energy on consoling him and making sure he stayed calm. Meanwhile, the rebels voices and footsteps grew closer. Shaylene could now make out a few words being said.

"They have to be in here somewhere. Let's turn this whole place upside down if we have to," the rebel soldier Owen said.

"I don't care if we have to wake up the dead to find them, we'll do it," Trent added. Soon their footsteps started coming very close. They sounded like they were about twenty feet away, ten feet, and then five feet. Shaylene was terrified for a moment, but relieved when they kept walking right past her hiding place. She could now see them through the brush, there were two of them. One of them was holding a sword and the other had a sword in a scabbard attached to his belt. They had walked down the pathway coming from the other end of the Memory Gardens. Shaylene realized they must have come in from the northern part of the cemetery grounds, which was an odd place to enter. No doubt they were searching another location when Stefan's scream attracted their attention. As they were walking away, the soldier on the left turned back and seemed to look directly at Shaylene's hiding place. It almost felt like he was gazing into her eyes with his eerily dark face, which was covered with some type of mud to hide his identity. Shaylene froze, wondering if she was spotted. A moment later, the soldier turned his face back around and kept walking towards the grave sites, tombstones, and memorial plaques of varying shapes and sizes.

The soldiers stopped about a minute later and talked to each other for a short time. Then, one of them called out with a loud voice, "Peasant woman, we know you are hiding somewhere in here. We're going to give you one chance. Come out now and turn yourself in, and we will spare your life. We will even allow you and your husband to keep your pitiful home." After there was no response to the offer, one soldier screamed out with rage and kicked over a tombstone standing in place next to him. Both of the soldiers started aggressively searching around the larger grave markers, memorial plaques, and statues.

When Shaylene was sure they were as far away from her as they were possibly going to get in their search, before turning back to come closer, she bolted. Holding Stefan firmly with both hands, she crawled out of her hiding place and began running in the opposite direction of the rebels. If she could make it over the small crest of the hill, she would be out of sight and headed down towards the river. But it wasn't to be. Shaylene slipped in the mud and landed on her back, with Stefan still in her arms. As she was getting back up, one of the rebel soldiers spotted her and both immediately went into pursuit. They were quite far away, but would be able to make up the time in a matter of minutes. Shaylene dared a quick glance back and saw she had been spotted, as she went over the crest and started running downhill as fast as she deemed safe. She hardly even noticed the pouring rain at this point, focused instead on the swiftly moving river a short distance away.

When she came to the bottom of the hill, she started pushing her way through some thick reeds which separated the hill from the river bank. She needed a plan, and needed it fast. There was no time to think though, because she looked back and discovered the two soldiers were coming over the crest of the hill behind her. A few more steps and Shaylene emerged out of the elbow high reeds onto the bank of the river.

Just to her right, buried slightly in the mud, Shaylene noticed part of a fallen tree trunk that extended out into the river. It was about eight feet long and half of it was floating on the water. With Stefan in her left hand, she used her right to try to free the tree trunk from the mud. It was no use, she didn't have the strength to do it. Shaylene glanced back and saw the soldiers already about halfway down the hill. Taking a few steps back, she gently set Stefan down on the bank. All the while, he was watching her with fascination. In fact, he had rarely seen what the world outside looks like at night, so every move and sound was like something new to him. With both hands, Shaylene pulled as hard as she could on the tree trunk. Finally, it budged. Mud and sand fell off the end she pulled up and quickly the current of the river tried to pull the makeshift floating device away from Shaylene. She didn't have the strength to fight the current, so she briefly let go, to pick Stefan back up. Returning with him held firmly at her side, she plopped into the icy water and wrapped her free arm around the floating log. She didn't need to do anything to get the log moving, as the current took care of that problem. Quickly they were picking up speed as the river flowed down toward the village center.

The two soldiers emerged at the river bank and could hardly believe their eyes. There was the peasant woman and her son holding on for dear life to a log, being taken down the river by the current. "Don't even think about jumping in after her," Owen said firmly. "It's much too dangerous and we'd have to ditch our swords here. Let's follow her along the river bank from a distance and when she tries to get out of the river, we will make our move. Maybe the rain will let up a little by then." The rebel soldier Trent agreed, so they followed close behind.

They maintained a jogging pace to keep up with the rapid moving current.

From Shaylene's vantage point, she couldn't see a thing. She was clinging for dear life to the log as she floated down the river. It was remarkable she could do this, but she didn't know how much longer she would be able to hang on. Her lower body was going numb from the coldness of the water, she didn't know what hazards could possibly lie under the water, and the pouring rain was limiting visibility to a few feet as it splashed off the water all around her continuously. Still, Shaylene held on to Stefan and held on to the log, realizing what was at stake. As the river rounded a bend and straightened out, Shaylene thought she knew where she was at. If she was right, she would travel through one more series of intense rapids before the river would level out and calm down, as it made its way into the village center. Once there, she could stay in the river and hide under one of the many wooden bridges which crossed from one side of Norwalk to the other. Or she could get out and try to find a new hiding place until the morning. Shaylene hadn't yet decided by the time she entered the final set of rapids, white water churning all around her. Stefan traded off between crying and spitting out water at this point. But his mother could do little to help him as they both made their way through the rapids. Remarkably, they didn't hit any rocks or get sucked under at any point, clearing the rapids intact. As the water became gentler and the ride more peaceful, Stefan calmed down. Shaylene tried to guide the log she was holding in the direction of the right side of the river bank. They were in the village center now, passing under the first of many bridges.

Shaylene managed to pull the log over to the side a few minutes later. Once she could touch the ground, she began wading out of the river. She looked down at Stefan. He was shivering intensely and not saying a word, seemingly traumatized by the whole experience. Soon she emerged from the water onto a bank of wet sand. She was exhausted, but needed to keep moving. Still carrying Stefan, she started walking up a small dune with her wet and worn out sandals. She figured that she would come out onto the main road one half block away from the exact center of town. At the top of the bank, she was astonished to find the two rebel soldiers waiting for her. They startled her so much, she almost dropped Stefan. But she didn't and she did the only thing left in her power that she could do, she screamed at the top of her lungs. "Help me, someone! Help, please help!" she cried out. One soldier quickly moved to quiet her down by putting a gag through her mouth. The other soldier took Stefan away and watched as Shaylene was tied up.

A few minutes earlier, the two royal guards assigned to their post in Norwalk were sitting near the King's Fountain, talking about old times. They had been in the village for several months on a six month assignment. Their purpose in being here, as clearly explained to them by the Chief Royal Knight, was to watch over the wealthy landowners of the town. They were to make sure the wealthy ones were not bothered in any way by the rebels or other criminals. At the same time, they were to safeguard and protect the royal family's property in Norwalk, places such as the spectacularly designed King's Fountain. Their conversation on this uneventful night drifted to two women they met on their previous assignment. "I think I've fallen in love," one royal guard said to the other. "This could be it for me."

The other royal guard laughed heartily and replied, "I hope so Mathieu. I expect to be the best man at your wedding, as you will be at mine." He rubbed his large belly and thoughtfully added, "And there better be some good food there as well."

Their conversation ended abruptly as a woman's scream pierced the night. The scream was close, perhaps coming from just around the corner, out on the river road. The two royal guards drew their swords and ran as fast as they could toward the woman's voice, which could no longer be heard. When they rounded the bend, they saw the rebel soldiers. One was holding a child and the other was leaning down tying knots around the woman's arms, which were being placed behind her. Without saying a word to each other, they knew what needed to be done. The rebels had to be stopped and taken into custody.

Though they were caught by surprise, the rebel soldiers had time to stop what they were doing and prepare for battle. The soldier holding Stefan dropped him to the ground and took out his sword. And the soldier tying up Shaylene dropped the ropes he was holding, doing the same. As they moved away from Shaylene, she loosened her ropes and picked up Stefan to hold him. She watched as the rebel soldiers went into a full on sword fight with the two royal guards. There was the sound of metal clashing against metal. Mathieu, the smaller of the two royal guards, moved slowly to one side as he was exchanging sword blows with his opponent. He was trying to separate the two groups who were fighting, to make sure nothing unexpected happened he was unprepared for. The other royal guard, who was stocky in build and named Reginald, saw what Mathieu was trying to do, so he moved in the other direction. With space to fight, Mathieu let his sword ability do the talking. Although he was a bit rusty, not being in a real battle since his last assignment, Mathieu quickly overpowered his rebel opponent, knocking his sword out of his hands and to the ground. The rebel pleaded for mercy as he dropped to his knees. Mathieu went over and picked up the rebel's sword and looked at what was going on in the other battle. His fellow guardsman was not able to move as quickly and screamed out in pain as the rebel's sword managed to clip his upper leg. The royal guard was still holding his own, but it was all in defense. With every swing of the rebel's sword, the guard was being pushed backwards. Mathieu arrived there just in time, holding his sword to the back of the rebel. "Stop now, if you value your life," Mathieu told him. Stunned by this development, the rebel halted what he was doing and dropped his sword to the ground. The stocky royal guard, now bleeding from his leg, came over and shoved his rebel opponent to the ground. "By order of the royal family of the peaceful land of Astoria, you are both being taken into custody to await trial for your crimes," Mathieu told them both.

Robbins, the rebel head of this mission, was growing more and more agitated back at Martin's home. He couldn't figure out what could possibly be taking the two soldiers so long. After all, the peasant woman could only have had a few minutes lead time on them, and she was carrying a child with her. Something must have happened. With

Martin still unconscious, Robbins decided to cut his losses and head back to the rebel camp, which was several hours away by horseback. Robbins couldn't afford to come back with nothing to show for himself. Even worse, Robbins couldn't allow himself to be taken into custody, which would land him in a prison cell for the rest of his days. So he picked up Lolek, who was now fast asleep, and went back out the open entrance, where the front door used to be located. Three horses were tied up to a post outside. Robbins untied his horse, climbed up on it while he was holding Lolek, and rode out of the town into the woods.

When the royal guards arrived at the home on horseback a little while later, Robbins was long gone. Helping Shaylene and Stefan down from his horse, Reginald asked them to wait outside while the place was checked out. A few moments later, he appeared back at the open front entrance and told them they could come in. Inside, Martin was slowly waking up as Mathieu untied his hands. And so Martin, Shaylene and Stefan were safe, but they would never again be the same, not without Lolek. They would spend the next decade wondering and worrying about his fate.

Chapter Two:

There Was a Royal Family

There was a royal family who lived in a castle, with daily banquets their guests would be dazzled. However, tonight's banquet, despite being an important one, would probably have a somber mood to it after the events of the day. A few hours earlier, two royal guards who were assigned to protect the village of Norwalk sent word they engaged in a sword fight with two rebels, which they defeated and took into custody. What was most disturbing about this news to King Charles was there had been a third rebel involved, and that rebel escaped with a one-year-old boy who belonged to a peasant family. King Charles didn't much care for peasants, but he did have a heart. And he felt for this poor family in Norwalk. Upon hearing this news, the king dispatched a full band of royal guards to Norwalk to take the two rebel soldiers into custody and transport them back to the prison located on the castle grounds. Norwalk was only an hour's ride away by horseback, so it wouldn't take long. He also ordered something be done for the peasant family who lost their child, to protect them in case the rebels came back. They were to be relocated onto the property of the landowner who the peasant Martin worked for. And a royal guard was to be posted outside of their residence at night for the next year. As compensation to the landowner, who was a kind man named Leon, King Charles sent him a gift of fifty gold coins, which was quite a generous bestowal indeed. King Charles also invited the landowner and his son to one of the royal banquets during the following week.

One of the reasons King Charles felt so deeply for this peasant family's loss, was he had his own daughter. She was only a year older than the boy kidnapped by the rebels, and Charles loved her dearly. Just before she was born, Charles stayed up nights, hoping and dreaming about having a son to take over his throne. In the land of Astoria, there was a way of life for the past two hundred years that had never changed. When the firstborn son or daughter of a king and queen reached the age of sixteen, he or she would become the new leader of the land. There were no exceptions to this rule. Being a man himself, King Charles thought a male could do a better job at handling the immense responsibilities, which is why he hoped for a boy. But it was a girl born on that night two years ago. A girl who would take over the throne as princess fourteen years from now, which would probably go by like a blur. King Charles and his wife Queen Delphine gave the future princess the name Stasia. It was taken from the name of a princess who ruled the land over one hundred years earlier. The Royal History Pages spoke highly of that princess, named Stasiana, from a long time ago. As Charles remembered it, the book even spoke of her as being one of the best rulers the land had ever known. That alone made it a fitting name for his firstborn, a girl with sparkling blue eyes and locks of blonde hair at two years of age.

With all of the trouble King Charles was dealing with on this day, he didn't have much time to take a break from his royal duties. And now it was late afternoon. The sun would be setting soon and the rest of his evening would be taken up with dinner and entertainment from the court jesters and musicians. Excusing himself from his throne, he instructed his Chief Royal Knight to stay at his post, but to come get him in case of another emergency. The Chief Royal Knight responded, "As you wish, your majesty. And where might I find you?"

"I will be with Princess Stasia in the Royal Gardens, and then taking counsel with the queen. Thank you, Chadwick," replied the king.

The king appreciated Chadwick's years of loyal service and knew he could be trusted to care for matters while the king took a break. Chadwick was King Charles' younger brother, born five years after the king. The king admired the way Chadwick had taken on a new role over the past few years, of not just staying at the castle, but traveling the countryside to do good for others. Chadwick would sometimes leave for weeks at a time, but always come back with reports of how he had helped those in need, while at the same time built up support for Charles' kingship. If only all of the wealthy landowners and noblemen were as supportive as Chadwick, there would be no problems in the land, Charles felt. Walking through the doorway located behind his throne, Charles exited the throne room and entered a short hallway. It led him into a central room which had three exits. To the right, one could walk out onto the Castle Terrace and look out at the vast castle grounds, which were mostly acres and acres of grassy field. It was there that King Charles delivered his yearly speech to the wealthy landowners. He also watched the games held twice a year on the castle grounds from the same spot. The Astorian Games, as they were officially known, brought together all the greatest athletes from around the land. Continuing straight from inside the central room, one would enter another hallway leading to the King's Chamber. That was where Charles and Delphine slept at night and took private counsel with one another. Nobody was allowed in that room, except for the king and queen themselves, and those assigned to do cleaning. At night, royal guards would be posted both in the central room and outside the King's Chamber.

King Charles did not take either of these two exits. Instead, he turned left and walked toward the Royal Gardens. The Royal Gardens were a special place, completely off limits to the general public, and even most of the guards and castle staff. The gardens themselves were enclosed by four walls, with a door on two of the sides which entered into different parts of the castle. Thus, in the midst of the heavily protected castle, there was a private outdoor area. In this small area there was a beautiful lawn containing flowers of every sort, which were brought in and planted from throughout the land. There was a pool of water in the middle of the lawn, continuously flowing by way of an underground spring which was diverted through here. As Charles walked out the door, a reddish brown fish jumped out of the pool and came back down with a splash.

Princess Stasia let out a scream of delight when she saw her father walking towards her. Stasia was sitting on the grass while her floppy-eared rabbit named Mandy hopped around in circles. Her caretaker was there with her, Chadwick's wife Delia. While Chadwick was given a life-long assignment as Chief Royal Knight, Delia served as attendant to the queen. When Stasia was born, Delia spent most of her days caring for the young princess-to-be, while Queen Delphine cared for royal duties.

"Look, princess, it's your father," Delia leaned over and whispered in Stasia's ear, as the king walked towards them. Stasia smiled widely as Delia looked up and told the king, "She's so happy to see you, your majesty. To what do we owe this precious visit?"

"We've had some tragic events in the land today, Delia. It seems the rebels are up to their old kidnapping ways once again. This time it was a peasant family from the nearby village of Norwalk who lost their youngest son." King Charles reached down and picked up his daughter, kissed her on the cheek, and continued, "The rebels are getting more and more daring with their actions. I mean, Norwalk is only one hour away by horse. They are no doubt trying to send me a message." A look of concern flashed across the face of Delia upon hearing this. The king continued, "But the good news is, we captured two of the three rebels who were involved with the plot. Two of my royal guards were posted there and managed to take them into custody, but not before the other rebel escaped with the child. I guess the reason I'm telling you all this Delia, is it makes me realize I need to spend more time with my daughter. It's so easy for me to get sidetracked with the concerns of the kingdom. But this little girl is going to be princess in fourteen years and I must make more time for her."

Queen Delphine walked out of the other door, from a short distance beyond the pool, as the king was finishing up his account. "I heard about what happened, Charles," she said. "Is everything all right with Stasia?"

"Yes my dear, she's perfectly fine. I just wanted to come and see her for a few minutes," Charles answered. Stasia was playfully trying to reach for Charles' crown, fascinated by the gold color and sparkling jewels which lined it. "Now, now, sweetheart," Charles said as he looked her in the eyes, "you're going to be wearing this soon enough." Charles handed the young girl back over to Delia and said, "It was good seeing you Delia. Take good care of her, like you always do. We will see you at dinner time." Queen Delphine took Charles' hand and the two walked back into the castle to further discuss the events of the day.

For Delia, this was her favorite part of the entire day. She enjoyed being the primary caretaker of the young girl. Stasia had such a radiance about her, a glow to her little face. The girl was fascinated by the world of small animals, insects, and flowers. It seemed she was happiest out here in the Royal Gardens, where the two spent much of each afternoon. Sadly, Delia carried with her a deep, dark secret she didn't want anybody to know about. While everyone else looked up to her husband Chadwick, the Chief Royal Knight, with admiration, Delia despised him. Behind closed doors he was sometimes abusive to her. Delia couldn't understand why he treated her so badly, when she offered nothing but love to him. During the day, Delia was free from his insulting behavior. And she was even more free when he would leave on one of his week long trips to "promote the king," as he put it. Delia looked over and saw Stasia once again chasing her rabbit Mandy around the garden. The rabbit changed course and started hopping over towards the pond. "Stasia, don't get too close to the water," Delia reminded her.

Two hours later as the sky was getting dark, there was a knock at the King's Chamber. Charles and Delphine were sitting in there discussing the best course of action to clamp down on the rebels. A message was slipped under the door and the king went over to pick it up. After reading it, the king looked over at his wife and said, "Ah, so it looks like our prisoners have arrived. Chadwick has notified me that they have been placed in the holding cell of the prison. Maybe now we'll be able to get some answers and find out where these rebels have been hiding out. I'm going to go over there and talk to them myself after the evening banquet." At that moment, a trumpet could be heard throughout the castle, notifying all it was time for the feast. "Speaking of the banquet, it sounds like it's time to go dine with our guests,"

Charles added. With that, they both headed toward the Grand Banqueting Hall.

Charles and Delphine had been awaiting this particular banquet for some time. Tonight, they were hosting very special guests from the neighboring land of Limekiln. They were being visited by King Dominic and Queen Bronagh, who arrived earlier this morning with hundreds of Limekiln army troops surrounding them in protection. There was a special ceremony held to welcome them in their first visit to Astoria's Castle to see King Charles and Queen Delphine in five years. They brought with them their five-year-old boy, known as Rackley. In thinking about tonight, King Charles was especially curious about one thing. The visiting king announced he had a proposal to share during the evening banquet. Apparently, it was a proposal which would bring many benefits for both lands for years to come. King Charles thought that perhaps King Dominic would suggest uniting their armies. Or perhaps he would want to start a building program to build higher walls across the border of the land. Whatever it was, King Charles was open to any suggestion to help make the land a safer place for the generation to come.

Charles and Delphine paused for a moment as they reached the entrance to the Grand Banqueting Hall. Right on cue, an attendant spoke loudly, "Attention everyone! I present to you the King and Queen of Astoria." Three musicians trumpeted their entrance and the fifty guests who were sitting at ten different circular tables all stood up at once. All eyes were focused on the king and queen as they walked to their seats at the head table and sat down. Shortly thereafter, the music stopped and all of the other guests sat back down. Conversation ensued at each of the ten tables throughout the room. Sitting at the king's table, clockwise to the king, were Delphine, Stasia (in her special chair), Delia, Chadwick, two royal knights, Queen Bronagh and King Dominic, their young son Rackley, and three dignitaries who arrived with them. As everyone was exchanging greetings, the table was swarmed with servers. The servers went around in a circle putting generous portions of food onto the golden plates and pouring the land's finest wine, Norwalk Red, into the golden drinking cups.

"I hope you enjoyed your afternoon," King Charles said to the other king. "I'm sorry that I wasn't able to spend the day with you, but there was an emergency situation which developed. These rebels have been giving me quite a headache lately."

"We totally understand," King Dominic responded. "After the ceremony, our delegation was taken out to the waterfall just beyond the castle. I must say, Astoria has some spectacular sights which are unmatched in the world. I think I can speak for all of us, in saying we were in awe of the beauty."

"Thank you for your kind words, my old friend. As you can imagine, I'm very interested in protecting the beauty of this land and making it a safer place for the future generations. That's why your proposal has definitely captured my attention. Although I must say, I'm not exactly sure what you are going to propose."

"I didn't mean to be cryptic about my proposal," King Dominic explained. "I only wanted to wait until we were all gathered here at the table to share it with you. I'm sure you would all agree with me that it's in the best interest of both our lands to work together in promoting peace and good relations with one another for the future. And sitting here at the table with us is our future." As he said these words, King Dominic pointed at the two young children, Rackley and Stasia. All of the adults looked at the children, and the visiting king continued, "I propose we form a marriage alliance involving our two children. When my young son has grown up and is known as Sir Rackley, Prince of Limekiln, he should be given in marriage to your daughter, who will by then be known as Princess Stasia. It will be a wedding the likes of which have never been seen before, uniting our lands, and our families, forever."

There was a brief moment of silence following King Dominic's speech. It was short lived, for King Charles stood up out of his seat and exclaimed, "What a wonderful proposition! We accept this grand idea. Our daughter Stasia will be given to your son Rackley in marriage one year after she begins her reign as princess, when she is seventeen." Upon hearing King Charles express his approval, all sitting at the table stood up and applauded. Those sitting at the nine other tables in the room all stopped eating and looked over at the king's table to see what the commotion was all about. Looking beyond his own table, at the other tables in the room, King Charles repeated what he said for all in the room to hear. With his booming voice, he proclaimed, "Let it be known to all present that Princess Stasia and Sir Rackley will marry when she is seventeen years old, one year after she becomes leader of Astoria!" As he finished his words, thunderous applause filled the room. Delia hesitated before applauding, but then joined in. It seemed she was the only one in the whole room who wasn't sure about this new idea.

A little while later, after the feast was finished, everyone moved from the banqueting hall over to the Grand Ballroom in anticipation of the evening's entertainment. Chadwick excused himself from the proceedings, to head over to the prison and begin questioning the two rebel captives. The Grand Ballroom was the most magnificent place in the entire castle. The walls were lined with spectacular paintings made by the most famous artists of the era. There was a large stage area, where performers would share in music, dance, poetry, and other arts. At times, important speeches were given from the stage. It was even the place where new rulers were coronated at sixteen years of age. At the foot of the stage was a vast, polished wood dance floor, used mostly for special events like balls and masquerade parties. Tonight, as with most other nights, the floor was covered with seats made of fine wood and crimson cloth. The seats were divided into two sections which stretched all the way to the back wall, with a walking path down the middle. Every night they were in use, all of the seats were occupied with castle residents, dignitaries, and the wealthiest of the landowners. Waving to everyone as he walked in, King Charles and his entourage sat down in the seats at the front, and the entertainment began.

The first act was an acrobatic juggler, who impressed the crowd with his every move. King Charles was watching, yet his mind proved to be elsewhere. He was thinking back to what transpired in the banqueting hall. When the visiting king made his proposition, it truly was the last thing on earth Charles was expecting to hear. But it was simply brilliant. Charles looked over at his baby girl, who was sitting in Delia's lap watching the juggler. The crowd applauded after the juggler made a particularly difficult catch behind his back. Seeing the reaction of the adults, Stasia slapped her small hands together in an attempt to mimic their applause. Charles smiled, looked back at the juggler, and continued thinking about the long term meaning of Stasia's future arranged marriage to Rackley. He wondered what the girl would think of marrying someone, not for love, but out of duty. He was sure she would understand, realizing it was in the best interests of her people, and she wouldn't hesitate to marry him. King Charles also reasoned she would grow to love Rackley over time, even if she didn't at first. But that was a long ways off. There would be many years to prepare for this event. After all, they were both still young children, Stasia being two years old and Rackley five. They needed to enjoy their youth and grow up first. Stasia had many years of royal training ahead of her, before she turned sixteen and became princess.

Charles' thoughts wandered to the situation with the rebels. As the second and third acts came on, a violin player and a visiting poet from another land, Charles became restless. At the first intermission, Charles left the rest of the group and headed across the castle grounds toward the prison with four of his royal guards. He wanted to check in on the questioning and perhaps even ask a few questions himself. As he arrived at the prison and was about to walk down the steps which led to the front door, Chadwick came out. Climbing up the last step, he was slightly surprised to see the king. "Your majesty," Chadwick said to him, "I didn't expect to see you over here. You should be enjoying the evening's festivities over at the Grand Ballroom. Let me take care of the dirty work for you. I already finished questioning the rebels."

King Charles asked, "Did you get anything out of them? Did you find out the location of the rebel fort?"

"They weren't in much of a cooperative mood it seems," answered Chadwick. "I pressed them hard for the past hour with threats, insults, and demands. But they wouldn't tell me anything except to say that terror will continue to fill the land. Really, your majesty, I wouldn't bother going in there. They are not going to tell you anything, at least not yet."

"Thank you, Chadwick, but I'll decide that for myself." The king walked past Chadwick and down the steps.

One of his royal guards moved ahead of him briefly to open the door, as King Charles walked into the underground prison. He had not been in here in a long time. When he walked through the door he almost choked on the stale air and musty scent of the place. The worst criminals of Astoria were kept in here, because it was the most secure prison in the whole land. There were no windows, no natural sunlight, and there was absolutely no way to escape. Unlike other prisons, which sometimes opened the way for a prisoner to escape with help from the outside, there was no possibility of that here. Astoria Castle was surrounded by high walls on each side. On every one of the four corners, where the walls intersected, there was a lookout tower. Each of these towers were manned twenty-four hours out of the day, every day of the year. The main way into the castle was through the open drawbridge at the front entrance gate. The drawbridge was lowered from sunup to sundown, being also let down at other times as needed. There was no other way to gain access to the castle grounds, except for the small servants entrance and bridge on the other side of the castle. Blocking any other approach was a deep moat which surrounded the castle on all sides, with hungry crocodiles living in the water. The fact was, no one had ever escaped from the underground prison on the castle grounds, and Charles suspected no one ever would.

The king ordered the jailers to take him into the holding cell of the two rebel soldiers. As the last of the locked barred doors were opened, King Charles walked into the cell, flanked by his four royal guards. The rebel soldiers, hands bound and feet tied to a chain, were clearly shocked to see the King of Astoria enter their cell. They dared not say a word to him, knowing he held their fate in his hands. Charles lifted his left hand to scratch his beard and started, "What you both did yesterday, what you've been involved with, is truly despicable. How could you possibly invade the home of a poor family and take away from them the most precious part of their lives? Don't either of you have families? I suppose not, or you wouldn't be involved with what the rebels are doing. Think for a moment about what it would have been like if this happened to you. What if you were taken from your parents' home in the middle of the night and brought into some cause you knew nothing about, away from your family and friends? Answer me!"

The rebel soldier Trent dared to look up at the king and respond. "Sire, I never knew my parents. They left me for dead when their food ran out and silver coins were gambled away. I'm only here today because one of the rebel leaders spotted me and took me into his own home. I owe everything to the rebels. And my mate here was fired a couple of years ago by the landowner who he worked for, when he was spotted eating a few grapes he was picking. The rebels were the only ones who would take him in, as no one else would give him a job." When he finished, the rebel soldier looked back down at his chains in embarrassment.

"If that's true," King Charles stated, "then now is the time to do the right thing. Help us track down and capture the rebels and their leader. We can make things right. You don't have to spend the rest of your days in this prison. If you help us, I will personally promise to set you free in ten years time. Think about it. It's a very generous offer which I'm only going to extend to you just this once."

The rebel soldiers didn't say anything to this, so King Charles turned to walk out of the room. The king knew they would never accept his offer. But the king had his principles and he wasn't going to break them. He did feel slightly sorry for them, if what the rebel soldier told him was true. There was no way he could commute their entire sentence in return for their help. It would have set a dangerous precedent throughout the land that others could capitalize on. No, justice demanded they spend some time behind bars for the crimes they committed. If King Charles had to track down the rebels without them, then so be it.

The next morning it was time to bid farewell to King Dominic and Queen Bronagh, and all those who came to Astoria Castle with them. After King Charles and Queen Delphine saw them off, they walked back through the castle and outside into the Royal Gardens. Delia was sitting on the grass in the morning sunshine with her back propped up against a rock. A few feet away from her, shaded by a fruit tree, was Stasia taking her morning nap. When Delia saw the king and queen, she extended a friendly greeting to them. The king responded, "And a good morning to you, Delia. I see you're enjoying the sun. It sure is nice considering the horrible storm which came through here two days ago. Listen, the queen and I have decided to take Stasia out to the waterfall this morning for a picnic lunch. Would you care to join us, or would you prefer to take the rest of the morning off?" Delia thought for a moment. It didn't take her long to make up her mind, because she enjoyed being with Stasia very much. Not only that, but it was a rare occasion when the king and queen took the morning off to do something fun. She said she would gladly accompany them.

Delia picked up Stasia, who opened her eyes briefly, but then fell back asleep. The four of them made their way out to the castle stables, which were divided into two sections. There was the royal stables, and there was the peasant stables. The king's group went to the royal stables, which held approximately forty horses at any given time. Most of the horses housed in the stalls were used by the royal knights and guards, as they fulfilled their castle protection duties or assignments in nearby areas. But there was also a special section which held the king's horses, four of them to be exact. The royal stables were divided from the peasant stables by a large wall that could only be accessed through one door. That door was kept locked, with a royal guard posted there at all times to make sure no peasants or other unscrupulous persons made their way through. The peasants used their section to hold their horses as they worked at the castle. It was quite a prestigious privilege for a peasant to be able to work in any capacity at the royal castle. Mostly Chadwick would hire young men and women from neighboring villages, such as Norwalk, when help was needed.

As King Charles, Queen Delphine, Delia and Stasia walked over toward the stables, a few of the horses started getting excited. The noise they were making woke up a sleepy Stasia. The young girl was only two years old, but it was already clear how much she loved horses. A couple of months ago, the king and queen were returning home from staying at their estate in the countryside, when they made a side trip to the village of Glaston and stopped at the vendors market being held that day. Leaving their horse drawn carriage, they walked through the market and created stunned silence as the locals stared in amazement at seeing the royal family. As Delia followed behind them carrying Stasia, the young girl seemed to be particularly taken with a collection of small, hand carved wooden toys one vendor was selling. Stasia tried to reach for them, even though the toys were several feet away. Seeing this, the vendor called to Delia and offered to give the young girl one of the toys for free. Delia turned around and walked over to the table, telling Stasia, "Go ahead, he said you could have one of them." Stasia smiled and looked around at all of the toys in front of her. What would she choose? There were hand carved trees, people, carriages, fruits, flowers, knight helmets, just about anything someone could imagine. The young girl's eyes lit up as she spotted a few hand carved horses on the right side of the table. She smiled brightly as she picked up not just one, but two of them. Delia objected briefly, wanting Stasia to only take one. But the merchant insisted, saying it was his pleasure to provide a small gift for such a beautiful little girl. "The young princess thanks you, kind friend. May your good deeds come back to you," Delia told him, as they returned to following the king and queen through the market. Ever since that day, Stasia and her two toy horses had been inseparable. It seemed the only thing she loved even more was petting the real horses in the stables and riding on one of them with an adult.

It wasn't long before the stable master had three horses ready. One for the king, one for the queen, and one for Delia and young Stasia. A contingent of twelve royal guards also mounted horses and followed right behind them as they rode towards the exit of the stable courtyard. Seeing the king and his family coming, the gate keeper immediately pulled open the large doors of the courtyard, which opened into the west side of the immense castle grounds. The group rode their horses across the vast field of green grass and crossed the open drawbridge, which led to the outside world. As they proceeded toward the waterfall, which was only a short ride away, they passed a couple of peasants walking on the road to the castle and several startled deer. Stasia was able to enjoy the ride, since the horses were trotting and not galloping. She looked out at the oak trees and hills to her right. But her eyes kept coming back to her horse and the horses in front of her. At one point, the group passed a fork in the road which went south to the village of Norwalk. There was a thick forest growing off in that direction, making the dirt road the most desirable way to get there.

Eventually the group took a short spur road, ending up at the picnic area by the river. After the royal guards checked the area to make sure it was safe, the king's group walked a short distance until the spectacular waterfall came into view. It was about two hundred feet tall, with thousands of gallons of white water cascading over the cliff. "It's so beautiful, dear," Queen Delphine remarked to her husband. "What a wonderful idea to come here today. I don't suppose you were inspired to do this because of the enthusiasm of the visiting king and queen last night, were you?" King Charles laughed because she was right. The visitors last night were so impressed with this place that it made Charles want to come out for a visit. Despite its close proximity to the castle, King Charles had not been out here in almost a year. He went over and took his daughter from Delia, walking a little closer to the falls. The young girl was watching the water with amazement. As they came closer, she turned her head away and kept wiping her eyes. The falls were creating a heavy mist, because there was so much water coming down. Stasia's face, hair, and light blue dress were getting drenched.

A little while later, the group was seated on a blanket spread out across the ground near the river. They were safely out of range of the mist, but still close enough to enjoy the sights and sounds of the waterfall. Stasia was eating pieces of apple which were cut up for her, while the adults were eating fresh baked bread and cheese. The conversation drifted between thoughts on the beauty of the area, Stasia's future coronation and marriage, and the troubles brought on the land by the rebels. Regarding the latter, Delia asked the king, "Do you think the rebels could ever possibly threaten our safety at the castle?"

"Not right now," King Charles replied. "Perhaps in ten years they may have the manpower, weapons and support to stage an attack on the castle. But the reports we're getting right now are of isolated cases of harassment. Essentially, the rebels are trying to create an environment of fear for people to live in. As long as we can find their hideout and put a stop to them within the next few years, I don't see any long term problems. I'm counting on Chadwick to live up to his title of Chief Royal Knight by tracking down the rebels and taking them into custody."

"I'm sure he will be able to do that," chimed in Queen Delphine. She glanced over at Stasia, who was picking some flowers at the edge of the blanket. "When our daughter takes the throne in fourteen years, we need to give her the best start we possibly can. Those first few years of ruling can be very tough. The last thing she needs to deal with is a group of people who have no respect for life or property."

Hearing this, the king responded, "Don't worry, that's a long time from now. I'm sure she is going to make a great princess. Like her namesake from long ago, the admired Princess Stasiana, our daughter will go down in the Royal History Pages as one of the greatest princesses Astoria has ever seen." Charles had more to say, but he stopped talking when Stasia came walking up to her mom.

The young girl was holding in her little hands a bouquet of wild flowers she had picked. There were probably six or seven different colored flowers all mixed together. With her hands full, she reached out with the flowers towards her mom and smiled. As she did this, Stasia said two simple words, "Here, mommy." Her mom accepted the gift but was left speechless. Water started to form under the queen's eyes and it wasn't because of mist from the nearby waterfall. She was overwhelmed with this precious gift from her adorable daughter. With the flowers now in her possession, the queen hugged young Stasia. It was a treasured moment, the kind that a mother never forgets.

Chapter Three:

A Peasant Who Slaved

It was an intensely hot, sunny day about ten years later in the village of Norwalk. A twelve-year-old peasant boy was working on his knees, with his forearms covered with dry dirt and dust. Sweat was dripping from his forehead and neck as his hands were continuously mixing soil, down a row of strawberry plants. It had been a long day working outside, made even harder with this humid summer weather. But it was Friday and that meant the peasant boy wouldn't have to work in the fields for the next two days. He would still have work to do on both Saturday and Sunday, but it was work he enjoyed. He had the great honor of being one of the locals chosen from Norwalk to work at the royal castle. There was no place he would rather be in the world than inside those castle walls scrubbing the marble and wood floors. Not only did he enjoy doing it, but he also earned a small wage for his weekend labors which helped to support himself and his parents.

As the boy reached the end of the row of strawberry plants he was cultivating, he moved over to the next row and began working back in the opposite direction. He couldn't help but smile, seeing this was the final row he needed to do today, and for that matter, for the week. As he moved from one plant to the next, the boy thought about something which made his smile change slowly into a frown. These past few months had truly been something of a nightmare for him. Up until then, he had a good employer who he enjoyed working for very much. It was a kind, old landowner named Leon, who helped his family immensely in their time of greatest need. But the kind man had passed away at the end of April, leaving his whole estate to his demanding son, named Rolf. After his father died, the son would go through wild mood swings, one minute telling the boy what good work he was doing, and the next yelling at him for petty things. Today was particularly bothersome, as the peasant boy had been minding his own business, carrying out his usual morning routine when the landowner's son walked by to check in on him. The boy was working up in the branches of a large apple tree gathering fruit when he heard a voice from down below, yelling at him to work faster. It startled him just enough that he lost control of the half full basket of apples he was holding on his forearm. He tried to regain a grip on it, but it spilled over, dropping apples everywhere onto the lawn below. Rolf was furious over the accident. He screamed at the peasant boy for several minutes before picking up one of the apples off the ground and throwing it at him as hard as he could. The boy was hit squarely in the face, after which Rolf stormed off towards the vineyards. As the peasant boy neared the end of the last row of strawberries, he stopped for a moment and put his dirty right hand up to his cheek, noticing the swelling was starting to die down.

"Stefan! Stefan!" cried a girl's voice from about twenty yards away. After the girl came up to the place where he was working, she stopped for a few seconds to catch her breath. Then she continued, "Hey Stefan, are you almost done? I finished my work a few minutes early today and was hoping to still find you here." The twelve-year-old peasant boy named Stefan paused to look up at his dear friend Yvonne. She was covered with dirt from head to toe. Up and down there were spots on her worn out clothing.

Stefan smiled at her and teased, "Yvonne, what did I tell you about playing in the pig pen with the hogs? It looks like they got the better of you today."

Yvonne flashed a look of irritation and playfully slapped him on the back. "Very funny, Stefan. I might be only eleven, and I might be only a girl, but you know I work just as hard as you do." Pausing briefly, Yvonne continued, "So are you finished? The reason I came over here to get you, is so we could go swimming in the lake. It's been such a hot day, the water will feel great."

"You know what, that's the best idea I've heard all day. Give me a minute to finish up these last few plants and I'll race you to the water. Here, take this!" Stefan picked a large, ripe strawberry and threw it towards Yvonne, who reacted quickly enough to catch it. As she started eating it, Stefan added, "But don't tell Rolf I gave it to you."

When he finished up his work for the day and put his cultivating tools away, Stefan and Yvonne raced toward the pristine water of Norwalk Lake. The race was no contest, as Stefan easily ran ahead of the young peasant girl. At one point, he was even briefly out of her sight, as he turned off on the road leading down to the water's edge. As Yvonne struggled to catch up, she turned off on the same road and was caught by surprise when Stefan jumped out from behind a tree, trying to scare her. "Gotcha!" he proudly stated, before continuing to run down toward the lake. Stefan's foot speed was only slowed down by the water as he began wading out into the lake. Yvonne followed and soon both of them were swimming around and splashing each other. When they burned up some energy, they began lightly treading water and talking to catch up on the developments of the past week. They had not seen each other since riding their horses home from the castle last Sunday night, where Yvonne also worked on the weekends. Stefan told her about how Rolf was getting meaner and more demanding of him. He also told her about getting hit in the face with the apple earlier in the day.

"That's horrible. I'm so sorry about that," Yvonne said back to him. "I was wondering why your cheek was so red. I wish you could work for someone nicer, like the lady of the house who I serve." Yvonne worked on the other side of Norwalk, past the village center, about twenty minutes by foot from where Stefan lived and worked. "Oh my, I almost forgot to tell you," Yvonne continued. "I heard some really good news today. Lady Ruth received a visitor this morning who came from far away, one of her nieces, I think. And guess what? The niece befriended me and even offered to teach me how to read and write while she's staying for the next month. Can you believe it? Me, Yvonne, humble eleven-year-old peasant girl from the lower class of

Norwalk. Soon I'll be able to add another title to that. Educated and smarter than any other peasant girl my age."

"Congratulations," Stefan responded, "that truly is good news. Make sure you hold her to it. Don't let her leave without teaching you all she possibly can. Because after you learn, I'm going to need you to teach me what you know."

"I'll have to think about that one. It depends on whether or not you deserve it. Maybe if you finally let me try riding your horse to the castle for a change," Yvonne said hopefully. The two dear friends continued swimming for a while in the deep blue water of the peaceful lake. Their only visitors were a family of ducks who happened to be swimming nearby. Four ducklings were following their mother. They kept dipping their heads and beaks into the water, probably to escape from the heat which filled the air. Soon, the sun started to go down behind the trees and Yvonne began swimming to shore. She called back to Stefan, "I better get home, Lady Ruth is going to start worrying about me soon."

"Yeah, I know what you mean, me too. I'm late for dinner, if you want to call it that," Stefan responded. The two came out of the lake and walked down the road headed for Stefan's place, leaving a trail of dripping water behind them. When they reached the landowner's estate where Stefan lived, the two said their goodbyes. "Have a safe journey home, Yvonne. I'll see you in the morning," Stefan told her as she continued walking down the road.

Stefan walked through the main gate of the landowner's property. After closing it behind him, he looked past the lawn and gardens at the large estate house where Rolf lived. Stefan couldn't understand how one person could live by themselves in such a large place, with so many rooms and windows. He figured it must have gotten lonely in there sometimes. Back in the day when the landowner's father Leon was still alive, the place received many more visitors, mostly from the upper class citizens of Norwalk. But lately, when the workers went home for the day, Rolf seemed to enjoy spending nights alone by himself.

Only a short walk away from the main house, just past the estate vineyards, was where Stefan and his parents lived. They moved into the small workers cottage on the property after the fateful events which transpired a decade earlier left their lives in shambles. Stefan didn't remember anything about the night when his younger brother Lolek was kidnapped by the rebels, and his parents didn't much talk about it anymore. About two years ago, Stefan was finally told the whole story when his father Martin thought he was old enough to hear it. Martin had the hardest time getting through the whole account all the way to the end. By the time he finished, Martin completely broke down and was holding Stefan close to him, resting his chin on Stefan's now brown hair. From what Stefan understood, his parents relocated with him from their original mud flat home at the edge of town to this cottage on the landowner's estate. The most interesting thing about them moving here, was it had apparently been the result of a royal decree of the king. The king even stationed a royal guard on the property for a year following the tragedy, after which the guard was reassigned somewhere else.

These days Norwalk was a much different place than it was back then. There were twenty royal guards residing full time in the village, stationed at strategic points throughout. Rebels hadn't been seen in the village for years, and except for the occasional property disputes between rich landowners, there weren't many problems. Compared to many people, Stefan did have a pretty difficult life as a twelve-year-old boy. Even so, he didn't ever complain, he knew what was expected of him. His father Martin could no longer work very much, his left leg having been severely injured in a fall about three years ago. The landowner took compassion on him though, because Martin was injured while working for him. The landowner let Martin turn his responsibilities of working in the fields over to his son, who was at that time only nine. Stefan's mother Shaylene suffered from bouts of depression, and although she tried to act happy around him, Stefan could see she was tormented inside. Shaylene would work inside the estate house during the day. Her tasks included cleaning, laundering clothes, and delivering baskets of fruit to the vendors market on Thursdays of each week. Shaylene was also in charge of managing the small amount of rice and bread provided for the family to eat each week. It was a simple life of hard work, but by peasant standards,

Stefan's family lived in a decent home and were able to all be together. That was the most important thing.

Shaylene woke Stefan up the next morning and reminded him that he needed to check in for work at the castle by eleven o'clock. A few minutes later he was up putting on the best clothes he owned. He searched through his wooden chest until he found the trousers and shirt with the least holes in them, and put them on. Kissing his mother goodbye and walking outside, he skipped over to the estate stables where one of his two most precious possessions was. Both of the things he treasured the most were given to him by the same person, the old landowner who recently passed away. The first was the necklace he wore around his neck, with the carved brasta wood pendant hanging from it. Stefan's parents told him that Leon gave it to him when he was a baby. When that happened, it was a real surprise to his parents. An even bigger surprise came a few months ago. When the old landowner started to get sick and realized his days were numbered, he took Stefan aside one day and made him the happiest boy in Norwalk. The kind old man told Stefan that he wanted him to have his horse. "It's not going to be of much use to me anymore, son. And I know you will take good care of him and give him plenty of exercise. From this day forward, he's yours," Stefan remembered him saying. The landowner's son initially objected, but relented a short time later when it became evident his father's sickness was serious. Rolf did lay down one rule for Stefan, which was there could be no riding on the property. So this morning, as he always did, Stefan walked ahead of his horse and led him down to the front gate. Once they were outside on the main road, Stefan jumped up onto his back and took off, leaving a cloud of dust behind him.

Yvonne was already waiting for him when Stefan pulled up to her place on his dark brown horse. "What took you so long?" she asked him.

"I couldn't figure out what to wear," he answered.

"Oh come on, you act like you're some dignitary visiting the castle or something. Don't forget, we're just kids who work there."

"I know, but someday I'm going to meet the princess and I want to look my best. She's bound to come into one of the rooms where I work eventually. Maybe she'll even invite me to do something with her, like go riding. We're both the same age, you know."

"Keep dreaming, Stefan. Keep dreaming," Yvonne told him as they pulled their horses away from Yvonne's place and headed off towards Astoria Castle.

Entering at the servants' bridge, Yvonne and Stefan dismounted and walked their horses across the narrow walkway. After checking out who they were, the royal guard stationed at the small gate opened it so they could pass through. They walked their horses for a few more minutes until they arrived at the peasant stables, where they tied them up in one of the stalls. Both horses immediately began feeding on some of the hay provided for them there. Yvonne and Stefan parted for the day, each heading off to work in different locations of the castle.

Stefan walked about ten minutes across one of the grass fields on the castle grounds to reach his work station. His station was located just past the underground prison, being attached to the far eastern side of the actual castle. When he checked in, the station guard reminded him that he was one minute late, and punctuality was important for workers at the castle. "Let's see," the station guard continued as he looked at his chart, "it looks like you're assigned to work today in the lower dining hall and the workers' quarters. All of the floors need to be scrubbed thoroughly in the lower dining hall, and you'll need to clean both the room floors and hallways of the workers' quarters. Go ahead and pick up the supplies you'll need and I'll drop by to check on your progress at about six o'clock this evening. If everything looks good, that will be it for the day. You can pick up a meal and head home." Just then another peasant worker walked in the front door and the station guard looked over at him, exasperated. As Stefan turned and walked down the corridor towards the supply room, he could hear the guard once again talking about punctuality.

Stefan picked up two wooden buckets in the supply room. One of them he filled with clean rags, while the other he filled with warm water and a powdery cleaning agent made in a nearby village. His assignment today was the one he received most frequently, cleaning floors in the eastern half of the castle. Most of the castle workers lived here, those who performed services which required them to actually live on the grounds full time. These workers included the cooks, the maids, the contingent of royal guards, and others who helped out in various capacities. Stefan had never seen any of the royal family in this half of the castle, but he figured there had to be a first time for everything. He did regularly see royal guards, and a few times even royal knights, eating meals in the lower dining hall. As he walked into the dining hall today, carrying his buckets, there were two lone royal guards sitting at one of the many tables talking with each other. They must have been taking a late breakfast, or perhaps an early lunch, Stefan figured. On weekends, which was when Stefan worked here, the place was usually not very busy, because most people were off spending time with their families. However, Stefan knew that the castle and castle grounds would be getting busier by the hour today, in preparation for The Astorian Games, which would be held on the great lawn tomorrow. The young peasant boy walked over to the far end of the dining hall and set his buckets down. He plunged a couple of the clean rags into the bucket of soapy water, dropped down on his knees, and started scrubbing.

An hour later, he was about finished with the first section of the dining hall, when the two royal guards stood up from the table they were sitting at. They started walking in the direction of Stefan on their way to another part of the castle, but for some reason they stopped in front of him. Stefan paused his work to look up at them. "Here you go, boy," one of the royal guards said to him as he handed him down a piece of sweet cake. "I hate to throw away food and my wife has me on a diet, so I better not eat this." Stefan happily accepted it and thanked him politely for his kindness.

As they walked through the door and down the next hallway, Stefan could hear one of the royal guards, the heavier one who was called Reginald, saying to the other one, "That was really nice of you, Mathieu. But I'll never let my wife stop me from finishing off my dessert." Laughter followed and echoed back into the room where a young peasant boy took a moment to stop scrubbing and enjoy his sweet cake.

Outdoors, near the edge of the great lawn, the young peasant girl Yvonne was hard at work tending to the flowering plants which surrounded the Castle Terrace. She was totally wrapped up in her work, trying to make every plant look perfect, not leaving one dead leaf or bad looking stem anywhere. She smiled and looked up at the sun in the sky, shining brightly overhead. It was a perfect day to be working outside, much cooler than yesterday. Though she was only eleven, Yvonne developed a love for working with plants. She enjoyed seeing small seeds she planted turn into beautifully sculpted works of art.

Yvonne did not have a normal life growing up, but then again, most peasants didn't. Her parents couldn't afford to keep her when their home was taken away from them over debts they owed. It was a painful time for her parents. She still remembers it like it was yesterday, though it was now five and a half years ago. Her mother walked up and down the streets of Norwalk with Yvonne in tow, knocking at the gate or door of every landowner in the village. Eventually she knocked at the door of the lady of the house where Yvonne now lives. The lady opened her door, took one look at Yvonne's mother, looked down at the young girl, then back up at Yvonne's mother and said, "I'll take her." It was as simple as that.

When the lady picked up Yvonne to bring her inside, the young girl cried out and said, "No, mommy, I don't want you to go! Take me with you. Don't you love me? Mommy!"

Yvonne's mother simply came apart and started crying profusely. She collapsed onto the porch of the lady's house, putting her face into her hands. The last words Yvonne heard her mother say before the door was closed were, "I'm sorry, my baby. I'll come back for you someday."

Yvonne's mother did not come back, and Yvonne had no idea where her mother or father were, or even if they were still alive. Yvonne vaguely remembers her parents discussing how they would have to go to some far off place to work off their debts, but that was about it. Still, Yvonne held out hope she would see them again someday. She was thankful that the lady of the house, Lady Ruth, treated her well. Lady Ruth required Yvonne to work hard in caring for the house she lived at, but allowed her the freedom to play with Stefan and her other friends when all of her tasks were done. Now that Yvonne was a little older, she even reluctantly agreed to let her work at the castle on the weekends. It didn't matter to Yvonne that when she came home with her small wages on Sunday night each week, she had to turn over the money to Lady Ruth. Of course, Yvonne didn't know it, but Lady Ruth was actually saving the money for a special reason. When enough funds were in place, Lady Ruth was going to surprise her with a new horse, since Yvonne's horse was getting very old.

When she thought she finished everything, Yvonne walked back along the lower portion of the small wall which supported the Castle Terrace to double check all of her work. Spotting something she missed the first time around, she went back to pruning one particular plant. While she was trying to make it look perfect, her overseer, an older woman named Elda, who had been in charge of the castle plants and flowers for thirty years now, came up to examine what she was doing. Surveying the plants lining the bottom of the Castle Terrace, the old woman was visibly impressed. "I've never seen the plants look so good," the woman told her. Yvonne looked up at her, blushing slightly, appreciative of the compliment. The woman continued, "Yvonne, now that you're finished here, I have a very important job for you to take care of. As you know, the games are going to be held on the castle grounds tomorrow. The royal family usually watches the games from right above where you've been working, up there on the Castle Terrace. For the rest of the day, I want you to give special attention to all of the plants and flowers up there, making sure everything looks the best it can for tomorrow. So, if you're done here, gather up your tools and follow me."

Hearing this, Yvonne was beyond excited. She couldn't believe she was going to be working, and actually physically standing on, the legendary Castle Terrace. This was where all of the important speeches were made to the people by King Charles. And like the old woman said, this was where the royal family would sit and watch the games held twice per year. She had never actually seen the games, or members of the royal family for that matter. But she was on the castle grounds working the last two times the games were held. The peasant workers were reassigned to other non-public tasks when the games were going on, usually something beyond the sight of the crowds of visiting dignitaries, wealthy landowners, and athletic achievers. Yvonne gathered up all of her things and followed the old woman towards the staircase which led to the Castle Terrace, twenty feet above where she had been working. Elda greeted the two royal guards who were posted at the bottom and spoke to them briefly. They looked over at the young peasant girl and nodded their approval. "Okay, you're all clear, Yvonne. Let's go up," the old woman directed her. The royal guards stepped to the side and let Elda and Yvonne pass by them. As they climbed up the staircase, which connected the great lawn with the right side of the Castle Terrace, Yvonne treasured each step.

Soon the staircase curved and they were at the top. Scanning her new surroundings, Yvonne looked around with a sense of wonder. To her right were four more royal guards. There were two of them on each side of the only entrance door leading into the castle. Standing mostly motionless, all four guards had swords in scabbards attached to their hips. The outside guards were each holding a lance, which had the dull end resting on the ground, with the sharp end pointing upwards. The guards wore a combination of thick clothing, dark green in color, and various pieces of body armor. None of them were wearing helmets or holding shields, which were probably reserved for use only in battle. When Yvonne met eyes with one of the royal guards, he gave her a friendly smile, causing her to smile back at him. She was happy to be up here. As her eyes shifted to the wide, polished stone platform she now stood on, she felt like she was on top of the world. It was an amazing view of the great lawn and castle grounds from here, that few subjects of the kingdom ever witnessed. She could see various castle workers out on the great lawn beginning to set things up for tomorrow's festivities. Yvonne followed the old woman around the outside edge of the upper terrace, where numerous plants were growing in full bloom. Elda gave her some further instructions, "Take your time and trim everything just right. It is very important not to miss anything. I'd help you, but I'm behind on my work designing the wreaths which will be worn by the victors tomorrow. Make me proud, Yvonne." With that, Elda departed and went back down the stairs. As she started working, Yvonne watched Elda as she crossed the lawn and went out of sight, appreciative that the old woman was giving her this opportunity of a lifetime.

Soon, Yvonne was once again absorbed in her work, trimming the boxed plants and cleaning around the different sized planters. As the afternoon wore on, she looked out at the great lawn to see what was going on. It was practically bustling with activity now. Yvonne's eyes caught sight of one group of workers in particular. They were setting up the archery targets which would be used in one of the competitions tomorrow. Yvonne was fascinated by the bow and arrow. She even had an old set back at her house that she liked to play with in her limited free time. Somehow, Yvonne had a natural talent for aiming at and striking targets from a great distance away. She laughed inside as she thought about the fact that every time she went into the woods to do target practice with Stefan, she beat him. What was more, she never missed hitting a target. The only question was whether she would hit the bullseye, or she would hit the inner ring right next to it instead. 'If only I wasn't an eleven-year-old peasant girl,' she thought to herself, 'I would probably grow up to be one of the most famous archers in the land.' She looked up at one of the four high castle lookout towers. She could make out the silhouettes of two royal archers standing up, with their backs to her, looking out at the horizon. How Yvonne wished she could be one of them, protecting the king and castle from the evil forces of the rebels. She imagined herself standing up there, spotting a group of rebels coming toward the castle to do harm. From way up high, she would take one of her arrows and fire it down right at their feet, stopping them in their tracks. Looking up, they would see the famed royal archer Yvonne standing tall, high above them in the lookout tower, and realize their attack was useless. In fear for their lives, they would turn and run, scattering into the woods, never to return again.

Abruptly, Yvonne became aware that some of the people down below on the lawn were stopping their work and staring up at her. She reminded herself that she was only daydreaming about being the famed royal archer, so she couldn't figure out why they would be looking at her. It was then that she realized they weren't looking at her, they were looking at someone else who walked out onto the Castle Terrace. Yvonne practically dropped her tools when she saw who it was. Standing twenty feet away from her was Astoria's young princess-to-be, Stasia. The twelve-year-old royal daughter was wearing a stunning red dress, with her long blonde hair blowing slightly in the gentle wind. Yvonne noticed there was a middle aged woman walking at her side, talking to her, probably one of her teachers. Yvonne didn't want to stare, so she quickly turned her head back and continued working on the plants. For the next ten minutes, the princess and middle aged woman continued talking, then they walked over towards the staircase. Yvonne dared another glance, thinking they were going to go down to the grassy fields below, but they didn't. They began examining one of the plants next to the staircase, talking about it. The young princess started feeling the stems, the leaves, and the flower petals of the plant. Finally, she leaned down slightly and smelled the flowers. When she was done, they moved over to the next plant and repeated the same ritual. This happened for the next few minutes, until it finally dawned on Yvonne that they were making their way around the outside of the upper terrace, gradually coming closer to where she was working.

Soon they were only two plants away from Yvonne, and she could hear what they were talking about. "And what do we have here?" the middle aged woman asked the princess.

"These are daylilies. Like this example here, they come in dynamic colors and can also take on a variety of shapes and forms," the princess answered. "We should really get some more of these at the castle, Delia. They're so beautiful." After the princess carefully checked out every detail of the daylilies, they moved over to another plant, which was directly next to where Yvonne was working.

"And this one? What is it and what are the most common types of colors it grows in?" the teacher asked her.

"That's easy. This is is a dahlia plant, which kind of rhymes with your name. In Astoria, the flowers grow mostly in red, but they can also be found in yellow." The teacher confirmed what she said was correct, and added she was quite impressed with Stasia's knowledge of plant life. She had correctly identified every plant so far today. Clearly, she was taking her studies seriously. The princess and her teacher took a few steps to the side, walking around Yvonne and over to the next unique plant. Yvonne was also working on a dahlia plant, like the one the princess was just tested on. Before the princess arrived at the next plant, she stopped. She turned around and walked back over to where Yvonne was working. Yvonne was stunned as the princess began speaking to her. "Peasant girl, would you please cut off one of those red flowers which matches my dress? I want to take it with me to brighten up my room."

Without hesitation, Yvonne replied, "It would be my pleasure, princess." Yvonne found the best looking of the red flowers in the planter she was working at, cut it off, and handed the stem to the princess.

The princess took the flower into her left hand and said, "Yes, this one is really pretty." Before leaving, she added, "Keep up the good work, it looks very beautiful up here."

"Thank you, princess, I will," Yvonne said, as the princess walked back over to rejoin her teacher.

A short time later, the princess and her teacher reentered the castle, the people on the fields down below went back to their business, and Yvonne was left alone to reflect on all that happened. Stefan was not going to believe this. She could hear herself telling him later, 'Me, Yvonne, humble eleven-year-old peasant girl from the lower class of Norwalk. Now I can add yet another title to that. One of the few peasants ever to meet, talk to, and do something for the future Princess of Astoria.' What a wonderful, life changing day it was for her.

Deep inside the eastern part of the castle, Stefan was about finished with his work for the day. He was scrubbing down the last of the hallways outside of the workers' quarters. Except for receiving the unexpected sweet cake, it had been a pretty uneventful day for him. His arms were growing tired and he was looking forward to receiving his evening meal before leaving to go home for the night. He was hoping that, as he did sometimes, he would be given a little extra food to bring home and share with his parents. Stefan felt great love for both of his parents. He wanted to make them proud by growing up to be a hard working, useful member of society. He couldn't change the fact that he was born into the world as a peasant. But he could make the most of each and every opportunity he was given. He realized there weren't many people out there looking to give him a break, or help him along in life. But the people who were in his life, were the ones he cared for, and that's what counted.

Stefan met his best friend Yvonne back when he was seven and she was six. He was out with his mother on a Thursday, bringing produce across town to the vendors market. As she was pulling the wooden cart filled with fruit down the main dirt road, a lady walked up and stopped her. Standing next to the lady was a small, young girl, with watery red eyes and tears streaming down her face. "Excuse me," the lady said to Shaylene, "but I was wondering if I could buy one of those oranges from you for my young girl here. She's been through a lot lately. She lost her mother." The lady ended up talking to Shaylene for a few minutes. At first, the two women didn't notice it, but the young girl and young boy, who were Yvonne and Stefan, also started talking. By the time the two women did look down, the children were sitting on the ground talking and playing with some rocks they found. Yvonne was no longer crying, but was smiling and laughing. Amazed, the lady asked Shaylene if she would allow her young boy to come over sometime to play with Yvonne. Shaylene reminded the lady that they were peasants, but if that didn't bother the lady, then Shaylene would be happy to drop Stefan off to visit from time to time. Arrangements were made, and Yvonne and Stefan grew up being the best of friends.

Stefan finally reached the end of the last hallway and collected his wooden buckets and rags. He took them back, cleaned them out, and put everything back where it belonged. As he walked out towards the exit, he stopped to check out with the station guard. The guard told him, "Hey, I wasn't able to come by and check on your work today like

I planned, but I'm sure you did a good job. Things started getting a little crazy around here with all of the work going on to prepare for the games." Handing Stefan his meager wage and a small bag of food, the guard added, "Thanks for your work, kid. I'll see you tomorrow." Stefan opened up the small bag as he was walking out the door, pleased to see he was given a little extra food. It made him happy to know he would be able to bring something home for his parents. Stefan skipped all the way back to the peasant stables, where Yvonne was already untying their horses.

"Guess what?" Stefan asked her. "I was given a little extra food today. My mother is going to be quite happy."

"That's really nice," Yvonne said, smiling. "But you're not going to believe what happened to me today."

Chapter Four:

A Princess To Be

That night a twelve-year-old girl was sitting in her room, looking out the window up at the stars. She was contemplating some complex issues that she was only beginning to understand. On her windowsill was a simple red flower. It was that flower, cut off from a dahlia plant earlier in the day, which caused the turmoil in her mind she was trying to sort out. She was to be the future princess of the land, but it was not something she ever asked for, or even selfishly desired. It was a role she was born to play. But she wasn't sure if she wanted all of this. Why couldn't she just have a normal life, like every other girl her age? There were just too many things she was being taught and attitudes she was being pushed to develop, which she didn't agree with. It wasn't in her heart to be the type of person they expected her to be.

It all started this afternoon, when she was walking on the Castle Terrace with her private teacher Delia, someone she had grown up spending a lot of time with. She loved Aunt Delia and appreciated all of the ways in which Delia was there for her through the years. Delia was giving Princess Stasia one of her weekly tests, at first in the Royal Gardens, and then out on the Caste Terrace. This week's test involved identifying and understanding the plant life and flowers of Astoria, something Stasia was well prepared for, because she always took her lessons seriously. The problem came when Stasia stopped her exam briefly to walk over to a peasant girl who was hard at work. Stasia asked the peasant girl to cut off the flower now sitting on her windowsill. That was it. It shouldn't have been a big deal, right? That's what Stasia thought anyway, as she continued looking out her window. Distracting her for a moment, a shooting star appeared and streaked across the night sky. After the trail of light disappeared, her mind returned to the mistake she made today, at least according to her uncle. Her Uncle Chadwick, who was Delia's husband, and served as Chief Royal Knight, was outside on the Castle Terrace briefly at the same time as Stasia. He was talking to the four royal guards about security for tomorrow's special event, when he observed the conversation which transpired between Stasia and the peasant girl. When Stasia walked back into the castle from the terrace a short time later, Chadwick was there waiting for her. He excused Delia and took Stasia into the Castle Library, saying there was something important he needed to talk with her about.

That's when he said some really hurtful things to her. Stasia reflected back on part of the conversation. Chadwick scolded her, "Have you ever once seen your father, the king, speaking to a peasant boy begging on the streets? Have you ever once seen your mother, the queen, speaking to a filthy girl working in rags? No, you haven't. And do you know why? The royal family does not interact with common peasants. No king, no queen, no prince, or no princess who has ever sat on this throne has ever been known to even speak with such a lower class citizen. That's what the Code of Honor scroll is all about." Chadwick was clearly irate and meant what he was saying. He then walked over to one of the shelves on the library and pulled down the most recent volume of the Royal History Pages. He brought it over to where Stasia was standing and threw it down on the table next to her. He continued with a nicer tone, saying, "Stasia, I'm only doing this for you because I love you. This might be hard to accept, but someday you'll appreciate what I'm saying. If we open up the door even a crack for the lower class people, they'll want to barge all the way through. What I want you to do for the rest of today and tonight, is to read through this book. As you do, think about how the leaders who came before you dealt with the common people. Learn from them, and strive to be like them in everything you do." As he finished up his speech, Chadwick walked out of the library. A moment later he reappeared at the door and added, "And Stasia, make sure you read it. I'm going to have Delia check in with you to make sure it's been read by Monday."

Stasia looked over from her seat by the window at the Royal History Pages, which was opened up and resting on her bed. To be completely honest, she didn't really like what she was reading. She found it interesting to learn about some of her ancestors, those who ruled before her. But Chadwick was right. They didn't much care for common people, at times even using them for slave labor in building projects across the land. She also read about how commoners received no rights in a court of law, no ability to own property, and were not permitted to have an audience with the king. Of course, she had been down this road before, having discussions about commoners with both her mother and father. Essentially, they agreed with Chadwick's view of matters. Her father did tell her one interesting story, about how when she was only a baby, he extended compassion towards one peasant family in a nearby village. It was only because the rebels kidnapped their son, and he didn't want any more trouble in the village, which was located so close to the castle.

Stasia felt confused thinking about all of these things. She realized that she wasn't going to be able to figure it all out tonight, so she decided to go to bed. She closed the shutters over her window and moved the book off her bed. Climbing under the covers, she drifted off to sleep, not feeling the least bit sorry about what she had done.

Her sleep was not very pleasant that night. Mixed in with other dreams she couldn't remember, was one she could. Although it seemed more like a nightmare to her. In her dream, she turned sixteen years old and was being coronated as the new princess in the Grand Ballroom. It was a great moment. There were people everywhere all around her, congratulating her and celebrating. But then she saw the peasant girl from earlier in the day walking up to her, holding another red flower. Suddenly, there was a lot of commotion, as people were moving to one side or the other, getting out of her way. They were scared of her. They didn't want to be touched by her. The peasant girl finally made it to the stage and reached out to give her the flower.

Stasia, wearing her new crown, reached down to take it from her. Before she could, the crowd who initially gathered for her coronation turned into an angry mob. They surrounded the peasant girl, picked her up, and threw her out of the castle. "No! Stop! No!" Stasia found herself saying aloud as she woke up.

When she realized it was only a dream, Stasia climbed out of bed and opened her window. She could see the first signs of daylight on the horizon. Putting her hand over her mouth, she yawned and thought about going back to bed. She decided not to and walked out of her room, feeling a bit hungry and lonely. She greeted the two royal guards who were standing attentively outside of her room and went downstairs, looking for something to eat. Just before she arrived at the kitchen, she spotted her father, King Charles. He was sitting down at a table, reading something, and sipping on a warm drink. "Good morning, father," she said to him.

"Stasia, my dear," he said, looking up at his daughter. "You're up early today. You must be really excited about the games. I hear Sir Rackley is going to be entering the archery competition. But you probably already know that, don't you?"

"Actually, I'm up early because I couldn't sleep," Stasia corrected him. "And yes, I've already been told by like ten different people that Sir Rackley will be competing today. I know that I'm supposed to marry him someday, or that I *have* to marry him someday, but right now it's the last thing on my mind. Can't everyone just let me be a girl right now?"

"Of course, my dear. I didn't mean to bring up Sir Rackley to upset you. You're probably too young to even be interested in boys right now. I want you to go out there and have fun today. Enjoy yourself. You've been studying so hard lately. It will be good for you to have a day off. Here, why don't you sit down with me for a while and enjoy some fresh fruit and warm bread."

"Thanks, father. I really appreciate that," Stasia said as she sat down next to her father and began eating a slice of watermelon. She glanced over at what he was reading and noticed it was an updated report on problems the rebels were causing throughout the land. Realizing her father had bigger problems to deal with, she felt kind of bad for snapping at him about the arranged marriage set for her in the future.

A few hours later, the castle grounds were filling up with people who came from all across the land. Athletes who excelled at every type of sport known were stretching and going through their training rituals. Wealthy landowners were jockeying for the best seats around the sporting areas. Game officials were carefully putting together the final pieces of equipment which would be used in the competitions. And castle workers were buzzing about, taking care of all kinds of tasks. While all of this was going on, Stasia was hanging out with two of her friends near the royal stables. One of them was Alana, the sixteen-year-old daughter of a royal archer. The other was Madison, the nine-year-old daughter of the royal guard Mathieu. They were laughing and making fun of one of the teenage stable workers who just walked by. He had turned to look over at them as he was passing, and said, "Hello there, girls." Somehow, he didn't see that there was a saddle somebody had left on the ground in his path. As he was winking at the sixteen-year-old, he tripped over it and fell on his face. The girls all let out a roar of laughter at the same time when it happened, leaving the stable worker totally embarrassed. He leapt up off the ground as fast as he could and ran off to parts unknown. It was the funniest thing Stasia had seen in some time.

Stasia and her friends had come out to the stables to visit with a few of the horses and sneak out for a ride. When their laughter finally subsided, Stasia led the girls into the special section holding the king's horses. It was where she kept her own horse, which she named Isobel. Isobel was an extremely rare white horse, magnificent, but as gentle as could be. One of the reasons for this was that Stasia spent a lot of time with her horse. Although she let the stable master and his workers groom and feed the horse, she preferred to come outside herself to tie the horse up each night. It gave Stasia an opportunity to bond with the horse, as she would rub the mane, neck, and head of Isobel for quite some time. Looking into the horse's eyes, she could feel the horse loving her back. The horse seemed to understand her, sometimes even better than humans did. Stasia took her horse out of its stall and the other girls went to get their horses as well. Stasia then led her horse and the others up to the door which separated the royal stables from the peasant stables. She asked the royal guard to open the door and let them out. She explained to him that they needed to exit the castle grounds from the servants' bridge, because the main drawbridge was too crowded today with spectators and athletes coming to the games. Before opening it, the royal guard asked her, "Does the Chief Royal Knight know about this?" The guard obviously being concerned for her safety.

"Of course he does. Now open up," Stasia told the guard. It wasn't exactly the truth. But if Chadwick, the Chief Royal Knight, knew about it, he would have either forbid Stasia from going, or sent a contingent of six royal guards with her. She really didn't want to go on a horseback ride with six guards, she wanted to go with her two friends. Besides, she was still rather angry with Chadwick and figured this would be a good way to get him back. The royal guard finally relented and let them pass through. After they walked across the servants' bridge, the three girls climbed on their horses and rode off into the nearby countryside.

Back in the castle, Delia and Chadwick were in their bedroom involved in another one of their arguments. This time, they were fighting about Stasia. Chadwick was upset that Delia had not corrected the young princess on the spot, when she was conversing with the peasant girl. "Delia, you can't let behavior like that go uncorrected," he was telling her. "That girl is going to be our new leader in four short years."

"We don't have the right to try to mold her mind to our liking," Delia responded. "If she has a love for all people, and not exclusively for the upper class, then why should we try to change that?"

"Because it has never been the way of our people. You may not have noticed, but there were quite a few citizens of Astoria staring up at the princess from the castle grounds down below. They saw everything which transpired. What kind of impression do you think it left on them?"

"To be honest, probably a good one," Delia answered. As she said this, a figure appeared outside of their door, standing in the shadows. Neither Chadwick nor Delia seemed to notice the eavesdropper.

Delia's answer was not what Chadwick wanted to hear. He showed his dissatisfaction by walking over and hitting a glass water container off a table in a fit of rage. Glass shattered everywhere as the container hit the floor. "You're not listening to me, Delia," he continued. "You're the one who spends the most time with her and has the most impact on her. It's your responsibility as her teacher to correct her thinking when it strays."

"Maybe I don't think her thinking has strayed. Maybe I think she's perfectly fine the way she is," Delia responded. Hearing this, Chadwick turned and kicked the table that the water container had been sitting on. One of the legs holding up the table snapped in half, causing the table to collapse onto the floor.

Ending the argument was the figure in the shadows, who now stepped forward into the room. It was Queen Delphine, who looked at them both for a moment without speaking. "Madam Queen," Chadwick finally said, his voice slightly shaking. "I didn't mean for you to see that. It was just a small disagreement we were having. I apologize for losing my temper."

The queen thought for another moment and began speaking. "I know you both have my daughter's best interests at heart. Please give her a chance to grow up. There will be times when she's going to let you down. But she has a beautiful heart and someday she's going to be an excellent ruler who will make all of us proud." After pausing to allow her words to sink in, the queen looked at Delia and asked, "Are you going to be all right, Delia?"

"Yes, I will be fine. And Stasia's already making us proud."

"I'm glad you feel that way. I know she cares for you both very much, and the king and I deeply appreciate all you both continue to do for her," the queen said. "Oh, I almost forgot. The reason I came up here in the first place was to see if you two could help me put the finishing touches on a gift I was putting together for Sir Rackley. The games are going to be starting soon, and I won't have any more time to get it wrapped up after that." Chadwick and Delia agreed to help her. All three of them went downstairs to finish putting the gift together.

A few hours later, Stasia returned from her secret ride. She was standing with her parents just outside the door leading onto the Castle Terrace. The princess-to-be was wearing a light pink dress, with white sleeves and a pattern of white daisies circling around at her waist and at the bottom of the dress. Her long blonde hair was being held in place by a hair clip studded with diamonds. Queen Delphine took her daughter's hand and squeezed it gently, saying, "You look so beautiful today, my dear." Stasia looked at her and smiled.

The Chief Royal Knight, Chadwick, came in the door and announced to the king, "Everything is ready, your majesty. All of the royal guards are in place. The crowd has been checked for anyone suspicious. And the royal archers have given us the all clear. Whenever you're ready."

King Charles thanked Chadwick and led his family through the door to the outside. As they stepped onto the terrace and walked towards their specially installed seats, applause, whistling, and screaming broke out in the crowd. The royal family walked together, side by side, waving to the thousands of ecstatic onlookers. It was the kind of moment the princess really enjoyed, seeing so many people, all of whom adored her and looked up to her family. Knowing they felt such affection for her made her want to fulfill her responsibilities and become princess. She wanted to return their love and do everything in her power to make their lives better. They were counting on her and she wanted to surpass their expectations. Stasia blew some kisses out to the masses, as the royal family waited for the applause to die down.

When the noise subsided, King Charles began to speak. "Welcome one and all to The Astorian Games of mid-summer! Today, we have gathered with us the best athletes and the fiercest competitors from throughout the land. The challenges are great, but the rewards for the victors even greater. All ten winners of the major competitions will have the honor of standing up here on the Castle Terrace, where they will each receive a wreath of victory and a prize of two hundred and fifty gold coins. May you all enjoy this great day." Raising his right hand in the air, and then dropping it with one fast motion, Charles added, "Let the games begin!" As applause once again sounded, trumpets and horns began playing in unison from the musicians standing on the terrace.

During the next hour, the games started with a jousting competition and a weight lifting challenge. All three members of the royal family sat on the terrace and watched with interest. The weight lifting challenge consisted of boulders of varying shapes and sizes that had to be moved from one marked area on the ground over to another. The boulders were pre-weighed to make sure all participants were given an equal and fair chance at winning. The person with the fastest time would move on to the next round. When the final two competitors were left, there was a twist thrown into the game. The boulders would have to be moved using only one hand, with the other hand tied behind their back. Onlookers gasped in surprise upon hearing this, thinking it was not humanly possible. The gasps turned to expressions of awe as both competitors showed their strength and agility in transporting the boulders one-handed. As the victor was named, Stasia asked her parents for permission to walk down to the grounds below, so she could have a first hand look at everything. Her parents agreed and Stasia headed over to the stairway. Seeing this, Chadwick signaled for four royal guards to accompany her out into the crowd. She walked down the terrace stairs with two of the guards in front of her, and two of them behind her.

Stasia's two friends were waiting for her at the bottom of the stairs. She hugged them both, before they started walking together out into the crowd. As the future princess made her way through, people were pressing in to get a closer look at her and say their greetings. The four royal guards did their job well, keeping a safe amount of space between the crowd and the three girls. "Where did you get that gorgeous dress?" her friend Alana asked her. "I've never seen you wear that one before."

"I know," replied the princess, "it's brand new. It was made especially for me for this special day. I can't believe how many people are here today. I think this is the most I've ever seen here on the castle grounds."

"Yeah, the games are getting more and more popular, it seems," Alana added. "If this keeps up, the castle workers are going to have to move the walls out to fit everyone inside at the next games in six months." The other two girls laughed, at hearing their friend suggest this impossible feat.

"Or maybe we'll have to start feeding the losers to the crocodiles outside the castle walls," Stasia added with her wry sense of humor. All three girls laughed again at the thought of this.

The girls walked slowly around the grounds, watching some of the different competitions for a few minutes, before moving on. Wherever they went, they would draw lots of attention. Suddenly, something a short distance away caught Stasia's eye. "Girls, girls, look! It's our favorite game," she said, pointing toward a stand with a game set up to cater to the crowd. The girls walked over to take a closer look. There was a small display stand with three wooden barrels in front of it which were standing upright. The tops were taken off the barrels, and they were filled up with water to the brim. Floating on the surface of the water were five red apples in each of the three barrels. Sitting on top of the display stand, behind the barrels, was a large bowl of delicious looking caramel apples.

"What I wouldn't give for one of those right now," Stasia's younger friend Madison said to her. As the girls were looking wishfully at the caramel apples, a man with a mustache, long sideburns, and curly black hair stepped out from behind the display stand. He was wearing a white glove over each of his hands.

"If you want one of those, you're going to have to win it, young lady," he said to her. Turning to Stasia, he added, "Welcome to 'Bobbing for Apples,' fair princess. How would you and your friends like to play the difficult game in front of you?"

Looking at her friends, who nodded back to her, Stasia answered him, "We'd love to play. We're kind of experts at this."

Taking his gloves off and tucking them into one of his trouser pockets, the man took a serious tone, "Well, to make sure all of you are familiar with the rules, let me explain how this works. As you can see, we have three barrels set up here, allowing for either two or three people to compete against each other at once. Since there are three of you, you will each choose a barrel and step forward in front of it. On my word, you will put your hands behind your back and keep them there throughout the game. Don't forget, I'll be watching from behind you, to make sure you don't move your hands away from your back in an attempt to gain some extra leverage." As the man with the mustache continued explaining the rules, more and more onlookers were crowding around the booth to see what was going on. The four royal guards kept reminding anyone who came too close to take a few steps back.

The man finished, "When you hear the signal, you'll dip your head down towards the top of the water and start trying to catch apples with your teeth. When you've caught an apple, take it with your mouth and drop it into the empty basket next to your barrel. The first girl to catch all five apples, dropping them into their basket, wins the grand prize. A sweet, juicy, tasty treat, that you can have all to yourself, one of these caramel apples." The now large crowd that had gathered applauded as the man held up the bowl containing the caramel apples for all to see.

The three girls stepped up to the barrels, with Stasia taking the middle barrel and one friend standing to each side of her. A hush fell over the crowd as they awaited the signal to begin. After looking around for a moment, the man rang a bell and the game was on. Alana immediately caught an apple and dropped it into her basket. Stasia bit for one of her apples, but she missed it, as it hit her nose and pushed away in the water. Madison was biting as fast as she could into her barrel, but was just managing to get water all over her face and hair. Her furious efforts were creating waves, which were spilling over the side onto the grass. Stasia moved into the lead, as she caught two apples in quick succession and dropped them into her basket. Seeing this, the crowd roared their approval and started chanting her name. Not to be outdone, Alana tied up the score, catching her second apple. Madison was still struggling, as every effort she made seemed to only make things worse. Soon, both Stasia and Alana had the hang of it, as each traded off catching apples until the score was even at four a piece. Finally, Madison caught an apple and dropped it into her basket. The crowd cheered its support, no doubt feeling a measure of sympathy for her. Then, Alana caught her final apple, a few seconds before Stasia was able to do the same. Victory within her grasp, her heart raced with excitement as she moved her mouth over toward the basket. Her nerves got the better of her. As she let the apple go from her mouth, it hit the corner of the basket, and bounced off onto the lawn. A moment later, Stasia dropped her final apple into her basket and the crowd went crazy. The future princess had done it! She was declared the winner of 'Bobbing for Apples.'

As the cheering continued, the man with the mustache walked over holding the bowl of caramel apples and said to her, "Congratulations, princess. In one of the closest contests I've ever seen, you came out the winner. Now for your grand prize. You may choose any one of these delicious caramel apples, whichever one appeals to your eyes." Stasia looked at the caramel apples in the bowl and then over at her two friends who she had just beaten. Madison appeared to be particularly dismayed over losing the contest. Stasia finally picked one of the apples, the biggest one she could see, and held it up in the air for the crowd to see. They once again cheered and started calling for her to take her first bite. Instead of bowing to their wishes, Stasia called one of the royal guards over to where she was standing. She asked him to take out his sword. When he did, the crowd gasped at the sight of it. Stasia next set her winning caramel apple down on the grass.

"Guard, cut this apple in half with your sword," she instructed him. With one quick swing, the guard hit the apple dead center with his sword, slicing it perfectly in half. She picked up the two halves and again held them up in the air. Wondering what she was going to do next, the crowd received their answer when she handed one half to Alana, and the other half to Madison, leaving nothing for herself. Spontaneous applause broke forth, continuing for nearly five minutes until Stasia motioned for them to quiet down.

As the three friends walked away from the 'Bobbing for Apples' contest, Stasia realized something special had happened. This was the type of ruler she wanted to be. One who was generous and kind, thinking of others before herself. It made her feel good inside, giving more to others than they could ever expect. It wasn't something she needed to think about doing, it came naturally to her. She may have been a twelve-year-old girl, but without question, she was wise beyond her years.

While Madison finished up the last remnants of her half of the apple, the three walked over to the archery competition, which was down to the last four contestants. Sir Rackley was one of the final four, despite being only fifteen. Stasia didn't know who the other three archers were, but they undeniably were proficient with a bow and arrow. The archers needed to hit both stationary and moving targets, which were getting smaller and smaller as the rounds went by. Seeing Sir Rackley again, for the first time in over a year, caused Stasia to think about the arranged marriage she was put into. It was another one of those things expected of her that she wasn't too thrilled about. Like she told her father this morning, marriage really was the last thing on her mind. Although, contrary to what her father thought, she had started to notice boys and enjoyed being around them. But she felt nothing special for Sir Rackley. Maybe with age, she would start developing the romantic feelings she observed other men and women regularly expressing towards one another. She wasn't too worried about it right now, so she stood and cheered for Sir Rackley.

Sir Rackley was losing to his final four opponent. It was the first time he ever entered a major competition like this. In Limekiln, the land where he lived, to be a good archer was considered the pinnacle of all achievements. The sport held legendary status there, and Sir Rackley practiced for all of his life as far back as he could remember. When his parents, King Dominic and Queen Bronagh, suggested he make the trip to Astoria Castle for this year's archery competition, he gladly obliged. Back home at his castle, he regularly beat every opponent he challenged, not having lost once during the past year. He didn't know if he was beating everyone because he was really that good, or if they were letting him win out of fear of reprisal. Thus, coming here to Astoria would answer the question for him. At the same time, it would provide a new and interesting way to test his skills against the best. Those were not the only reasons Sir Rackley wanted to come on this trip. The girl he was to marry in five years time lived here, the royal princess-to-be. Though he knew little of her and spent hardly any time around her, he thought he was in love with her. Perhaps his love came out of a sense of duty to his parents or the people of his land, or perhaps it came from the thought of marrying a mysterious princess. Whatever the reason, he was hoping to see her today and looking for some kind of sign she actually felt affection for him and remembered that he existed. So far, he was tremendously disappointed. She hadn't even shown up to watch his archery competition. And it had appeared to him that right when the archery competition started, she left her seat next to King Charles and Queen Delphine, and went to do something else. Discouraged, he kind of went through the motions in the early rounds of the contest. He was winning his matches and advancing, but his heart wasn't into it. As the field narrowed down to the last few archers, his half-hearted effort was no longer enough to carry him through. He no longer cared if he won or lost.

Those feelings all changed for Sir Rackley when he set his bow down after another low scoring shot. Scanning the crowd out of habit once more, his eyes finally locked in on his girl. It was really her, the princess was here watching him. And wait a minute, she was even vocally supporting him. With new resolve, Sir Rackley wanted to impress her. He couldn't afford to lose this match now. On his next three turns, he fired three consecutive, difficult bullseyes, the last one hitting a moving wooden rabbit right between the eyes. With his amazing comeback in winning this match, it was now smooth sailing to victory. His final opponent was nearly twice his age, and even a bit taller than him, but Sir Rackley made quick work of him and was declared official winner of the archery competition. The crowd was cheering, the king and queen were applauding, and the young girl he was infatuated with was shouting his name. It was the best day of his life.

As darkness set in and the games came to an end, the crowds massed together near the bottom of the Castle Terrace. Even the officials and workers stopped what they were doing to gather around and watch the awards ceremony. The lamp torches were lit all across the castle grounds, casting bright firelight down on everyone. Out in the middle of the great lawn, a nine-year-old girl walked up to her father, who was the royal guard Mathieu, and gave him a hug. Mathieu, who was standing next to his friend Reginald, also a royal guard, leaned down and lightly tickled her. As she was giggling, he asked her, "Did you have fun today, Madison?"

"I always have fun with the princess," she answered. Madison started to tell him the whole story about bobbing for apples and the caramel apple prize, but her story was cut short as trumpets once again sounded for all to hear.

"The king is about to speak. Why don't you finish telling me about it later," Mathieu told his daughter. His daughter turned around, and the three of them joined everyone else on the castle grounds in silence, waiting for King Charles to begin.

When the trumpets and other instruments died down, King Charles stepped forward. "Today has been a grand day in our kingdom. The greatest athletes from all over the region have traveled here in search of victory and glory. And they did not disappoint. The queen and I would like to first of all congratulate all who had the courage and desire to enter The Astorian Games. There were no losers today, only winners. Every athlete who qualified and participated today will have his name forever etched into the Royal History Pages. That being said, let us now welcome onto the Castle Terrace our ten event champions!" After saying this, the king motioned to his left. In perfect sync, the ten champions walked out and lined up in a straight row, near the front edge of the terrace. When the applause finally started to subside, the king continued his speech. "And now, the part you have all been waiting for. Each winner will receive the prize they have been promised, two hundred and fifty gold coins. In addition, the most beloved girl in our land, princess-to-be Stasia, will put a wreath of victory on each champion's head. Princess, if you will do the honors, please."

That was Stasia's cue and she stood up, walking down the line of winners. First, she would wait for King Charles to announce the name of each winner and what the event had been. Then she would hand them the bag of gold coins and gently put the wreath of victory onto their heads. When she reached the end of the line, Sir Rackley was standing there, the second to last person. She saw him staring at her, and it made her feel the slightest bit uncomfortable. But she did what she was supposed to do. And then she had one of those impulsive ideas she came up with every once in a while. It was the kind of thing where she did something without really thinking about it. After she finished putting the wreath on the head of the final winner, she went back over and kissed Sir Rackley on the cheek. If this was the best day of Sir Rackley's life, then that was the best moment of his life. When her parents saw what she had done, they both looked at each other and smiled. And the young, twelve-year-old princess-to-be, wearing a beautiful pink dress with daisies on it, sat back down, wondering what she had done.

Chapter Five:

Secret Scheme of the Rebels

Earlier that day, a rebel spy spotted the princess and her two friends riding away from the castle and into the countryside. There wasn't much he could do about it at the time. The spy, who walked with an obvious limp, did, however, make a mental note to tell Prince Agis about it the next time they met. The spy was a large man named Robbins, who was traveling with Herman, a wealthy landowner sympathetic to the rebels' cause. They were on their way to attend the games at Astoria Castle. Also in their group was Sebastian, an eleven-year-old boy who Robbins had raised as his own son for the past decade, at the personal request of Prince Agis. Today was to be an important day in Sebastian's upbringing and transition into a young man. After years of being brought along on rebel raids, only to watch things from a distance, Sebastian would no longer be a bystander. This would be his first assignment, giving him the chance to demonstrate his loyalty and commitment to the rebels' cause. The task involved helping to break two rebel soldiers out of the castle prison, who had been imprisoned there for ten long years now. It was a very important assignment, one that benefited the two long-time prisoners, the rebels as a group, and Sebastian. The plan would be executed later that night, after the games concluded and the awards ceremony was taking place. Until then, Robbins and Sebastian had another vital task to fulfill. Prince Agis wanted them to do surveillance on the castle grounds, looking for weaknesses they could exploit later when it was time to carry out their ultimate secret scheme.

General Robbins and his group arrived at the drawbridge leading into the castle. There were people everywhere out front, including merchants, beggars, athletes, landowners, even a small group of castle musicians. But of more interest to Robbins were the two contingents of royal guards standing near the drawbridge. The first group consisted of five royal guards stationed at the beginning of the bridge. They were carefully eyeing everybody who walked by. Robbins noted that anybody who looked the least bit suspicious was stopped and carefully searched before they were allowed to pass. The second group consisted of only two guards, which were stationed on opposite sides of the entrance gate at the end of the drawbridge. Robbins looked up at the two lookout towers visible from where he was standing. Each of the lookout towers had two royal archers standing in it. One of the royal archers was watching the people who were milling about outside of the castle. The other royal archer was attentive to the surrounding countryside, scanning it back and forth for any signs of a threat. As Robbins and his group started to walk across the drawbridge, one of the royal guards looked at all of them carefully. The guard's eyes first checked out Sebastian and Herman, but quickly moved on to Robbins. When the group passed by the royal guard, Robbins breathed a sigh of relief. It was short lived, as he heard a voice calling from behind him.

"You there, stop and come back here for a moment," the voice said. Robbins' heart almost stopped as he turned back and looked at the royal guard who was speaking. "Not you, the young man with you," the guard said to Robbins. "I want have a look inside the bag he's carrying."

Sebastian cast a nervous glance at Robbins. Robbins took control of the situation, telling him, "It's all right, son. Let him check out the bag." Sebastian took the bag off his shoulder, walked over to the royal guard, and handed it to him. The guard opened it up and began taking out the contents to inspect them.

"Let's see what we have here, young man," the guard said. The guard took out the items, naming them off. "One small wool blanket, five silver coins, two changes of clothes, a writing instrument, one tablet of papyrus paper, and a set of newly pressed keys. It looks like everything here is okay. Just out of curiosity, what are these keys for? They almost look like dungeon keys." Robbins started to answer the question, but was quickly cut off by the royal guard. "Not you, I asked the boy."

His eyes shifting ever so slightly, Sebastian answered, "Um, those are a new set of keys which were made for our stables. Recently, two of our horses were stolen at night, while we were sleeping. So we installed barred gates over each of the stalls, to protect them from thieves."

Satisfied with the boy's answer, the guard handed him back his bag. As the group was leaving to walk across the drawbridge, the guard added, "I hope it's not those despicable rebels stealing from you. They have no respect for private property." Robbins and his group pretended to laugh, assuring the guard they had no such trouble and had never seen rebels before.

Robbins paused for a moment when he arrived at the middle of the drawbridge. He looked down into the thick moat that went under where he was standing, which completely surrounded the castle. The moat was dirty green in color and quite wide from one bank to the other. "Father, look!" Sebastian called to him, pointing out towards the middle of the moat. Robbins looked and saw a huge crocodile surface, its long snout and the top half of its scaly head, neck, and back visible. "That thing looks terrifying," Sebastian added a moment later. Robbins wanted to object, because he wasn't afraid of anything. But he couldn't do it, realizing he shared a portion of the boy's fear. Prince Agis once spoke to the rebels about the guardian crocodiles of Astoria Castle, but hearing about them and seeing one of them in person were two completely different things. The bottom line was there would be no way to cross the moat safely without jeopardizing one's life, or at the very least, one's limbs. Any overthrow or attack on the castle would have to be direct, across either the drawbridge they were standing on, or the small servants' bridge on the other side of the castle.

Unexpectedly, someone came up behind Robbins as he was still watching the crocodile and lifted up on his waist, shouting, "Over you go!" Robbins nearly reacted by hitting the assailant with his elbow, before he realized it was Sebastian pulling a prank on him.

"This is not the time for jokes, son," Robbins scolded him. "We have work to do here and we don't want to draw attention to ourselves. We need to keep our focus on our mission."

"Sorry, father, I couldn't resist," Sebastian managed to say while he was still laughing. "And didn't you once say the element of surprise is critical to our success?"

The group continued walking across the bridge and through the open entrance gate onto the castle grounds. Sebastian was instantly struck with the vast, wide open space which existed inside the castle walls. Bumping into several people as he was looking around, he apologized and tried his best to keep up with everyone else. Robbins needed something to eat, so he led the group over to a food vendor set up close to the entrance. He ordered two meals of chicken legs and potatoes, since Herman didn't want anything. Herman paid for the food, after which he left the group to get involved in some of the activities going on and to look for some of his wealthy friends. Robbins and Sebastian took their meals away from the crowded areas and found a shady spot where they could sit down and eat. They found a place with relative privacy, so they could review both aspects of their mission one last time. After they were finished eating and talking, Sebastian and Robbins each went to different areas of the castle grounds to do the surveillance part of the operation. While Sebastian headed east, Robbins headed west across the great lawn, looking for guard stations and any observable weaknesses.

Robbins felt good about being placed in charge of this mission today. It was a real show of faith on the part of Prince Agis to entrust him with what needed to be done. Recently, he was promoted to general, which was near the top of the rebel hierarchy. Prince Agis was the unquestioned leader of the rebels, as he formed them some twenty years ago as a small group of dissidents opposed to King Charles and the royal family. What started out small back then had now grown into a large network of opposition, numbering into the hundreds. While they were based in one central location, deep in the forest, far from any roads or villages, the rebel camp was set up in such a way that it could be moved at a moment's notice. In its current location, the camp was set up at a small clearing in the forest, in between a river and a small rocky hillside. The dining and residence tents were located at the outer areas of the camp, which is where the rebels would eat and sleep. Right next to these was the new recruits tent, which housed both willing and unwilling new rebels. To maintain the horses, a small section of forest was enclosed, with long tree branches and logs used as fencing. At the heart of the camp was the sword fighting circle, where all of the rebels practiced fighting on a daily basis. Finally, there were larger tents set up near the river for the generals, special visitors, and Prince Agis.

So far, the rebels only needed to relocate one time in the twenty years they were in existence. It was several years ago, when a party of two royal guards and one land surveyor stumbled onto their camp. The party had been out deep in the forest, mapping uncharted land, when they came across the rebels. Realizing they made a discovery which could end the threat of the rebels forever, they all turned their horses around and immediately rode as fast as they could to get out of the forest. However, the rebels knew the territory much better and quickly caught one of the royal guards and the land surveyor. The other royal guard managed to escape, though, and so the rebels were forced to pack up and move to another strategic, deeply hidden location. Not wanting to feed any prisoners, the rebels left the two captured men at their old camp, half naked and tied to a tree. The rebels painted a message in big red letters across their backs, which read, 'IN SERVICE OF KING CHARLES.' Knowing a vast army of royal guards would descend on their former camp, the message and half naked men would be all that remained. Since relocating, there were no signs of anyone coming anywhere near the vicinity of their new camp. As increased protection, rebel soldiers were now posted in the forest area surrounding their new camp.

When Robbins was promoted to the rank of general by Prince Agis, one of the added benefits was that Robbins could finally see his face. It was something he looked forward to for a long time. Prince Agis was very sensitive about keeping his identity a secret, worried that if one of the rebels defected and exposed who he was, it would bring down the entire operation. Prince Agis would arrive and depart from the rebel camp with a creepy looking mask over his face. He would keep the mask on when walking around camp, when giving directions or speeches to rebel soldiers, and even when he led attack groups into villages. Prince Agis would only take the mask off when he went into his central command tent to discuss operations with his generals. That night when he was promoted to general, it was a real surprise to Robbins to find out who the man behind the mask actually was. It gave him a strong boost of confidence, making him realize the secret scheme in the works for years could indeed become a reality.

One of the reasons Robbins received the rank of general was that Prince Agis was impressed with the way Robbins handled raising Sebastian. Sebastian was one of the many kidnapped boys the rebels collected over the years, with the intention of building up their numbers and creating fear. About ten years ago, Robbins returned with a young baby boy after a botched operation in the village of Norwalk. It was difficult for Prince Agis to understand what could have gone wrong, because he sent Robbins in with two well-trained soldiers, who were heavily armed and faced little or no resistance. Prince Agis was initially terribly upset when Robbins rode back into camp with only one baby, and without the other two soldiers. But over time, Agis came to appreciate that Robbins acted with wisdom in aborting the operation, otherwise he would have been captured as well. As punishment to the two rebel soldiers who failed him, Prince Agis let them rot in prison ever since, without making arrangements to allow for their escape. But enough time had gone by, so he finally sent in his team of Robbins and Sebastian to get them out tonight.

Walking on the eastern part of the castle grounds, Sebastian looked at the entrance leading to the underground prison where his first operation would take place later tonight. As the surveillance report indicated, there were no royal guards stationed at the top of the stairs. That was a good thing, because Sebastian didn't want any surprises tonight. His hope was to go in, do exactly what he had been told to do, and get the prisoners out without any problems. His father, Robbins, emphasized to him how important it was to get this first operation right, in order to please both his father and Prince Agis. Sebastian wanted to make them happy, so he would do his very best.

Although he enjoyed seeing what life was like here at the castle, Sebastian missed his friends he had grown up with back at the camp, and was looking forward to returning there so he could play with the other boys in the nearby caves. At eleven years old, the rebel camp life was all Sebastian had ever known. From time to time, he would see young baby boys brought into camp, so they could be raised there. He learned some of them were brought in by kidnapping, which kind of disturbed him. When he expressed his concern to Robbins about it, Robbins tried to justify why kidnapping sometimes needed to be done. Robbins also reassured Sebastian that he was not a kidnapping victim, but had been rescued and adopted by Robbins when Sebastian's birth parents died in a tragic accident. As Robbins told it, they were victims of the cruelty of King Charles and his reign, as King Charles issued a royal decree relocating Sebastian's parents to another home, wanting the land they were living on for himself. A short time later, there was a massive mudslide from the hills above, which buried Sebastian's parents and all of the others who were relocated, resulting in their untimely death. Sebastian could think of no reason to doubt the story. By sticking with the rebels, he hoped to someday avenge their deaths by assisting in the overthrow of King Charles and the royal family. As he thought about this, Sebastian reached up towards his neck to feel the necklace holding a brasta wood pendant on it. He rubbed the carved piece of wood between his thumb and index finger, recalling how Robbins told him it was the only thing left by which he could remember his birth parents. It only served to strengthen his desire to make King Charles and the royal family pay for what they had done to his parents, and that payback would start tonight.

A while later, after he completed his surveillance assignment, Sebastian was left with a few hours of free time. He decided to use it to listen to some of the live music playing at various spots around the castle grounds. Sebastian spotted a group of musicians performing for a small crowd outside of the castle blacksmith building, playing some of the royal songs which were famous throughout the land. The two piccolo players and three flute players were blending together in perfect harmony. As they finished up a short number known as 'The Queen's Intermezzo', Sebastian joined the rest of the crowd in applauding. Sebastian deeply loved music, often wishing he could have an instrument of his own. Back at the rebel camp, collecting musical instruments was not a high priority, which meant they were in very short supply. Among what they did have, there weren't any piccolos or flutes.

As the group of musicians finished another piece of music, the band leader announced to the crowd, "Thank you very much, everyone, thank you. We are going to take a short break now, but don't go anywhere. We will be back in one hour to refresh your ears with more of the sweet sounds of Astoria." The musicians set down their instruments on their stools and walked away together towards one of the refreshment stands. Some of the gathered crowd began dispersing, but Sebastian sat down and began thinking about something. He was looking at one of the bronze flutes, wishing it was his own. He reasoned that Robbins didn't say anything to him about what he could or could not do in his free time. And he was confident that if he really wanted to steal the bronze flute, it would not be very difficult for him. The only challenge would be with so many people on the castle grounds, he wouldn't be able to account for every set of eyes when he made the swipe. But this was his one chance, and perhaps only chance, to get his own musical instrument. There weren't many bronze flutes in the land, so it would be a valuable prize to have. Soon, the perfect opportunity to make his move presented itself.

Seeing a commotion in the crowds of people behind him, Sebastian looked over and saw what appeared to be a group of important people coming his way. As those around him began debating who it might be and were all looking in that direction, Sebastian slowly stood and started backing up towards the stool which held the bronze flute. When the people realized it was the future princess with two of her friends, many of them started running over to get a firsthand look. Others just stood where they were, watching the three girls walk by and speaking highly of the princess. Then, he decided to go for it. With one swift motion, Sebastian moved the bronze flute from the stool into his bag. Thinking he was in the clear, he moved off to his side, hoping to disappear into the crowd.

Just when he thought he was safe, Sebastian felt the tight grip of a hand around his right arm. "Young man, what do you think you're doing?" a voice said to him. A jolt of fear cascaded through Sebastian's body as he realized he was caught. He tried to make a break for it, but the grip on his arm was too strong. Turning around to look at his captor, Sebastian was surprised to see one of the musicians who was performing earlier. Sebastian stared at him with wide open eyes, fearing his stupid decision had jeopardized the entire operation. "Did you really think you would get away with stealing that flute?" the musician asked him. "Our instruments are too valuable for us to let them out of our sight at any time. Whenever the five of us take a break, one of us is always assigned to watch over our instruments. Open up your bag and show me what's inside of it." Sebastian had no choice but to open up his bag and pull out the bronze flute he had stolen. Taking it back, the musician released his grip on Sebastian's arm, but continued speaking to him. "Young man, where are your parents today? Haven't they taught you it is wrong to take something which does not belong to you? This flute cost a lot of money, and the person who owns it worked a lot of hours to pay for it." Then, the musician asked once again, "Where are your parents right now?"

Even though he was now free, Sebastian decided not to run away, realizing it would be better to try to talk his way out of this predicament. "My father is on the other side of the castle grounds. I'm not sure what he's doing, but he's probably watching some of the competitions. I'm sorry I took the flute, mister. If you let me go, I promise to never do anything like that again."

"That's sad to hear," the musician said in response. "I find it disappointing when parents don't take the time to be with their children, but send them off on their own on days like this." After thinking for a moment, the musician continued, "I didn't get a chance to introduce myself earlier. My name is Nathaniel. I tell you what I'm going to do for you. I'm not going to hand you over to one of the royal guards, because they would take you to your father and expel you both from the castle grounds. So I'm willing to let you go, on one condition."

"What's that? I'll do anything," Sebastian said.

"You have to spend the next hour with me, because I'd like to talk with you more and take you on a short tour of the musicians building. You can look at and try out all of the instruments we have stored there, and I might even have a surprise for you. So, what do you say?"

"You would do that for me?" Sebastian responded in disbelief. "I would love to see some of the instruments." The two turned and walked away, discussing every question about music that Sebastian ever had.

Slightly under an hour later, Sebastian was standing outside of the musicians building. He said goodbye to his new, older friend named Nathaniel, and was holding a gift in his hands. It was a wooden piccolo, not nearly as valuable as a bronze flute, but valuable nonetheless. Nathaniel mentioned something about a surprise, but this was totally unexpected. Sebastian began feeling something inside he never really felt before, guilt for what he had done earlier. He never could have imagined somebody would give him something for nothing, just out of the generosity of their heart. But that was what the musician had done. To Sebastian, it was more than a gift, it was a lesson in life, something he could take with him and influence the way he viewed others. After thinking about what happened for a while and trying out his new prized possession, Sebastian put it into his bag and walked over to the western side of the castle grounds, to wait for Robbins at their prearranged meeting place. When he arrived there, Sebastian found a spot where he could lay down and take a nap, placing his bag under his head to use as a pillow.

A while later, he was awoken by Robbins. "It's almost time for your first assignment, Sebastian. You should get up and start preparing. It's getting dark outside." Sebastian sat up and his eyes began adjusting to the change in light. Instead of sunlight, there was now just the firelight shining down from the lamp torches above. The last of the athletic games had concluded, and people were starting to gravitate toward the Castle Terrace, where preparations were underway for the awards ceremony. Sebastian picked up his bag and took out the set of keys, looking them over.

"You're sure these are going to work, right, father?" Sebastian asked, seeking reassurance.

"Prince Agis promised they would open all of the necessary locks, so you have nothing to worry about," Robbins answered. Robbins took Sebastian's bag and opened it up to put his writing tablet and instrument back inside. Seeing the new piccolo, Robbins took it out and asked, "And what is this, Sebastian? You know better than to risk stealing something when we are on an important mission."

"I didn't steal it, father. One of the musicians gave it to me as a gift."

"Sure he did. Nobody is that generous. I will overlook your stupidity this time and let you keep it if you complete your assignment, okay?" Robbins returned the pack to his son and left to get the wealthy landowner they were traveling with. They would meet up later with Sebastian at the final meeting point. Sebastian put the keys into his hidden pocket, and carried his bag as he walked off toward the assignment which would make or break him.

When King Charles started speaking to the crowd, that was Sebastian's signal to walk down the stairs into the underground prison. Despite being so well prepared for what he was about to do, Sebastian was a nervous wreck. He rehearsed what he was supposed to say over and over in his mind, but nothing would compare to the real thing. Finally psyching himself up enough, Sebastian opened the door and went inside.

As he walked into the entrance area, he saw one jailer standing at a desk, reviewing some paperwork. The other jailer who was supposed to be there wasn't anywhere to be seen. Sebastian figured he was probably off making the rounds, checking on the prison cells, or maybe even giving the prisoners their nightly rations. The jailer, who was named Bailey, looked up from what he was reading and spoke to the boy, not the least bit concerned at seeing him. "Son, if you're looking for the privy, you've come to the wrong place," Bailey said.

Sebastian began his rehearsed lie with a short sentence. "I've come here to see my father," he said. Upon hearing this, the jailer set down his papers and expressed surprise.

"Your father? Here, at the castle prison?"

"Yes, I've traveled here today all alone from a great distance to see him. Shortly after I was born, he was taken into custody and has been imprisoned ever since. My mother won't talk about him anymore, and I have never met him. I only want to see him one time and tell him that although I disagree with the crimes he has committed, I still love him. It's been hard growing up without a father, and I have been wanting to see him for many years now. When I found out the games were taking place today, I asked my mother if I could come to find him. She said that she felt I was finally old enough to make the trip. So here I am." Sebastian finished his remarks, and awaited the jailer's response.

Bailey was quite dumbfounded at hearing the boy's plight. He told the boy to hold on for a few minutes, while he went to discuss the matter with his fellow jailer. Sebastian could hear the two talking for several minutes in a nearby room, debating what course of action to take. Finally, both of the jailers walked back in and stood next to the boy.

"Son, this is a very unusual request you have made," Bailey stated. "It's usually our policy never to allow visitors to talk with a prisoner without the express permission of the Chief Royal Knight, or at least, one of his assistants. However, this evening they are very busy with security detail for the royal family, so we're going to make an exception. My friend here will take you back and let you spend five minutes with your father in his cell, if your father is willing to see you. But you're going to have to leave your bag here, until you get back. I'm sorry, that's the best we can do for you."

Sebastian was relieved to hear that, as everything was going according to plan. He set his bag down over by the entrance door and gave Bailey the name of his 'father'. When Bailey heard the name of the criminal, he knew who it was immediately, and realized that part of the boy's story checked out. Owen, the prisoner mentioned, had been held in a cell for the last ten years, his life wasting away. Sebastian followed the other jailer back into the depths of the underground prison, until they arrived at the door of the captured rebel soldier. The jailer put his key into the lock and pushed open the cell door. Lying on the ground was a man who looked worse off than any beggar you might find in a village. The man had long, graying hair and a lengthy beard. The prisoner's ears perked up when the jailer said, "Owen, your estranged son is here to see you. You can have five minutes to talk to him, if you want to see him." When Owen agreed to see him, the jailer added, "Make it count. I will be right back." The jailer closed the door behind them and went to a bench at the end of the hallway to sit down and wait for the five minutes to elapse.

"What is the meaning of this?" the rebel prisoner named Owen asked Sebastian.

"I'm here in behalf of Prince Agis to secure your freedom tonight," the boy answered, as he took a set of keys out of his hidden pocket and tossed them to him. "Prince Agis has provided this set of master keys, which will open every door in this prison. Once I leave, wait until the coast is clear, and let yourself out of your cell. Find the other rebel soldier who is imprisoned here and let him out of his cell. Both of you together are to sneak up on the two jailers and do whatever is necessary to take them by surprise and subdue them. Use one of the swords, or knives, hanging in the entrance room to quickly shave off your beards, and open the door to the outside. You will find waiting there for you two changes of clothing. Get rid of your prison suits, put on the new clothes, and meet me at the castle entrance. Did you get all of that?" When the rebel prisoner confirmed he understood the plan, the boy added, "Make sure you carry this out as quickly as possible, but with caution, to make sure you don't get caught." A few moments later the cell door opened and the jailer told the boy it was time to leave. To complete the ruse, the boy finished by saying, "Father, don't forget I love you. I will be there for you if the king releases you someday." The boy followed the jailer out to the entrance room, thanked both of the jailers, picked up his bag, and walked outside. When the door closed behind him, he took the two changes of clothes out of his bag and set them off to the side of the entrance door. Sebastian then walked upstairs and across the great lawn to the meeting point, knowing he executed his first assignment perfectly.

Back in his cell, Owen held the set of keys in his hand. He could hardly believe after ten long years, he was this close to getting his freedom. The prisoner spent many nights tormented over the fact he remained loyal to Prince Agis, and refused King Charles' offer to release him after ten years if he cooperated. He thought about it more and more as the ten year anniversary of his capture approached. Despite the growing regrets, he kept his loyalty to the rebels all of this time, and now it paid off. A short time after the boy left and he was certain the jailer was long gone, Owen walked over to his cell door and started trying some of the different keys. One of them fit perfectly into the lock, and he pulled his cell door open. As he went out, he didn't look back into his cell, because he never wanted to see it again. He did close the door behind him and lock it, as an extra precaution. The prisoner knew exactly where the other rebel soldier was imprisoned, because both of them were held in the most secure area since they first arrived. In the beginning, they were imprisoned together, but then they were separated when a nearby cell became available. The prisoner quietly walked over and used the same key to open the cell of his trapped rebel friend named Trent.

Once everything was quickly explained, both of them relocked the second cell and moved cautiously down the hallway. Soon they encountered the main door leading into this wing of the prison, which was also locked shut. It didn't take long for Owen to figure out which key opened the lock. The prisoners closed the door behind them and pressed on, trying to make as little noise as possible. Passing cell after cell in yet another hallway, they could now almost taste their freedom. Just before they reached the end of the hallway and the next locked door, they heard somebody walk up and insert a key from the other side. Quickly they went through an open door to their left and ducked into the unlighted room. It was just in time, because it was one of the jailers. They could hear the jailer turn around and lock the door behind him. As he walked past their hiding place, the light from his small hand torch intruded into their room. "Should we take him down?" Trent asked.

"No, leave him be. I have a much better idea," Owen responded.

After the jailer disappeared around the bend, the two prisoners came out of their hiding place and unlocked the door he had just come through. They opened it and went through into the next hallway, which was much larger. They could see the way out, it was just ahead. Creeping up to the final locked door, they spotted the other jailer beyond it a short distance, looking through some papers. When they found the correct key, they unlocked and swung open the final door separating them from their freedom. Owen then told Trent to go hide behind a large food cart sitting nearby, as he took off his shirt. He lifted his shirt up to one of the candles burning along the wall, allowing it to catch on fire. Once it started burning, he threw the shirt on the ground, a few feet past where the food cart was sitting, and yelled, "Fire!" Finally, he went and hid next to the other prisoner.

Bailey, the jailer standing in the entrance room, heard him and ran into the large hallway without really thinking about what he was doing. He went straight for the burning shirt, trying to smother the flames. As he passed by the food cart, Owen stuck out his leg and tripped him. The moment Bailey fell to the ground, the two prisoners were all over him, knocking him unconscious. They stamped out the fire and walked out into the entrance room, locking the two jailers behind them. Before they went outside, the two prisoners took one of the swords hanging in the entrance room and slammed the tip of it into the lock several times, rendering it useless. There would be no way the jailers could get out and come after them or find help. They would have to wait until somebody stumbled upon them, which probably wouldn't be until the next shift arrived.

A short time later, two clean shaven, nicely dressed, former prisoners met up with Sebastian, Robbins, and Herman at the meeting point. Without saying a word, the group turned and walked across the drawbridge along with the thousands of other people who were exiting the castle grounds. They had done it. They carried out a masterful escape plan, the first time in history there was an escape from the underground castle prison.

It was a couple weeks later when Prince Agis came riding into the rebel village to see the two newly freed rebel soldiers. Upon seeing their leader, who was wearing his creepy looking mask, both of them pledged their continued support for the rebel cause, thanking the prince profusely for their freedom. To this, Prince Agis said from behind his mask, "That's good to hear, for the time of our attack on the castle is nearly at hand. I have chosen a month to carry out our secret scheme, a few short years from now, which will inflict the worst possible pain on King Charles and his family. When the time comes, he will spend the rest of his life suffering in anguish." Prince Agis followed up this news with loud, evil sounding laughter, which seemed to echo off the trees of the forest.

Chapter Six:

Their Lives Crossed Paths

It was on an October afternoon, four years later, that two best friends met up and sat down under an apple tree during a work break at the royal castle. One of them was the peasant boy Stefan, from the village of Norwalk, who was now sixteen years old. The other was the peasant girl Yvonne, also from the village of Norwalk, but one year younger than he was. They had been working hard all afternoon in different locations of the castle, but favorable scheduling permitted them to share this thirty minute break together. Before sitting down, Stefan reached up and plucked two red apples from a branch of the tree. He handed one of them to Yvonne, and began eating the other one. "So, how has your day been going, Yvonne?" Stefan casually asked.

"It's been good so far. I don't have any complaints," she responded. "But I will say this. Things have been kind of crazy, with people hurrying here and there. I've been working on the floral team all day. We've been putting together all of the flowers and vases that will be used during the coronation ceremony tonight. I've never seen so many flowers in my life. After break, we're going to start setting all of them up in the Grand Ballroom."

"Wow, you're so blessed, Yvonne. How come you always get all the prestigious work assignments?"

"You know why," she answered. "Ever since I learned to read and write, Elda, the woman who is in charge of the castle plants and flowers, has found me more useful. I can actually read the work orders and make sure everything is done right, without having to always be told."

"Yeah," Stefan responded, "but you taught me how to read and write, too. And it didn't result in me suddenly getting to spend more time in close proximity to the royal family in the western half of the castle."

"Oh, Stefan," Yvonne sighed, "are you going to start whining once again about how you've still never actually met the princess, or even seen her in person? One of these days I will tell her there is a peasant boy who has been dreaming about meeting her every day for the past four years. I'll tell her how you vividly imagine the moment when she will someday walk up to you, tell you that you are the boy of her dreams, and ask you to marry her." After finishing her sarcastic statement, Yvonne tried to reassure Stefan by scooting over next to him, and resting her head on his shoulder. As she was gently rubbing his back with her right hand, she added, "Don't feel bad, Stefan. You've accomplished a lot already. You're probably the highest ranking peasant boy who has ever worked here at the castle. With the long record of floor cleaning you have built up, you must be a trusted, valuable worker."

"Thanks, Yvonne," Stefan responded. "That means a lot."

The two best friends spent the rest of their break time peacefully sitting under the apple tree in silence, thinking about different things, until it was time to head off in opposite directions. In view of tonight's historic importance to the land of Astoria, both were asked to stay and work the night shift. Yvonne went back to work with the floral team, while Stefan went over to the eastern side of the castle, to continue scrubbing floors.

The past four years brought lots of developments in the lives of both Yvonne and Stefan, as well as their respective families. Yvonne still had not heard from her birth parents, but continued living with Lady Ruth. Her routine in life was much the same as it always was, except at fifteen she felt like she was wiser and more mature. She wanted Lady Ruth to give her more freedom in making decisions, but Lady Ruth was slow to comply. Lady Ruth still required her to report her whereabouts at all times, and maintain a large home workload in addition to what Yvonne did at the castle. Still, Yvonne loved Lady Ruth as if she was her own mother. About a year ago, Yvonne received one of the best surprises of her life. Her horse had died of old age a few weeks earlier, so she started riding double with Stefan, on the back of his horse, to her job at the castle on weekends. One Sunday night, though, Stefan pulled up to her house, and they both stared over into Yvonne's front yard. Behind the fence, there was a young looking, brown horse quietly grazing on the lawn. The horse stopped chewing for a moment to look up at them, before putting his head back down to continue feeding. A few moments later, Lady Ruth appeared on the porch with the biggest smile. Yvonne would never forget Lady Ruth's next three words, "He's all yours!" Yvonne jumped down from Stefan's horse, tears swelling in her eyes, and practically ran through the gate, trying to get inside the yard. She started to run over to her new horse, but abruptly changed direction and ran up the porch steps to give Lady Ruth the biggest hug she ever received. Lady Ruth held her for several minutes, before letting her go meet her new horse. After waving to Stefan, Lady Ruth went back inside the house. Stefan was so happy for Yvonne that day, and pleased he was there to share the special moment with her.

What Stefan failed to realize to this point, however, was that his best friend Yvonne had started to develop romantic feelings for him. About six months ago, she realized that she liked him more than just as a friend. But she was afraid to tell him. In fact, she didn't think she would ever tell him how she really felt inside. She was content to be best friends with him, spending virtually all of her free time with him, doing things together. Besides, she had nothing to offer him as a peasant girl. It was true he was a common peasant, too. But it seemed as if he was always dreaming of achieving a better life for himself, with his farfetched dreams of meeting the princess. And while Stefan had never even seen the princess, Yvonne had become acquainted with her on brief occasions. At times, Yvonne's work assignment would involve taking care of the plants in the Royal Gardens. Several times over the past four years, the future princess came out into the gardens while Yvonne was working there, to study her lessons in the fresh air outside. Every time, the princess said a brief greeting to her, even once asking what her name was. Yvonne couldn't have realized that the future princess was doing this in defiance of Chief Royal Knight Chadwick's instructions involving not speaking to peasants. Still, Yvonne appreciated the kindness the princess showed her, which always cheered her up and made her feel better about herself as a person.

In contrast with Yvonne's somewhat normal life of the past four years, Stefan faced some ongoing adversity. Much of it came from Rolf, the landowner who employed him. As Stefan grew older, the landowner kept pushing him to do more work, and to get it done faster. It left Stefan near the point of total physical exhaustion at the end of each work day. Compared to what he was doing on Rolf's estate, Stefan's work at the castle felt like a breeze. But his own workload wasn't what bothered Stefan. At sixteen years of age, his body could handle the toll of hard work. What bothered him was that the landowner had forced his father Martin to go back to work. This, despite the fact that Martin suffered a severe injury to his leg in a fall seven years ago. After which, Leon, who was then in charge, permitted him to retire, taking the strain off his injured leg. But Rolf became greedy, wanting to increase his profits at any cost, so he forced Martin to work every day, despite being in constant pain. Stefan wished there was a way he could make more money for his family, or find a better employer, but there didn't seem to be anything out there. Options truly were slim for a peasant family, especially with one member not at full health. Stefan's biggest source of support through all this was his best friend Yvonne. Yvonne became to him the sister he never had. She understood him, she cared about him, and she was always there when he needed somebody the most. If only he could somehow repay her for all the kindness she showed to him. Although, he thought perhaps he didn't need to, because it seemed that her kindness was already being returned to her with all of the good things happening to her at the royal castle.

While Yvonne and Stefan were working hard, the sixteen-year-old princess-to-be, Stasia, was sitting in a chair in her private changing room, being attended to by four different maidens at the same time. One maiden was working on her hair, another was putting makeup on her face, and a third was tending to her nails. The fourth maiden was spot checking every detail of the dress she would wear tonight, which was hanging nearby. Sitting in a chair a few feet away from her was Aunt Delia, her most trusted friend and tutor. "I can't believe this day is finally here, Delia. I've waited so long for this, to be able to make a difference in the lives of the people of Astoria. In a few short hours, I'm going to go from being the daughter of the king, to being royal princess, the new leader of our people. To tell you the truth, Delia, I'm kind of scared right now. How can I possibly do this right?"

"Relax, Stasia," Delia said in a comforting tone. "Everything is going to be fine. You're going to be wonderful tonight. I believe in you."

"I know you do, Delia. I'm just not sure I believe in myself. There are so many different people trying to give me advice about what to do, that it's overwhelming. It seems like I can't even think for myself, with Chadwick and everyone else breathing down my back at every turn. Why does everybody want to control me so much?"

"I'm going to tell you a little secret, Stasia, and I want you to remember this," Delia replied. "After tonight, it doesn't matter what other people want from you, or what they want you to do. Once you are crowned as princess, the rest is up to you. Astoria's future has been placed in your capable hands, to do what you feel is right and in the best interests of your people. From now on, when so-called advisers suggest things to you, it is up to you to determine if you want to follow the course they are suggesting, or if you want to choose your own path." As Delia was finishing up her thoughts, Stasia's father and mother, King Charles and Queen Delphine, walked into the room. "I'm going to say goodbye for now, Stasia," Delia finished up, "to give you some time to talk with your parents. But I will see you down in the Grand Ballroom very soon." Delia left the room and the royal family was together again, one last time before King Charles would hand over the throne to his daughter. Meanwhile, the three maidens who were tending to Stasia's appearance continued working diligently at their tasks.

Seeing her dress, which was still being prepared by the fourth maiden, Queen Delphine remarked, "Look at your dress, it's stunning."

"I know, mother," Stasia replied, making eye contact with her in the mirror, "I sure hope it's going to fit."

"We know you're busy right now," King Charles said, "but we wanted to come by and tell you how proud we are of you. It has been our privilege to raise you the best way we knew, but our work is now finished. You're a young woman now, one who is ready to step out into the spotlight and lead our people."

"Stasia, you have shown us your intelligence, your kindness, and your love for many years now," the queen chimed in. "You've shown us that you have a beautiful heart. Now it is time for you to show these things to the people of Astoria. We have no doubt you are going to be wise and good to our people."

"Thank you both for your kind words," Stasia responded. "I know that I still have a lot to learn, which I can only gain from real life experience. At sixteen years of age, I don't feel like I'm very old yet. I still feel very young. But I am ready to accept the role waiting for me since the day I was born, and I will always do the best I can."

"We know you will, sweetheart," the queen added. Looking over at the king, the queen said, "Let's leave her be, Charles."

"One more thing," Charles said, "try and enjoy the moment tonight. It is a moment which will never be repeated in your life, so cherish every second you are walking down the floor of the ballroom, as you complete your journey from young lady to princess." Finished sharing their encouragement, Charles and Delphine walked out of the room, leaving Stasia and her four maidens alone to their preparations.

Over in the Grand Ballroom, scores of dignitaries started to arrive from all over the land. Only the most noble of noblemen, the most wealthy of landowners, and those who were extended family members of the royal family were invited on this special night. The best wine in the land was being served at the back of the ballroom, and people were gathered in small groups there, talking joyfully to each other. One dignified young man, nineteen years of age, appeared at the entranceway to the Grand Ballroom. A royal guard stopped him briefly to check his identity. After looking at his official invitation, the guard looked down at a list of names and asked, "What did you say your name was again?"

"Sir Rackley," the young man replied.

"Ah, yes, we have you right here. You may go through," the guard told him.

"Thank you," Sir Rackley said as he walked through the door into a ballroom that was larger and grander than anything he had ever seen in his own land. Red carpet had been placed over the wooden floor, from one end of the room to the other. There were rows and rows of seats, but not many people were sitting down yet. Most were involved in conversations, laughing and having a good time. Sir Rackley walked over to the counter to pick up a glass of wine. When the worker was done serving a man and woman, he moved over and asked Sir Rackley what he wanted.

"I'd like a glass of your best stuff," Sir Rackley told him.

"That would be our vintage Norwalk Red," the worker told him, as he filled up a clean glass with wine which came from a barrel. When he was finished filling it, he handed the glass to Sir Rackley, who put it to his lips to taste it.

"This is really good, thank you," Sir Rackley told the worker as he walked away with his glass of red wine. Sir Rackley looked around and couldn't find anybody he recognized, so he walked over to one of the walls and started admiring the paintings lining it. When he came to the third painting, he stopped to study it more carefully. It was a picture of a much younger King Charles, when he was in his early teens. Standing next to him was his younger brother Chadwick, and behind them were their father and mother, the previous king and queen. Everyone was smiling, except Chadwick, who showed an expression of indifference. After studying it for a while, he moved on and came to another painting at the end of the ballroom, close to the stage, that aroused his curiosity. It was a painting of Princess Stasia made recently, perhaps only one or two years ago. She was standing outside in the royal stables next to her horse Isobel. Stasia had flowers in her hair and was feeding the horse an apple. It was a touching scene, perfectly captured by the artist who painted it. Sir Rackley looked at the painting for some time.

"Beautiful, isn't it?" a voice said as somebody came up behind him. Sir Rackley turned to see Queen Delphine standing behind him.

"It sure is. *She* sure is," he answered.

"Stasia has always felt a deep love for her horse. Every day these past few years, Stasia tried to finish up her studies as quickly as possible, so she could go outside and take Isobel for a ride. Those two will always be inseparable," the queen said. Her eyes moved down to the belt he was wearing. "I see you're still wearing the gift Charles and I gave you four years ago at the games. You never know, someday we might give you something even nicer." The gift had been a black leather belt made of the finest materials available. On the front of the belt were five words etched in gold, 'For the love of Stasia'. It came wrapped up really nice, along with some chocolates imported from a distant land.

Sir Rackley smiled, and replied, "This belt was the best gift I have ever been given. I only wear it on very special occasions, because it's so valuable to me. The words written express what always has been written on my heart."

"Well, I'm sure my daughter feels the same way about you," the queen replied, before walking away to visit with someone else. Sir Rackley looked at the painting once again, before walking to the back to get another glass of vintage Norwalk Red.

About two hours later the Grand Ballroom was completely filled with the elite class of Astoria. The room was lively with conversation and royal musicians were lightly playing music in the background. A worker carried in a new barrel of wine through the side entrance, and set it down on the refreshment counter. Most people were now in their seats, in anticipation of the event about to begin. A hush soon fell over the room as King Charles walked out and sat down next to Queen Delphine, who was already in her seat on the left side of the stage. Chief Royal Knight Chadwick was standing off to the side of them, on the stage but up against the wall. Across the back of the stage were a mixture of royal knights, royal guards, and royal archers. On the right side of the stage were the musicians, who finished up the musical number they were playing. The court judge, who was host of the proceedings, was sitting just right of the center of the stage. There was a table set up next to him which held two objects, a golden crown and the Code of Honor scroll. When the music stopped for a moment, the court judge stood up and spoke to the crowd. He directed them, "Ladies and gentlemen, please find your seats, as the coronation ceremony will begin in five minutes. Thank you." He sat back down and the royal musicians started playing one final musical piece. A few dignitaries hurried off to the back counter to get another glass of wine, which they brought with them to their seats. Several older women, who were admiring the elaborate vases and flowers across the front of the stage, also went to their seats.

By the time the musical piece finished, everyone was sitting down. There wasn't a single vacant seat in the entire ballroom. The court judge stood up again and spoke, saying, "Welcome one and all to the greatest of all nights in the land of Astoria. It is a night that will be forever recorded in the Royal History Pages. For those of us privileged enough to be here, it is a night which will be forever etched into our minds and hearts. Before the ceremony begins, it is my privilege to direct your attention to King Charles, ruler of Astoria, who will now deliver his final address." The court judge sat down once again as King Charles stood up and walked over to the center of the stage, to the sound of deafening applause.

"Dignitaries and noblemen, landowners and wealthy citizens, family and friends, tonight is both an ending and a beginning for all of us. It is the end to what I hope has been a prosperous time for all of you under my leadership. I have done my best to carry out the Code of Honor in my dealings with the citizens of Astoria. Though I was not able to completely eliminate the threats posed by the rebels, I have done my utmost to contain them. As I look out at you tonight, I give you my solemn word and personal assurance that my daughter is both fit and ready to lead you from this night forward. At sixteen years of age, she has impressed both the queen and I with wisdom beyond her years."

As the king continued his speech, there was a slight commotion towards the back right area of the ballroom. It was caused by the faint sound of broken glass, muffled, but still audible. A royal guard walked over to where the sound originated from to see what the problem was. He saw an older woman who appeared to be in her nineties, who was sitting in the outer aisle seat of the row, visibly upset. When he asked her what happened, she explained, "I am so sorry. I can't believe I did this. I was holding my glass of wine, when my arm started shaking because of a chronic illness I'm dealing with. Before I even knew what happened, my glass fell out of my hand and onto the carpet below."

The royal guard looked down and could see shattered glass everywhere, with red wine spilled all over the carpet.

"Don't worry about it," the guard said to her. "I'll call someone in here right away to get this cleaned up." The royal guard, who was known as Mathieu, turned around and walked out of the side entrance to find someone who could do the job.

Stefan had been working for the past few hours on his knees, cleaning the floor of the hallway which divided the two sides of the castle, which was known as The Gateway. It was almost a bridge between two worlds, as the western side of the castle was essentially a private area for the royal family, those working directly for them, and those protecting them. The eastern side of the castle was where the workers, guards, and other employees lived and took in their meals. As Stefan cleaned, several people crossed through The Gateway from one side to the other over the past few hours. A worker walked by him carrying a barrel of wine, a few soldiers came from one direction or the other, and most recently, a chef crossed back into the eastern wing. At the entrance door to the western side, there was a single royal guard checking everyone who walked in, making sure they had clearance to enter that part of the castle. Stefan looked up from what he was doing when another royal guard appeared at the door, rushing through it as if he was in a real hurry to get somewhere.

"There you are!" the royal guard said to Stefan, as he ran up to where he was working. "I've been looking for you."

"You've been looking for me?" Stefan said in surprise, not understanding what the royal guard could possibly want with him.

"Yes, you are the one. I've seen you working here at the castle for quite a few years now, and you always do such a great job in keeping these floors polished and clean. Right now, we have an emergency situation over in the Grand Ballroom. Some red wine has been spilled and there's broken glass on the floor, which is a real hazard to our guests. I need you take your cleaning supplies, and come with me, right now." Upon hearing this, Stefan was in disbelief, not sure if this was actually happening. Was this some sort of dream he was having, or was this real? If it was a dream, he didn't want to wake up, so he immediately picked up his supplies and followed the royal guard out of The Gateway and into the western part of the castle.

Yvonne had spent her evening finishing up some pruning and trimming out in the Royal Gardens. She was happily at work, humming to herself, thinking about Stefan. She truly enjoyed the quiet time on their break earlier in the day, when she sat on the ground resting her head on his shoulder. He had so much adversity going on in his life that she wanted to be there for him, in any way she could. Maybe someday he would come to have the same feelings for her which she had developed for him. Maybe not, but there was nothing wrong with hoping for it. She smiled, just thinking about it. A beautiful orange butterfly fluttered over and landed on a small branch near where Yvonne was working. "Hey, girl, what are you doing outside so late?" she asked the butterfly, not expecting an answer. "Don't you have a home you can fly into to keep warm?" The butterfly remained stationary on the small branch it was sitting on. "No, I guess you don't. The world is probably your home, isn't it?" Yvonne's conversation with the butterfly was cut short when she saw two people walking by one of the open doors leading into the Royal Gardens. They didn't enter, but kept walking right past it. Yvonne looked twice, because one of the persons walking by was clearly a royal guard, but the other person looked exactly like Stefan. Not using her usual discretion, Yvonne dropped her pruning tools and ran across the Royal Gardens toward the door. She stopped when she arrived at the door and peeked her head around to see who it was walking by. The two people were further down the hallway now, but the second person still looked like it was Stefan, although she couldn't be sure, because she was now looking at him from the back. "Stefan, is that you?" she called out, again showing a lack of discretion. Stefan heard her voice and turned around, waving to her briefly before rounding a corner. Yvonne was totally shocked. It really was Stefan, and he was actually in the western half of the castle. He must have been working, because he was carrying a bucket in one of his hands. But what Yvonne found strange, was that he was headed straight in the direction of the Grand Ballroom, where the new princess would be crowned only a few minutes from now. Yvonne went back into the Royal Gardens and continued her work, the butterfly now gone from the branch it was sitting on. As she did, she thought back to all of those times over the years when Stefan dreamed of seeing the princess. It almost became an obsession to him, she thought, and now he was headed into the room where the princess was about to have the biggest night of her life. She found it simply amazing, and hoped she was right, for his sake.

Stefan walked into the Grand Ballroom and the scene in front of his eyes was surreal. The king was up on the stage, standing tall, his voice carrying throughout the room. There were countless people in the seats, all focused intently on what he was saying. After they entered at the side door, the royal guard turned left and headed towards the back half of the crowd, and Stefan followed. The guard brought him over to where the spill had taken place. Sharp pieces of broken glass were still sitting there, scattered across a small area of the red carpet. "This is the spot. Get this cleaned up and make sure you get all of the broken glass," the royal guard directed him. The royal guard left him there, returning to the place where he was posted.

Watching every moment of this development was Chadwick, who was standing on the stage, up against the left wall. It was his job to notice and analyze anything at all out of the ordinary taking place in the room. He would determine if it was a threat and act accordingly. Chadwick heard the wine glass fall to the ground a few minutes earlier. His eyes zeroed in on the royal guard who went over to help the old woman. And his eyes followed the royal guard as he walked out of the side entrance. Chadwick assumed he went to get one of the long-time castle workers, or perhaps even one of the maidens, to clean up the spill. Chadwick thought the royal guard may have even planned on cleaning up the spill himself, which would be understandable in this type of situation. So, it was quite a surprise to him when the guard came back through the door a few minutes later with a teenage peasant boy, who was carrying a bucket with him. Chadwick wanted to run off the stage and correct the situation, but he couldn't. The king was speaking and there was nothing he could do at the time. If he had his way, Chadwick would've thrown the boy out of the ballroom and fired him from his job at the castle on the spot, for even thinking he could set foot in here. Then, he would have severely reprimanded the royal guard, who he could see was Mathieu, reminding him that the Code of Honor forbids interaction between the royal family and peasants. Putting them together in the same room was a formula for disaster. If anything, it was going to cost Mathieu any chance of becoming a royal knight in the foreseeable future, Chadwick would make sure of it. Not aware of any of these ill feelings, Stefan began working to clean up the spill. There were sharp pieces of glass everywhere, so he carefully picked them up one by one, and placed them into a small trash bag attached to his bucket.

On the stage, the king was finishing up his speech. "So then, guests, it is time for the moment you have all been waiting for. These will be my last words as your king. Henceforth, my daughter will now serve as your new leader. May I present to all of you here tonight, the girl who holds the future of our land in her hands, your Princess Stasia!" As the king finished, he gestured out with both of his hands, palms up, towards the back of the Grand Ballroom. Immediately after his last words, the royal musicians on the right side of the stage started playing a new song they composed for this moment. All heads in the crowd turned with keen anticipation towards the back entrance, waiting for the new princess to walk through the main door. Chadwick even found himself caught up in the moment, forgetting about the peasant boy and the transgressions of the royal guard Mathieu, as he joined all eyes in looking to the back.

Stasia was standing outside of the door, knowing that the moment she walked through it, her life would change forever. A few of her maidens were continuing to straighten out and perfect every inch of her dress. She wished Delia was here with her to give her a few more words of encouragement, before she walked through the door. But she knew Delia was on the other side, sitting somewhere out in a vast crowd of people. Like Delia told her a few hours ago, everything would be fine. The path to be taken from now on by the people of Astoria would be hers to choose. As the music continued playing from the other side, Stasia excused her maidens. She looked down at her dress one last time, brushed her hair back slightly with her fingers, and walked through the door into the Grand Ballroom.

Thunderous applause was there to greet her when she stepped through to the other side. She paused for a moment, and then continued taking deliberate, slow steps forward, as she was encouraged to do. Far at the other end of the ballroom, she could see her parents sitting up on the stage, smiling down at her. This was her moment, her time to shine. She looked and felt every bit the part of the princess she was supposed to be. She realized that despite her fears growing up of being inadequate and not good enough, this was where she wanted to be. Seeing so many people here tonight, all applauding and looking at her with affection, really touched her heart. She began walking past the first few rows of people at the back of the ballroom.

Stefan finished picking up the broken glass, and was dipping his rags into his water bucket to start cleaning up the spilled wine, when he heard the king announce the entrance of Princess Stasia. He heard the music start and saw everyone around him look towards the back of the ballroom. Stefan tried to continue working, pushing his wet rags into the red carpet to get the wine out of it. But he stopped what he was doing completely as the princess came through the door. As she passed by the first few rows of people, she was not too far away from him, although she was walking down the middle, and he was working near an outer aisle seat. After years of dreaming about what it would be like to see her in person, his first look at her surpassed any dream he ever had. She was absolutely beautiful, the prettiest girl he had ever seen in his life. She had amazing locks of long blonde hair, which dropped down about a foot below her shoulders. She was wearing a gold necklace with a sparkling diamond attached to it. Her dress was pure purple in color, made of the most expensive looking fabric imaginable. Her eyes were shifting back and forth, looking at everyone as she passed by, smiling all the while. It may have been part of his wishful thinking, but Stefan even thought she briefly looked at him and smiled. No matter what, he was stunned by her radiance and purple garments, as she gracefully strolled down the red carpet.

Stasia had indeed taken note of the peasant boy as she walked by the area where he was working. She wondered briefly how he managed to get past the watchful eye of Chadwick, who felt such disdain for lower class people. She hoped he would still be there in a little while, because seeing him gave her an idea which she wanted to carry out. As she continued past the midpoint of the ballroom and started getting closer to the front rows, Stasia was able to make out some of the faces looking at her. She spotted Aunt Delia, sitting off to the right. A couple of rows in front of Delia was Sir Rackley. She was happy to see him, but refused to allow her mind to start thinking about the arranged marriage scheduled to take place between them one year from now. This wasn't the time for her to worry about something she couldn't change. Stasia walked past them and up the stairs onto the stage of the Grand Ballroom. She turned around to look at the crowd and saw that their eyes were still glued to her, watching her every move. She looked over at her father and mother, who looked like proud parents as they smiled at their daughter. Soon the music died down and another round of applause took its place. When that finished, the court judge stood up and walked over to where Stasia was standing, holding a shining object between his hands. The object was a golden crown.

As the court judge approached the princess, Stefan thought about the magnitude of everything that had just happened. Of all the possible places where their lives could have crossed paths, this was the place where it happened. In the Grand Ballroom at the coronation of the princess. Stefan realized he now felt something new in his heart, something very special. It was love at first sight, and it wasn't a dream, it was real. He fell in love with her on this majestic night.

Chapter Seven:

First Act as Princess

As the princess accepted the crown from the court judge, she held it in her hands for a moment. In the shiny gold, she could see a distorted image of her face looking back at her. The crown was pure, solid gold, with a band of studded diamonds wrapped all the way around it. She lifted the crown above her head and slowly pulled it down over her blonde hair. The crown fit perfectly on her, and now she would have to spend much of her time wearing it, whenever she would care for royal matters. Stasia continued smiling elegantly out at the crowd, as they applauded and cheered their approval. Now that she was wearing the crown, she was officially the new leader of Astoria. That could not be changed until either her death or the time when her firstborn reached the age of sixteen. She realized having that knowledge would possibly be the only thing which would give her the courage to do what she intended to do next.

As the next part of her coronation ceremony, the court judge walked up to her holding the Code of Honor scroll. This was a time-honored tradition in which the new ruler would accept the Code of Honor written by the previous ruler. Accepting it would demonstrate to all that the new ruler would follow the same laws and rules of conduct the previous ruler set forth. Once it was accepted, the new leader would at some point copy it word for word and keep the new copy in the throne room. It was mostly done for the sake of appearances, but in two hundred years time, no one ever changed the Code of Honor for any reason. They simply accepted it and continued to follow carefully everything it set forth. That's what made Princess Stasia's intended action so difficult to carry out. If she went through with what she was planning, she had no idea how the gathered crowd would react. Stasia looked over at Delia sitting in the audience, unsure if she could do this. Delia nodded her head, trying to give her the encouragement she needed to continue. Stasia accepted the Code of Honor from the court judge, now holding the ceremonial scroll in her hand. Several seconds went by, and Stasia started to lose the perfect composure she was maintaining up until now. With the exception of Delia, she felt like every person in the entire room wanted her to accept the scroll she held. Tears started to form in her eyes as the time came for her to make her final decision. Then, from somewhere deep inside of her, she found the courage to do something nobody in the audience ever would have expected. She took the Code of Honor scroll and tore it completely in half. She then dropped both halves onto the ground in front of her. There was an immediate, collective gasp from the audience. Right away she heard a voice yell out, "That's treason!" Looking over, she saw that it was said by her Uncle Chadwick, who looked like he was completely enraged.

Stasia moved her eyes from Chadwick to King Charles, saying through her tears, "I'm sorry, father."

The audience was now murmuring, with several people arguing with each other loudly. A couple of dignitaries stood up from their seats and headed for the exit. Stasia was starting to self destruct inside emotionally, as things were quickly spiraling out of control. She heard a loud smash, and looked back over to where Chadwick was standing. He was so angry that he literally had punched his fist through a painting hanging on the wall next to him, destroying it completely. Then something happened she didn't expect. Sir Rackley stood up out in the audience and spoke up with a loud voice. "Please, everyone! Please, give me your attention for a moment. I know you are all no doubt very surprised by what you have seen. But Princess Stasia, your new leader for many years to come, is standing on the stage. Please, give her a chance to explain why she has done this. Give her the respect she deserves." When he was finished speaking, Sir Rackley sat down and the murmuring in the audience quickly died out. Things were improving, until Chadwick made it clear he wasn't willing to listen to Sir Rackley's suggestion. Once again he yelled out, "You can't do that! That's treason!" He started to walk towards the new princess, anger seething out of his bones. King Charles saw this and stood up to stop him. But he didn't need to, because Chadwick was instantly surrounded by other royal guards and royal knights, the very ones he commanded. They restrained him and started to take him away.

"Guards, stop!" the princess said to them. "Let him go." The guards looked at her in surprise and released Chadwick, who slowly walked back to where he had been standing. The royal guards stayed where they were and kept a watchful eye on him, in case he decided to try something else. Her tears now gone, Stasia turned to everyone in the audience and began speaking. "I am sure many of you out there feel the same way my Uncle Chadwick does, that the Code of Honor scroll is too sacred to be changed. As your new leader, I must do what I feel is right and in the best interests of all of our citizens. Let me assure you that most of the laws and rules of conduct written down in the Code of Honor will be upheld with the strongest determination by me. There are just a few things written in it which are not in my heart to do. With these things, I must guide you in a new direction. All I'm asking of you is to give me a chance to prove to you that I have good intentions, and that what I'm doing will make your lives even better." Stasia stopped for a moment to compose herself. The ballroom was so quiet you really could have heard a pin drop. Stasia continued, "You will find many of the changes I will be instituting involve the lower class people of our land, the peasants and the poor people. As I have grown up, I have realized something about myself, despite those who have tried to change me. I have realized I have a love for all people. I simply cannot look down on somebody simply because they don't have a lot of money, or they weren't born into a noble family. It is my desire to make sure the poor people in our land have rights of their own, and have enough food to eat."

Stasia looked over at where the peasant boy was working. Seeing he was still there, no longer working, but listening intently to her speech, she continued, "I would now like to give all of you a real life example of the type of ruler I plan to be." She pointed towards where the boy was kneeling and instructed, "Guards, bring that peasant boy who is cleaning the floor up here to the stage." Two royal guards, including the royal guard Mathieu, walked over and helped the boy up. As he was walking with them, the boy, who was Stefan, was in such shock that he didn't realize he was still holding his cleaning rag in his hand. The royal guards brought him up and dropped him off next to Stasia. He stood there looking at her, holding a dirty white rag with streaks of red wine in his hand. Stasia put her hand on him and turned him out towards the audience. Stefan followed her lead, and looked out at everyone, not saying a word. "My first act as the royal princess will be to give this peasant boy food and clothes fit for a guest. He is without question the only poor person among us here tonight. It is my order that he is to be bathed, clothed, and then fed tonight at my coronation banquet. He will eat and drink along with the rest of us, all together in one room." Stasia looked over at King Charles and asked him, "Father, will you see to it that this boy is cared for?" King Charles started to agree, but another person stepped forward who wanted to do it more.

"Please, princess, let me help the boy." Stasia couldn't believe her eyes, because it was her Uncle Chadwick speaking. She wondered how he could have experienced a change of heart so quickly and be so willing to follow her new ideals. Chadwick explained, "Princess, I owe an apology to you and to everyone present for my shameful behavior tonight. The old way of thinking was so heavily ingrained in my mind that I reacted without even listening to you. Please, princess, permit me to make things right by doing all you ask with the boy." Although his words seemed to be sincere, in his heart Chadwick didn't mean a thing he said. But he realized quickly when the royal guards surrounded him that if he didn't pretend to go along with the princess and her new plans, he would probably lose his job as the Chief Royal Knight, and perhaps even be asked to leave the castle. So he stood there hoping she would take the bait.

She did. "Okay, uncle. It's very kind of you to make that offer." Realizing his plan worked, Chadwick walked over and took the rag out of the boy's hand. Chadwick led him down from the stage, out towards the main entrance at the back of the Grand Ballroom. Something extraordinary happened when he did that. One by one, the members of the audience began applauding and standing up. In a short time, everybody was standing and the entire room was thundering in applause on a scale never before seen. The applause continued long after Chadwick and the boy walked out of the room and disappeared from their sight. Stasia simply stood on the stage, wearing her new golden crown, and took it all in. She looked over at her parents and exchanged smiles with both of them. Then, she looked over at Delia and exchanged a smile with her. Finally, she looked at Sir Rackley and mouthed the words to him, 'Thank you.' His intervention was what turned this whole thing around. She felt like she was on a sinking ship, before he stood up and pulled her from the depths with an act of true kindness. Or perhaps it was an act of true love. Several more minutes went by, and the applause wouldn't stop. So Stasia finally spoke over the noise, "Thank you, everyone, but that's enough. Thank you so much." After the clapping stopped, she concluded her remarks, "I hope all of you will stay and come to my dinner banquet tonight. I promise all of you that I will do all I possibly can for each one of you, and for everyone else in Astoria, with the love I have in my heart guiding me." With that, her speech was over and her coronation ceremony came to an end. Stasia went over to her parents and hugged both of them, while everyone else started talking with one another and enjoying more wine.

Stefan's mind was reeling as the series of events involving him unfolded. In a short span of time, he went from never having seen the princess, to being one of the key components of her coronation ceremony. It was really true, he was involved in her life now. Against all odds, of all the thousands, perhaps tens of thousands of teenage peasant boys who lived in Astoria, he was the one who was in the right place at the right time. And she even touched him on the shoulder. The hand of the princess touched him, as it gently prodded him to turn around and face the crowd. The things she said on the stage, that he was to be her example of how she was going to change things for poor people everywhere. He thought of his parents, who regularly had only rice and stale bread to eat. He couldn't wait to tell them everything that had happened here tonight. But the night was not over, there was more yet to come. The princess said Stefan would be dining with her tonight at her coronation banquet. He wondered if this meant he would get to sit next to her. It didn't matter, because he would at the very least be in the same room with her.

Stefan didn't care much for the man he was following through the hallways of the castle. He was scared of Chadwick and didn't trust him after seeing his explosion of anger take place on the stage. Chadwick's actions reminded him a lot of the landowner Stefan worked for, who would also have outbursts of anger. While the princess forgave Chadwick in front of everyone, Stefan would have preferred it if her original choice to help him, King Charles, was the one he was following. As they stopped in the clothing and laundering room of the castle, Stefan listened to a conversation Chadwick was having with one of the workers.

"I'm going to need a nice change of clothes for this peasant boy. Something that looks really good. Do you have any garments which would fit him?" When Chadwick finished with his question, the worker carefully looked over Stefan, and walked over to him to take a few measurements. The worker then went through some articles of clothing hanging above the wash basin.

"Here we go. This should fit the lad perfectly," the worker said, as he pulled down a nice looking outfit, which looked like it belonged to a dignitary. He added, "Don't worry about returning this, it was left behind by a visitor many months ago."

"Yes, this will do just fine," Chadwick said to the worker, taking the outfit and handing it to Stefan. Chadwick started to head out of the room, but stopped when the worker wanted to tell him something else.

"One thing before you go, Chadwick," the worker said. "A large supply of royal guard uniforms disappeared from here recently and nobody can seem to find them. I thought you should be made aware of this."

"Don't worry about it," Chadwick replied. "I gave an order for those uniforms to be destroyed. They weren't up to my standards, and I wanted new uniforms to be made so that all the guards would look their best for the new princess."

"Wow, that was brilliant of you. You think of everything, don't you?" the worker asked, obviously trying to win favor by his use of words. Chadwick walked out of the room, with Stefan following, as they headed for the royal bath house.

A short time later, the coronation banquet was underway in the Grand Banqueting Hall. Seated at the head of the main table was Princess Stasia, still wearing her regal purple dress and golden crown. Seated at the table with her, were King Charles and Queen Delphine, Delia, Sir Rackley, Alana and Madison, and several notable dignitaries. There were also two open seats at the table, one of them being right next to her. The group was conversing about the coronation ceremony, which was no doubt the conversation topic at each one of the tables in the room. Stasia was trying to explain her actions to King Charles.

"Father, I'm sorry again about tonight. I'm not sorry for what I did, but I'm sorry I didn't have the courage to tell you my intentions before I carried them out. It's just that I was worried you wouldn't understand and you would try to talk me out of it. As it was, I didn't know if I was actually going to be able to do away with the old Code of Honor until the moment came."

"My dearest girl," King Charles replied, "you don't have anything to apologize for. You have every right to rule this land in the way you see fit. However, I do have to disagree with one thing you just said. You said that you lacked courage, but it took more courage than I've displayed in my whole life for you to tear that scroll in half in front of all those people."

"We're all behind you, Stasia," the queen added. "We're all going to support your new Code of Honor." After the queen said this, everyone sitting at the table also expressed support for the princess and her new plans. One of the dignitaries, though, added a request.

"Yes, you have my complete support as well, princess," he said. "But while you're helping the poor and needy, don't forget about us either."

"Don't worry, my friend," the princess told him, "I'm not going to forget about anybody. You're going to always have everything you need. I feel that my plan for the lower class will only make the lives of landowners and dignitaries better. Because peasants will now have rights of their own, I think it will motivate them to be harder workers, as they will feel better about themselves and know their lives are meaningful." As the princess was talking, servers brought more water and juice over to the table, refilling all the golden drinking cups which were empty.

King Charles changed the subject by announcing he had a surprise to share with everybody. "Sir Rackley, what you did out there for my daughter tonight will never be forgotten by our family. By your actions, you have shown yourself to be more than deserving of the gift that the queen and I were planning on giving you this evening. Now that the queen and I will be retiring from public service for the most part, we want to give everything we have in support of our daughter. And being that the two of you are going to be getting married next year..." The king stopped short of finishing his sentence and turned his head to ask his daughter something. "Stasia, you *are* still planning on marrying Sir Rackley, aren't you?"

Stasia looked, not at her father, but at Sir Rackley as she answered, "Yes, father, Sir Rackley and I will get married next year. Just because I did some things unexpected tonight, it doesn't mean I'm going to throw away everything you've spent your life doing for this land."

Satisfied, the king continued, "Being that the two of you will marry next year, the queen and I want to give Sir Rackley our country estate as a gift." Looking directly at Sir Rackley, he added, "We would like you to have it as your own, so you can move closer to the royal castle and spend more time with our daughter. We think it's unfortunate the two of you have barely seen each other over the years, so this will give you both an opportunity to build up your relationship."

"Thank you, your majesty," Sir Rackley replied. "I would be pleased to accept your most generous gift. Nothing would make me happier than to spend more time with the princess during the next year."

The conversation was interrupted as two late arrivals came up to the table. It was Chadwick with the peasant boy Stefan, who now resembled a dignitary. All who were sitting at the table were visibly impressed with the boy's new look. "Excellent job, Chadwick," the princess said as she looked at Stefan. "You made him look like a new man." Chadwick thanked her and took his seat next to Delia at the other side of the table. Stefan continued standing in place, feeling embarrassed over all the attention he was getting. "Please, don't be afraid. Sit down next to me," the princess told him, after which he took his seat. As soon as he did, a server brought over a full plate of food, which included a large piece of pork, a mound of broccoli, and some delicious looking bread rolls, all resting on a golden plate. Another server brought the same thing to Chadwick. Stefan picked up his utensils to eat, too shy to say anything, but feeling wonderful inside because he was sitting next to the princess, the girl of his dreams. The princess and Delia started talking about something, as did Chadwick and the king and queen. Breaking the ice for Stefan was one of Stasia's friends who was sitting at the table, a thirteen-year-old girl.

"So, what is your name?" she asked him. Before he could reply, he had to finish chewing his food and swallow it down.

"My name is Stefan. What's yours?"

"My name is Madison. It's nice to meet you, Stefan," she said. After a brief pause, Stefan thought of something he could ask to keep the conversation going.

"Madison, what village do you live in?" he inquired.

"I don't live in a village. My parents and I live here at the castle. My father is one of the royal guards protecting the princess."

"Do you get to attend a school if you live here?" Stefan further asked.

"You mean do I *have* to attend school? Yes, I do, and I spend a lot of my time studying with my class. We meet every weekday and have our own teacher. When the teacher can't make it, Delia, the woman sitting next to Chadwick, comes over and teaches us." Stefan and Stasia's young friend Madison continued talking for a while as they were finishing their food. Then, Stefan realized he had forgotten something important.

He abruptly blurted out, "Oh no, I forgot about my friend Yvonne. I was supposed to meet her twenty minutes ago at the peasant stables."

The princess heard this, looked at him, and asked, "Do you mean Yvonne, the young peasant girl who takes care of the castle flowers?"

"Yeah, that's her," Stefan answered. "We always ride our horses home together after work to our homes in Norwalk. She's probably wondering what happened to me."

Stasia looked over at Delia and asked her, "Delia, could you do me a big favor if you're finished eating? Being that this young peasant girl is waiting for Stefan, and we can't let him leave just yet, I think it would be really nice to invite her to join us."

"Sure, I'll be glad to," Delia replied. "But all things considered, she's probably not going to be very presentable."

"Yes, you're right. Why don't you take her to be bathed and clothed, also. Then, see if she's hungry and wants some of the leftovers from the banquet. When she's all finished eating, bring her over to my coronation ball." Delia agreed, and left to get Yvonne, while everyone else at the table continued talking and finishing their meals.

Yvonne was waiting outside of the peasant stables for Stefan to meet her, tired from working the extra shift. She had been sitting down on a bale of hay, impatiently playing with her hair. When he didn't come after twenty minutes, she figured something must have happened. Perhaps he was asked to do some urgent floor cleaning in the Grand Ballroom after the coronation ceremony ended. It was getting pretty late at night, so Yvonne stood up and untied her horse, preparing to ride home alone for the first time in as long as she could remember. "Hey there, boy," she told her horse with a hint of sadness in her voice. "It looks like it's just you and me tonight." She led him out of the stall and started to walk toward the exit, with her head looking down at the ground. She stopped when she heard a voice calling to her.

"Yvonne! Are you Yvonne?" a woman was asking her, as she ran in her direction. When Yvonne didn't reply right away, the woman spoke again, "Please tell me you're Yvonne."

"Yeah, that's me," Yvonne finally said.

"Oh, I'm so relieved. I was worried that I missed you. The princess asked me to come out here and find you. When your friend, the peasant boy, told the princess he was late in meeting you, she sent me to get you. Out of the generosity of her heart, the princess would like to invite you inside the castle tonight to receive a new dress, some exquisite food, and a visit to the Grand Ballroom where her coronation ball will be taking place later." Yvonne's eyes lit up as the woman explained these things to her. It was one of the greatest things that had ever happened to her. The princess was always nice to her, but this was totally unexpected.

"I would love to go with you and do those things," Yvonne said. "But something you said doesn't make sense. Did you say my friend Stefan was talking with the princess?"

"I guess you two have a lot of catching up to do later," Delia replied. Yvonne put her horse back in the stall and followed Delia into the castle, as excited as she had ever been.

Shortly after midnight, the coronation ball got underway in the Grand Ballroom. The ballroom looked a lot different than it did a few hours earlier, when Stasia stood up on stage to receive her crown. All of the chairs in the room were stacked up and removed. The wall to wall red carpet was rolled up and put away into storage. Castle workers removed the painting which was badly damaged by Chadwick's fist, and replaced it with a new one. All that remained was the polished wood floor, the refreshment counter at the back, and about twice as many musicians, who were sitting on the stage, playing appropriate music. On the floor, there were many couples of all ages dancing and enjoying themselves a great deal. The mood was festive, as everyone awaited the entrance of the princess and her parents.

When Stasia arrived, she walked into the room with the king and queen standing next to her, one to each side. Most in the room stopped their talking or dancing and gave them brief applause. As they resumed their activities, the rest of those who were at Stasia's dinner table followed them into the room. Stefan came in at the back of the group, as he was walking with and talking to his new friend Madison. Soon she said goodbye and went off to visit with some of her other friends. Stefan looked over at the back counter, and noticed there was a worker serving drinks. Since he was thirsty, Stefan walked over and asked if he could have something to drink.

"Would you like some champagne or red wine?" the worker asked him.

"I've never tasted either before, so I wouldn't know which one to pick," Stefan told him, realizing his answer must have sounded unusual to the worker. The worker studied him for a moment and figured out who he was.

"You're the peasant boy from earlier tonight, aren't you?" the worker asked. When Stefan confirmed he was, the worker continued, "It's my privilege to serve the person who the princess chose to represent what she stands for. Since you don't know what to try, I'm going to pour you a glass of our red wine. Take it down slow, if you're not used to alcohol." The worker put the glass under the wine barrel and filled it up, after which he gave it to Stefan. Stefan took his first sip and the wine tasted bitter, causing him to show a funny expression on his face. The worker laughed at seeing this, as Stefan walked away into the crowd, looking for a place to sit down.

A short while later, as another musical number finished, Sir Rackley walked up to Stasia and tapped her on the shoulder while she was talking to three visiting noblemen. "Pardon me, princess, but might I have the next dance?" he asked.

"Of course you may," she replied, before excusing herself from the conversation she was in. Sir Rackley walked her out to the middle of the dance floor, where they stood motionless for a moment with their hands locked, waiting for the music to start. "I hope you're a good dancer," Stasia teased him, "because I've been known to kick people in the shins when they step on my feet." Sir Rackley didn't have time to reply, because the music started again, and Stasia pulled him right into a dance.

Stefan was not able to find a place to sit down, so he leaned against the wall for some time, taking quick, short sips of his wine. He was feeling kind of lonely and completely out of his element. A few people greeted him as they walked by, but for the most part, nobody was really paying attention to him. At least from the wall he was leaning against he could see the princess as she danced with Sir Rackley. That alone made his feelings of discomfort worth enduring. While he was looking at her, a familiar girl's voice greeted him.

"Hello, Stefan!" Stefan looked around and was surprised to see Yvonne standing next to him, wearing an elegant blue dress.

"Yvonne, you made it! It's so great to see you. I thought maybe the woman who went out to get you, I think her name was Delia, arrived too late and missed you. But you're here, and you look stunning!"

"Yes, I'm here, and you don't look too bad yourself. We could actually pass for a wealthy couple visiting the castle," she said. Stefan didn't catch the hidden reference Yvonne made to them passing for a husband and wife.

"Hey, you have to try this red wine, it's something else," Stefan told her.

"No thanks, I don't care for wine. Lady Ruth let me taste it once and it didn't go over well with me." Yvonne paused and looked longingly out at the dance floor. Then, she continued, "As long as we're both here in this amazing place, would you please dance with me?" Stefan tried to get out of it, saying he wasn't comfortable going out onto the dance floor and didn't know how to dance. But Yvonne kept pleading with him, "Please, Stefan, just this once. It would mean a great deal to me to share a dance with you here. It doesn't matter if you don't know how to dance, all you need to do is follow my lead. Trust me, it's not too hard." Reluctantly, Stefan allowed Yvonne to take him out into the crowd, and they started dancing. It wasn't as hard as he expected, although it was clear that his movement was not totally in rhythm.

While the coronation ball was taking place, there were a couple of worried parents sitting down in their small home in the village of Norwalk. Stefan's mother, Shaylene, stood up from her chair and looked out the window once again. "There's still no sign of him," she said to her husband Martin. She started pacing back and forth, not knowing what else to do with herself. "Stefan should have been home hours ago. Something terrible must have happened."

"Calm down, honey," Martin said to her. "I'm sure he's perfectly safe. There are so many royal guards now posted in Norwalk that I'm sure he will be okay."

"Yes, but something could have happened to him on the way from the castle to Norwalk. Or worse yet, the rebels could have even attacked both Stefan and Yvonne on the way, perhaps to try to rob them."

"That's not very likely," Martin replied. "That road is one of the safest in Astoria, at any time of night. Just to be on the safe side, why don't we take a walk down to Lady Ruth's house, where Yvonne lives, and see if she's heard from them." Shaylene agreed, glad to finally be doing something more productive with her time. They both put on an overcoat and walked out the door toward Lady Ruth's house. Many years ago, Martin wouldn't have dared to go outside at night, as the village of Norwalk was a frightening place to be after dark. But with all of the royal guards, Martin didn't hesitate to suggest the course of action they were taking.

When Martin and Shaylene arrived at Lady Ruth's house, they found her sitting outside on her porch, with a blanket over her shoulders. She stood up to welcome them, and invited them to sit down with her on her porch. "So I take it Yvonne's not home yet either?" Martin asked her.

"No, she's several hours late now. And she's never been more than a half an hour late before," Lady Ruth answered.

"What do you think we should do?" Shaylene asked.

"Nothing at all but wait," Lady Ruth said. "We don't have any more horses, and without them it would take much too long to walk to the castle. Yvonne's been pushing me to have more freedom and space lately, so this is probably just the result of that. At least we know they are together, which goes a long way towards putting my mind at ease." All three family members sat quietly on the porch, willing to wait the entire night if it was necessary.

Back at the castle, Stefan and Yvonne were still dancing, oblivious to the concern of their family members. At one point, they passed close by the area where Stasia and Sir Rackley were sharing their dance. Sir Rackley observed them struggling a bit, and said to Stasia, "Look at those two. It looks like they are dancing for the first time ever. They kind of make a nice couple, don't you think?" Stasia looked at them, just in time to see them accidentally bump into another couple on the floor, and she couldn't help but laugh.

"Aw, they look so cute together," she said. Sir Rackley joined her in laughing, and then took a more serious tone. There was something he felt he really needed to say to Stasia.

"Stasia, I think you are a remarkable young woman." Stasia looked into his eyes as he continued. "I only hope someday you can grow to love me, as I love you." Stasia allowed Sir Rackley's words to sink in for a short time, not saying anything in reply back to him. She would have preferred it if he hadn't said such a serious thing to her, just yet. She didn't let it bother her, though, she just looked for an opportunity to change the subject. Finally, she came up with an idea that would give her a way out.

"Hey, I want you to do something for me," she told Sir Rackley.

"Sure, anything," he said.

"I haven't spent very much time talking to the peasant boy Stefan, tonight. And he was a big part of my coronation ceremony. When this dance finishes, I'd like you to dance with his friend Yvonne, and I'll take a dance with him. It will help me finish setting the precedent which I started earlier tonight, in plain view of everyone here." Sir Rackley gladly agreed with what she asked him to do, and continued dancing with her through the rest of the musical number.

Right when it ended, Sir Rackley and Princess Stasia headed over to the place where Stefan and Yvonne were standing. Sir Rackley spoke first, looking at Yvonne. "Excuse me, young lady, I would like to introduce myself. My name is Sir Rackley, and I was wondering if I might have a dance with you?" Yvonne looked over at Stefan and smiled as she accepted Sir Rackley's invitation. Sir Rackley led her off to another part of the dance floor.

"So, I guess that leaves us two," the princess said to Stefan. "Would you give me the honor of dancing with you on this majestic night?"

To this offer, he replied, "The honor, the privilege, would be all mine."

Sir Rackley and Yvonne talked as they danced, and found out they shared a common interest in something. Sir Rackley asked her, "What kinds of things do you enjoy doing, Yvonne?"

"I'm quite good at archery," she replied. "Don't tell anyone, but I have a great secret. To some, I am known as Yvonne, humble fifteen-year-old peasant girl from the lower class of Norwalk. But to others, I am known as the greatest archer in the entire land."

"Is that so?" Sir Rackley asked her. "I do a bit of archery myself. I'd love to challenge you someday, if we ever get the chance."

Princess Stasia and Stefan were also having a conversation as they danced. Stasia asked him, "How long have you worked at the castle? Have you always cleaned the floors?"

"I've been working here a long, long time, ever since I was a young boy," he replied. "And, yes, I've always been a floor cleaner, mostly in the eastern side of the castle."

"Now that I'm in charge of things here, perhaps I could get you another job you might enjoy more," Stasia said.

"That would mean the world to me, princess. I will do whatever you want me to do. You know, it was my dream these past few years to someday see you in person. And to be here dancing with you, or at least trying my best to dance with you, is the greatest feeling in the world." As he said this, the princess noticed Stefan was looking at her with dreamy eyes, totally overwhelmed by the moment. It brought a smile to her face.

In reply, the princess said to him, "Well, then, I'm glad that I was able to bring a little bit of happiness into your life tonight."

Section 2

A Young Princess

A young princess
With so many plans
She loved her people and had their respect
Giving more to them than they could ever expect

Chapter Eight:

A Beautiful Heart

"Is that the last of your things, Yvonne?" the boy shouted across the yard.

"Yes, that's everything." she replied. "You can go ahead and finish tying it down with the ropes."

On a June morning, eight months after the coronation ceremony of the princess, two best friends, Stefan and Yvonne, were packing up the things they would need on top of Lady Ruth's carriage. Lady Ruth was still inside her house completing some last minute tasks, and Yvonne was outside leading her horse over to the gate. When she brought it through to the other side, she tied it up loosely next to Stefan's horse. She looked up at him working on top of the carriage, and said, "Oh, Stefan, this is going to be such a wonderful trip. I am so glad your parents are letting you come with us."

Upon hearing this, he replied, "Yeah, me too. I couldn't imagine just sitting around Norwalk for the next two weeks. Especially when there is a whole world out there I've never seen before."

Stefan and Yvonne were the recipients of some unexpected time off from their work, as were many other peasants throughout the land. It was all a part of something known as 'Stasia's Reformation', which laid down new guidelines for the proper and fair treatment of lower class citizens. Among the new guidelines were allowances for peasants to be able to own property, to be able to bring grievances over mistreatment to the attention of the princess, and to receive a mandatory two weeks of either rest or vacation during each work year. Those who had not received any time off during the past two years were to be granted an immediate two week break. Thus, everything lined up perfectly for Yvonne to be able to travel with her foster mother, Lady Ruth, as she went on her yearly visit to see some of her relatives in the distant village of Langston, about two days away at normal travel speed. Yvonne had pleaded with Lady Ruth for several days, as she really wanted to invite Stefan to go with them. Lady Ruth finally gave in, on the condition that Stefan's parents approved of the trip, and that they both stayed on their best behavior when they were in the company of Lady Ruth's relatives. Most importantly, Lady Ruth didn't want them disappearing again for almost an entire night, as they did during the night of Princess Stasia's coronation. That night, Lady Ruth waited with Stefan's parents until nearly the crack of dawn before the two returned home. Both Yvonne and Stefan assured her it would not happen again on this trip. Also, Stefan's parents gladly agreed to let him go on the trip, knowing that as he approached seventeen years of age, going to Langston would be a good eye-opener for him. It would help him see there were other places out there, not just the life he was accustomed to living in Norwalk. So here they were, preparing to set out on an amazing trip. As Stefan finished tying down the last pieces of luggage to the carriage, Lady Ruth emerged from the house, ready to depart.

"Yvonne, I hope the two horses we rented to pull the carriage are in good health. It is going to be a long journey to Langston."

Looking at the horses, Yvonne replied, "I am sure they will be fine, Lady Ruth. They look like they are almost as excited to get going as we are." Lady Ruth came through the gate, closed it, and climbed into the carriage to sit down. One of her house servants, a young man in his early twenties, was sitting at the outside front of the carriage, ready to steer the horses. As they prepared to depart, Lady Ruth shared some final instructions with Yvonne and Stefan.

She poked her head out of the carriage window and said to them, "Make sure you two don't ride too far ahead of us. We don't want to lose you along the way." After Lady Ruth brought her head back inside the window, Stefan and Yvonne looked at each other and laughed. With that, they were off on their two day journey to Langston, on the other side of Astoria. Stefan and Yvonne rode their two horses ahead, and Lady Ruth followed behind them in her horse carriage.

That night, the travelers pulled into a village about halfway between Norwalk and Langston, called Kifissia. Kifissia was a much smaller town, and there was only one place where accommodations were available. As Lady Ruth's servant stopped her carriage outside of the inn, Stefan and Yvonne dismounted their horses and tied them up to the wooden post outside. "This is it. This is where we'll be staying tonight," Lady Ruth announced to them, as she stepped down from her carriage. The servant helped her with her bags, and Stefan and Yvonne took their belongings off the carriage as they all walked inside. After they checked in, the innkeeper showed them where they would be lodging, in a spacious four bedroom suite. They then ate dinner together in the dining area, discussing everything they had seen along the way. When they were finished, Lady Ruth announced she was retiring for the night, and the servant went back outside to finish securing the horses and belongings for the night. Stefan and Yvonne, however, walked off to explore the town a little bit.

Soon, they found a nice spot to relax, on a small rock wall spanning one side of a bridge. Stefan and Yvonne swung their legs over the rock wall and sat on it, looking down at the river which flowed below them. After sitting and staring for a while, Yvonne gently rested her left arm across Stefan's shoulder. She looked at him and said, "Stefan, it makes me so happy you are here with me on this trip. I couldn't imagine it any other way."

He continued looking down at the river and agreed, "Yeah, we really needed this. We've worked so hard, basically all of our teenage years, so it feels great to have a little time off for a change."

Seeing he wasn't getting her point, Yvonne tried to be a little more direct. "That's true, but the important thing is we are here together."

To this, he replied, "You're right. We're going to have a lot of fun doing things when we get to Langston. Although, half of me kind of misses being at the castle, because that's where the princess is." When Yvonne heard this, it made her feel a touch of sadness inside, and she slowly took her arm off the back of his shoulder. She couldn't force him to fall in love with her if he didn't want to. If he wanted to continue dwelling on his impossible romantic fantasy, that was his choice. Yvonne thought maybe it would simply take some more time for him to realize that the girl of his dreams was sitting right next to him, and not inside the throne room of Astoria Castle. She soon stopped worrying about it as the two best friends talked about other things for a while, before heading back to the inn.

When they went back inside, they saw a lively bunch of people all sitting around in the public area, having conversations and playing games. There was a local musician from Kifissia lightly playing a stringed instrument on a small stage set up for that purpose. Stefan and Yvonne went over to listen to what he was playing, and sat down on a small couch which was unoccupied. After listening for about thirty minutes, Stefan found himself distracted, eavesdropping on a conversation taking place behind him between a dignitary and landowner who were playing cards.

"I must say, I never expected that Princess Stasia's reforms would work out so well for Astoria."

"Neither did I. It goes to show why you or I are not running this land. She has a knack for improving the spirits of our workers."

"No kidding. The work production of my servants has actually increased since the people received their own rights. And here I was worried it was going to make them slow down and cost me money."

"I have found the same thing with all of my employees. Show them a little love and appreciation, and they want to work harder to make you happy." The two continued talking, heaping praise upon Princess Stasia and the changes she made. Stefan found the conversation to be very interesting, because it revealed that the chance she took was paying huge dividends. And he and Yvonne were enjoying some of those dividends right now, having received the vacation time to go on this trip. Stefan realized his shoulder was beginning to feel sore. Discovering why, he looked down and noticed Yvonne was asleep with her head resting against him. He didn't want to disturb her, so he let her sleep as he continued listening to the musician.

The next morning, everyone in the group woke up early, as they continued their journey over a mountain pass and down into the village of Langston. At the same time, Stefan's parents, Martin and Shaylene, were being dropped off outside of the royal castle by a friend, who took them in an old, beat-up horse carriage he owned. The friend promised them he would be waiting for them when they came back out. As they arrived at the drawbridge, a royal guard checked their papers, and allowed them to pass through onto the castle grounds. "Are you sure we did the right thing by not telling Stefan about this?" Shaylene asked Martin.

"Absolutely, it was the right thing to do," he answered. "If Stefan knew what we were doing, it would have made him skip out on his trip with Yvonne to Langston. And like I told you earlier, I don't think it would be right for the princess to know that he is our son. She looks with favor upon him, and it might have caused her to be impartial in rendering her decision about our case. I don't want any special favors or special treatment, I only want the right thing to be done. Whatever she decides, I'm sure it will be objective and fair." Martin and Shaylene continued walking toward the west side entrance, where they were scheduled to have an audience with the princess.

Among the many new changes Princess Stasia had instituted was one which proved to be exactly what Martin and Shaylene needed. For many years, they felt as if Rolf, the landowner they worked for, was treating them with an unusual cruelty. Not only was he harsh and demanding, but he went back on promises made to them by his father Leon, before he passed away. When word came out that peasants were now allowed to bring their problems to the attention of the princess, Martin and Shaylene were quick to put their names down on a waiting list growing by the day. Sometime this morning, their names would be called, and they would have a chance to go into the throne room and plead their case directly to her. She would then talk with the landowner, who was required to be present to defend himself, and render her decision.

As they came up close to the entrance, Martin and Shaylene felt hopeful she would see things their way. They climbed the stairs and saw Rolf standing outside the door, waiting for them with one of his friends, a man named Wilfred. The friend he brought was someone who had a bad reputation in the village of Norwalk, being known as a drunk and troublemaker. Martin tried to extend a friendly greeting to the two men, but the landowner laughed at him. He then gloated, "You are wasting your time here today. You don't have a chance of getting a favorable ruling."

"The princess will decide that, not you," Shaylene said in response.

"Yes, but I don't see anybody with you today. Like, perhaps, some witnesses to back up your claims. As for me, I've brought somebody with me who will testify that you both, and your worthless son, are all a bunch of lazy, no-good workers." Upon hearing this, Martin and Shaylene's hearts both sank. They didn't have any way to prove to the princess that the things they would tell her were true. They could only give their word. However, Rolf brought somebody to support his side of the story. And the princess couldn't have possibly known about the man's bad reputation. To her, he would probably appear to be an honest person, there to expose Martin and Shaylene's claims as false. But it was too late. There was nothing they could do, except hope for a miracle.

When their names were called by the court official, Martin, Shaylene, Rolf, and Wilfred all followed him into the throne room. Princess Stasia was sitting on her throne, wearing her golden crown and regal garments. The court official directed Martin and Shaylene to take seats on the right side of the room, while Rolf and Wilfred were told to take seats on the left. The princess started talking to them.

"Welcome, my dear citizens, to the throne room of Astoria Castle. Before I start, I would like all of you to know that words of truth are very important to me. Should you be caught speaking lies before me, your crime is punishable by time in the castle prison. That said, let us begin. First, I would like to hear from those who are here to file grievances. Please, introduce yourselves and tell me how you have been wronged."

"Your highness," Martin began, "my name is Martin and this is my wife Shaylene. We are peasant workers who live in the village of Norwalk. Shortly before Shaylene and I were married, I began working for a landowner, putting in long, hard days of labor. Then, almost fifteen years ago, my family and I moved onto the landowner's estate, where we were given a small cottage to live in as I continued working. At that time, my wife also started working. While in the act of working, about eight years ago, I suffered an unexpected fall, severely injuring my leg. The injury has left me with continuous, shooting pain which rarely stops. As compensation, the landowner I worked for said I could stop working and my nine-year-old son could take my place. However, the landowner died, and his son, of whom my complaint is against, took over the estate. The landowner's son forced me to go back to work, despite the promise made to me by his father."

Shaylene added to what her husband said, "Your majesty, not only that, but he has increased my workload, and my son's workload, to a nearly unbearable level. He is abusive towards us, treats us as if we are worthless, and only gives us a small portion of rice and often stale bread to eat for the week. We can live with being treated badly, as people have looked down on us all of our lives, but we ask that you at least allow my husband to discontinue working because of his injury."

"I see," the princess stated at hearing this. "These are serious charges in my eyes, as I have no tolerance for those who harshly treat others, no matter what their class or status." Looking at the landowner, she asked, "What do you say to these charges brought against you today?"

"Your highness, I say they are telling you lies," Rolf answered. "I have always been good to their family. My father allowed them to move onto our property against my wishes, and I have allowed them to stay there, even after he died. Out of the kindness of my heart, I gave their oldest son a horse he could ride. Every day, I give them enough food to survive, I give them a reasonable amount of work, and I give them a safe place to live. Yet, this is how they show their appreciation. And I have to be honest with you. In my opinion, they are somewhat lazy. Martin, here, is just looking for a free pass, so he can have an excuse to sit around all day and do nothing. I wouldn't mind if he did retire, but the work his son does is practically worthless. Every time I go outside and check up on him, he's either working really slow, or doing nothing at all. I've even caught him taking naps under the trees of my orchard when he was supposed to be gathering fruit. He's the laziest one of them all."

"What he says is true," Wilfred chimed in. "I've seen it for myself. He does everything he can to get out of working. Worse yet, he even stole from me last weekend when I visited the estate. I went inside the main house to have lunch, and when I came back out, the silver coins I left in my saddle bag were all gone. It wasn't the first time he has taken something from me, either." Finally, with a raised voice, the landowner's friend pointed over at Martin and Shaylene, and said, "Their son Stefan is nothing but a common thief!"

When the princess heard this last line, she started trying to put all of the pieces together in her mind. She thought for a moment, and asked the landowner, "You said their son is very lazy. Just as I don't tolerate harsh treatment of others, I don't tolerate laziness or those who try to take advantage of their employers. Tell me, if you will, what was his name again, and how old is he?"

Feeling like he was about to win the case, Rolf happily answered, "Their son's name is Stefan and he is almost seventeen years old."

"I see," the princess said to him upon hearing this. Looking at the landowner's friend, she asked, "Just to clarify something, on what day of the week and at what time did their son steal the silver coins from you?"

"He stole them from my saddle bag at around noon, last Saturday. And I would like to be compensated for what he has taken."

Upon hearing his response, the princess looked over at Martin and Shaylene, asking them, "Why did you not tell me that you had a peasant son named Stefan? And why is he not here to defend himself today? Where is he?"

Martin answered, "Your highness, we didn't think it was necessary. Or, appropriate might be a better word. He is traveling with a friend on a trip to Langston."

Princess Stasia asked all of them to stand up. When they did, she continued, "I have considered all of the evidence and made my decision. My ruling is in favor of Martin and Shaylene, the peasant couple. I hereby give my order that Martin be permitted to retire from work, that all in their family receive better treatment, and that better food rations be given to them. I will have one of my royal guards check in with them each month to be sure my orders are carried out. You are all excused."

Standing there in utter shock, the landowner and his friend didn't move. Rolf finally asked the princess, "Your highness, how could you possibly rule in their favor? They presented no proof to their claims, while I brought an eyewitness to back up what I was saying."

"You really want to know, do you?" the princess replied. "And I am willing to tell you. But first, let me remind you that if I find out either of you have lied to me today, you will be taken directly from here to the castle prison. I am going to give you one last chance to confess the truth to me, if you would like. Would either of you like to tell me something?"

All of a sudden, the landowner's friend shouted out, "He's the one who put me up to this!" Pointing at Rolf, he added, "He offered me money if I would come here today and support the lies he was telling you. He's the one who should go to prison, not me!"

"Shut up, you idiot!" Rolf said back to him. After that, Rolf started becoming really afraid, so he stood there looking at the princess with a measure of terror in his eyes.

"You two are a disgrace to our people," the princess finally said. "It wouldn't do any good to put either of you in jail. I'm going to have you do something more useful with your time. As further punishment for lying to me, I hereby give the cottage where they have been living, over to Martin and his family, to retain full ownership and rights to it for as long as they and their offspring may live. And both of you are required to perform one month of free labor in behalf of the village of Norwalk. Report to the royal guard station, effective tomorrow morning." She concluded by saying, "You may not say anything further in reply to this. Leave me at once!" At hearing this, everyone stood up to leave, but the princess stopped Martin and Shaylene, "Not you two. Stay for a moment, I would like a word with you."

As soon as Rolf and Wilfred walked out of the throne room, Princess Stasia stood up from her throne and walked down to where Martin and Shaylene were standing. She gave each of them a hug. She then asked them, "Why didn't you tell me that you were Stefan's parents? It would have made my job here a lot easier today."

"I know it would have," Martin replied, "but we didn't feel it was the right thing to do. We felt you would be able to see the truth."

"It is so wonderful to meet you both. I was able to see through their lies once I figured out that the Stefan involved was your son and not somebody else with the same name. That's why I asked you where he was today. I knew where he was because I saw his friend Yvonne working the other day in the Royal Gardens, and she told me they were going on a trip to Langston. I can't believe they had the nerve to accuse your son of being a lazy worker. He's the exact opposite. He's a very hard worker. And that elaborate story about him stealing silver coins. I know he always works every Saturday and Sunday here at the castle, and he would never take something which does not belong to him."

"You have such wisdom at a young age," Shaylene replied. "Thank you so much for the kindness you have shown us today, and the kindness you show to our son as well."

"I adore your son," the princess said. "He is a really nice boy."

"He adores you, too," Shaylene said. "Probably more than you know. You're practically all he ever talks about at home."

"Aw, that's sweet," the princess replied. "I've been meaning to give him a promotion here at the castle. How do you think he would like to be either the head of grounds keeping or the assistant jail keeper? Both positions are opening up soon."

Martin answered, "If I had to guess, I would say that he would take whichever job would let him see you more often." At hearing this, the princess smiled.

While Stefan's parents were having this conversation with Princess Stasia, Delia was teaching a small class of students in another part of the castle. Her relationship with Chadwick continued to deteriorate lately, and they were barely on speaking terms at the moment. Chadwick left recently for another one of his long trips into the countryside, supposedly to continue gathering support for the princess and her new ideals. Delia was glad that he was gone, and she was enjoying filling in as a substitute teacher for the young ones who lived at the castle while their regular teacher was out sick. As part of their learning experience, students would regularly receive guest speakers and experts from every field of study.

Today, a specialist in the birds of Astoria happened to be visiting the class. When he walked in, Delia introduced him to everybody. "Students, our special guest has arrived. I would like to introduce you to Anton, who is going to give you a lesson on the rarest bird in the land." The students looked at the back of the classroom and saw a tall, long-haired man walking towards the front. He was wearing an extended leather glove which covered most of his arm. Perched on the glove was an Astorian eagle. Anton arrived at the front and greeted everybody.

"Hello, students," he said.

"Hello, Anton," they all answered, somewhat in unison. Delia took a seat near the back of the class, as she listened in with interest.

"I would like to introduce all of you to J-Bird, one of the few remaining Astorian eagles in the land. Sadly, they have been hunted nearly to extinction. At last count, there were less than ten Astorian eagles with active nests within our borders. Today, you will all get a chance to touch this rare, magnificent bird. But first, let me tell you more about his lifestyle and habits." Anton continued teaching the class for some time, after which he allowed the students to come up one by one to cautiously pet the bird. One girl in particular, a fourteen-year-old named Madison, was quite impressed.

"Wow, his feathers are so soft and pretty," she said. "I wish I could take him home with me and keep him in my room." Anton laughed at hearing this, and soon Delia and the rest of the class were laughing as well, causing Madison to blush.

King Charles and Queen Delphine had been enjoying themselves these past eight months, slowly being involved less and less with daily activities at the castle. King Charles still wanted to be kept aware of any developments involving the rebels, as he was hoping to somehow assist in putting a stop to their terrible deeds. They were both very pleased with the way their daughter asserted her authority, although they wished she would spend a little less time hearing grievances from unhappy peasants and leave a little more time for herself. But her heart kept propelling her to do all she could to help other people, and they understood that. Charles and Delphine were arriving at their former country estate, which they gave to Sir Rackley as a gift on the night the princess was coronated. They were here to visit with Sir Rackley and discuss with him some of the wedding arrangements. As it stood now, Princess Stasia and Sir Rackley were supposed to be getting married in four months. That time would go by quickly, so it was smart to begin finalizing some of the arrangements now. As they pulled up to the wide gate in their horse carriage, two servants opened it, allowing them to enter. Queen Delphine noted to her husband that Sir Rackley had made some changes to the landscaping, and that the estate was looking better than ever. As they pulled up next to the portico, Sir Rackley was waiting there to meet them.

"Charles and Delphine, it's good to have you here," he told them.

"We're glad to be back," Charles said. "Stasia sends her greetings but was way too busy to come with us. You've sure made some improvements since the last time we were here."

"Oh, I simply told my servants to make a few slight modifications. Please, won't you both come inside and join me for some tea out in the back?"

"We would be delighted to," the queen answered.

King Charles and Queen Delphine followed Sir Rackley through the large estate home which was once their vacation residence, back when Charles was in power. As they were passing through, Delphine reached up to touch one of the crystals attached to a chandelier hanging in the main room. "I remember when we were given this chandelier," she said to Charles. "You just turned twenty-five, and Chadwick and Delia were recently married."

With a hint of sarcasm, Charles looked at her and said, "Let's hope they stay married. They've been having a lot of problems lately."

"It's understandable," Delphine replied. "Living at the castle and serving the royal family is not an easy thing to do. It's a very stressful environment, to say the least." The three walked through another door and onto a veranda built out in the back. The veranda was built to take advantage of the grand view of the surrounding countryside, which was very scenic and beautiful. There were green hills as far as the eye could see, dotted with many different kinds of trees. As everyone sat down, Delphine pointed to a small family of deer who were feeding on the grass nearby. "Aren't they precious?" Delphine asked, to which Sir

Rackley and King Charles agreed. The three of them spent the rest of the afternoon sitting on the veranda, drinking tea and discussing Sir Rackley's desired arrangements for his upcoming wedding.

Far away from Sir Rackley's country estate, Stefan and Yvonne spent another day on the road together. A few minutes ago, they finally arrived in Langston, awestruck as they rode their horses down the main dirt road into town.

"This village is so modern," Yvonne said of her first impressions.

"I've never seen anything like it," Stefan agreed. "I didn't even know homes could be built this big." The group arrived at one of the large houses near the center of town, where Lady Ruth introduced everyone to her sister, Lady Rachel, and two young boys who were staying with her.

"These are my two grandsons," Lady Rachel said. "They are going to be staying with me all summer while their father and mother are traveling the Limekiln region." Once Stefan and Yvonne went inside and visited for a while, Lady Ruth gave them permission to go out into the village for a few hours.

"I need you to do me one favor while you're out," Lady Rachel asked them, as she handed them a copper coin. "Before you come back tonight, could you please stop by the market and pick me up a few oranges for tomorrow's breakfast?" Stefan and Yvonne promised they wouldn't forget, and walked out the door into the streets of Langston.

In the forest a short distance outside of the village of Langston, a small group of rebel soldiers gathered about two hours later, equipped with swords, bows, arrows, and torches. Among the group were General Robbins and his assistant Sebastian, who was now sixteen years old. They were listening attentively to an address by the rebel leader Prince Agis. As usual, Prince Agis was wearing his creepy mask and some dark clothing. "Rebel soldiers, this is a very important operation we are carrying out tonight. I don't want any mistakes. I want you all to stand your ground, no matter what happens. Is that understood?"

"Yes!" they all shouted.

"Good," Prince Agis continued. "Since our strategy is clear, we have a little business to discuss. We have lost the support of three more formerly sympathetic landowners, which has put a strain on our resources. They have taken a liking to Princess Stasia, causing them to withdraw their funding. We even lost the support of Herman, one of our strongest financial backers. As a result, we will have to plunder more villages and take more aggressive action against royal guards scattered throughout the realm. Remember, all of these things are leading up to our imminent attack and overthrow of the castle. So, do not lose heart, stay strong, and keep your heads up. We are only months away from being in power, and each one of you will be rewarded handsomely for your loyalty. You will all be part of the new leadership of the land of Astoria." When he finished, Prince Agis took his sword out, a masterful looking weapon, and held it up in the air, shouting, "May we have success tonight!" After he put his sword away, he kicked his horse in the side, causing it to take off in a gallop. Behind him, fourteen rebel soldiers followed, all of them on horseback.

Stefan and Yvonne took their time walking through town, talking and admiring the buildings they were passing. They were particularly fascinated by the royal guard station built next to the library in the village center. It was a large, stone building, that had two giant swords crossing each other, attached to the wall, above the entrance doorway. Stefan and Yvonne walked up the stairs to take a closer look at the two swords. As they were talking about them, a royal guard walked outside and greeted them.

"Hey there, kids. Can I help you?"

"Hello, sir," Yvonne said to him. "We were admiring these swords. Are they real?"

"No, those swords aren't real," the guard said as he was laughing. "It would take three men just to pick one of those up, much less use it in battle. My name is Callum. I haven't seen you kids around here before. Are you locals?"

"No, we are from Norwalk," Stefan answered, "but you could also say we're from the royal castle, because we both work there."

"Yeah, and we even know the princess," Yvonne added.

"I'm sure you do," Callum said. "Well, the next time you see her, could you please tell her to send some reinforcements out here? We only have a few guards in town, and we sure could use the help. That is, unless you two want to enlist." The guard was now laughing again, and Stefan and Yvonne could see that he wasn't taking them seriously. They said goodbye to him and walked off towards the market, which they passed earlier.

Entering the market, Stefan and Yvonne went over and started putting some oranges into a small box they could carry home. When they had all they could buy for one copper coin, they carried the box up to the merchant who owned the place. "Will this be all for you tonight?" the merchant asked Stefan and Yvonne. Before they could answer him, a terrified woman who had just walked out of the door with her groceries, ran back inside screaming.

"We're surrounded! We're surrounded! Somebody help us," she was saying. Stefan, Yvonne, the market owner, and three other people who were inside the store, all stopped what they were doing and looked out the two open windows to see what she was talking about. When they saw what caused her to have such fear, they were just as frightened. Outside of the market, rebel soldiers, too many to count, surrounded the store. All of them, with the exception of a man with a mask, were holding a hand torch burning with fire. Yvonne reacted by closing her eyes and pulling herself tight against Stefan, holding him for dear life. She had heard stories of the rebels burning down buildings before. She didn't want her life to end here tonight, not without first telling Stefan how she felt about him.

Thinking this could be her last chance, she lifted her head off of him and whispered in his right ear, "I love you, Stefan." Stefan heard what she said and clutched her tightly, realizing she was afraid for her life.

Not entirely sure of their safety, he whispered back to her, "I love you too, Yvonne. Don't worry. Everything is going to be okay."

The rebel leader, who was wearing the mask, approached one of the open windows and shouted inside, "Market owner, prepare to have your store burned to the ground!"

Chapter Nine:

Years of Royal Training

The market owner went into a panic when he heard the masked man's threat. While Stefan and Yvonne were standing in place holding each other, the other three shoppers and the woman who had run back into the store were all trying to find hiding places. But not the market owner. To the surprise of the rebels outside, he ran out the front door, straight toward the masked man. When Sebastian saw this, he immediately dropped his torch onto the ground and tackled the market owner before he could get to the masked man, who was Prince Agis. Sebastian held him down, keeping his face planted in the dirt. Prince Agis looked down at the market owner and started making fun of him.

"What did you think you were going to do, fight me?" Prince Agis asked him in a mocking tone. "I am the greatest sword fighter in the entire land. What were you going to do, attack me with peaches and pears?" Realizing he was in a precarious situation, the market owner decided not to speak. Sebastian slowly released his grip on him, before standing up and kicking him in the back as hard as he could. The market owner grimaced as the pain shot through his body. Prince Agis looked at Sebastian and commended him, "Well done, Sebastian. That's what I like to see in my soldiers, a willingness to protect their leader." Sebastian thanked him and went back over to where he was originally standing, picking up his torch along the way.

Stefan watched these developments from inside of the market, feeling quite disturbed over the cruelty being displayed. As Yvonne continued holding onto him tightly, he thought about his options. His first concern was for Yvonne's safety. He wanted to get her out of here and as far away as possible. Perhaps he could turn himself over to the rebel soldiers, asking them to take their anger out on him instead of the others. Certainly there was no way he could put up a fight against them, as he had no skills with weapons of any kind. Even if he did, there were no weapons in the market, only fruits and vegetables. He looked around and felt terrible as he saw everyone else in the store hiding down on the ground, behind tables of produce. He didn't want to see anyone get hurt tonight, and trying to fight against the rebels outside could only result in making things worse. Stefan needed to do something, and realized he had to act fast. He finally decided his best option was to try to gather everyone up, so they could walk outside and beg the masked man for mercy. Speaking to the girl clutching him, he said, "Yvonne, I need your help. We have to get all of these people outside before something tragic happens."

Yvonne opened her eyes once again and looked up at him. "Okay, if that's what you think we should do, Stefan, I will try my best." She then transformed herself in front of him, from a girl overcome by fear into a young woman of great courage. She went over and started urging three people who were hiding to get up and follow her. Stefan saw this and went over to get the other person who was hiding, practically yanking him up. The people hiding were all too disheartened to resist, and were ready for someone to take control of the situation.

Stefan directed them, "Everybody, follow me outside. It is not safe in here, as the rebel soldiers have threatened to burn the market to the ground. We need to get out while we still can." When he was finished, and saw several people nod in approval, he turned around to go outside, confident they were coming behind him.

Prince Agis was still humiliating the market owner when he saw six individuals walk out of the front door of the market. It caught him by surprise, so he asked them, "Well, what do we have here? More residents of Langston who want to stand up against the mighty Prince Agis?"

Stefan spoke up in behalf of the group. "No, we're not interested in fighting you, sir. We know you are much stronger than us and we wouldn't dare try anything to provoke you. I beg of you to let everyone else go, and do what you want with me. Please, sir, these are all innocent people who have nothing against you. Please don't hurt them."

Prince Agis was impressed upon hearing this. He responded from behind his mask, "Boy, for someone so young, you have great courage. I can respect that and will grant your request. I will release everyone here tonight, including you. Someday soon, I will be the leader of this land, and thus you should know something about me. I did not come to Langston this evening to do harm to you or anybody else. I came with my fellow rebel soldiers simply to resupply our camp with the necessary provisions of life. And that's exactly what we are going to do right now." Looking at his men, Prince Agis ordered them, "Bring the horses in and empty this store of every last fruit and vegetable being sold."

When he heard this, the market owner pleaded, "No, please, I need to sell these things to earn money for my wife and children." Prince Agis was tired of dealing with the whining of the market owner, so he ordered Robbins to take him and the other six people across the road and hold them there. The prisoners were forced to watch as the rebel soldiers brought their horses up to the front of the market. On each horse was an enormous saddle bag, which could fit a large amount of supplies inside of it. It wasn't long before all the fruits and vegetables in the entire store had been plundered by the rebels.

After the horses were backed away, Prince Agis told the market owner, "I wouldn't want to leave without giving you a goodbye present, for you and all residents of Langston to remember me by." He started laughing and threw his torch through the window of the market. All of the other rebel soldiers did the same, throwing their torches into the two windows of the market. Soon, a small fire turned into a blazing inferno.

When the market owner saw his store burning to the ground, he put his hands into his face and said, "I can't watch this any more. I just can't watch this." As the fire raged, Prince Agis held his sword up high in victory, ordering his men to follow him out of town. The last rebel soldier to follow him was Sebastian, who had been staring at Stefan for the past minute. Stefan noticed it, and was worried the rebel soldier was thinking about harming him in some way, before leaving. So he kept his head down, looking toward the ground, trying not to provoke the rebel in any way. In reality, Sebastian was simply curious as to why Stefan was wearing a necklace which looked exactly like his own. Sebastian had never seen another one like it, anywhere, in his entire life. Without saying a word, he finally decided to kick his horse and follow the rest of the group out of town.

When the rebels were out of sight, the small group of people who were originally inside the store together quickly dispersed. The four customers who were shopping at the time of the raid ran off into the streets of Langston, all heading towards their homes. The market owner turned and slowly walked off toward his home. And Stefan and Yvonne decided to return to the royal guard station they visited earlier, to report the shocking events. As they were walking, Yvonne asked her best friend for a favor. "Stefan, I'm scared. Would you take my hand, please?" When she asked this, Yvonne wasn't making the request as a romantic gesture. She was just feeling the after-effects of what happened and needed some support. Stefan didn't take it as a romantic gesture either, and was happy to take her hand into his as they walked toward the guard station.

After a short time, they were once again climbing the steps of the large, stone building. They walked under the two giant, crossed swords and into the entrance area of the royal guard station. Callum, the royal guard who teased them earlier was still there, cleaning some weapons with a rag. When he saw the two teenagers again, he joked with them, "You've come back to enlist, have you?" Upon hearing this, neither Stefan or Yvonne laughed.

In a firm tone, Stefan replied, "No, we have come back to report some terrible news to you. My friend Yvonne and I were at a nearby market, shopping for some oranges, when a large group of rebels surrounded the store. We managed to get outside, along with the market owner and the other customers. The rebels took all of the fruits and vegetables from the store, after which they burned the store to the ground."

The royal guard looked at him and said, "You're serious about that, aren't you? Where are the rebels now?"

"They rode away as the store was burning down. I heard the leader, who went by the name Prince Agis, say something about stealing the fruits and vegetables to resupply their camp. That's probably where they are headed. And, you know, I swear I've heard his voice somewhere before. It sounded familiar to me for some reason."

Callum added, "This is a high priority matter. There is only one other guard on duty tonight. He left a while ago to check some of the roads at the other end of town, but he should be back any minute. When he returns, I want you to show us exactly where this took place. And I may need one of you to ride with me tonight to the royal castle to give a firsthand report to the princess and the Chief Royal Knight. You two weren't serious earlier when you said that you knew the princess, were you?"

Yvonne spoke up, "Yes, we really do know her. We have both worked at the castle for many years."

"Okay, then, it would be very helpful if one of you could ride with me. I am going to be riding at top speed all night, which should get me to the royal castle by tomorrow morning. Think about it, and let me know. You two can sit down over there in the waiting area until the other royal guard gets back." Stefan and Yvonne, who were still holding hands, went over and sat down.

They sat there for a few minutes before Yvonne said, "Stefan, there is no way I can ride back with him to the royal castle tonight. Lady Ruth would never allow it."

Stefan replied, "I understand. She's probably going to be pretty freaked out after she hears about what happened to us. I suppose I could take my horse and go with him."

"But I don't want you to go, Stefan. I want you to stay here with me. I need you."

"I know you do, Yvonne. But you heard what he said. This is a serious matter and they need our help. We might be able to provide some details which could lead to the capture of the rebels and bring an end to the horrible things they are doing."

About a minute passed before Yvonne conceded, "All right then, if you must go. But it's going to be lonely around here without you."

When the other royal guard returned, he was filled in on the events which had transpired. The guards left the station, riding their horses over to the market, where they found it still smoldering. Stefan and Yvonne were riding on back, sitting right behind the two guards. They continued on, arriving a few minutes later at the house of Lady Rachel. Once again, Lady Ruth was sitting outside on the porch, worried because Yvonne and Stefan stayed out so late. When she saw them pull up, she stood up and said to the royal guards, "I hope these two didn't somehow get into trouble."

"No, ma'am," one of the royal guards responded. "They were the victims of a rebel attack which took place tonight in Langston. They were in the wrong place at the wrong time. The market they were shopping at was raided and burned down by a group of rebels."

"Oh, my," Lady Ruth replied at hearing this. "Yvonne, are you okay, my darling? I didn't realize this village was such a dangerous place, or I never would have let the two of you go out at night."

"It's not a dangerous place," the royal guard said. "This type of attack has never happened here before. Otherwise, we would have more royal guards stationed here to provide protection. Ma'am, I really need to get going, and I would like to take this boy with me back to the royal castle so he can give a firsthand account of the events that took place." After it was discussed for a few minutes, Lady Ruth decided to let Stefan take his horse and ride with the royal guard back to the castle. Stefan said a quick goodbye to Lady Ruth and Yvonne, and rode off with Callum on the longest, fastest, and hardest horseback ride he had ever been on.

The next morning, Princess Stasia was having breakfast with her parents, who had returned from their visit to Sir Rackley's country estate. Delia joined them, and was telling them about the fascinating visit of the bird expert to the class she was teaching. "The Astorian eagle was magnificent," Delia said. "It's one thing to see one flying high above you up in the sky, but it's quite another to be standing right next to one, touching its feathers. I only wish there was a way we could protect the few remaining birds, before they are all gone."

"Maybe there is," the princess replied. "Perhaps I could enact a law to ban any type of hunting or contact with them. I could even announce the new law by holding a special gathering of village statesmen in front of the grand Astorian Eagle Monument standing at the top of the mountain pass just before the village of Sorensen. It would be a sad day, indeed, when we lost the last of our mighty Astorian eagles." Changing the subject, Stasia asked her parents, "So, how did your visit go with Sir Rackley yesterday?"

"It went well," Queen Delphine answered. "We spent a good part of the afternoon sitting out back on the veranda, enjoying the view of the countryside and discussing wedding arrangements."

"And what type of wedding has Sir Rackley envisioned us having?" the princess further asked.

"His vision is of the grandest wedding the land has ever seen. He would like dignitaries and noblemen from all over the region to attend. Sir Rackley wants to marry you outdoors, standing on the Castle Terrace, in plain view of the thousands of people he would like to attend. After the ceremony, he would like to have a massive celebration with an abundance of food, wine, and cake, spread throughout the entire castle grounds." As the queen was finishing her description, Stasia looked kind of disappointed.

King Charles could see the unhappiness in her face, so he asked, "What's wrong, sweetheart?"

"It's just that I always dreamed of having a small wedding," Stasia replied. "With only my close family and friends there, those who have been an important part of my life. My coronation ceremony was large and elaborate, and I was hoping that my wedding could be the exact opposite, simple, yet special."

"Well, nothing is set in stone," the queen pointed out. "There is still plenty of time to discuss things with Sir Rackley and come to some sort of compromise." The four family members continued talking about other matters until they finished eating, and went their separate ways for the day.

A few hours later, Stefan and the royal guard from Langston rode into the royal castle and went straight to the main guard station. After they gave a brief explanation of why they were there, the guard on duty sent for one of the royal knights. Soon, Mathieu walked into the room where Stefan and Callum were waiting. Mathieu had been recently promoted to the rank of royal knight, in an order coming directly from the princess. She was frustrated with the fact that Chadwick was always gone on trips, and wanted a new royal knight to be her special security advisor. Appreciating Mathieu's long record of outstanding service, she chose him. Recognizing Stefan, Mathieu asked him, "Hey there, my friend. Isn't today one of your days off?" Stefan told him about the rebel attack, divulging every detail he could possibly think of. When he was finished, Mathieu said, "I would like to thank you for cutting short your vacation to ride back here to the castle with the royal guard. It took real courage to do what you did, leading those people outside and pleading in their behalf to Prince Agis. I think the princess would prefer it if you came with me and told her the whole story in person, instead of her hearing it second hand from me. Would you mind doing that?"

"Of course not," Stefan replied, "I would be happy to see her." Stefan and Callum followed Mathieu over to the throne room, where the princess was currently hearing another case involving the mistreatment of a peasant worker.

When she saw Mathieu and Stefan walk in, the princess interrupted the proceedings. "Pardon me, everyone, but I'm going to need to take a brief recess. Wait here and I will be back to hear the rest of the dispute in a few minutes." Princess Stasia walked down to the back of the throne room and gave Stefan a hug. She told him, "It's good to see you, Stefan. I thought you and Yvonne were away on a trip to Langston."

"We were," Stefan said, "and she still is. But something tragic happened, and the royal guard asked me to ride back here to tell you about it. Yvonne and I went into a market last night to buy some oranges. While we were paying for them, a group of rebels, led by a man named Prince Agis who was wearing a fearsome looking mask, surrounded the market and threatened to burn it down. Fearing for their lives, I managed to convince everyone in the store to walk outside. Prince Agis forced us to watch as the rebels emptied the market of every last fruit and vegetable, before throwing their torches inside, burning it to the ground." Stefan then backed up in the story and filled in each and every detail he could think of that happened. When he was finished, the princess looked over at Mathieu with concern on her face, and then back at Stefan.

"Is Yvonne safe?" the princess wanted to know.

"Yes, she was unharmed," Stefan answered. "Right now she's still with her family members at their home in Langston. But she was still feeling quite frightened over everything that transpired, at the time when I left."

"You did the right thing, Stefan, by coming here to tell Mathieu and I about this. The rebels seem to be getting more aggressive. In the past, it has been somewhat rare for Prince Agis to be directly involved in raids. Eyewitness reports have said he usually watches raids take place from a distance, allowing his rebel soldiers to do all of the dirty work. You're one of the few people who he has actually talked to."

"The boy showed remarkable courage by his actions," Mathieu said to the princess. "He put the welfare of others ahead of his own. He even had the wise sense to go directly to the royal guard station and report the attack, whereas everyone else went running off to their homes."

"Yes, you are right," she said. Looking at Stefan, she continued, "Stefan, we appreciate everything you have done. I appreciate it. You've had a long night riding without any sleep, so you may return to your family in Norwalk to get some rest." The princess thought for a moment, and added, "While you're here, I've been meaning to ask you something. You have spent many years scrubbing the castle floors, doing a wonderful service for all who live here. I have been wanting to offer you another job, something which would be more meaningful to you. What do you think about that?"

"Princess, I would be happy to take on any job you need me to do," he said.

"Well, then, I will let you choose between two jobs, both of which will allow you to maintain your current schedule of working here on the weekends. The first job is the weekend head of grounds keeping. You would be responsible for overseeing five workers, making sure the inside and outside of the castle are not only presentable, but appealing to the eye. The second job available is the assistant jail keeper. You wouldn't be able to work outside as much, but it is a much heavier responsibility to care for. Two royal guards work in the castle prison at all times. You would help arrange their schedules, process their reports, and bring all of the necessary food and provisions into the prison. You would also have to take the swords used by the guards over to the blacksmith building to have them sharpened on a regular basis." Pausing for a moment, she smiled as she added one more small point, "Oh, and the assistant jail keeper is also required to meet with me once per week to report on the condition of the prison, and share any relevant needs, concerns, or problems. So which one will it be, Stefan?"

Without hesitation, Stefan revealed his choice. He would become the assistant jail keeper. Stasia told him to meet with Mathieu the next time he came to work, and he would see to it that Stefan was given the proper training for his new assignment. She said goodbye to them both, and thanked Callum for coming to the castle to immediately report the rebel attack. A few minutes later, Stefan was on his way home, riding his horse back to Norwalk to get some much needed rest. He couldn't believe he was now the assistant jail keeper, with the great honor of being able to give a personal report to the princess each week.

One week later, Princess Stasia was standing near the top of a mountain pass, addressing a large gathering of village statesmen who traveled from all over Astoria to be there. When the princess heard the detailed report about the rebel attack in Langston, she consulted with Mathieu and planned a trip to see for herself the remains of the market. She also was going to meet with the market owner and his family to make arrangements to have his market immediately rebuilt at no cost. Finally, she would visit the royal guard station in Langston, to announce that an additional ten royal guards would be permanently posted there. But first, the princess was carrying out an idea Delia planted in her mind a week earlier. Delia told her about the decreasing numbers of Astorian eagles, and she wanted to try to save them if it was at all possible. Things worked out just right, because to reach Langston, she needed to pass right by the famous eagle monument, which stood high in the mountains, just before the city of Sorensen. So the order was given, and all people with any type of governing authority were required to be present. After they received the details of the new law from Princess Stasia, they would return to their villages and make sure every single citizen was informed. With the princess on this trip were

Delia, the royal knight Mathieu, several royal archers, and fifty royal guards as protection.

The princess had been speaking for twenty minutes now to the large crowd gathered around her. Behind her was the Astorian Eagle Monument, a large representation of the bird, carved out of a giant stone many years ago. "In view of all these facts I have shared with you today," the princess said, "I feel it is time for us to do something to protect this mighty creature. That is why I am enacting this new law, to protect the Astorian eagle and to educate our people about the importance of not allowing it to go extinct. I am counting on all of you who are here today to help me with this. The Astorian eagles are counting on you." Pointing to the monument behind her, she added, "This monument, which has stood for many years, was built by those who felt a deep love and appreciation for the bird and its great wisdom. Please, my dear friends, let us make a difference for the sake of our children, and our children's children. Let us save the Astorian eagle." As the princess concluded her speech, everyone applauded and vocalized their commitment to seeing that the law protecting the eagles was obeyed.

To finish the special ceremony, the bird expert Anton, who visited Delia's class a week earlier, stepped forward with his eagle perched on his arm. Anton's eagle was one of only two tame birds left in the land, as it was taken out of the wild several years ago. The purpose was to see if the eagle pair would start reproducing in captivity, thus leading to an increase in the amount of eagles in the land. So far, it had not worked. Anton spoke to the crowd, "Let me now give you all a demonstration of the great wisdom of this bird." Speaking to the bird and pointing towards a nearby grove of trees, Anton told him, "J-Bird, go seek out prey. Fly!" The crowd watched in fascination as the Astorian eagle started flapping its wings and flew off into the grove of trees. After a few minutes, some in the crowd started talking with one another, wondering where the eagle went. A few started asking Anton if the bird was ever coming back, or if he had flown away to his freedom. To this, Anton said, "Patience, my friends. J-Bird is on the hunt." When a few more minutes passed, more and more people started to express their doubts. But then, they spotted him. The Astorian eagle named J-Bird was flying back from the grove of trees, carrying something in his talons. As he flew in close to the crowd, he dropped a squirrel he captured to the ground, just before landing back on Anton's arm. The crowd applauded, totally impressed by what they had seen.

Delia walked over to the bird expert and said, "Thanks, Anton. I think that display made a real difference in helping these people to appreciate the intelligence and value of the eagle." A short time later, the statesmen were on their way back to their respective villages, and Stasia continued with her group towards the villages of Sorensen and Langston.

Stasia arrived in Langston, not inside a royal horse carriage, as most leaders were accustomed to doing, but riding her white horse Isobel. There was a vast crowd of local residents gathered outside, having heard that the princess would be coming to town today. As Stasia followed her royal guards into the village center, onlookers waved to her and expressed their support and appreciation for her. The large delegation came to a stop outside of the burned down market, and Stasia climbed down from her horse. She walked over and looked at the ruins of the formerly busy marketplace. There was nothing left of it. The rebels had completely destroyed it by their actions. She shook her head in disgust, saddened that something so cruel had happened. The market owner and his family were standing nearby, next to the foreman of a local work crew. Stasia went over to them and introduced herself. "Hello, and thank you for meeting me out here today. I know it must be hard for you to return to the place where such a horrible deed took place. Let me assure you, my royal knights and guards are doing everything in their power to track down and capture the perpetrators. They will be brought to justice. Until then, I want to help your family in any way I can. Therefore, I've made arrangements for your market to be rebuilt as soon as possible. When it is finished, the royal family will donate to you an entire month's supply of fruits and vegetables for you to sell and earn money from."

The market owner's wife spoke up, saying, "Thank you so much, princess. We never expected to be on the receiving end of such goodness. We were worried that our lives had been forever shattered, and thought we would soon end up living on the streets. How come you are such a caring person?"

The princess appreciated the compliment, and she answered, "I'm not perfect, but I want to do my best to help the good, hardworking people of our land. The years of royal training I received before becoming princess have guided me to act on the direction of my heart. And my heart goes out to anybody who has been savagely victimized by the rebels."

"Thank you, my good princess," the market owner said in response. "Your thoughtfulness will always be remembered by our family, and by everyone in Langston." Princess Stasia turned her attention to the foreman of the local work crew, who was standing with the market owner and his family.

"Greetings, and thank you for meeting me here as well. I would like you and your workers to begin reconstruction of the market immediately. Please use the best materials available, and rebuild the market just as it stood before it was burned down. The royal castle will provide all of the necessary funds, which you can pick up at the royal guard station tomorrow morning." The foreman assured her the market would be rebuilt and ready to open for business within a couple weeks. Satisfied, the princess and her delegation continued on to their final stop in Langston, the royal guard station. When they were finished with the necessary business there, they retired for the night at the large estate house of a wealthy landowner who lived in the village. The next morning, they left to return to Astoria Castle.

As the princess and her delegation approached the mountain summit where she announced the new law in protection of Astorian eagles a day earlier, she was riding next to Delia. They were discussing Stasia's idea to hold a large feast for the poor on the castle grounds. The princess wanted to make it an annual event, where poor people from all over the land could come to the castle grounds and be served a free meal. The princess continued telling Delia more about her idea. "And I could even participate in the special event by helping to serve food to some of the families. What do you think, Aunt Delia?"

"I think it's another one of your wonderful ideas." The conversation was cut short when there was a small commotion among the royal guards who were riding ahead of the princess. Several were pointing to the west, in the direction of some trees that continued up a hillside. The royal knight Mathieu, who was Stasia's special security advisor, soon dropped back from the pack to talk to her.

"What is it, Mathieu? What did you see over there?" the princess asked him.

"One of our guards thought he saw a rebel soldier sitting on a horse, just behind some trees. But nobody else saw it."

"What do you think we should do?" the princess further asked.

"I recommend we stop here and send some of our guards up to look around in the trees, just to be safe. Once we're given the all clear, then we will proceed over the mountain pass. It won't be long until we come out of the thick forested areas, which should be safer."

Just when Mathieu finished explaining his strategy, the royal guards started shouting and pointing in the direction of the trees once again. Mathieu and Stasia looked over and saw several rebel soldiers emerge from the canopy of trees on horseback. More kept coming, and before long, there were close to fifty rebel soldiers standing at the edge of the tree line, staring down at the princess and her delegation. Some of the rebel soldiers were holding bows and arrows, while others were holding swords. The royal guards, who were all there to protect the princess, took out their weapons and sat on their horses, ready for battle. One and all, they were willing to fight to the death, if necessary, to safeguard Stasia's life. Mathieu directed all of them, "Hold your places, men. The rebels are nearly equal in number to our forces. While they are not as well trained as we are, they currently are in a superior fighting position, being up on the hillside. We don't want to attack, because it could be a trap. They could have more rebels waiting behind the trees to pick us off one by one. So stay put, let them make the next move." About a minute later, when he was sure the royal guards weren't going to attack, the rebel general named Robbins dropped his sword to the ground, in plain view of everyone, and rode his horse down toward the princess.

One of the royal archers who was sitting on his horse near the princess, yelled back to Mathieu, "I have a perfect shot. Do you want me to take him down?"

The princess answered for him, "No, don't shoot. He's coming down unarmed. He must have something he wants to say to me." The royal archer let up slightly on his bow, waiting for the rebel to arrive.

When Robbins was within fifty yards of the delegation, he stopped and yelled out, "Princess, I come in peace. We mean you no harm today. Prince Agis has sent me here with a message, which I will deliver to you if you promise to allow me to safely leave."

"Then come forward and tell us why you are here," the princess answered. "I'm not interested in seeing any bloodshed today, so you have my promise."

Robbins closed about half the remaining distance, and explained, "Prince Agis demands that you revoke all of the reforms you have instituted for the lower class. If you do, he is willing to stop raiding villages and burning down buildings. If you do not, he wants you to know that his actions will only worsen, causing fear and chaos everywhere. The raid which was carried out recently in Langston was an example of this. What do you say in reply?"

Stasia directed her horse Isobel to walk a little bit closer to where Robbins was. She stopped just behind two royal guards at the outside of the line and gave her answer. "You can tell Prince Agis that the people of Astoria will not be intimidated. And you can let him know I will soon be hosting a special feast for the poor, which will provide an abundance of food for the lower class. It is but one of the many steps I will continue to take as I help the less fortunate to better their lives."

"Prince Agis will be very unhappy to hear that," Robbins said.

"One more thing, I have an offer of my own for your Prince Agis. If he comes forward and turns himself in, confessing to all of his crimes and disbanding his rebel army, then I will commute his sentence to life in prison. Now, leave us, before I change my mind about taking you into custody." Upon hearing this, General Robbins immediately turned his horse around and rode back up the hillside, into the trees. He stopped only long enough to pick up his dropped sword, and then he was gone. The rebel soldiers who were waiting, turned and followed him, until they were also out of sight. Meanwhile, the princess continued her trip home to the castle, which proved to be uneventful the rest of the way. In view of everything, Princess Stasia was more determined than ever to help the poor people of the land.

Chapter Ten:

Wise and Good to Her People

'Come to Princess Stasia's First Annual Feast For the Poor', announced a canvas flyer passed around the countryside. Lady Ruth was holding one of the flyers in her hand, debating whether or not it would be appropriate for her to attend. She certainly wasn't poor, as she owned a nice home and held lots of wealth. On the other hand, her foster daughter Yvonne was very poor, owning nothing except for a horse. As Lady Ruth returned home from an early morning stroll at the crack of dawn, she intended to talk to Yvonne about this. When she walked in the front door, she called out, "Yvonne, are you awake yet?"

A sleepy sixteen-year-old girl awoke from her slumber when her name was called out. She had put in a double shift working yesterday, in order to get the day off today. After working so hard, she went to bed exhausted, and was counting on sleeping in at least a little extra this morning. She realized she couldn't as Lady Ruth once again called out, asking if she was awake. "Yes, Lady Ruth, I am now," she said. Yvonne stretched her arms and yawned several times. Soon, Lady Ruth appeared at her bedroom door.

Lady Ruth was holding a copy of the canvas flyer which distributed by the thousands throughout the land of Astoria. This was done by the order of Princess Stasia, who wanted copies to be made and given out in every single village, especially in the poorer parts. "Is this where you were planning on going today, Yvonne? I found one of these while I was out for my early morning walk, and I would sure like to attend. But this canvas flyer says that the feast is for poor people."

"Yes, that's true," Yvonne explained. "But there are going to be many landowners and noblemen there as well. You see, it's the landowners and wealthy people who are providing most of the food today. If you want to go, rent a horse, and fill up your carriage with as many groceries as you'd like and bring them to the castle grounds."

"That's a great idea, Yvonne. I think I will do that. Would you like to ride over to the market with me and help me fill up the carriage with produce?"

"I'm sorry, Lady Ruth, but I can't. I was planning on riding my horse over to the castle as soon as I woke up. Now that you've woken me up, I'm going to get dressed and be out the door. It's an important day for the princess, and for me, so I want to be over there as soon as possible. But I will look for you among the thousands of people later."

"Okay, I understand," Lady Ruth replied. "I can get the servant boy to help me. I hope to see you later."

Yvonne stayed in bed for five more minutes and then started getting dressed. She began going through her clothes, looking for something nice to wear. How she looked wasn't one of her usual concerns, but this day was important to her. The only thing nice she could find was the blue dress she was given at the coronation of the princess, eleven months ago. She didn't want to be stuck wearing it all day, so she went ahead and found an outfit with very few holes, and put it on. Then, she practically ran downstairs and out of the house, saying goodbye to Lady Ruth as she sped through. It felt kind of funny to her, untying her horse and riding off to the castle alone. This was very rare, because she was always riding there with Stefan. But she couldn't wait around today. She needed to be at the castle right when people started arriving. Yvonne's grand hope for the day was that she would be able to find her birth parents, her long lost mother and father. She didn't tell Lady Ruth about what she was hoping for, because she didn't want her to feel sad, as if the love she gave Yvonne wasn't enough. Lady Ruth's love was enough, and it was deeply appreciated by Yvonne. But lately, Yvonne started thinking about her birth parents again, and how they dropped her off on Lady Ruth's doorstep when she was only six years old. She still couldn't forget her real mother's last words, promising to come back for her someday. That was ten years ago, and outside of personally knocking on every door in every poor area of Astoria, today was her best shot to find her parents. Because today, all of the poor people in the land were invited to the special feast the princess was hosting. Thus, Yvonne rode toward the castle with hope, something she hadn't allowed herself to feel for a long time.

An hour after Yvonne arrived there and began her search, Stefan was awake and eating breakfast with his parents. Today's special feast at the castle was to be a family outing, giving Martin and Shaylene a rare opportunity to spend the entire day with their son. In the past couple of months, a lot of things changed in their lives. For starters, they now owned the small cottage they lived in. It was given to them by royal decree of the princess when the landowner they worked for was caught lying to her right in her throne room. After that dramatic day, Martin and Shaylene barely saw the landowner for the next month, because he received a further punishment of having to work for free for an entire month to better the village of Norwalk. Now that they did see him every day, things were much different than they were before. The landowner never scolded them, yelled at them, threw things at them, or even pressured them. Essentially, he let Stefan and Shaylene work at their own pace, and allowed Martin to retire peacefully, never asking him to do anything. As the princess further instructed, the landowner now gave them a decent amount of food to eat, with some variety to it. The day before the royal guard was scheduled to come by and check on things last month, the landowner even invited Martin and his family into his estate house to enjoy a large meal with some wine. Stefan had been initially surprised when his parents told him that they went in for an audience with the princess, but he could see why he was kept out of the loop. His parents didn't want any handouts. They only wanted a just and fair decision from the princess, which was exactly what happened.

Stefan's own life also changed, as he was now the assistant jail keeper at the castle. Mathieu spent a few weekends training him, but soon realized Stefan only needed to have things explained to him once, observing he was quick to take the initiative in learning about his new job. It helped that Stefan knew how to read and write, which was something he learned from Yvonne about five years ago. At seventeen years of age, Stefan was now the youngest person working at the castle with such an important post. One of the things about his new job which surprised him was the opportunity to learn about some of the secrets of the castle, things unknown to others. For instance, there was a vast network of underground tunnels and secret routes, some of which were made so long ago that they had not been explored for many years. Mathieu showed him the main underground corridors, but Stefan noticed there were many passageways either sealed up or blocked off. Upon discovering these things, Stefan decided he would take on a new hobby. His goal was to map out the entire network of tunnels in his spare time. During one of his weekly meetings with the princess, which was always the fifteen minutes Stefan looked forward to the most each week, he told the princess of his idea. After she heard about it, Stefan was thrilled when she authorized him to begin mapping out the tunnels during his work hours, if he had extra time with nothing important to do. So, armed with a hand torch and papyrus paper, he started his mapping work a few weeks ago. It was going well. But so far, he was only scratching the surface. It would take at least several more months for him to figure everything out. What Stefan was most curious about was whether or not he would stumble across a secret route leading from the castle to the outside. He doubted it, but he had already been surprised to find several things he was not expecting.

As Stefan and his parents were finishing up breakfast, there was a knock at the door. It was the family friend they were waiting for, who despite being poor, owned a horse carriage. It was quite old and beat up, but it was much better than walking. Soon, the family was all loaded in, and they began their ride to the castle grounds. Shaylene decided to ask her son about the day's events. "Stefan, what are going to be the highlights of the special feast today?"

"Well, the highlight for me," he answered, "and probably everybody else, is going to take place at six o'clock this evening, when the princess will appear on the Castle Terrace to personally serve dinner to some poor families. Right before she does that, she will deliver a speech to everyone present, which should be fantastic, like all of her speeches are."

"And where is your friend Yvonne today?" his father asked.

"Yvonne went over to the castle grounds early this morning. She has this idea that she's somehow going to find her birth parents today."

"What makes her think that?" his father further inquired.

"She figures all of the poor people from the entire land, at least those who can make the trip, will be at the special feast. So, she sees it as her best chance ever to find them. I only hope she doesn't get her hopes up too much. I would hate to see her disappointed at the end of the day, if she spends her whole day looking for them, but can't find them."

"I agree," Shaylene said. "Yvonne is almost like a member of our family, and it would be sad to see her let down. Let's all hope for the best, for her sake."

While Stefan and his family were riding towards the castle, the Chief Royal Knight, Chadwick, was having a heated discussion with one of the royal knights. They were talking in the main guard station about security arrangements for the special feast, and particularly, for the royal family. "Why can't you learn to follow my orders, without questioning everything, Mathieu?" Chadwick was saying. "There is a reason I am the Chief Royal Knight. I know what's best, and my long record of protecting the royal family shows that. In my many years of loyal service, no harm has ever come to them."

"I understand that, sir," Mathieu replied. "But Princess Stasia has made me her special security advisor, and I don't think some of the decisions you've made today are very wise."

"That's because you haven't been with me during the past two weeks," Chadwick continued. "I've been out following up on reports of rebel activity. My sources have informed me that the rebels are in retreat mode, as they have been running extremely low on provisions, including food. I've even been told they may be preparing to cross our borders into another land, in search of a better place to live."

"If that's true, it is good news," Mathieu responded. "But even so, do you really think it's wise to give half of our royal guards the day off?

And why are you posting so many of the royal guards outside of the castle?"

"Look, I don't have time for this today," Chadwick said, as he started getting angrier. "But just to ease your mind, in the spirit of this special feast and because of the low threat level, I thought it would be nice to allow some of the guards to have a day off. And by posting a majority of the guards outside, they will be able to quickly identify and put a stop to any unexpected rebels, before they even enter the castle grounds. I've given all of them orders to carefully watch all of the peasants entering, to see if any of them look suspicious, as if they might be rebels in disguise. Now, can I get back to my duties?"

"All right, let's do this your way," Mathieu finally said. "But let me go on record as saying I disagree with some of the decisions you've made today."

"You can disagree all you want, but I'm the one who is in charge here." After he said that, Chadwick stormed out of the main guard station.

Mathieu looked over at a royal guard who was standing in the room, and said, "Boy, he sure is testy today, isn't he?"

Princess Stasia was sitting in her bedroom, looking out her window as more and more people were coming through the front entrance gate into the castle grounds. She had set aside a couple of hours this morning to prepare her speech, which was to be given later tonight from the Castle Terrace. But she found herself distracted, watching all of the lower class citizens arrive for her special feast. She also looked on with appreciation, as she saw lots of landowners and wealthy citizens hauling in food and setting up tables to be used both at lunch time and dinner time. The princess had been slightly worried that not too many poor people would actually come today. First of all, because it was a long trip to the castle for many of the citizens, as villages were spread out somewhat far apart in Astoria. And second, while she put forth every effort to get as many canvas flyers spread throughout the land, she knew that many of the lower class citizens couldn't read, so she wasn't sure if they would even know what she was inviting them to. But, judging by the amount of people who had already arrived, the message did get out, and people were willing to make the trip. It made the princess happy to see that, because never before had such a thing been done at the castle. According to the Royal History Pages, commoners were only brought to the castle in previous years when there were building projects in need of workers. People were then brought in by the hundreds, and even thousands, to do slave labor. What a reversal today was, with the wealthy class actually laboring on behalf of the lower class, in both providing food, and helpers to cook and distribute it. They were glad to do it, as the princess was enjoying unprecedented popularity in the land. Her reforms resulted in nothing but improvements for people everywhere. While there was initial doubt and opposition to her ideals, people were eventually won over when they saw how successful things turned out.

Princess Stasia's train of thought was interrupted when there was a knock at her open bedroom door. She looked over and saw it was the royal knight Mathieu. "Excuse me, princess," he said. "I'm really sorry to bother you, but I felt that I needed to talk to you about something."

"Come in and sit down, Mathieu," the princess told him. "I'm not doing anything important, for a change. I'm just trying to figure out what I'm going to say later."

"Thank you, princess." After taking a seat, he continued, "I have a disagreement with Chadwick over the way security is being handled today. He has given half of the royal guards the day off, and on top of that, he has posted a majority of the active royal guards outside of the castle, to spot rebels before they can even get through the gates. I feel we would be better served with more guards, not less. And I also think we need to be at maximum strength inside the castle walls, just in case something happens."

Princess Stasia thought for a moment about what he said, and replied, "Mathieu, I really appreciate your concern for me and your desire to make sure I'm completely safe. But Chadwick has been watching over me ever since I was a baby. I think it is best to trust his judgment. You are doing a great job though, and I want you always to bring your concerns to me."

"Yes, princess. Thank you for easing my mind a little bit. I will be ready to escort you when it is time to make your appearance at six o'clock."

"Very good, Mathieu. By the way, how is your daughter Madison doing?"

"She's wonderful. Thank you for asking. She's helping to serve food in one of the lines today, with the rest of her class. I think your Aunt Delia is with them, along with the regular school teacher."

"Well, make sure to give her my greetings when you see her. It's too bad I can't spend as much time with her, or my other close friends from growing up anymore. Such is the duty of being princess."

"Don't worry, I will tell her," Mathieu promised. He stood up and walked out, more confident about the security arrangements Chadwick put in place for the day.

As the morning went on, approaching the noon hour, Yvonne thought she spotted a woman who bore a resemblance to what she remembered her mother looking like. She saw the woman's face briefly from a distance. The woman appeared to have the same eyes and facial features of her birth mother. Trying to weave her way through the crowd was difficult, but she finally reached the spot where the woman was standing. The woman was no longer there, so Yvonne looked around, trying to figure out where she went. Finally, she spotted the woman again, not too far away now. The woman had her back turned to Yvonne, and was talking to somebody. Full of hope and with her heart racing, Yvonne ran towards her and called out, "Mother, is that you? Mother, it's me, Yvonne." The woman didn't answer or even turn around, but kept talking to the other person. Yvonne finally came up right behind her, and said, "Mother! Mother! It's me, Yvonne!" The woman turned around this time, and when Yvonne saw her face close up, she realized she made a mistake. As the woman stared at her with a puzzled look, Yvonne said, "I'm sorry, I thought you were somebody else." Yvonne turned around and walked away with her head slumped down. So far, her efforts today were a complete failure. She had started by spending several hours watching people come into the entrance gate. When that proved to be fruitless, she started to walk around looking carefully at every single person, figuring she might have missed her parents when they entered the castle grounds. Yvonne now noticed that food was starting to be served and lines were forming all over the place. But she wasn't hungry, because she was feeling totally dejected and depressed. The hope she came into the day with was now all but gone. She found a place to sit down on the great lawn where she could rest her back against the side wall of a stone building. She closed her eyes and tried to stop herself from crying. She wanted to be a strong girl, not one who was emotionally fragile.

Soon, a voice called out to her, and she opened her eyes. "Yvonne, what are you doing over here all by yourself?" It was one of Yvonne's neighbors, a young girl who was eleven years old named Annette.

"Oh, hello, Annette," Yvonne said to her. "I've been walking around all morning and I needed a break." Yvonne's eyes spotted movement inside of Annette's shirt. She couldn't figure out what was causing it until she saw a small kitten poke its head out of one of her large pockets. "Annette, you brought your kitten to the feast today?"

"Yes, my parents said it was okay. I couldn't leave her at home all day by herself. She would have been much too lonely without me. Do you want to hold her?"

"Sure," Yvonne answered. Annette took her kitten the rest of the way out of her large shirt pocket and handed her to Yvonne. As Yvonne was petting her, she commented, "She's so adorable, Annette." The kitten was enjoying the attention, softly purring as Yvonne scratched her behind the ears. When she was finished, Yvonne handed the kitten back, and added, "Make sure you let me watch her for you, if you ever go away on vacation or anything."

"Don't worry I will," Annette promised, before saying goodbye and walking away. After the short visit from her young neighbor, Yvonne was feeling a little bit better about life. Seeing how happy the girl was over having her own kitten made Yvonne realize that sometimes you need to find happiness in other places, if it doesn't come to you in the way you're expecting it.

King Charles and Queen Delphine were working hard at one of the tables, as they helped to serve a long line of poor people. Stasia wanted them to serve the poor during the noon hour, while she would take a turn serving the poor in the evening. It wasn't something the king and queen were used to doing, but they were enjoying themselves. It was a beautiful day outside, and they had never seen people display so much gratitude over a simple meal. As people walked up and received a plate of food, they would thank the king and queen profusely. At the same time, Charles also kept hearing everyone saying really nice things about his daughter, making him feel proud inside. King Charles had received the shock of his life about eleven months ago, on the night of Stasia's coronation. When she ripped up the Code of Honor scroll right in front of everybody, he may have been the most surprised person in the whole ballroom. But when she so passionately described her reasons for doing so to everyone gathered that night, she won him over to her side. He was going to support and stand by her ideals for the rest of his life. That's why he was out here today, to do his part in promoting the new Code of Honor, which Stasia recently finished writing and made public.

A few tables away from where the king and queen worked, there were a couple of landowners helping another long line of people. Near the middle of the line were Stefan and his parents. "I can't believe how many people are inside the castle today," Stefan said. "I've never seen anything like this."

"This is certainly a big turnout," his father agreed. "I hope they don't run out of food before we get up to the front."

Shaylene laughed at hearing this. "It's not likely," she said. "This has been so well organized, I couldn't imagine something like that happening."

Suddenly, a familiar voice broke into the discussion. "Hello, everyone!" It was Yvonne, who took cuts and jumped into line with them. Stefan and his parents greeted her and asked how her day was going. "It hasn't been going exactly as I would like it to, but it is good to be here, nonetheless. My search efforts have not panned out, but at least I was able to find you all. And just in time, because I started getting hungry a few minutes ago."

"Hey, Yvonne," Stefan said, "I have something I want to show you after lunch. Do you have like a half an hour or so?"

"I always have time for you, Stefan," she replied. "I am getting really tired of searching for my birth parents, anyway. Has anybody seen Lady Ruth anywhere? She said she was going to try to help out with the food today." Nobody had seen her yet. With so many people, numbering into the thousands, finding somebody would be purely chance. When they finally reached the front, one of the wealthy landowners who was serving food asked if he could take their order.

"Hello, good folks," he said. "My name is Petros. What would you like to eat this afternoon? We have just about every kind of meat, including ostrich, pig, duck, and my personal favorite, rabbit. We also have every type of fruit and vegetable you could possibly desire." Everybody gave Petros their order, and soon they were each walking away with heaping plates of food. They went to find a place where they could sit down on the great lawn to enjoy their meals and time together.

Meanwhile, outside the castle, four royal guards walked towards the drawbridge and started crossing it. This caused another royal guard, who had been standing outside all day watching all of the peasants who went in very carefully, to remark to the guard standing next to him, "There go another four royal guards. That makes like twenty in the past hour. They must all be coming back from a tour of duty out of town, in another village or something."

To this, his companion said, "Yes, you're right. It's funny that I haven't seen anyone I recognize, though. Then again, new recruits always get the least desirable postings around the land."

"That's for sure," the other guard said, laughing. "I remember back in the day when I first became a royal guard, I was sent off to a small border village for several years. It felt like I was in exile, or something." Someone else then caught the attention of the two guards. "Hey you, over there, stop for a minute," one of the guards shouted at an older peasant who started crossing the drawbridge. They went over and did a routine check of his bag and pockets, before allowing him to continue across.

When the four royal guards entered the castle grounds, they immediately walked together towards two guards stationed near the blacksmith building. When they arrived there, one of the four royal guards stepped forward to speak. "Greetings, fellow guards. We've been given orders to come over here and increase security for the rest of this day and tonight. You two have been given permission to take the rest of the day off, as a reward for your good service."

Surprised, one of the royal guards who was stationed at the blacksmith building said to his companion, "Well, what do you know? I guess our efforts do get noticed." The two walked off towards their rooms in the eastern half of the castle, ready to change out of their guard uniforms and into some civilian clothes.

A short time later, a similar event transpired inside the entrance gate. Four royal guards walked up to the three guards who were stationed there and excused them for the rest of the day, saying that they were assigned to take over. During the next two hours, this happened at nine other locations around the castle grounds, including outside of the main guard station.

After they finished lunch, Stefan took Yvonne with him over to where his new job was based, at the underground castle prison. When Yvonne first walked into the entrance area of the prison, her nose adjusted to the musty odor permeating the place. The two royal guards who were working inside greeted them both, after which, Stefan introduced them to Yvonne. Stefan told them that he wanted to show Yvonne where he now worked, which they said would be fine. He used his key to open the door leading into the first large inner hallway. Candles along each side of the wall provided some light, but it was not very bright. "It's kind of dark and scary in here, Stefan," Yvonne half joked.

"I'll take care of that," Stefan said, as he picked up a hand torch and lit it on fire. Soon, the whole large hallway was engulfed in firelight, allowing Yvonne to see everything. "Follow me, I want to show you something very few people know about," Stefan said. He led her down the hallway and turned left into one of the supply rooms. When they both were inside, Stefan handed Yvonne his torch, asking her to hold it while he did something. He moved some equipment and chairs away from the back wall. Then, he took down some wood planks to reveal a small opening which led into a secret passageway.

When Yvonne figured out what he had in mind, she said, "Oh, Stefan, I don't want to go in there. I'm going to get all dirty."

Overcoming her initial objection, Stefan pleaded, "Come on, Yvonne. It will be fun. Once you get through the opening you can stand up in there." To show how easy it was, he went through first, took the torch as Yvonne passed it through, and offered to help her through with his other hand. Soon, the two best friends were exploring some of the tunnels which spread out from the underground prison.

Back in the entrance area of the underground prison, four royal guards walked down the stairs and came inside. The two jailers who were working there gave them a friendly greeting. One of the four royal guards said to them, "We have been sent here with orders to take over for the rest of the afternoon and evening, to provide additional security. You two are excused for the rest of the day, to enjoy some much deserved rest and relaxation."

One of the jailers who had worked at the castle prison for a long time, named Bailey, looked at the other and said, "That's strange. Stefan didn't say anything to us about an adjustment in the scheduling. He usually keeps on top of those types of things."

The new royal guard interjected, "This order came directly from one of the royal knights at the top. It's partly a reward for your faithful service here."

To this, the other jailer replied, "Well, I'm not going to question somebody else's decisions. If they want me to take an evening off, I'll take an evening off." The two jailers gathered up their belongings and exited the castle prison. As they walked up the stairs, Bailey said to the other jailer, "I don't like this. I'm going to go over and check in with Mathieu to make sure this is okay."

"Suit yourself, but I'm getting out of the castle for the rest of the day. I will see you tomorrow," the other jailer replied.

The two jailers parted ways at the top of the stairs. While one went to enjoy himself, the other started to search through the vast crowds of people for Mathieu. He was unsuccessful for quite some time and almost decided to give up altogether. But then he decided to check outside of the castle, and that's where he found him. Mathieu was patrolling the perimeter of the castle, keeping watch on everything and everyone entering and leaving. Since Chadwick wanted the protection efforts to focus on the exterior, Mathieu stayed out there for most of the day. Coming up to him, the jailer greeted him and asked,

"Mathieu, I wanted to make sure it was okay to take the rest of the day off from working in the prison."

"The rest of the day off?" Mathieu repeated back to him. "Who is working in your place?"

"The four royal guards sent over by the main guard station."

"Who authorized this?" Mathieu asked.

"I thought you did, sir. I was told that I could spend the rest of the day relaxing, because of my good work."

"You are a good worker, but I didn't authorize anything. Let's go over to the prison right now, and get to the bottom of this thing. Somebody is going to be in big trouble if they didn't clear this with me or Chadwick."

In a short time, Mathieu and Bailey walked back onto the castle grounds and downstairs into the castle prison. The four royal guards who were now working in there looked surprised to see them. Mathieu looked at them and demanded, "Guards, who authorized your transfer over here to work for the day? We have a very strict policy about who is allowed to work in the castle prison." The four guards looked at each other and didn't answer right away. "Speak up, guards! I need to know who authorized this transfer." Finally, one of the four royal guards provided an explanation.

"The royal knight did," he said.

"Which royal knight?" Mathieu wanted to know.

"The one who is working down the hallway," the royal guard answered, as he pointed in the direction of the prison interior. "He said that he needed to check on something important in there."

"Something's not right here," Mathieu said to Bailey. "Let's go talk to him and find out what is going on." As Mathieu and the jailer turned to walk toward the prison interior, they took a few steps and suddenly fell to the ground, unconscious. They had been attacked from behind by the four royal guards, who were impostors.

Chapter Eleven:

On the Castle Terrace

For a while now, Stefan had been showing Yvonne some of the passageways he previously discovered. Stefan led her to several dead ends and also down one passage which started getting muddy, causing Yvonne to want to stop. After she saw enough, the two started walking back toward the storage room where the small entrance was, being guided by firelight from Stefan's torch. "So, do any of these secret tunnels lead anywhere?" Yvonne asked him.

"So far, I haven't been able to connect with any other parts of the castle," he told her. "But I've had limited time with which to do my exploring. I know some of them must meet up, because there are similar tunnels that can be accessed from both the western and eastern sides of the main castle complex."

Yvonne became concerned about something, so she said to him, "Stefan, please be careful when you're down here. I wouldn't want you to get lost or hurt down here, where nobody would ever find you. Are you sure these tunnels are structurally safe?"

"Absolutely, Yvonne. These tunnels have stood for over a hundred years, from what I've been told. In the past, they were used a lot. But they are no longer considered useful. That's why the memory of them has been forgotten by most people. Don't worry, I am always careful down here and I've started making maps, to learn my way around."

When Stefan and Yvonne came to the small opening they first climbed through, Stefan set his torch down on the ground. He helped

Yvonne climb through into the other room, which was dark, because very little firelight was shining through. Yvonne right away heard a lot of voices coming from the hallway, so she turned around to look out into it. Because there was a small amount of light from the candles burning along the wall, she could partially see what was going on. Three royal guards passed by, and they were pulling two other people by the arms. Yvonne thought she recognized who they were. When Stefan climbed out with his torch, Yvonne looked at him and said firmly, "Put out that torch, Stefan. Something weird just happened." He wasn't used to her using that tone, so he didn't question her, but reached back through the opening and dropped the torch on the other side. He covered it with dirt and left it there. When he pulled his upper body back through the opening, Yvonne explained, "I think I just saw Mathieu and one of the jailers who was here when we first came in. They were being dragged down the hallway towards the prison cell areas by three other people. It could have been somebody else, because there isn't much light out there, but I am pretty sure of what I saw."

Stefan's mind started spinning when he heard this. The only thing he could think of to do was to get out of the prison as soon as possible, before those three men came back. Stefan led Yvonne out into the hallway, which was now quiet and empty, and back toward the prison entrance. When they reached the entrance, they were stopped by a royal guard.

"Hey, where did you two kids come from?" he asked them. Stefan explained to him that he worked at the prison, and was inside a supply room taking inventory with Yvonne for the past hour.

The royal guard pointed toward the prison interior and asked, "Did you see anything in there?"

"Did we see what? What is there to see?" Stefan answered.

The royal guard dropped his suspicion when he heard this and told Stefan, "Don't lie to me, young man. You two were probably making out in there, weren't you? Well, I'm going to have to ask you to leave now, because I have business to attend to. If you have any more work to do, you can come back and finish it tomorrow." When they heard this, Stefan and Yvonne turned and walked out of the prison, and up to the castle grounds, where they breathed a huge sigh of relief.

After their eyes adjusted for a few seconds to the bright sunshine, they quickly walked away from the stairway and mixed in with the crowd. Stefan didn't know what to make of what just happened. More than that, he had no idea what to make of what Yvonne apparently saw. Stefan had never seen the royal guard before who was now working in the prison entrance area, and Stefan was the one who was in charge of making the schedules. The two jailers who were assigned to work were both there when Stefan and Yvonne first walked in, but when they left, there was no sign of them. If it was really one of the jailers and Mathieu seen by Yvonne being dragged away into the back of the prison, then something unlawful must have been happening. Stefan came up with a theory which seemed to make a lot of sense to him. As soon as they were safely mixed in with lots of other people, he stopped her so they could talk. "Yvonne, I think we're safe now."

"Stefan, what happened in there? What were those three people doing to Mathieu and the jailer?"

"I think there is another jail break going on right now. When Mathieu was training me for my new job, he told me about a breakout that happened about five years ago. Back then, the rebels used a young boy to help two of their captured soldiers to escape. That was the one and only time anybody has ever escaped from the castle prison."

"If you're right, though, why was there a royal guard on duty?"

"I think he's switched sides and is with the rebels. Somehow they must have convinced him to join their cause, or bribed him with a lot of money, or something. And those other three people you saw are probably rebel soldiers."

Yvonne asked, "What are we going to do?"

"Right now, we have to get into the castle and talk to the princess. If we're not able to, then the best thing we can do is to report this situation to Chadwick, if we can find him." Satisfied with the plan, Stefan and Yvonne headed over to the western entrance of the castle, hoping to get inside.

When Mathieu regained consciousness, he was lying face down in the dirt. "What? Where am I?" he said aloud as he used his arms to push himself up. When he was on his knees, he looked over and saw Bailey laying on the ground. And then it all came back to him. Bailey had come to get him, telling him about something unusual going on in the prison. When Mathieu followed him back here, they encountered four royal guards who turned out to be impostors, as they misled Mathieu and Bailey and then attacked them from behind. Still groggy, Mathieu crawled over to where Bailey was resting and checked his pulse. He was still alive, just out cold. Mathieu looked around to see where he was. Although it was dark, he realized that he was locked in a prison cell. There would be no getting out of here. And there would be no calling for help. All he could do is wait and hope that somehow, somebody came for him.

Although it was getting late in the afternoon, and the king and queen finished serving the lunch meals a long time ago, they continued to stay out on the castle grounds. When lunch ended, they started visiting with many of the landowners, noblemen, and even peasants who were around them. So far, the day was a complete success. It served a good purpose in feeding the poor people of the land. But it also united people of all different classes, something that had really never happened before. There were poor people mixing with rich, peasants mixing with noblemen, and even commoners mixing with the king and queen. As they finished their current conversation, a familiar face came up and greeted the king and queen. "Hello, Charles and Delphine. I'm surprised to see you still outside."

"Oh, hello Delia," the queen answered. "We have been having such a great time visiting with everybody that it's like time slipped away. We've seen many old friends and made many new ones. How have you enjoyed the day?"

"I enjoyed it as much as you did," Delia answered. "I was able to serve food alongside the students I sometimes get to teach. It was such a good idea to have our young ones from the castle involved in this cause. They have all learned a lot, and they enjoyed it so much that all of us are going to come back and serve again at dinner time, after Stasia's speech."

"Speaking of her speech," the king said, "she is going to be delivering it about one hour from now. Maybe I should go back inside the castle to see if she needs any help putting the finishing touches on it."

"No, you should probably just let her be," the queen suggested. "This speech means a lot to her, so I'm sure she already knows what she's going to say, word for word."

"Are you two going to watch her speech from down here?" Delia asked.

"Yes, for a change, we are," the king answered. "Since we are having such a good time visiting with everybody, we thought we would stay down here through the end of the speech. It will be interesting to watch Stasia from out here, being among the people. I think it will give us a new perspective on how she affects everybody."

"That sounds like a good idea," Delia said. "Enjoy the rest of your afternoon and evening, and I will see you back in the castle later tonight." Delia turned around and started walking back over to where she was working with the children, to start setting things up for the dinner meal.

When Stefan and Yvonne arrived at the main castle entrance, they tried to walk through so they could get inside. But four royal guards who were stationed out front stopped them. "Hey, wait! Where do you two think you are going?" one of the royal guards asked.

"We are going inside," Stefan answered.

"No, you're not. You don't have permission to go inside there," the guard said.

"What do you mean?" Stefan asked. "We are always allowed to go inside the castle. We work here."

"Not tonight, you can't. There have been new security arrangements set up for the special feast. All castle workers have been given the rest of the day off. Why don't you come back tomorrow if there's something you need to do."

"You don't understand, I really need to talk to the princess. I think there are some rebels here tonight who might be attempting a jail break right now, as we speak," Stefan said with an urgent tone.

"Rebels? At the castle? Nonsense, young man. Why don't you two run along now and go wait for dinner to be served."

Yvonne tried another approach. "If we can't talk to the princess, then do you know where Chadwick is? He could help us." The royal guard was starting to get frustrated with Yvonne and Stefan. So they would stop bothering him, he offered a compromise.

"I tell you what I will do," he told Yvonne. "I will take you inside to voice your concerns to Chadwick. But your friend here is going to have to wait outside for you until you come back. How does that sound?" Yvonne looked at Stefan to see if he was okay with the idea. When he nodded his approval, Yvonne followed the royal guard inside the castle, while Stefan went to sit down and wait.

When she was finished preparing her speech and spent enough time looking out at the vast crowd of poor people, Stasia laid down on her bed to rest. She was extremely tired, as she put a lot of time and effort this past week into organizing her special feast. At the same time, she kept up her normal schedule at the castle, which meant she was really expending herself. As she was resting, Stasia thought about Sir Rackley. He wasn't in attendance at her special feast because he was busy at his country estate continuing to work on their wedding arrangements. Princess Stasia and Sir Rackley were now due to be married in less than a month, right after she turned seventeen. They had initially disagreed about what type of wedding to have. Sir Rackley wanted a large, outdoor wedding. But she wanted to have something more down to earth, with only his family, her family, and those they cared about the most being in attendance. Eventually, they came to a compromise. They would have the small wedding she wanted, on the stage of the Grand Ballroom. But for the reception, many more would be in attendance, and that would be held outside, directly following the wedding ceremony. Stasia was happy with it, although she wasn't totally happy about getting married. Sir Rackley was a nice enough boy, and he gave evidence of his love for her through both his speech and actions, but the princess was not completely in love with him. Even so, she would go through with the wedding, because she didn't want to ruin everything her father worked for, and she felt that she owed it to her parents and to the people of both lands. As she was thinking about these things, the princess drifted off to sleep.

When she finally woke up from her nap, she realized there was now less than an hour to get ready. She got out of bed and walked downstairs, calling for her maidens. When three of them came to her, the princess told them that she needed to have her face and hair prepared, so they followed her into her private changing room. They began working on her, as always, to make her look as beautiful as they possibly could. Of course, with Stasia this wasn't very difficult, as she had a natural, radiant beauty to her face. While she was sitting there, Stasia reflected on Mathieu's visit earlier in the day. He was concerned with Chadwick's security plan for the feast, thinking it wasn't good enough. But she told him not to worry about it, because Chadwick always knew best. It seemed like lately those two were always disagreeing about something. For some reason, they just did not get along. Stasia figured part of it stemmed from how she went around Chadwick and promoted Mathieu to a royal knight, by herself. Usually that was a decision Chadwick made, but the princess wanted Mathieu to be her special advisor, because he had built up such a fine record of good service. Stasia hoped they would get along someday, and start working together, instead of against each other.

Yvonne followed the royal guard into the castle, relieved to have an opportunity to tell Chadwick about what was going on in the prison. She hoped that she was not too late, because she wanted to see the rebels and traitorous royal guard captured and taken into custody. That is, if Stefan was right about what was going on in there. He was only guessing, but his guess sounded like the most likely scenario to her. Yvonne continued following the royal guard as he stopped and talked to three fellow guards along the way. The last guard he spoke to turned and walked off into the castle. The guard she was with then said to her, "Okay, he is going to get Chadwick right now. Hang on a minute and you can talk to him."

"Thank you, sir," Yvonne said to him. Finally, she had caught a break. Soon, Chadwick would be here and he would know what to do. It was too bad Stefan was told to wait outside, because he probably could have done a better job explaining everything. But she would do her best. A few minutes later, she received her chance, as Chadwick came walking into the room.

"Hello, my young friend," Chadwick said to her. "I have been told that you have some suspicious activity you would like to report to me. Tell me, what is going on?"

"Thank you for seeing me, Chief Knight Chadwick. My name is Yvonne, and I work here at the castle. A little while ago, I was with another worker over in the castle prison. He was showing me something in one of the supply rooms when I thought I saw Mathieu and one of the jailers being pulled along the hallway by three people, just outside where I was standing. They looked like they were unconscious. When we went back to the prison entrance area, there was a new royal guard working there in place of the jailer, and he asked us to leave. I think the three people I saw might be rebels and the royal guard who was working may have been helping them. They might even be planning a jail break tonight." Chadwick was listening intently to every word she said, with obvious concern on his face. Yvonne could see that he appreciated the seriousness of the situation.

"Yvonne, I would like to thank you for bringing this situation to my attention," Chadwick said in reply. "We certainly don't want to allow another jail break to happen. Don't you worry, I am going to look into this immediately. I will go over to the prison myself and find out what is going on. Now, why don't you go enjoy the rest of your night with your family or friends. Everything will be fine."

"Okay, I am so glad I was able to talk to you, to tell you about this," Yvonne said with relief. "But don't go over to the prison alone. Make sure you bring some royal guards with you."

"Thanks for the tip, I will," Chadwick said, before turning and leaving the room. The royal guard who originally brought her inside, led her back out to where Stefan was waiting. Yvonne was smiling as she walked up to him.

"I did it, Stefan. I told Chadwick everything!" she exclaimed.

"Great job, Yvonne. What is he going to do about it?"

"He is going to gather up some royal guards and go over there right now," she said. "Chadwick told me not to worry, he would take care of it." Both Stefan and Yvonne were glad that the Chief Royal Knight was now aware of the situation. There was nothing more for them to do, so they went off looking for either Lady Ruth or Stefan's parents.

Near the entrance to the castle grounds, four impostor royal guards relieved the two royal guards who were assigned to control the opening and closing of the drawbridge. Like in the other cases, one of the four guards told them that they were free to take the rest of the day off. Initially, the two royal guards were surprised. But after discussing it with each other, they gladly took advantage of the opportunity to leave work early and spend time with their families. As the new operators of the drawbridge were standing there, they heard the signal they were waiting for. The castle bell tower rang one time, telling them it was five forty-five in the evening. All who lived and worked at the castle kept track of time by listening for the regular bells. Every fifteen minutes, the bell would ring one time: at fifteen, thirty, and forty-five past the hour. When the hour changed, the bell would ring an equal number of times to represent which hour of the day it was. For instance, at five o'clock, the bell would ring five times, and so on. The bell tower was really helpful for all who spent their lives within the castle walls. However, on this night, the bell tower proved to be helpful for the impostors.

When they heard the bell ring, two of the impostor guards went out onto the drawbridge and cleared it of the few people who were walking across it. At this point, nearly everybody was already seated somewhere on the great lawn, inside the castle grounds, as they waited for the princess to begin her speech in fifteen minutes. Once it was clear, the other two impostor guards began raising the drawbridge, to close access to the castle. As it slowly moved up, some of the genuine royal guards working outside began shouting across the moat, asking what was going on. One of the impostors shouted back to them, saying they were under orders to close the drawbridge for the next two hours. He then backed away, being unwilling to answer any more of their questions. Within a few minutes the drawbridge was closed, becoming one with the castle walls. Now there was no way anybody could either enter or leave the castle grounds, except for through the small servants' bridge on the other side. However, that had also changed.

Two impostor guards had taken over the castle entrance used primarily by workers at the servants' bridge. When they heard the bell ring, they started to do the same thing being done at the main entrance. They immediately raised the bridge, which was a much easier process, thus cutting off the only other route into or out of the castle. But when they were finished, they did something a little different, that was not done at the main drawbridge. The two impostor guards used their war hammers to destroy the turning mechanism, which was used to lower or raise the servants' bridge. Without the turning mechanism, it would be impossible to ever drop the bridge down again, unless somebody first spent several hours fixing it. Once they were done, and completely certain the servants' bridge was rendered useless, the two impostor guards walked off to take care of another assignment they needed to complete.

Yvonne and Stefan found the familiar faces they were looking for, five minutes before the princess was to begin her speech. They spotted Lady Ruth first, but soon realized she was sitting with Stefan's parents, talking to them. Yvonne and Stefan went over to join them, taking a seat on the grass not too far away from the lower wall of the Castle Terrace. Lady Ruth greeted them as they sat down. "Hello there, Yvonne and Stefan. I'm glad you found us. I ran into Martin and Shaylene a while ago, and we've been catching up ever since."

Shaylene asked Yvonne, "What did Stefan take you to see, Yvonne? You two sure were gone for a long time."

"He took me over to the castle prison, to see where he is working now. We did some exploring in there," she answered.

"Sounds exciting," Shaylene said. "And where at the castle are you working now, Yvonne? Are you still caring for the flowers and gardens?" Yvonne started to answer her but was cut off when somebody started speaking to the crowd from the Castle Terrace. The person informed everybody that the princess was preparing to come out and give her speech.

Among the impostors, General Robbins and his assistant Sebastian had taken over one of the most important and strategic locations on the castle grounds. Hiding undercover in royal guard uniforms, they were standing at the bottom of the stairway which led up to the Castle Terrace. It had been very challenging for them to take over this position and convince the other guards, who were two royal knights, to leave. When Robbins and Sebastian first approached them, using the same ruse being used everywhere throughout the castle grounds, the royal knights were difficult. They told Robbins and Sebastian that they were not going anywhere without a receiving a verbal or written change of orders. A short time later, when Robbins and Sebastian brought back a new set of written orders, the two royal knights finally relented and left their post. With the addition of this spot, rebel soldiers dressed in disguise as royal guards now controlled virtually all of the castle grounds. Most of the real royal guards were either stuck outside the castle or were now off duty relaxing in their rooms. Knowing this, Robbins smiled as he realized the overthrow of the castle was finally at hand.

Just inside of the doorway leading out to the Castle Terrace, Princess Stasia was now a couple minutes late for her speech. She was waiting for Mathieu, wondering where he was. Earlier in the day, he promised to escort Stasia out and watch over things during her speech. But now, he was nowhere to be found. Chadwick finally said to her, "We can't wait for him forever, princess. I am sure there is a good reason why he wasn't able to make it. Perhaps he encountered a rebel trying to sneak onto the castle grounds and took him into custody." Although she was slightly worried, Stasia realized Chadwick was right. She was glad he was there, because if both Mathieu and Chadwick had been gone, she definitely would have postponed her speech until one of them arrived.

"All right, let's go out," Stasia said to him. She walked through the doorway, right behind Chadwick as they moved out onto the Castle Terrace. When the crowds of people saw her come out, they erupted in cheers. Cheering louder than anybody else were Stefan and his group of family and friends, who all stood up as the princess walked out. Also cheering loudly were the king and queen, and Delia, who all were watching the princess from a greater distance away. Sebastian even got caught up in the spirit and started cheering his pretend support.

When Robbins saw Sebastian doing this, he smacked him across the stomach, saying, "Quit fooling around, Sebastian. Royal guards don't cheer. They stand still and look around for people like us."

As the cheering and applause slowly came to a finish, the princess was looking out at everyone, smiling. It was now a few minutes past six o'clock, and there was still plenty of sunlight left in the September day. Stasia looked elegant, wearing a light yellow dress made for the occasion that was quite exotic looking. Soon she began speaking to the crowd. "Good evening, my dearest friends. It makes me so happy to see that all of you made it here to Astoria Castle. Thank you for the sacrifices you have all made in being here today. I would like to thank the landowners, noblemen and noblewomen, and the wealthy citizens, who contributed food and supplies in such great quantities. Without you, this special feast could have never taken place. And I would like to thank all of the volunteers, castle workers, and my parents, King Charles and Queen Delphine, who shared in serving food earlier today. Most importantly, I would like to thank all of the poor citizens of Astoria for coming out, some of whom have made the trip despite living a great distance away. For those of you who received one of my invitations, you probably noticed that today's event was called 'Princess Stasia's First Annual Feast For the Poor'. What that means is today's special feast is not a one time event. It is a special event to be held each year in September, here on the castle grounds, for as long as I am your princess." Upon hearing this, the crowd once again erupted in cheers.

As the speech continued, King Charles and Queen Delphine were taking it all in, as members of the crowd. The queen told her husband, "See, she didn't need any help with her speech. She is doing fine."

"Yes, I can see that," the king responded. "The people out here really adore her and are listening carefully to her every word."

"Well, perhaps it is time for us to head up to the Castle Terrace," the queen added. "Stasia's speech will be finished soon, and she probably would like us to be up there."

"That's a good idea," the king said, "because after her speech she is going to be serving some of the poor people herself. I would like to be there by her side, when she is doing that." The king and queen both agreed it was time for them to leave the crowds of people and make their way up the side stairway to the top of the Castle Terrace. So, they started walking off towards the bottom of the stairs.

Stefan and Yvonne were standing up at their location in the crowd close to the bottom of the Castle Terrace, watching the speech take place. While Stefan was looking up at the princess, hinging on her every word, Yvonne was thinking about Stefan. She slowly took his hand into hers, trying to do it as naturally as possible. While the last time she tried this was not with romantic intentions, this time it was. Stefan accepted her hand, but did so without even thinking about it. Up on stage was the girl of his dreams, the girl he felt that he was in love with. Yvonne noticed he was watching the princess with great intensity, but she didn't mind. At least he gave her his hand, which must have meant something. There was no way she could compete with the princess for his affection, but at least she could offer him something real, not imaginary. Martin, Shaylene, and Lady Ruth were standing behind Stefan and Yvonne, and Shaylene noticed the two were holding hands. She leaned close to Lady Ruth's ear and whispered, "Have a look at those two. It appears there might be some romance starting to blossom."

Lady Ruth saw them holding hands, and responded, "Well, it's about time. Yvonne has been crazy about him for some time now. There is nothing better than falling in love with your best friend, or so I've heard."

When the king and queen reached the bottom of the stairway leading up to the Castle Terrace, the two royal guards did not move out of the way as they usually did, to allow them to go up. One of the royal guards, Robbins, said to them, "I am sorry, your majesties, but we have been told not to allow anybody to go up these stairs, even you."

"You can't be serious," the king said to him. "I can go anywhere I want in the castle, at any time."

"Not this time, you can't," Robbins responded. "If you would, please, go back and enjoy the rest of the speech. This stairway will be reopened later." This was totally unacceptable to King Charles. Nobody had ever before tried to stop him from going somewhere on the castle grounds. And this royal guard didn't even have some kind of reasonable explanation in denying entry. King Charles would have understood it if perhaps the stairway was hazardous to walk on, or if there was some kind of other danger. But he wasn't going to stand for this.

Speaking with a forceful voice, the king demanded, "Move out of the way, guard, right now." The two royal guards still wouldn't budge. The king tried to physically move them aside, but Robbins pushed him back. As the king was getting angrier, his wife was trying to calm him down.

"Charles, why don't we just wait?" she said to him. "We don't want to cause a scene, right in the middle of our daughter's speech." But King Charles didn't even hear what she was saying. He was so upset that he was now shouting at the two royal guards. Some in the crowd who were standing nearby heard the commotion, and looked over to see what was going on.

As the princess was winding down her speech, she started to notice the dispute going on between her father and the two royal guards who were posted at the bottom of the staircase. She tried her best to continue talking, but it was really distracting to her, and made her lose some of her thoughts. Finally, she stopped speaking and looked down to find out exactly what was going on. From her vantage point, it seemed like her parents wanted to pass by and come up to the Castle Terrace, but the guards didn't want to let them. With an authoritative voice, she called to the two royal guards, saying, "Guards! What is going on down there?" They didn't respond, or even look up at her, so she demanded once again, "Guards, let the king and queen pass through, right now!"

When the two impostor royal guards realized they were now the focus of the princess, and even the vast crowd of people, they sprung into action. Robbins and Sebastian both pulled out their swords and grabbed hold of the king and queen, taking them hostage. Those in the crowd who could see what happened all reacted with utter shock. Within a matter of seconds, more royal guards appeared. But they didn't help the king and queen. They began building a wall of protection between Robbins and Sebastian, and the crowd, holding their swords out in a threatening manner. The princess could not believe her eyes. It seemed to her that two royal guards had turned bad, and that a growing number of other royal guards were all in league with them. The king and queen were really being held at sword point, with their lives in danger. Stasia became extremely frightened, not knowing what was going on. She turned around and called out to Chadwick for help. "Chadwick, you have to help them. Please, do something, before it is too late." For a moment, Chadwick didn't say anything back to her in response. Slowly, a wicked grin came over his face, as he prepared to reveal his intentions. He pulled something out which was hidden away under his shirt. It was a creepy looking mask that looked like something out of a nightmare. He put the mask over his face with one hand while his other hand took out his sword. Then, he finally spoke to the princess.

"Allow me to introduce myself to you, princess. My name is Prince Agis, leader of the rebels."

Chapter Twelve:

Extraordinary Wisdom

As Princess Stasia registered Chadwick's words, she almost fainted. Her entire world was now collapsing, and she was all alone. There was nobody, anywhere, who could help her. How could all of this have happened so fast? A couple of minutes ago, she was giving her speech to all of her beloved poor citizens. And now she was just betrayed by someone who she spent her entire life trusting. Her parents had been betrayed too, especially in view of the fact that Chadwick was the younger brother of King Charles. Stasia realized she needed to compose herself, and quickly. What was now happening was in plain view of thousands of people. She needed to make it clear that she was a strong leader and would not cower in fear before Chadwick. So the princess spoke up to him, while he was laughing and waving his sword around in the air. "Chadwick, you cannot go through with this. Please, think about what you are doing. All of us: you, me, my parents, Delia, we are all family here. You don't want to betray everyone who loves you. Put down your sword and release my parents, and we can all talk this out."

"What do make me out for, a fool?" Chadwick said in reply. "This is not something I suddenly decided to do. I have been planning and waiting for this moment for many years, for decades. There is no turning back now. I will ascend to my rightful place as ruler of this land."

Looking down at her parents as Chadwick was rejecting her offer, Stasia wanted to know something. "And how did you get my royal guards to turn against me?" Stasia asked.

"Are you almost seventeen, and yet still so naive, princess?" he answered. "Those men who have taken the king and queen into custody are not royal guards at all, but they are my rebel soldiers. Almost a year ago, I removed a large supply of royal guard uniforms from the castle, without being detected. My men are now wearing those uniforms. Even as we speak, most of your royal guards are locked outside of the castle walls, with no way to get back in. And what few guards are still on duty inside of the castle will soon be removed and taken into custody."

Stefan and Yvonne were listening closely to every word being said up on the Castle Terrace. They were just as much in shock as everybody else was. After all, Yvonne had personally met with Chadwick only a short time ago, asking him to look into the strange things going on in the castle prison. But both Stefan and Yvonne realized this was no longer about a simple jail break, this was about an overthrow of the castle. Chadwick, or Prince Agis as he now wanted to be addressed, intended to be the new ruler of the land. What Prince Agis had told Stefan and Yvonne a few months ago outside of the market was now proving to come true. Yvonne turned to Stefan and said, "Stefan, we need to do something. We need to help the princess." Stefan agreed with her, but as he looked around, he couldn't see anything that they could do. There was a large blockade of impostor royal guards, who had now been revealed to be rebel soldiers, blocking entrance to the Castle Terrace and the king and queen. Yvonne suggested something. "Perhaps we could somehow get the princess into the underground tunnels you showed me earlier and find a way to get her out of the castle." Stefan liked the idea at first, but then realized it could never work.

Stefan replied, "It's a great idea, but there are too many drawbacks. For one thing, we don't know our way around down there, or even if any of the passageways lead outside of the castle grounds. It would slow us down way too much. However, what you said first is something we have to do. We have to get to the princess." He thought for a few more minutes and came up with a plan. "Okay, Yvonne. I have an idea, but I need your help. We already know that there is no way to get into the castle through any of the main entrances. We have to assume that any guards we see posted are actually rebels in disguise. But if you run around into the eastern side of the castle, and pick up some supplies to make it look as if you're working, you might be able to get by the guard who is posted in The Gateway, which is the hallway connecting the two sides of the castle. Once you do that, you have to get to the entrance door leading out to the Castle Terrace, and signal the princess to run inside. Meanwhile, I will run around to the other side of the castle, and be waiting for you and the princess at the stables. Hopefully, we can get our horses and use the servants' bridge to ride out of the castle, and get the princess away safe." It took a moment for Stefan's entire plan to sink in, but Yvonne thought she understood it.

"Stefan, there are a lot of things that can go wrong," she said in reply. "But if somehow I can get through that hallway and get to the princess, I will take her outside to meet you at the stables."

"Be strong, Yvonne," Stefan told her. "You can do this. You're much more likely to get through that hallway than I am, since you are a girl. I will see you at the stables, very soon."

"Okay, Stefan," she said. "I'm leaving now, but if anything goes wrong, please know that I love you." With that, Yvonne turned and pushed her way past people as fast as she could. As she did, she noticed there was a wide range of emotions people were showing, including fear, anger, pain, and panic. Once she was out of the area where everybody was all bunched together, she ran as fast as she could for the workers' entrance in the eastern part of the castle.

On the Castle Terrace, Prince Agis was continuing to boast about his accomplishments, things he carried out behind the backs of the royal family. He bragged about how he was the one who arranged every aspect of the jail escape of the two rebels which took place five years ago. He had maneuvered things so that the rebels were provided with a set of prison keys, paving the way for their easy escape. Speaking of the jail, he laughed and informed the princess that Mathieu was one of the first persons the rebels captured today, and he was now sitting behind locked bars. "You better not bring any harm to him," the princess said upon hearing this, "or you will suffer his same fate."

Prince Agis didn't like hearing this, so he snapped back, "Princess, you are no longer in charge here. Haven't you realized that? I am the new ruler."

When Delia first saw the shocking events taking place on the Castle Terrace, she literally dropped a basket of fruit she was holding, and headed over towards the stairway where the king and queen were being held. She knew that Chadwick had some personality flaws, but she never suspected anything like this. Although they rarely got along and barely spoke much these days, she still loved him. When she reached the stairway, the rebel soldiers stopped her, telling her that she could not pass. She argued with them, and even tried yelling up to Chadwick, all to no avail. When the rebel soldiers figured out who she was, they immediately took her into custody, and pushed her over to where the king and queen were standing.

As Yvonne arrived at the workers' entrance at the eastern side of the castle, she slowed down to catch her breath and survey the scene. There was no guard of any kind posted outside, so she would have no problem getting inside. Once she entered, she started taking the route towards the connecting hallway, which would give her access to the other side of the castle. Then she realized she was forgetting something. She looked for the nearest supply closet and finally found what she needed. She wanted to make it appear to any rebels she encountered that she was working the whole time, unaware of Chadwick's treachery. She finally picked up two buckets she came across which held dirty water and used rags in them, and continued towards the connecting hallway. When she went through the door leading into The Gateway, her heart sank. Waiting at the other end was a rebel soldier in a royal guard's uniform. She tried not to show any surprise, and walked slowly toward him and the door at the other end, with her two buckets in hand. The guard stopped her when she came close to the entrance door into the western side of the castle. He said to her, "Young lady, you are not allowed in that part of the castle right now. The princess is holding her special feast and giving her speech." Yvonne didn't know what to do, so she tried the only thing she could think of. She dropped her buckets and ran for the door, grasping at it, trying to get through. But the guard grabbed her by the arm, stopping her. As he pulled her back, she lost all hope, and came close to crying. The guard scolded her, "What are you trying to do? Didn't you hear what I just told you? You can't go in there tonight. Mathieu told me earlier not to allow any workers through." Yvonne's eyes lit up a little bit after she heard Mathieu's name mentioned.

She asked the guard, "Did you say Mathieu? But aren't you one of the rebel soldiers?" The guard looked dumbfounded as he heard Yvonne's question. She had asked him if he was a rebel soldier, but why would she ask such a thing?

"Of course I'm not a rebel soldier, young lady. Are you high on something?" he finally said in reply.

"Sir, if you are a genuine royal guard, then you don't know what has happened. A large number of rebels have taken control of the castle grounds, dressed up as royal guards. They took the king and queen hostage, and right now Prince Agis is holding the princess prisoner on the Castle Terrace. I was trying to get through here to help her." When the royal guard heard this, he was so alarmed that he pulled out his sword immediately. Then he moved into action. Telling Yvonne to wait behind, he opened the door and headed for the Castle Terrace. As he moved away from her, Yvonne shouted a reminder to him. She urged him to slow down, because rebel soldiers may have infiltrated the castle interior. The royal guard would need to keep his defenses up.

Prince Agis was now holding the princess with a firm grip on her upper arm. He led her out to the edge of the Castle Terrace, continuing to speak of his brilliance to all who would listen. While some in the crowd tried to find a way out of the castle, most stayed where they were and watched to see what would happen. None in the crowd dared to take any kind of heroic action, seeing that the king and queen were being held at sword point. Prince Agis directed his next comments to those in the crowd. "And to all of you poor people out there, just to let you know, I despise you. You make me sick. If you were born to be a slave, then that is what you should be until the day you die. I have spent the last year taking trips into your villages, burning down your buildings and stealing from, or I should say taking back from you what never belonged to you in the first place. As your new ruler, I am going to restore dignity to the throne."

Stefan watched as Prince Agis inched closer to the edge of the Castle Terrace, all the while holding on tightly to Stasia. It gave him an idea that he thought just might work. It was an idea which popped into his head because of something he personally experienced and suffered through five years earlier. He figured there was nothing to lose by trying it. So he asked his parents if there was any fruit left over from lunch. They didn't have any. But Lady Ruth, who was still standing there with them, had an uneaten apple, which she took out of her pocket and gave to him. Stefan's crazy plan was to aim for the mask of Prince Agis, which he was still wearing on his face. He hoped that a direct hit thrown hard enough would cause Prince Agis to lose his balance and fall over the twenty foot drop from the Castle Terrace to the lawn below. With all of his strength, he went for it. He threw the apple as carefully and as fast as he could. To Stefan's great surprise, he scored a direct hit.

Prince Agis was in the middle of praising himself in yet another way, when he was beaned in the head. As the apple hit him, it caused him to drop his sword out of one hand and lose the tight grip he had on the princess with his other hand. Prince Agis reached up to take off his cracked mask and feel his head where he was hit. But at that moment, he received an even bigger surprise. The princess was looking right at him when the apple ricocheted off his head, cracking his mask. She saw him struggling and did the first thing that came to her mind. She lunged toward him and pushed him over the edge. Prince Agis was screaming as he fell, but his voice went eerily silent as he hit the ground below, being knocked unconscious. While the other rebel soldiers were trying to figure out what to do, the princess turned and bolted for the inside of the castle. She made it through the door just as the royal guard sent by Yvonne arrived at the same place. The timing couldn't have been better. Princess Stasia was very relieved to see one of her real royal guards when she rushed through the door. The guard immediately started jamming the door handles with his sword to prevent the rebels from coming through after her.

After a few minutes of chaos took place, Robbins assumed command of the rebel soldiers who were all gathered near the stairway. He first sent a few of them over to help Prince Agis in any way they could. Next, he told Sebastian to watch the prisoners, and ordered ten rebels to follow him up the staircase and into the castle. When they arrived there, they were locked out, unable to open the door. Somebody had jammed something through the door handles, preventing anybody from coming in after the princess. Robbins kicked the door in disgust and led the soldiers back down to the bottom of the stairway. He ordered all rebels who weren't involved in watching over the prisoners to storm the castle from all entrances. The priority was to capture the princess and eliminate anyone who tried to stop them from achieving that. As the rebel soldiers shouted their agreement, they all headed off in groups of four in different directions.

At the same time, Stefan arrived to wait for the princess near the stables. He noticed there were no guards on duty to stop him from walking from the peasant side into the royal stables. He walked right through the door and found some hay stacked up nearby to hide behind. He was sitting there for about five minutes, when four rebel soldiers rushed past his hiding spot and into the royal castle. On the one hand, it was really alarming for Stefan to see that, because surely they would capture the princess if she was on her way out here. But, on the other hand, the urgency with which they rushed through must have meant that the princess had still not been taken into custody, which meant there was still a chance she could escape. When he had nailed Prince Agis in the head with the apple and seen the princess push him over the edge, Stefan took off immediately for the stables. Those in the crowd who saw what he did, commended him as he passed by them. He also heard his parents calling for him as he ran away, but he didn't have time to explain to them what he was doing.

Just as four rebel soldiers rushed into the castle at the entrance outside of the royal stables, similar groups of soldiers entered the castle everywhere else. They were now flooding the hallways, looking for her. About ten minutes later, the princess was following the royal guard back towards The Gateway, the connecting hallway where Yvonne had first spoken to the royal guard. Shortly before they reached the door, it opened from the other side and four rebel soldiers came rushing through. The princess and the royal guard turned around and started running the other way. And the rebels gave chase, with one of them shouting, "It's the princess. Get her!" Soon, other rebels in the castle heard the excitement, and came towards the princess and the royal guard from another direction. Once they were cornered, with no way out, the royal guard threw down his sword and surrendered, not wanting a fight. Thus, the princess and the royal guard were taken into custody by the rebel soldiers. Robbins soon arrived on the scene, walking up with an obvious limp, and congratulated the soldiers on capturing her.

He came close to the princess and laughed at her. "You really thought you could escape, with so many of us here? Nice try. But for your sake, you better hope that you didn't seriously injure Prince Agis when you pushed him off the edge." Turning his attention to the soldiers, he directed, "Take her back outside, and place her into custody next to the king and queen. Hopefully, Prince Agis will be feeling better and be able to tell us what to do next.

King Charles, Queen Delphine, and Delia were all hoping the princess would be able to find a way to escape from the rebels after her dramatic display of courage on the terrace. Someone in the crowd had pelted Prince Agis with a piece of fruit, and Stasia had taken advantage of the unexpected event by pushing him over the edge. The three prisoners then watched as Princess Stasia ran inside, shutting the door behind her. Somehow, she locked the door, because when the group of rebels tried to go in after her, they were unable to do so. But now, as they looked up at the entrance door, it was opening again, and rebels were walking back through it to the outside. Charles, Delphine, and Delia were devastated when they saw the princess with them, along with a royal guard. Despite her best efforts, it looked as if the rebels had captured her. This would be the end for the royal family. With everyone now in custody, the rebels would be able to rule the land unchallenged. Sebastian took custody of the princess as she reached the bottom of the stairs and pushed her over next to her family. He heard the queen say, "Hello, my daughter. I'm sorry you weren't able to escape, but at least we're all together now. Everything is going to be okay." Sebastian laughed and walked back over to wait for further instructions from either Robbins or Prince Agis.

Prince Agis was now sitting up on the great lawn, with pain throbbing through his head and right shoulder, which he landed on. Robbins walked up to him, asking if he was okay. "Of course I'm not okay. I could have been killed in that fall. Did you find the princess?"

"Yes, master," Robbins answered. "We found her in the castle, trying to escape with the help of a royal guard. We captured her and have her in custody, along with the rest of the royal family."

"Good work, general," Prince Agis said. "And what of my wife?"

"She is also being held by our soldiers. She tried to go up the stairway while you were speaking to the crowd."

"Release her at once. I do not want her treated like the rest of the criminals. Speaking of the crowd, we are going to have to let them out of here soon. They are starting to get unruly. Right now, I am going to speak with the prisoners before they are escorted to the castle prison, which will be their new home. I want you to send as many soldiers as are needed to take full control of the lookout towers. Then, line up at least forty rebel soldiers and lower the main drawbridge, to allow everybody to leave the castle grounds. Give standing orders to the soldiers in the lookout towers to take down any royal guard who tries to come anywhere near the drawbridge." When Prince Agis finished giving General Robbins these orders, Robbins went to gather up some men, and carry out what he needed to do.

A few minutes later, Prince Agis walked towards the prisoners, and saw Delia being separated from them. A rebel soldier was telling her that she was free to go, and she walked off into the crowd, looking heartbroken. Getting closer, Prince Agis stopped to talk with Sebastian. He wanted to know which of the rebel soldiers was responsible for capturing the princess, so they could be rewarded for their good work. Sebastian said that the first group to spot her was made up of four rebel soldiers, and he gave Prince Agis their names. Two of those four rebel soldiers were Owen and Trent, who had been the ones that Prince Agis helped to escape from prison five years ago. Prince Agis took note of that, and walked over to where the king, queen, and princess were all standing. The princess was keeping her head down, with her face looking at the ground. "Don't be too sad, princess," Prince Agis said to her. "You gave my rebel soldiers a little exercise and training. And it was good you had a chance to do some running, because you will never again see the outside world, for the rest of your days."

"Leave her alone, Chadwick," the queen said, coming to her defense.

"How could you do this to us?" the king asked him. "You are my brother, my flesh and blood."

"You feign ignorance, Charles," Prince Agis answered. "If you really don't know, perhaps someday I will pay you a visit in prison and explain it to you."

Over at the stables, Stefan was looking out from his hiding spot when he saw a peasant girl who looked like Yvonne walk out of the castle door. The princess was not with her, which caused Stefan's hope to begin fading. If the princess had been captured, Stefan knew it would be nearly impossible to get another chance like this. There would be too much security around her to ever help her escape again. And that would mean Prince Agis could do as he pleased, as he ruled the land of Astoria. Stefan looked at his surroundings. Once he was sure there were no rebel soldiers around, he came out from his hiding spot. As the peasant girl came closer, Stefan asked her what had gone wrong. "Yvonne," he said to her, "what happened? Where is the princess?"

Below the Castle Terrace, Prince Agis finished talking to King Charles and ordered the soldiers to take the king, queen, and princess away to be locked up in prison. But as the princess raised her face a little, to see where she was going, something caught the eye of Prince Agis. "Wait a moment, soldiers," he told them. Prince Agis walked around until he was standing directly in front of the princess, who was once again looking down. With one of his hands, he pulled her face up to make eye contact with him. The girl could see it immediately in his eyes, Prince Agis knew that she was not the princess. "Sebastian! Get over here right now!" Prince Agis shouted.

"Yes, Prince Agis. What is it?" Sebastian said as he rushed over.

"This is not the princess, Sebastian. Where is the princess?" As Prince Agis said this, his anger was building up inside.

"I don't understand," Sebastian answered. "This is certainly the princess. She's wearing the same dress she had on earlier. And is that not the golden crown on her head?" Not happy with his answer, Prince Agis pulled the golden crown off the head of the princess and put his hand on her hair. With one swift motion, he pulled a blonde wig off her head, throwing it to the ground. Sebastian was stunned. He didn't know what to say, or what to do.

"You still think this is the princess?" Prince Agis demanded to know. "You better gather up some men and find the real princess, or our position in control of the castle could be in jeopardy." As Sebastian took some men and hurried off, Prince Agis pulled out his sword and slammed it against a nearby wooden table. The fury of his sword put a huge dent in the wood. At the same time, Prince Agis felt a rush of pain in his right shoulder, which was injured in the fall. He walked over to talk to the girl who was pretending to be the princess, who was more frightened than ever, pointing his finger in her face. "You, you did this. You were the one who talked to me earlier about the prison. For causing me so much trouble and helping the princess escape, I should put you in prison." Prince Agis was interrupted as an older lady came up from behind, pleading with him.

"Please, sir, have mercy. Don't put my little girl into prison." It was Lady Ruth, with Stefan's parents standing behind her. Lady Ruth looked absolutely traumatized as she fell to the ground, pleading for Yvonne.

"You want me to let her go, after what she has done to me? Very well, let it be done. Soldiers, release the young girl." The rebel soldiers did as they were told, and brought Yvonne over to Lady Ruth. As Lady Ruth stood up and was hugging her, Prince Agis added a stipulation. "And soldiers, find out where these two live, get everybody out of their home, and burn the house to the ground." Prince Agis then walked away looking for Robbins, wanting to give him some new orders, as Lady Ruth began screaming out from behind him. Along with giving Robbins the new orders, Prince Agis was going to see to it that Owen

189

and Trent never messed up another operation. The two rebel soldiers had made their final mistake and were going to prison.

Thirty minutes earlier, when the royal guard who Yvonne met in the connecting hallway told her to stay behind, Yvonne did for a moment. Then she realized that she needed to explain Stefan's plan to the princess, which she forgot to tell the royal guard about. Yvonne chased after the royal guard, never being able to catch up, but always keeping him within sight. When the royal guard finally reached the door leading to the Castle Terrace, he ran into Princess Stasia who was running inside. While he was jamming up the door, Yvonne finally caught up to where they were. Yvonne told the princess about Stefan's idea to escape the castle by way of the servants' bridge. "That idea might work," the princess told her, "but only if you're willing to help me do something."

"Of course, princess. What can I do?" Yvonne replied.

"We have to trade places," Stasia explained, "and make the rebels think you are me, the princess. Chadwick is either dead or knocked out, and most of the other rebels have never seen me up close or spent any time with me. So if you and my royal guard give them a brief chase and allow yourselves to be caught, they will think they have captured me. They will then call off the search, and I will be free to escape with Stefan. You should know that if you're willing to do this, you may be risking your life."

"I will be happy to do that in your behalf, princess," Yvonne said. "But how are they ever going to think that I am you? We might be close to the same age, but we don't exactly look the same."

"Leave that to me," the princess said. "It's just a good thing that the rebels haven't taken over the inside of this part of the castle yet." When the royal guard finished what he was doing, Stasia quickly led everyone towards her private changing room.

When the princess, Yvonne, and the royal guard arrived at the private changing room, Stasia began explaining her plan. She first asked the royal guard to wait outside to keep watch, and told Yvonne to follow her in. "Here's how we are going to trade places," the princess explained. "We need to first of all change our clothes. You put on my dress, which is very conspicuous, and I will wear your peasant clothes." After looking around the room for a few seconds, Stasia spotted something else they would need. "Here we go," she said. "We can use a couple of these wigs which are kept in here for the masquerade balls. I will give you this blonde headed wig, and I'll take one that matches your brown hair color." After the girls traded outfits and put on their wigs, they stared into the mirror for a moment. They really did resemble the other person. There was one more missing piece, which Stasia put on Yvonne's head, the golden crown.

"I can't believe I actually look like you," Yvonne said to the princess.

"For the final part of the plan, here is what is going to happen," Stasia continued, as she opened the door to include the royal guard in the conversation. "Anytime, now, this place is going to be flooded with rebel soldiers, looking for me. I'm going to hide in here until it is clear you two have been captured. Once that happens, I will go for it. I will try to walk out of here and hope for the best. Thank you both for doing this, for risking your lives for me."

"It's an honor to do it," the royal guard said to her.

"May you find Stefan and escape safely," Yvonne added. With that, the plan was implemented, and 'Princess' Yvonne and the royal guard started running in the opposite direction that Stasia needed to go, trying to make noise and attract attention.

As they hoped, 'Princess' Yvonne and the royal guard were soon spotted as they headed for the connecting hallway, and taken into custody after a short chase. As 'Princess' Yvonne was being escorted outside and down the stairs towards them, Queen Delphine was the first to notice they captured the wrong person. She leaned over to the ear of King Charles and whispered, "That's not Stasia. It's a girl who is wearing her dress and has the same type of hair, probably one of her maidens." Queen Delphine told the same thing to Delia, but added, "Let's play along, and pretend they have captured Stasia." When the rebels brought the new prisoners down to the bottom of the stairs, Sebastian took the princess and pushed her over to stand with her family. The queen greeted her by saying, "Hello, my daughter. I'm sorry you weren't able to escape, but at least we're all together now.

Everything is going to be okay." Yvonne looked up at her and nodded her head, glad to see the queen was playing along.

Things quickly calmed down inside the castle after Yvonne and the royal guard were led away. Stasia waited a few more minutes, until she could no longer hear any voices. Then, she slipped out into the hallway and started walking towards the door leading out to the royal stables. As the final part of her disguise, she had put some mud on her face that was usually used by her maidens to give her beauty treatments. She tried to spread the mud around her exposed skin as much as she could, and even added some on her wig. Stasia nearly reached the door, when a rebel soldier yelled to her from behind. "You there, what are you doing in here?" the rebel asked her.

Stasia froze for a moment before realizing she needed to keep up the disguise. She turned around and looked at the soldier, saying, "I have been working in the garden this evening, and now I have to clean up after the horses." When the rebel soldier saw what 'peasant' Stasia looked like from the front, he was repulsed by her.

"Get out of here, you filthy peasant," the rebel told her. "And don't come back in here tonight, or you're going to be out of a job." Stasia nodded her agreement, and turned around with a slight smile on her face as she walked through the door and towards the royal stables.

The disguise was working so well that when Stasia walked out of the door and down towards the stables, Stefan thought it was Yvonne. He looked around, making sure nobody else was there, and emerged from his hiding spot. "Yvonne," he said to her, "what happened? Where is the princess?" Stasia couldn't help but laugh a little bit when she heard this, despite everything that had happened to her and her family. When she reached Stefan, Stasia put out her arms to hug him. After the hug, Stefan looked at her, trying to figure out what was going on. The person he hugged reminded him of Yvonne and was even wearing her clothes, but it wasn't Yvonne.

"It's me, Stefan, it's Princess Stasia," she finally told him. He felt so stupid after she said that, because he should have known right away. He didn't dwell on his embarrassment, though, because there wasn't time.

He told her his plan, "It is so good to see you, princess. I was thinking we could get two horses and ride out of here through the servants' bridge."

"That won't work," the princess said. "Chadwick told me he has most of my royal guards trapped outside, unable to get into the castle grounds. If they can't get in here, then we can't get out. But we can't stay here either, so let's go see if we can get the servants' bridge back down."

"Should we bring some horses with us?" Stefan asked. Stasia thought about it for a moment, but only because she really wished she could bring her horse Isobel with her. But bringing horses would attract way too much attention, so she told him that they better go on foot. Besides, if they needed horses, the royal guards would have plenty of them outside of the castle grounds, where they were trapped, walking and riding around in circles.

Just before they came to the servants' bridge, Stefan realized somebody was missing. "What happened to Yvonne? Why isn't she with you?" he asked the princess.

Stasia looked at him with a measure of sadness and answered, "I'm sorry, Stefan, but the rebels captured her. We traded identities, to fool them. She gave herself up so I could be free. I really hope she will be okay." This news hit Stefan like a ton of rocks. His best friend had been taken into custody by the rebels, who probably thought she was the princess. And when they realized they had the wrong person, Stefan figured they might get so angry that they could possibly throw her in prison for the rest of her life.

Stefan and Princess Stasia looked at the raised servants' bridge for a minute before they realized the turning mechanism had been deliberately dismantled. This was a major setback, but at least there were no rebel soldiers anywhere in the area. They walked outside of the gate and looked across the moat. There was no way to get across to the other side without jumping into the green water and swimming. The light outside was starting to fade now, and they needed to find a way out as quickly as possible. As they were debating what to do, small waves started rippling out in both directions from the middle of the moat, an obvious sign of a crocodile swimming by. Then, two royal guards on horseback appeared on the other side of the water. They were probably riding around the castle in circles, feeling helpless as they were trapped outside. They looked at the two peasants standing on the other side, and started riding off again. Pulling off her wig, Princess Stasia shouted to them, "Guards, it is me, the princess!" The two royal guards stopped as soon as they heard this, and guided their horses back over to where they previously were.

"Princess, what can we do to help you?" one of them shouted across the moat.

"We are trapped over here, with no way to get across. The servants' bridge has been disabled, and cannot be let down. Do you have any ideas?" she said back to them. The two royal guards looked at each other and started talking about the predicament. Stefan wanted to feel useful, so he went back over to the gate and looked around to see if the coast was still clear. It wasn't, because he saw two rebel soldiers running in the direction of their location, and several other rebel soldiers running back towards the stables.

"Princess, we have to act now! They're coming for us!" Stefan said with an urgent tone. "We have no choice but to jump in and swim across." The princess started to say no, but she was pulled off the embankment by Stefan, down into the thick green moat. After briefly going underwater, Stefan and Stasia were pushed back up to the surface by the thick composition of the moat. They started swimming as fast as they could toward the other side. The crocodile that had been swimming by took notice of them and changed direction to head towards them. Stefan and Stasia were about halfway across when the two rebel soldiers walked through the opened gate. They saw two people swimming in the moat, two royal guards on the other side, and also the wig left behind on the bank. But they didn't notice the crocodile, which was swimming almost entirely underwater, creating small surface waves.

"That's the princess, trying to escape!" one of the rebel soldiers yelled, as he jumped off the embankment into the moat. He could hear his fellow soldier telling him to wait as he was jumping, but he had no interest in waiting. If he could capture the princess, Prince Agis would consider him to be a hero. Perhaps he would even be named the second in command.

As Princess Stasia and Stefan reached the other side, the crocodile continued to close in on them. But the royal guards reached down and were able to pull them both out of there, just in time. Seeing that its initial prey was now gone, the crocodile turned and swam toward the rebel soldier. The soldier finally spotted the crocodile and started swimming back the other way. He almost made it all the way when he felt the pain. With tremendous force, the crocodile came up behind him and snapped its jaws onto his legs. The soldier started flailing his arms around in the water, trying to stay afloat. When his fellow soldier saw this, he leapt off the embankment with his sword out. He drove his sword into the side of the crocodile, causing it to start thrashing. At the same time, the crocodile released its grip on the rebel, and his fellow soldier was able to pull him back out of the moat to safety.

On the other side of the moat, Stasia and Stefan were drenched with smelly, green water. But they were safe, now under the protection of two royal guards. Several other royal guards rode up about a minute later, stopping to help and protect the princess. Stefan looked to the other side of the moat while the princess was talking to them, and saw the rebel soldier carrying off his severely injured companion. Stefan figured that some of the rebels at least had the courtesy to help each other, if nothing else good could be said of them. The princess spoke to Stefan, saying, "Thank you for helping me to escape. I couldn't have done it without you or Yvonne. It is because of your extraordinary wisdom that I am free, and someday I will be able to reward you both for what you have done, risking your lives in my behalf."

"Where will you go now?" Stefan wanted to know.

"I have decided to ride off with six royal guards, on the road towards Norwalk, making sure some of the rebels see which direction I am heading. When I am halfway there, I will change course, and we will take a cross-country route through the forest to Sir Rackley's country estate, where I will go into hiding until we can gather our forces and attempt to retake the castle."

"But princess," Stefan said with concern, "won't the rebels come looking for you at Sir Rackley's?"

"They might, but it is not likely," Stasia answered. "After all, should the rebels bother Sir Rackley, they would face severe consequences, being that he is the son of a foreign king. The rebels wouldn't want to risk having Sir Rackley's father bring an army of soldiers into Astoria, because they would face a fierce fight."

"I understand, princess," Stefan responded. "That sounds like a great plan. Could I please go with you?"

The princess thought for a moment, and told him, "You may ride with me for a short while, since you live in Norwalk. After we are an hour into the forest, though, I want you to turn around and go back to your home. I will explain why in a little while. There is something I need you to do for me, if you can. Right now, we must leave this place." Two of the royal guards climbed down off their horses, giving them over to Stefan and Princess Stasia. Several more rebel soldiers were now gathered at the gate, watching to see what the princess and her royal guards would do next. The rebel soldiers who stood there could only watch helplessly as the princess and her protectors rode off towards Norwalk.

Chapter Thirteen:

To Pretend She Was Poor

Lady Ruth's house did not end up getting burned down that night, as Prince Agis had threatened. He only said it to make Lady Ruth and Yvonne suffer some mental anguish. In effect, giving them a form of punishment. The rebels were way too involved with securing the castle grounds in every way possible to take a side trip to Norwalk which would accomplish little in the big picture. So, a couple of rebel soldiers led Lady Ruth and Yvonne up to the entrance gate, and then inexplicably pushed them into the crowds of people, leaving them behind and walking away to do something else. When Prince Agis learned for a certainty that the princess was no longer on the castle grounds, and his men finished taking over the strategic positions in the lookout towers, he ordered the drawbridge to be lowered. There were no royal guards waiting on the other side when that happened. The moment the drawbridge came down, the thousands of people who were trapped on the castle grounds began pouring out into the surrounding land. It was a chaotic scene, as the crowd was so agitated over the events of the day that several people were almost trampled, and a few others were nearly shoved over the side, into the moat below. Because there was so much at stake, Prince Agis didn't send a contingent of rebel soldiers to chase after Princess Stasia. He knew there wasn't much he could do once she was off the castle grounds, and he didn't want to divide his forces, which would have left the castle less secure. But with the exception of her escape, the night was a complete success.

The reason there were no royal guards waiting when the drawbridge was lowered was they had all gathered together and rode off towards the village of Glaston. Glaston was the village closest to Sir Rackley's estate. The plan was for the royal guards to make the guard station in Glaston their base of operations. They would secure the village and maintain their position there as long as possible, posting two guards to do surveillance a few miles outside of the village. If rebel soldiers were spotted coming to attack the guard station, they would retreat to a hiding place in the forest, somewhere in which they could keep in close contact with the princess. The princess had taken six of the royal guards with her, to guide her safely through the forest to Sir Rackley's, taking a cross-country route. Once she was safely there and in hiding, those six royal guards would join their fellow guards in Glaston. Unfortunately, rebel soldiers now outnumbered the royal guards by a ratio of almost two to one. Many of the royal guards, royal knights, and royal archers had been captured, and taken into custody in the castle prison. Others fled into the countryside, not knowing what to do. It was going to be a very difficult task to take back the castle, if it was even possible.

As Stefan rode away from the castle on a horse given to him by a royal guard, following the princess and six royal guards, he finally had a chance to think about all that had happened. It was dark outside now, and it felt like it had been one of the longest days of his life. At least he was safe, and he was able to make a real difference in helping the princess escape. She even spoke of rewarding him at some later date, which would be something he could dream about from now until then. Not lost in his thinking was the concern he felt for his best friend Yvonne. Like Stefan, she willingly risked her life to help the princess escape. But unlike Stefan, she wasn't riding safely away from the castle. Instead, she was facing the wrath of the rebels and Prince Agis. He decided to check up on her later tonight in Norwalk, to make sure she was able to get home safely.

A short time later, the princess and her group turned off the main dirt road, heading directly into the forest. It was slow going, because clouds rolled into the sky and covered the moon, making it darker than usual. Stefan followed the group at the rear, as they navigated their way through trees, around rocks, and through the brush. They led the horses across a small stream, spooking a bobcat that was drinking from the water. About an hour into the ride, when a light drizzle started coming down, the royal guards called for a break. Princess Stasia pulled her horse back to where Stefan was riding and told him to follow her. She then told one of the royal guards that she and Stefan would be taking shelter nearby, under a tall, thick tree, if they needed her. Stefan and the princess rode their horses a little further, before dismounting and tying them up. They went to sit under the branches of the tree, where it was relatively dry. As they sat down and remained silent for a minute, Stefan was taking in every second. If it wasn't for all of the tragedy, this would have been the type of moment that lived in his dreams. He was sitting next to the princess, the most beautiful and wonderful girl in the whole world, under a dark sky, with rain gently falling around them. He closed his eyes and tried to freeze the moment in his mind, so he could remember it in case something like this never happened again. The princess spoke to him, "Stefan, I want you to know how much I care for you. I love you and Yvonne both, for the kindness and love you have both shown to me. I consider you and Yvonne the dearest of my friends, and I hope one day we can all be together again at the royal castle."

"Thank you, princess. I feel the same way about you," Stefan said in reply. He forgot to add the part about his love involving more than just friendship, but he knew it was not appropriate to do so, in view of Princess Stasia's engagement to Sir Rackley. Even if she was not engaged, he probably wouldn't have said it anyway. The princess continued with what she wanted to say to him.

"When I chose you at my coronation ceremony to come up onto the stage, in representation of all poor people, I couldn't have imagined you would end up being such an important part of my life. I could also never have imagined that my Uncle Chadwick would end up betraying my family in such a horrible way, as he did today."

"There has to be something we can do about that," Stefan said as he shivered. The cold air and slightly wet clothes he was wearing were starting to have an effect upon him.

"There is something that we can do. Actually, something that I am going to ask you to do, for me. I understand if you don't want to do it, because it is unfair of me to ask you to risk your life in my behalf, any more than you already have."

"Princess, whatever it is that you need me to do, I will try my very best, even if it costs me my life," Stefan said in reply.

"All right, then, here is what I ask. I want you to go to work as usual at the royal castle. If I am right, the rebels will allow you to keep your position working in the castle prison. They may not allow you to still be the assistant jail keeper, but they need workers. They can't do everything by themselves. Do whatever is necessary on your part to win their favor. Then, if you can, find a way to help my father and mother escape, and bring them to me." Stefan was somewhat surprised to hear this request from the princess, because what she was asking of him sounded completely impossible. How in the world would he be able to get the king and queen out of their prison cells and off of the castle grounds? Stefan didn't know, but he would at least try.

"That will not be easy, princess. But you know I will try with all my heart. If there is a way to keep my job at the prison, and if I can find a way to get your parents out, I will do so without hesitation," he finally told her.

"Thank you, Stefan," the princess said. "Your willingness to try is all I can ask of you." She thought for a moment, and added something which might give him some incentive to try his hardest. "One more thing, Stefan. If you can rescue my parents and bring them back to me, I will give you something in return. I will give you anything you ask of me, no matter what it is. If you wish to become the village statesman of Norwalk, it will be yours. If you want to become a royal archer, you will be trained. Whatever you seek, you will receive. That is my promise to you." When Stefan heard this last part, the promise made to him, his mind started racing. He knew without hesitation what he wanted to ask her for. Of course, that would depend on whether or not she had already gotten married. But if she wasn't, and if by some miracle the wedding to Sir Rackley fell through, he would not hesitate to tell her what he really wanted. He almost felt like getting up right then and there, and racing off to the castle to rescue the king and queen. His thoughts were brought back to reality when he felt a nudge on his shoulder. "Stefan, did you hear what I said?" the princess was asking him.

"I did, princess," he answered. "And, believe me, I will do everything in my power to break the king and queen out of there." A few minutes later, the royal guards wanted to press on, so Stefan and Princess Stasia parted ways. While the princess headed for Sir Rackley's country estate using a slow route that would take the entire night, Stefan headed back towards the Norwalk dirt road. The whole ride back, Stefan couldn't stop thinking about the opportunity which presented itself, if he could only save the king and queen.

When he finally returned to his home village of Norwalk, it was still raining lightly. Stefan figured it must have been close to two o'clock in the morning. Still, he tied up his horse and knocked on the door of Lady Ruth's home. When he did, he heard somebody come down the stairs, but they didn't open the door. He knocked again, this time calling out with a loud voice, "It's me, Stefan!" Soon, the front door was opened by Lady Ruth, who looked relieved to see him.

"Stefan, I am so glad it is you," she said to him. "The rebel soldiers threatened to burn down my home. So, when I heard a knock at the door, I thought they were here to make good on their threat."

"They threatened to burn down your home?" Stefan asked, repeating her words back to her. "I'm sorry for coming by so late, but I've been worried about Yvonne. Is she safe?"

"Come in and see for yourself," Lady Ruth said. Stefan followed her into the home and up the stairs to Yvonne's room. Lady Ruth gently opened Yvonne's bedroom door, and Stefan could see her peacefully sleeping in the dark. Lady Ruth whispered to Stefan, saying, "Perhaps you would like to go in and wake her, and give her a kiss goodnight. I know she would be happy to see you." Lady Ruth then walked away, going back into her own room, leaving Stefan standing outside of Yvonne's bedroom.

Stefan quietly walked into Yvonne's room and sat down in a chair next to her bed. He looked out the window at the rain continuing to fall. Then he looked back at Yvonne, not wanting to wake her. He finally stood up and leaned over her, kissing her on the forehead, as Lady Ruth suggested. When Stefan did this, she slowly came out of her sleep and woke up looking at him standing close to her. "Oh, Stefan," she said, "I am so happy you are here. I was just dreaming about you."

"Yvonne, I've been worried about you all night. It's good to see you home safe, in your own bed."

"Yes, we made it home safe. I will tell you the whole story tomorrow. I think I lost my job at the castle."

"Everything is going to be okay, Yvonne. Don't worry about it. I will help you find another job until the princess is back in power."

"Oh, thank you, Stefan. Would you mind doing me a favor, before you go?"

"Sure, I would be glad to," Stefan told her.

"Would you watch over me, until I fall back asleep? It has been a really frightening day for me, and I would feel better knowing you are here."

"Of course, I will," he said. Stefan stayed there for another fifteen minutes, sitting by her bedside. After he was certain that she was once again asleep, he stood up and walked out of the room, finally on his way back to his own home.

The next morning, the weather continued to be gloomy and overcast, much like the mood of the entire land, as Astoria woke up to a new leader in power. Stefan woke up after only a few hours of sleep and started getting ready to go to work, as he usually did on the weekends at the castle. His mother was also awake at the early hour, and she tried to convince him to stay at home. She didn't think it was a good idea for him to show up at the castle, worried about what the rebels might do to him. She even thought one of the rebels might recognize him as the boy who threw the apple at Prince Agis, ultimately resulting in his fall off the Castle Terrace. Stefan convinced her that the rebels had no idea it was him, and told her how the princess had personally asked him to continue working at the castle. So, she stopped trying to persuade him, deciding to trust his judgment in this matter.

When Stefan arrived at the castle, he rode his horse to the servants' bridge, but it was still raised up. It was kind of hard for him to look across the moat, seeing the exact spot where he and the princess had jumped into it a day earlier. But he needed to move on, so he rode his horse around to the main entrance gate, where he found ten rebel soldiers standing guard out front. "Halt, there!" one of the soldiers told him, with his hand out, palm pressed forward. "What business do you have at the castle?" the soldier asked, as Stefan climbed down off his horse.

"Good morning, sir," Stefan said. "I am reporting for work this morning, as always." When they heard this, three of the rebel soldiers came over and checked him out very carefully, searching him, his work bag, and the saddle on the horse. When they were finished, the first rebel soldier spoke to him again.

"Before you enter the castle, be advised there has been a change in power. Prince Agis is the new leader of Astoria, as Princess Stasia was removed last night for the crime of treason. If you do not wish to work for the new leader, you may leave now and return home. But if you agree to support Prince Agis, you may continue with your usual duties at the castle. You will continue to receive any small wages you have been earning up until now."

"My loyalty will be with Prince Agis," Stefan lied. "My family cannot afford for me to lose this job, which covers much of our living expenses." Satisfied with the answer he heard, the rebel soldier permitted Stefan to walk his horse across the drawbridge and report for work as usual.

As Stefan guided his horse across the great lawn, over to the peasant stables, things felt so different at the castle. Everything he was used to seeing and being familiar with was gone. It was a different atmosphere, with no royal guards walking around, very few familiar faces among the workers, and no royal archers up in the lookout towers. Stefan did not want to be here right now. He felt so uneasy, and even lonely. But this is what he had been asked to do. So, he opened a stall and put his horse away for the day. Yesterday, Stefan rode to the feast with his parents, but ended up taking the royal guard's horse home at the end of the night. To avoid suspicion, he decided it would be better to ride his own horse back to the castle today. He walked across the great lawn and down the stairs into the castle prison, arriving right before the ring of the eight o'clock bell.

Sebastian was the one who was there to greet Stefan when he walked into the entrance area of the prison. Sebastian had been placed in charge of the entire prison, which included watching the prisoners, giving orders to the other rebel soldiers who were assigned there, and monitoring the activity of any workers who still desired to keep their jobs. It was a very important assignment, as King Charles, Queen Delphine, and the royal knight Mathieu were all being held prisoner deep in the underground cells. Sebastian thought it was kind of ironic, because five years earlier he was the one who deceived his way into the prison, helping the two rebel prisoners escape. And now, he was entrusted with watching over all the prisoners. Sebastian had already reviewed the official schedule Stefan made for the upcoming week, detailing which royal guards usually worked there and which workers were assigned to do what tasks. As Sebastian was only able to take a couple hours of sleep himself, he had been in a rush to get down to the prison this morning. Along with forgetting his coat, Sebastian also forgot to put on his necklace, which held a brasta wood pendant, something he usually wore every day. When Stefan walked through the entrance door, Sebastian greeted him. "Good morning. I take it you are one of the workers here at the castle prison. Are you aware there have been some changes made here at the castle?"

"Yes, sir, I am," Stefan answered. "But I assured the soldiers outside that this job was an important source of income, so the new ruler has my complete support."

"That's good to hear," Sebastian said. "We are expecting to be very short staffed, so we're going to need all of the workers we can get. For some reason, you look somewhat familiar to me. Tell me, please, what is your name, age, and work assignment?"

"My name is Stefan. I am seventeen years old. I've been assigned the job of assistant jail keeper. Mostly, I see to it that all of the prisoners are fed and have water. I also care for the weapons stored here, stock and organize the supply rooms, and make up work schedules."

"Ah, so you are Stefan," Sebastian said. "I've been reading your schedules. It looks like you are very organized. I want you to know that trust is a big issue if you're going to keep this job. I need to know I can trust you and that you will keep your eyes and ears open. You need to become familiar with all of the rebel soldiers who will be working in here. If you see any former royal guards, or anyone who doesn't look like they belong here, you must let me know immediately. Because if any of these prisoners end up escaping, it will be you, me, and everyone else working in here who will pay the price. Is that understood?"

"Yes, sir, completely."

"Good, and you can call me Sebastian. I am a year younger than you, at sixteen. From now on, you will take all your orders from me. You may keep your title of assistant jail keeper, but you will essentially be my assistant. Go about your normal routine, and if there is anything I want adjusted, I will let you know." As Sebastian was finishing, he noticed that Stefan was wearing a necklace similar to his own. It caused Sebastian to shout out, "That's it! I knew I had seen you somewhere before. You were at the market in Langston when we burned it down."

"Yes, I was there," Stefan acknowledged, starting to get slightly worried.

"After we left that night, Prince Agis spoke to us several times about his admiration for you. He told us that you would have made a model rebel soldier, with the courage you displayed in bringing those people out of the market. And now, what do you know? You are working for Prince Agis here in the prison. He will be very pleased when he hears this."

"Thank you sir, I mean, Sebastian," Stefan said. "I will try my very best to make him proud by continuing to work as hard as I can." That answer really pleased Sebastian, and gave him a boost of confidence and trust in him. Sebastian then wanted to ask Stefan something about the necklace he was wearing.

"Tell me, Stefan, where did you get the necklace you are wearing? It seems like it is probably very rare."

"You are right, it is extremely rare," Stefan answered. "The brasta wood pendant comes from a distant land, so you won't find another necklace like it anywhere around here. It is very valuable, probably my most valuable possession, besides my horse."

"And you've never seen another one of these before?" Sebastian wanted to know.

"I haven't, but my parents have. They originally were given two of these as a gift when I was only a baby. It was a gift from the wealthy landowner who my father worked for. One was meant for me, and one was for my baby brother, who was one year younger than me."

"Does your brother still wear his to this day, as you do?" Sebastian asked.

"I have no idea, Sebastian. My baby brother was kidnapped from our home when I was only two years old. I don't remember him at all, and my parents rarely talk about him anymore. It brings them too much pain."

"I understand, my new friend. Well, I am going to let you get to your work assignment, and I am going to continue with mine. Perhaps we could spend a little more time together soon, to become better acquainted."

"That would be nice," Stefan said, as he walked toward the castle interior to begin his work. Before he started to prepare the food order for the day, Stefan stopped by the supply closet he had been in the day before with Yvonne, when he was showing her the tunnels. He carefully put the wood planks back over the small opening in the wall and pushed the supplies and equipment up against them, to ensure that no rebels would stumble across the secret passageway.

Sebastian's mind was filled with all kinds of thoughts as he tried in vain to concentrate on his work. He was fairly certain there was at least a possibility Stefan was actually related to him, being his brother. Everything appeared to fit together. Stefan was a year older than he was. And Stefan said that his baby brother, who was one year younger, had been given a necklace matching his own. Sebastian was one year younger, and did have the same necklace. And the story about his baby brother being kidnapped fit in with what the rebels were doing fifteen years ago. The only part which didn't make sense to Sebastian was that Robbins had told a completely different story of Sebastian's family, saying they died in a tragic mudslide after King Charles greedily took over their land and relocated them to a less desirable location. Robbins had even personally assured Sebastian that he was not the victim of a kidnapping. Yet, Sebastian wanted to believe he still had family alive. That's why he couldn't stop thinking about Stefan and what he had said. Sebastian decided to keep his thoughts about the matter to himself and leave his own necklace back in his room, while he tried to do some investigating on his own. Perhaps he could talk Stefan into inviting him over to share a meal with Stefan and his parents. That could be the first step he could take. One way or another, though, Sebastian would get to the bottom of this mystery. He would find out if this was all just a coincidence, or if he had family he never knew about.

That morning, Princess Stasia and her six royal guards finally arrived at Sir Rackley's country estate. The princess was tired, her clothes were wet, and her hair and face were covered with dirt and mud. It was a long journey through the forest, in miserable weather conditions. As the princess and her protectors arrived at the back of the estate, Sir Rackley came running out to meet them. "Princess, I am so glad you are safe," he said when he was halfway there. "Some of my workers attended your special feast yesterday, and brought back the terrible news about what happened. I was hoping you would escape and come here."

"Hello, Sir Rackley," she replied. "I am here to stay for a while, to pretend I am poor. I must dye my hair, change my appearance, and become one of your workers, for the time being."

"Do you think the rebel soldiers will come here looking for you?" Sir Rackley asked.

"I would expect a small group of two or three to come here, eventually. But the rebel soldiers do not want to provoke you in any way, knowing that your father would bring in his forces and retaliate, should the rebels attempt to harm or control you. So I think this is one of the safest places I could be."

"Good thinking, princess," he said in reply. "Would you like to come inside now and get cleaned up, and maybe even get some food or rest?"

"Thank you, but it is best to start now in playing my new role as a peasant girl. I will go into your workers' quarters to change, eat, and rest. If you could provide me with some clothing that looks the part, I think it would be enough for now."

"I will take care of that for you right away," he promised. "There is something I need to ask you, that has been worrying me all night. But if it would be a better time later, I can wait." Stasia climbed down from her horse and walked over to where Sir Rackley was standing, because she could see the concern on his face.

"What is it, Sir Rackley? What is on your mind?" she asked.

"It's just we were supposed to be married in less than a month. What will become of our engagement and wedding, in view of all that has happened?" Stasia felt really bad about what she had to say next, but she figured he may as well know now.

"Sir Rackley, I think you already know the answer to your question. I am no longer the leader of this land, which means there is no basis for our engagement, anymore. I fully intended to marry you, next month, but our parents arranged this marriage on the basis of it uniting our two lands. That can no longer be done, at least not right now. I doubt your parents would want you to marry a fugitive, which is what I have become. If circumstances change in the future, and our forces can find a way to retake the castle, we may revisit this topic again. But for now, my focus cannot be on a relationship. It can only be on finding a way to rescue my parents and save Astoria from the bleak future it is headed for."

"I understand. You are right," Sir Rackley said, clearly disappointed. He said goodbye to the princess for the time being and went off to make all of the arrangements that would be needed during her stay. Princess Stasia didn't want to hurt him, but there were more important concerns on her mind as she led her horse toward the workers' quarters. The six royal guards who accompanied her checked the perimeter of the property to make sure everything was safe, and then rode back off towards the village of Glaston.

At the castle, Delia didn't know which would have been worse for her, the mental state she was in right now, or if she was locked up in prison like the king and queen. She had watched in horror as her husband Chadwick betrayed the princess in front of the vast crowd of people. Now she felt numb inside. Her willpower, her desire to live, and her resolve were all sucked out of her, leaving an empty shell of the strong person she once was. The only thing more surprising to Delia than the betrayal was how Chadwick allowed her to stay free, while every other person who was close to the princess was now sitting in prison. Delia tried to sleep in her own bed last night, walking back into the castle after most of the crowd went home. But she found herself unable to. Finally, she got up and did the only thing she could to bring her a little bit of comfort. She went and slept on top of Princess Stasia's bed, in the bedroom of the princess. She was still lying there, thinking about everything, when Chadwick appeared at the open door. He knocked on the door several times before speaking. "Delia, my dear, I know you must be angry with me," Chadwick said to her. "But what I have done is what needed to be done, for the land, for the castle, for us." Delia couldn't bring herself to look at him as he spoke. He continued, "I hope you will forgive me in time, and we can begin the healing process. You and I have not been getting along for some time now. Perhaps you will see that your best option is to begin treating me with the respect and appreciation I deserve." Chadwick waited at the door for another minute, before continuing his lecture. "From now on, I would like you to address me as Prince Agis, for it is the name I wish to be known by. You will continue to have full access and privileges throughout the castle, as long as you do not turn against me. Do not attempt to visit or help any of the prisoners escape. Is that understood?"

Delia still didn't make eye contact with Chadwick, but she realized it was in her best interest to give him an answer, so she said, "Yes, Prince Agis, you have made yourself very clear. I will not disobey you."

"I am glad to hear that," Prince Agis said. "I don't expect you to move past all that has happened overnight. But I do require your obedience." Prince Agis turned around and walked downstairs, out of Princess Stasia's bedroom, to head for a planned morning meeting with General Robbins.

Robbins had been assigned by Prince Agis to watch over all departments in the castle, making sure there was a smooth transition in power to the rebels. He met very little resistance as he walked to all the different areas of the castle, accompanied by a group of rebel soldiers. About the only trouble came from several royal guards who were hiding out in their rooms, in the eastern side of the castle. Those remaining guards were finally all taken into custody, being chained up and hauled away to the castle prison. But, as Robbins walked back towards the other half of the castle, he encountered another disturbance. A fourteen-year-old girl named Madison ran up to him, whining about how her father Mathieu did not come home last night. "Do you know where he is, sir? My mother is so worried. She stayed up all night crying." Robbins felt no sympathy for the young girl, or her mother, and he didn't want to be bothered by either of them.

"Get lost, little girl. The best thing you and your mother can do, would be to pack up your things and get out of the castle. Your father has been locked away in prison, where he is going to spend the rest of his life." Robbins didn't think he could make himself any clearer than that. Madison started crying when she heard the cruel words Robbins said, and she turned to walk away. She only took two steps when she turned back and lunged at him, hitting her fists against his chest. Her boldness surprised him, and two rebel soldiers quickly grabbed her, pulling her away from him. She was still kicking and shouting at him, so he became firmer with her.

"How dare you attack me. Didn't your parents ever teach you any manners? I don't want to ever see your face again, or I will put you in prison with your father."

Robbins threatening words had the opposite effect on Madison than what he was expecting. She stopped throwing her fit and asked him politely, "Would you please put me in prison, so I could be with my father?" Robbins laughed, and continued walking toward his meeting with Prince Agis, leaving the young girl behind, fatherless and heartbroken.

When General Robbins and Prince Agis were done reviewing all of the successful changes made, Prince Agis headed over to the castle prison. No longer in need of wearing his creepy looking mask, Prince Agis was now free to show his face outwardly to both his rebel soldiers and the whole world. Prince Agis greeted Sebastian and asked how things were going at the prison. Sebastian informed him that all was going well. He mentioned how only a few workers had shown up today, desiring to keep their jobs, but that they all expressed support for Prince Agis. That pleased Prince Agis, and he commended Sebastian for doing such a fine job, before asking to be taken back to talk with the imprisoned royal knight Mathieu. Sebastian led him back through the hallways, to the very back of the prison, deep underground, and opened the cell door of Mathieu. Mathieu was sitting against the back stone wall of his cell, next to Bailey, the jailer who was also imprisoned. While Prince Agis talked to Mathieu, Sebastian stood there with his sword drawn, pointed towards the prisoners. Prince Agis was holding a burning torch in his hand and spoke to Mathieu, saying, "Mathieu, my old friend, how are you enjoying your new home?" Mathieu sat there, glaring back at him in the firelight, anger showing in his face. The moment Mathieu saw him, everything became very clear in his mind. He could see that Chadwick was wearing rebel clothing and realized Chadwick must have been Prince Agis. Prince Agis continued, "It seems that just like my wife, you don't wish to speak with me. Have it your way, but except for receiving your daily food rations, I may be your final visitor for who knows how long, the next month, the next year, perhaps even the next five years. As punishment for your crimes, I am sentencing you to spend the rest of your life in this prison. You may as well know, for your own peace of mind, I have overthrown the princess, imprisoned the king and queen, and I am now the new leader of the land." Prince Agis then gloated about his success, saying, "You never saw it coming, Mathieu, none of them did. I was way too intelligent for you. You could almost say it was your ignorance which led to the overthrow of the castle. I hope you can live with that." Prince Agis turned to walk out of the room, but stopped when Mathieu spoke to him.

"Your scheme will never last, Chadwick. The people of the land will not tolerate you as their ruler. Mark my words, they will take back the castle. It is only a matter of time." Prince Agis scoffed at Mathieu's foolish suggestion and walked out, as Sebastian closed and locked the door behind them. Soon, the prisoners were once again engulfed in total darkness and isolation.

During his lunch break, Stefan chose not to eat, but rather, to do some exploration in the underground tunnels. When he was sure nobody was watching him, he went into the supply room, closing the door behind him. He carefully moved everything out of the way and once again took down the wood planks covering the small entrance. He picked up the torch used the day before, and after shaking the dirt off and relighting it, walked down the secret passageway. He brought with him a writing tablet, and he spent the next forty-five minutes mapping out several more dead ends. But then, he experienced his first breakthrough. He followed a passageway requiring him to walk through ankle-deep mud, which he had not taken before. It kept going, long past where the other ones stopped in dead ends. Soon, he reached a junction. The muddy trail continued to his left, but he stepped onto the dry dirt which continued straight. After a few more minutes, he finally came to what he thought was a dead end. But this dead end was different, because he could see small glimmers of light shining through. He brought his torch close to examine the dead end, and realized he had discovered an opening, very similar to the one in the castle prison. He pressed his eyes against the wooden planks covering the opening and was shocked to find he was looking into the clothing and laundering room of the castle. There appeared to be a sink, or something large, propped up against the boards his eyes were pressed against. It was a good thing the boards weren't perfectly lined up, or he would have had to push them down to figure out exactly where he was. In the clothing and laundering room, he could see several servants at work, cleaning as they usually did. Stefan realized it was time to turn around, as he needed to get back to work on time. But he took a moment to first make some notations on his map. After he put his writing tablet away in his pocket, Stefan headed back to return to the prison through the other end of the secret passageway. He felt thrilled as he walked, realizing he finally caught his first break. He could now access the western half of the castle. And the only thing left that he wanted to discover was whether or not there was a tunnel leading all the way outside of the castle grounds. If he could find that, he knew it would be much easier for him to help the king and queen escape. As he climbed back into the storage room in the castle prison, Stefan was feeling more upbeat then ever. His optimism was quickly dashed, however, when he realized there was somebody waiting for him. Sebastian was standing there, watching Stefan intently as he stepped back out, holding a torch that was still burning. "And just where have you been, Stefan?" Sebastian demanded to know, with a threatening look on his face.

Chapter Fourteen:

Winning Their Confidence

Stefan realized he was going to have to think hard and fast to give an answer. A lot was at stake with how he ended up handling this situation. His job at the castle prison, the trust he was starting to build up with Sebastian, and ultimately, the potential escape of the king and queen. But he couldn't just say anything off the top of his head. His explanation would have to check out with Prince Agis, if Sebastian ended up passing on what Stefan said. Sebastian asked once again, "Where have you been, Stefan?" Using the best story he could think up, Stefan tried to calmly give his answer.

"Hello, Sebastian. I am glad you came in here," Stefan said. "I was on my way to look for you, to tell you about a problem we've been having in here." Stefan pointed down to the muddy boots he was wearing, and continued, "As you can see from my boots, we've been having some flooding problems back in these old tunnels. Part of my job assignment has been to look back in here, each day, to make sure the water and mud don't start getting too close to this small opening in the wall. The last thing we want is water pouring into the hallways of the prison, if you know what I mean."

Sebastian relaxed his angry stare as he listened to Stefan's explanation. Sebastian then told him, "Okay, keep me posted on the status, if anything changes. Has anyone ever thought of sealing up this opening, so we don't have to worry about this problem? Are these tunnels actually used for anything?"

"No, they are not," Stefan answered. "They were used a long time ago, over a hundred years ago. But now, they are just a hazard and a problem. I could try to seal up the opening if you would like, but castle engineers have suggested against it in the past."

"Well, whatever," Sebastian said. "I will let you worry about it, since it is your job. I was actually looking for you, because I wanted to ask you for a favor. I would be interested in getting to know all of our workers and their families here in the prison, and since you are one of the head workers, I thought I might start with you. Do you think we could get together tomorrow night and have dinner? Perhaps at the house of your parents?" Stefan found this request to be quite odd, but by granting the request, he realized it would help distract Sebastian from thinking any more about the tunnels. Stefan didn't know what his parents would think, if he was to ask them to have one of the rebel soldiers into their home to share a meal. But he would have time to explain it to them tonight.

"I'm sure that would be fine with my parents," Stefan told him. "I will talk to them when I get home tonight, to set up all the arrangements."

"Thank you, Stefan. You would have my gratitude," Sebastian said. He turned to walk out of the supply room, leaving Stefan behind, relieved that his efforts to map out the tunnels had not been shut down.

When he was done working for the day, Stefan rode his horse back to Norwalk. He didn't return home right away, deciding instead to stop by Lady Ruth's house to see Yvonne. She was outside in the front yard, cultivating some planted vegetables. As she saw Stefan dismount his horse and tie it up, she dropped what she was doing to run out and meet him. She gave him a long hug and kissed him on the cheek. Then she said, "Thank you for coming to see me, Stefan."

"Do you want to get out of here for a while?" he asked her.

"Of course I do. Where would you like to go?"

"I was thinking we could take a walk down to the King's Fountain, to sit down and talk for a while." Yvonne thought it was a great idea, and after running back inside to tell Lady Ruth what she was doing, Yvonne walked with Stefan down to the village center. On the way, she explained to him every detail of what happened to her last night after she and Stefan each headed off in different directions to help the princess. She recounted the horrible threat Prince Agis made to Lady Ruth, although he didn't end up carrying it out. When she was finished, Stefan told her about the frightful swim across the moat, and how a crocodile was pursuing them, but changed course and attacked one of the rebels. Stefan ended by telling about his trip through the forest with the princess and the request she made to him.

"Stefan, that sounds much too dangerous, what she wants you to do," Yvonne told him. "You are only one boy. How could you possibly break the king and queen out of prison without being caught?"

"I have no idea, Yvonne," he replied. "But I do have all of the keys and I do have full access to the entire prison. I just need to focus on winning their confidence a little more, and perhaps then, there will be less people looking over my shoulder, scrutinizing everything I do. The funny thing is, the head rebel soldier has taken a liking to me. He seems to trust me, never doubting anything I tell him. He even wants to come over to my house tomorrow night, to have dinner and meet my parents."

"That's strange," Yvonne said. "Are you sure it is not some kind of trap?"

"No, don't worry, it's not a trap. My guess is that he wants to do a background check on me, before passing more of his responsibility in the prison on to me."

After a short walk, the two friends arrived at the King's Fountain, the grandest designed monument in the village of Norwalk. It was fifteen feet high, being circular in shape, nearly half the size of a house. Water was diverted from the nearby river, one block away, allowing the King's Fountain to flow all year round. Stefan and Yvonne walked over to it and sat down near the lower portion of the fountain. Stefan took off his boots and Yvonne took off her sandals, after which they both soaked their bare feet in the cool water. It gave them a slight chill, but it was also very refreshing. "Great idea, to come down here," Yvonne remarked.

"I thought it might be nice," Stefan said, "because it's been an unusually hot day for September. The morning started out so gloomy.

I can't believe how the weather changed this afternoon. I sure hope the rebels don't come through here and rename the King's Fountain, Prince Agis' Fountain." Yvonne laughed at the suggestion, telling Stefan that the rebels had better things to do than rename the famous monuments throughout Astoria. As she sat by the fountain next to Stefan, Yvonne couldn't help feeling truly happy, being with the boy she loved. If only he would realize the fact that she wasn't a little girl anymore. She was grown up now, and had feelings for him. If he would just tell her something, like how beautiful she looked tonight, or how much he thought about her during the day, everything would be perfect. Instead, he suggested something that would result in them being apart.

"Yvonne, I've been thinking today," he said, "about what you could do for work. I came up with an idea which seems to makes sense. As I told you earlier, the princess is staying at Sir Rackley's for the time being, to pretend she is a peasant girl. But besides Sir Rackley, she doesn't have any friends there. I was thinking that you could go there and work for Sir Rackley. I'm sure he would hire you on. That way, you could accomplish two things at once. You could earn some money and you could keep her company. She did tell me that you were one of her dearest friends, while we were out in the forest." Yvonne thought about Stefan's suggestion. It really wasn't what she wanted to do. Even if she had to go without making any money for a while, she would rather have stayed in Norwalk to be close to him. But she didn't want to disappoint Stefan.

So, she finally said, "If that's what you want me to do, Stefan, I will do it. I will go to Sir Rackley's and ask for a job. Lady Ruth could probably give me a ride there in her horse carriage, because my horse is still locked up in the castle stables."

"Great, Yvonne, I thought you would like the idea," Stefan said. "And don't worry about your horse. I will be checking on him every day. I will try to find a way to bring him home for you, as soon as I can."

"I know you will, Stefan. I'm sure going to miss you while I'm gone. Will you promise to think about me?"

"Yvonne, I'm always thinking about you. You know that." The two best friends kept talking for a little while before they walked back to Lady Ruth's, saying goodbye for the time being. Stefan continued home, having to talk his parents into going through with the dinner tomorrow night. It wasn't easy, but Stefan finally convinced them it was very important in the grand scheme of things.

The next morning, Lady Ruth and Yvonne departed for Sir Rackley's country estate. It would take most of the day to get there, but at least the dirt road passed through some of the most scenic parts of the land. At the same time, Robbins and Sebastian were holding a meeting on the castle grounds to discuss the current status of the prison. Robbins wanted to know if there was anything he could do to help his adopted son. "Everything is going well, father," Sebastian told him. "We have plenty of rebel soldiers taking shifts working in there, and we also have at least one castle worker who takes his job seriously."

"Remember, Sebastian," Robbins suggested, "don't try to do everything yourself. The key is to delegate as much as you possibly can, so you can spend more time doing the important work."

"I will, father," Sebastian promised. Robbins then noticed that Sebastian had somewhat of a distant look on his face, as if something was on his mind.

"Is there something you want to tell me?" Robbins asked him.

"There is something I have been thinking about lately, but I wasn't planning on talking to you about it right now," Sebastian answered. "If you must know, it's about my past. I mean no disrespect by saying this, but the fact is, I'm not sure if what you told me about my past, about my family, about how you adopted me, has any truth to it. I think you told me what I needed to hear at the time. But I'm older now, and I think you owe me an explanation. Please, father, I need to know where I come from."

"You are a very smart boy, Sebastian," Robbins said upon hearing this. "And you are right, many of the things I told you when you were younger were not true. Perhaps someday I will share with you the entire story of how you came to be part of the rebel family. But, right now is not the proper time. Someday, my son. Someday." Sebastian was not happy to hear this from Robbins, and he turned around and stormed off. It was bad enough that Robbins admitted to lying for all of these years, but when exposed, he refused to tell Sebastian the truth. Sebastian would have to figure it out on his own.

Delia was back in the castle classroom, finally feeling useful again. Prince Agis had asked her to take over as the new teacher, since the old teacher left the castle during the overthrow. It was an assignment she happily accepted, without any hesitation. Of course, Prince Agis had reminded her that she needed to promote him as being a good leader to her class. But, besides that, she was ready to help and support the remaining children who still lived at the castle. The class size initially shrunk, going from being a full room of students to only five who still remained. Around ten o'clock, though, Robbins walked in with eleven new students who would be joining the class. Yesterday, they were moved from the rebels old camp in the forest to their new home at the castle. Robbins decided it would be good for them to start experiencing a normal life, since Prince Agis would be the permanent ruler of the land. During the first hour of teaching, Delia realized they were an unruly bunch, but she would endure and teach them as best she could.

A little while later, Delia was in the middle of a history lecture, teaching the students about a ruler from one hundred and fifty years ago, when one of the rebel boys interrupted her, shouting, "That king was a nobody compared to Prince Agis!" The other ten rebel students then shouted their agreement, and further insulted the former king who Delia was trying to teach about. Delia tried to ignore the comments and start lecturing again, but she noticed a young teenage girl was crying in the back row. She asked the students to excuse her for a few minutes, and she took the girl outside to talk with her.

"Madison, what is wrong, my darling?" Delia asked. Madison didn't answer, but reached out, needing Delia to hold her. Delia let her cry for a few minutes on her shoulder. When she finally stopped, Delia said, "Madison, I am sorry about your father being locked up in prison. This must be a terrible thing for you and your mother to be experiencing right now. We have to be patient for the time being, because there is nothing we can do to change what has happened."

Madison looked up at Delia, wiping away some of her tears, and asked, "Will the princess ever come home to the castle, to save us?"

"Of course, she will," Delia answered. "But it will be when the time is right. If she can find a way to come back to help us, she will. You were one of her best friends growing up, and I'm sure she cares about you. Like I said, right now we must have a little patience."

"Thank you, Delia. That makes me feel a little better."

Prince Agis was on his way back to the castle prison, to take care of some unfinished business. Yesterday, he faced Mathieu and informed him of his lifetime sentence. Now he needed to do the same with King Charles and Queen Delphine. Once Prince Agis talked with them today, he didn't want to ever see them again. This would be the last time, he hoped, that he would ever have to look at the face of his older brother, who had taken all the glory for himself when he was the king. Prince Agis walked into the entrance area of the prison and ordered the rebel soldier who was working to take him to the prison cell of the king and queen. When the soldier unlocked the cell door, Prince Agis withdrew his sword, and excused the rebel soldier, desiring some privacy. He then went inside, holding a torch in one hand and his sword in the other. The firelight revealed that the king and queen were sitting down on the dirt, holding each other. "Charles and Delphine, you look comfortable. How have you been enjoying the prison food? Is it as good as the daily banquets you used to enjoy?"

"Chadwick, why have you done this to us?" the queen demanded to know. "We have shown you nothing but love throughout our lives, and this is how you repay us? If your parents were still alive, what would they think of your actions?"

"I don't care what dead people would have thought," Prince Agis said, with bitterness in his voice. "The only thing they ever thought about were themselves and Charles. I was always the odd one out, the one who was born five years too late to be worth anything."

"You know that's not true, Chadwick," the king interjected. "You were loved by them the same as I was. It's not my fault I was the firstborn, which required me to become the new leader when I turned sixteen. How could you despise me for something I had no control over?"

"I have always despised you, Charles, every day since you became king instead of me. You were the one who received all the glory, all the admiration, and all the praise. I was forced to follow behind you, watching and waiting for my turn to come. And, after many years of planning, my time has now come. I am the ruler of this land."

"Forget about us for a moment, Chadwick," the queen pleaded, "but think about your niece, Stasia. She looked up to you and loved you. Even though you were hard on her sometimes as she was growing up, she knew you were only trying to make her a better person."

"Then why has she spent the last year destroying everything that has ever been held dear in this land? The poor people have never had any rights or say in things. It's going to take me some time to undo all the damage she has done. Look, I have no need to justify myself to either of you. I came by out of the kindness of my heart, to let you both know that I have sentenced you to life in this prison, with no possibility of parole. But I have an offer for you, if you wish to see the outside world again. If you come out and publicly support me as the new leader, I will allow you to spend one hour per week outside of the prison, heavily guarded of course, to walk on the castle grounds."

King Charles was quick to reject his offer, saying, "I wouldn't come out and support you, even if it meant saving my life."

"Very well, then," Prince Agis said. "But know this, I will not be making this offer again. These past few years, when you thought I was taking trips into the countryside and villages to build support for your kingship, well, I was actually doing everything I could to tear it down. I was leading my fellow rebels on raids, bringing misery to as many people as I possibly could. Now, I will leave the two of you in misery. Goodbye." Prince Agis walked out of their prison cell, feeling he had finally closed the door on the worst chapter of his life. Now, he would finally get some attention and glory, instead of his older brother. And he had carried out the secret scheme of the rebels at the worst possible time for King Charles, when it caused him the maximum amount of pain.

Prince Agis emerged from the underground prison, fully taking in the breath of fresh air which awaited him. Before eating his lunch, he wanted to check on the rebel soldiers who were guarding the drawbridge to make sure everything was in order. As he was walking over there, his eyes looked up into the sky and spotted an Astorian eagle soaring up high, circling around some prey. The eagle probably had its sights set on a squirrel or rabbit on the ground below. Prince Agis thought of an idea when he saw this, a thought that would increase the pleasure he was feeling at the moment. With no hesitation, he shouted up to the rebel soldiers who were manning the nearest guard tower, and ordered them, "Shoot it down!" The rebel soldiers didn't obey immediately, wondering why Prince Agis was asking them to shoot down the rarest bird in the land. They didn't realize he was doing this to openly defy the new law that Princess Stasia recently put into effect. By harming the innocent eagle, he would be able to make a statement, at least in his own mind. When he saw that his rebel soldiers were not obeying him, he shouted again, "Shoot the eagle down, soldiers, now!" They looked at each other and shrugged, before one picked up his bow and pulled an arrow back tight. Then, he fired it. The arrow went sailing into the sky. Despite its amazing intelligence, an Astorian eagle was no match for a trained archer. Fortunately, the bird changed course by coincidence, just at the right moment, causing the arrow to sail past. Prince Agis watched as the arrow missed and fell to the ground below, almost too close to a small group of workers who were caring for some plants. The rebel soldier didn't get another chance to take a shot, because the Astorian eagle flew off, away from the castle. Seeing this, Prince Agis cursed out in anger before continuing on to the drawbridge.

Later that night, Lady Ruth and Yvonne pulled into Sir Rackley's country estate. They were not expected, but they were welcomed with open arms. When they arrived at the front gate, a servant came down from the main house to open it for them. The servant then followed them back up the short road to where they parked, next to the portico, to help unload their belongings. Sir Rackley soon appeared at the front door, saying, "Well, if it isn't my dancing partner from the coronation ball. Welcome to my country estate, Yvonne."

"Hello, Sir Rackley," Yvonne replied. "This is my adopted mother, Lady Ruth. I know this is short notice, but I came here looking for a temporary job."

"Of course, Yvonne, that will not be a problem. Now, why don't the two of you come inside and we can discuss this further. We were all sitting down to eat dinner, so I hope you're hungry." Yvonne and Lady Ruth were glad to hear that, because they both were very hungry. They joined Sir Rackley and two of his friends, both young men who were visiting from his homeland, at the dinner table. As they started eating large helpings of roasted duck and asparagus, Sir Rackley was curious if Lady Ruth and Yvonne knew about his special visitor. He asked them, "Are you aware that I have somebody special staying on the property for a while?"

Yvonne smiled and answered, "You mean the princess? Yes, that's one of the reasons I am here. I'm not sure if she told you, but I was involved in helping her to escape. The end result of that is I was fired from working at the castle, which has left me without a job. So I was hoping you could hire me on here as one of your workers. At the same time, I could spend some time with the princess, so she would have another friend around."

"What a great idea, Yvonne," Sir Rackley said. "I'm sure you will make a great addition to the staff here. The only problem I see in giving you this job is that it's going to be hard to let you leave someday. The boars will miss you too much." All at the table laughed upon hearing this. Sir Rackley continued, "Lady Ruth, I'm sure that you're going to want to spend the night, before returning home. I will have one of my servants prepare a room for you."

"That would be splendid. Thank you, kind sir," Lady Ruth said to him. The small group of five continued eating their meals, getting to know one another. When dinner was finished, Yvonne gave Lady Ruth a hug and wished everyone a good night at the table. She was anxious to go out to the workers' quarters and visit with the princess. Before she left, Sir Rackley stopped her to remind her about something.

"Yvonne, I have a proposition for you. Do you remember the night at the coronation ball, when we shared a dance?"

"Yes, of course I do, Sir Rackley," she said.

"Good, because I seem to remember you telling me that you were gifted at archery. Isn't that right?" Lady Ruth didn't give Yvonne a chance to answer, because she answered for her.

"Yvonne is as good as any royal archer at the castle," Lady Ruth bragged.

"That's very interesting," Sir Rackley said upon hearing this. "The reason I ask is that I have not lost an archery match in several years now. I would like to challenge you, Yvonne, to a contest. If I can beat you, I get to choose your work assignment here at my country estate.

But if you beat me, you can choose your own work assignment. What do you think?"

"I would be glad to shoot against you. I might not look like much, being a sixteen-year-old peasant girl, but I sure do know how to hit targets. The thing is, it doesn't really matter to me what my work assignment is. I am truly happy doing any type of labor. So, if I beat you, I'm going to ask you for something else. I would like your help with something which has been troubling me, but is very important to me."

"Okay, whatever you say," Sir Rackley replied. "I will have my servants prepare a target challenge for us at three separate distances, within the next few weeks. Have a good night, and take my greetings to the princess when you see her." Yvonne walked out of Sir Rackley's estate house, and down a small hill to where the workers' quarters were located.

Yvonne opened the door when she arrived, carrying with her a bag filled with clothing and personal items. She went into the main room and saw there were ten beds, with three of them taken with workers who were relaxing after a hard day. One of them was Princess Stasia, who looked up at Yvonne as she walked in. The princess was writing in her journal, which she had kept for many years now, calling it 'Majestic Times'. Since her main journal was still in her bedroom at the royal castle, Stasia started a new one here at Sir Rackley's. "Yvonne, what in the world are you doing here?" the princess screamed out with delight, as she jumped up from her bed and ran over to give Yvonne a hug. "You are safe, that is so good to see. Now I will be able to sleep a little better at night."

"Hello, princess, and thank you for your kind words," Yvonne said. "I was fired from the castle, so Stefan thought it would be a good idea to come here to work, where I would be close to you."

"That boy sure thinks up some good ideas," the princess stated. "It will be great to have a friend here to spend my time with."

"You mean another friend? You already have Sir Rackley here," Yvonne pointed out.

"Actually, I can't really hang out too much with Sir Rackley, because he has a lot of visitors who come and go every day. We can't risk letting word get out about me being here. That's the whole point. I am here to fit in as a worker."

"I see what you mean, princess. It must be hard to have the boy you're going to marry so close to you, but at the same time, so far away."

"Well, I guess you may as well know," the princess revealed. "Our engagement is off, at least for the time being. After everything that has happened, we could never get married, unless things go back to being the way they used to be in Astoria." Yvonne was shocked to hear this, and immediately thought of Stefan. He would view the broken engagement as giving him new hope, making him think he still had a chance to win over the heart of the princess. That wasn't good news for Yvonne.

"And what of you and Stefan?" the princess asked. "Are you two just best friends, or is there something more?" Yvonne couldn't believe the princess was asking her this. By asking Yvonne such a personal question, it meant she truly viewed Yvonne as a close friend. Up until now, Yvonne had not revealed her personal feelings about Stefan to anybody, except Lady Ruth. She was happy to have another person who she could open her heart to.

"Princess, Stefan and I are best friends. We have been for a long time. In all honesty, I do have romantic feelings for him, but he doesn't seem to have them for me. I have tried everything I can think of to let him know how I feel, outside of blurting it out. Since you asked, I don't think Stefan could ever see past you long enough to notice me, in that way." This last statement caused the princess to frown, as she tried to understand its implications.

She asked, "Do you mean that Stefan has romantic interest in me?"

"That's exactly what I mean, princess. He has lived in a fantasy world for the past five years, or so. You're all he talks about, all he thinks about, and all he dreams about. I've given up on trying to get him to live in the real world with me."

"Well, I will take it as a compliment," the princess finally said. "I probably should have noticed it sooner, since I was spending more time with him lately at the castle. But, being the princess, I get a lot of admiring looks and compliments from people, so I usually don't pay much attention to that when it happens. Would you like me to talk to him for you? I could tell him how you feel about him."

"No, please don't, princess," Yvonne pleaded. "If he finds out I told you these things, it's possible he would never forgive me. Actually, that's why I have to beat Sir Rackley at archery. He challenged me a little while ago, while we were eating dinner. And he promised he would help me with something if I can beat him. I intend to ask him to convey how I feel to Stefan."

"That sounds like a much better idea," the princess conceded. "But unless he lets you win, I'm not sure if you can beat him."

"We will see about that," Yvonne said. The two friends continued talking for a while, until more of the workers arrived and everyone went to sleep for the night.

The next morning, Yvonne woke up early and went to work with the princess. Their assignment for the day was to care for the animals, to feed them, clean up after them, and give exercise to those in need of it. Sir Rackley kept quite a lot of animals on his country estate, with most of them being left over from the days when the king and queen used the estate as a vacation home. Some of the animals were there to provide food and dairy products, while others were kept around to provide enjoyment for any young guests who would visit the estate. The animals included horses, cows, chickens, regal peacocks, wild boars, and ostriches. Of all the animals, the wild boars were the most entertaining, as they had been captured in a nearby forest and brought here. Princess Stasia and Yvonne started their work by cleaning up the horse stalls. While Yvonne was used to doing it at home, the princess had never done any type of cleaning before. As she was working in the stalls, the princess was thinking about her white horse Isobel. She hoped Prince Agis would not do something cruel to Isobel.

That night was the special dinner held for Sebastian at the cottage owned by Stefan's parents. Martin and Stefan were sitting in the front room, anxiously awaiting the arrival of Sebastian. Meanwhile, Shaylene was busy continuing to cook in the kitchen. Though the family did not have a lot of money, they tried their best to put together an elaborate meal, wanting to leave Sebastian with a good impression. Stefan's motive was to try to build up a friendship with Sebastian, hoping it would lead to more trust with his work at the castle prison. Stefan told his parents how important this was, and they agreed to do everything they could. Soon, there was a knock at the front door. Martin stood up to answer it, thinking it was Stefan's workmate Sebastian. But when Martin opened the door, he found out that he was wrong. Instead of being Sebastian, it was Rolf. The landowner pushed past him, walking into the cottage as if he still owned it. After recovering from his initial shock, Martin asked him, "What do you think you're doing? This is our home now. You can't just walk in here without our permission." Rolf laughed at him, picked up a chair, and threw it out the front door. Stefan saw this and began getting really upset. He started to walk over to the landowner, intending to use force to get him out of the house and stop what he was doing. But Martin came over and restrained him, after which Martin told the landowner, "You'd better leave right now, or I am going to report your actions to the authorities."

"What authorities?" Rolf said, with sarcasm. "The word is out everywhere. The princess has gone into exile and there is a new ruler, Prince Agis. From what I hear, Prince Agis has rolled back all the reforms, and poor people no longer have any rights. So, you need to pack up your things. I am evicting you from my cottage. If you don't get out of here, I will round up some of my friends in the village, including Wilfred, and have them get you out." The landowner started throwing more things out of the front door, while Martin and Stefan stood there, not knowing what to do. Finally, Shaylene came out of the kitchen and started screaming at him, telling him to stop, as Rolf picked up some books resting on a table and threw them outside. Rolf didn't intend to stop. He wanted to make things very clear to Martin and his family.

Rolf next carried out a vase full of flowers, which he tossed to the ground. It shattered everywhere, causing Shaylene to chase him outside, still yelling at him. The landowner laughed at her, telling her that he could do whatever he wanted. The dispute was interrupted, though, when a young sixteen-year-old boy walked into the picture. He had observed what was going on for the past two minutes, and felt it was time to get involved. "Hey, you! Stop what you are doing, right now!" Sebastian ordered the landowner. Rolf didn't even bother to look at him, but walked back into the house to do more damage. If the landowner had looked at him, he would have noticed that Sebastian was dressed in the outfit of a rebel soldier, wearing a sword by his side. When Stefan heard Sebastian's voice, he raced out the front door and ran up to him. "What is this man doing to your home, Stefan?" Sebastian asked.

"He is ruining it. He showed up at our door suddenly, barged in, and began throwing our property out the door. The princess ruled against him in judgment and awarded us this house because of his long lasting cruelty towards our family. Now that the princess has been removed as the leader, he thinks he can do whatever he wants."

"Wait out here. I will handle this," Sebastian instructed. He walked in the front door of the cottage and observed the landowner pulling on the table which was set for dinner. The landowner looked like he wanted to pull the entire table out of the house. Sebastian walked over to him, grabbed him, and threw him down to the ground with tremendous force. Rolf groaned as he hit the ground, in both surprise and in pain. Sebastian picked him up by his shirt, tearing it as he lifted him. With one hand on the landowner's hair and one hand on his ripped shirt, Sebastian led him out the front door and shoved him away from the house. Rolf landed near some pieces of the broken vase, cutting himself in several places. Sebastian pulled out his sword and started walking towards the landowner, who finally realized the predicament he was in. Sebastian was on a mission, and he was going to teach Rolf a lesson he would never forget. Just before he reached the landowner with his outstretched sword, Sebastian stopped when he heard Shaylene's voice calling.

"Sebastian, stop. Please, that's enough," she said to him. Sebastian snapped out of his rage as he heard her voice. He turned back to look at her, the way a son looks at his mother. A moment later, he looked back at the landowner, who was bruised, cut up in several places, and completely shaken by the beating.

Sebastian told him, "The princess may be gone, but Prince Agis is now in charge. Just so you know, I am one of the main soldiers who serves Prince Agis. If I ever hear of you bothering these folks again, I will come looking for you, and you will be putting your life in jeopardy. Is that understood?"

With his voice shaking hysterically, Rolf answered, "Completely, sir. I will never trespass on their property again."

"You had better not. And these things of theirs that you have broken, I want you to repay double what they are worth."

"Yes, sir. It will be done immediately," the landowner said. Sebastian was finally satisfied, so he ordered the landowner to get up off the ground and leave his sight. The landowner was happy to comply, running off to get some of his wounds looked at. When the landowner was gone, Shaylene thanked Sebastian for what he had done. All four then went back inside to enjoy the meal she prepared for them. As Sebastian sat down at the table to eat, he realized that he had protected his long lost family, and he began looking for the right opportunity to tell them who he was.

Chapter Fifteen:

One Moonlit Night

Sebastian wanted to know all about the family history of those he was dining with, so he asked question after question. Martin and Shaylene were happy to relate everything, not keeping anything from him. They told him about how they first met and were married, settling down for a simple life in Norwalk. And it appeared that Stefan was headed for the same future, as he enjoyed living in the village and cherished his job at the royal castle. Sebastian wanted to know if anyone in the family played musical instruments. When Shaylene heard this question, she excused herself from the table and went to get her old wooden flute. She brought it back to the table to show Sebastian, and he looked at it curiously. "Could you play something for me? It doesn't have to be anything special, perhaps a short song you like," he asked. Shaylene played a melody for him, one of the songs she used to play for Stefan when he was growing up. Sebastian found the song eerily familiar for some reason, although he couldn't remember where he might have heard it before. In response, Sebastian pulled out his piccolo from the small bag he brought with him, and showed it to everybody. "I was given this five years ago, during a visit to the castle," Sebastian related. He decided there was no harm in being completely honest, because he was growing more certain by the minute that this was his long lost family. "To tell you the truth, I was at the castle on my first assignment from Prince Agis. He had ordered me to break two fellow rebels out of the castle prison. While I was there that day, I was caught stealing a flute which did not belong to me. The musician who caught me didn't get angry over my theft, but gave me this piccolo instead. It was a gesture I will never forget. Since I am now living at the castle, I haven't been able to find that kind, old musician. He probably fled the castle with most of the other workers. But his deed has always meant a great deal to me."

"Sebastian," Shaylene said, "I know you are a rebel soldier who is loyal to Prince Agis. But how do you feel about some of the things he has done throughout the land, like burning down buildings, stealing what does not belong to him, and kidnapping innocent children?" Martin frowned at Shaylene, shaking his head quickly, side to side, trying to tell her that this was a bad direction to take the conversation in. But, Sebastian didn't mind the question. He was willing to share his views.

"I have never felt good about taking things from others, or causing them hurt and pain. But, it is the way I have been raised. My adopted father, Robbins, has helped me to progress up the rebel chain of command at a very fast pace. I have done a lot of things I regret along the way, but it was all a part of helping Prince Agis to take over his necessary role, that of being the leader of Astoria." Sebastian added something he thought was pertinent, saying, "Stefan has promised his full support for Prince Agis, as I hope you both will." After Martin and Shaylene did not express their agreement, Sebastian decided to change the subject. "Tell me, have you always lived in this nice cottage?"

"No, we have not," Martin answered. "We originally lived in a mud flat home on the outskirts of Norwalk, a short distance past the village cemetery. One night, a tragedy happened to our family in that home, and King Charles kindly moved us over to this cottage, so we could restart our lives."

"I'm sorry if I'm imposing," Sebastian said, with curiosity, "but I was wondering if you wouldn't mind telling me what happened. Stefan told me that your youngest son was kidnapped, but he didn't share any other details." Martin and Shaylene exchanged glances, knowing this was a difficult subject to talk about. Finally, Shaylene summed up everything that had happened fifteen years ago with five words.

"The rebels destroyed our lives," she said. As her words sunk in, everything started hitting Sebastian very hard. He needed to know the truth, but it was causing him pain and anguish inside. Shaylene noticed that tears seemed to be forming on his eyes, which really surprised her. She didn't take Sebastian for a particularly sensitive boy, especially after the display of rage toward the landowner, earlier in the evening.

"Could you please tell me more?" Sebastian pleaded. Martin thought the conversation was starting to go a little too far, so he stepped in.

"Sebastian, this is painful for my wife. Please, if you don't mind," he said. But, seeing how affected Sebastian was, Shaylene wanted to tell him the story, figuring it might drive a wedge between him and the rebels he served.

"Thank you, Martin, but it's okay," she said. "Sebastian, one night we were all resting quietly in our home. I was asleep, and our two young babies, Stefan and Lolek, were asleep in their baskets. Martin was sitting next to me, when rebels pounded on our door, demanding we pay them money which we did not lawfully owe to them. As soon as I heard them, I fled with Stefan out the back window. But Martin stayed and watched them break down our door, coming into our small home with torches and swords. They chased me for a long time that night, but I eventually was saved by two royal guards. Martin wasn't so fortunate. He was brutalized, and our youngest son Lolek was kidnapped. We have never seen or heard from him since. For all we know, he is dead." More tears became evident on Sebastian's eyelids as he listened to this detailed story of what had transpired that night. He had one question which he needed to have answered.

"Could you describe the rebels that came into your home? What did they look like?" Sebastian wanted to know.

"It was a long time ago," Martin replied, "but I can tell you one thing I remember as if it happened yesterday. The rebel who was in charge that night, the one who beat me up the worst, and ultimately kidnapped our youngest son, well, he walked with a distinct limp." These words cut into Sebastian so deeply that he could not stand it anymore. He could not hold back his tears, and he began weeping openly. Martin had described Robbins in the most obvious way possible. Robbins had always walked with a limp, being born with one leg slightly shorter than the other. There was no question about it anymore. Sebastian was Lolek, and this was Sebastian's family. Martin, Shaylene, and Stefan all looked at each other, feeling uncomfortable, not knowing what to say or do. Sebastian continued crying for several more minutes. He then took something out of his pocket and put it around his neck. It was a necklace with a brasta wood pendant on it which matched Stefan's perfectly. When Shaylene saw him do this, she almost fell out of her chair in total disbelief. Sebastian stood up at the table, tears continuing to flow.

With emotions running high, he exclaimed to Martin and Shaylene, "I believe that I am your son Lolek." He couldn't say anymore, he just walked over to where Shaylene and Martin were. They both stood up, and took the crying teenage boy into their arms, holding him, trying their best to comfort him. Martin and Shaylene both knew it, Sebastian was indeed Lolek, they didn't have any doubts. Stefan watched all of this, now understanding why Sebastian was so curious about him and his family. All of the pieces fit together now, and it brought a painful realization to Stefan. In order to help the king and queen escape, Stefan would have to betray Sebastian, who was his own brother. That is, unless he could somehow get Sebastian to switch sides and help him. The thought of betraying Sebastian after all that had happened seemed too hurtful to carry out, and Stefan didn't know if he could ever go through with it.

The family of Martin, Shaylene, Stefan, and Sebastian spent the rest of the evening talking about everything. It was a night that had changed all of their lives. It brought an end to fifteen years of wondering and grief for Martin and Shaylene. It reunited Stefan with the brother he never knew. And for Sebastian, it made him feel like he finally had a place in the world, a real family, which had been torn away from him when Robbins kidnapped him all those years ago. Sebastian didn't know how to feel about Robbins anymore, thinking of all the pain that his actions brought upon Martin, Shaylene, and Stefan. He almost felt like he hated Robbins, which was a strange way to feel about the only father he had ever known. It would take some time for Sebastian to come to terms with all of these new feelings and figure out what to do about it. For now, he was the happiest he had ever been, as he realized that the life he always dreamed of having was finally now beginning.

Three weeks later, Sir Rackley's estate was buzzing with excitement over the archery contest set to take place between Sir Rackley and Yvonne. Sir Rackley had invited some of his friends from around the countryside to come see the historic contest. For the first time since he competed at the games about five years ago, Sir Rackley knew that his opponent was not going to let him win. He had observed Yvonne practicing, which quickly dismissed his thoughts about her not being any good. She was nearly as good, if not just as good, as Sir Rackley was. And if he wasn't on the top of his game today, there was a real possibility he could end up losing this match. Of course, that was exactly what Yvonne had in mind. She had never really been in the spotlight before, so she was enjoying every moment of this. All of the workers at Sir Rackley's estate, including the princess, who now had long, dark hair, received the afternoon off from work. They were invited to come out and watch the competition. The challenge was simple, as it was set up in three parts. The first target was medium distance away. With Sir Rackley's great sense of humor, he ordered the face of Prince Agis to be painted onto two grapefruits. They were set perfectly in place on top of a small post, the challenge being to hit the face of Prince Agis right through his nose. The second target was a bit further, and it was a moving target. A unique pulley system was installed, which would be moved by one of the workers, who had been practicing for hours. He needed to get his timing just right, not slowing down or speeding up at any time. When the signal was given, the worker would pull on the ropes in a continuous motion, resulting in three wooden sparrows moving across the field, all at once. The challenge was to hit the center sparrow with a flaming arrow. This particular target was more difficult than anything ever used at the games before. The shot needed to be executed perfectly, because if the flaming arrow was even an inch off, it would light one of the outside wooden sparrows on fire. The final target was a long distance shot, a single circular piece of wood propped up. If somebody won the first two rounds, they would be declared the winner. But if it was a split, then it would go down to the final tiebreaker, with the shot taken from an impossible distance away. Most people trying this shot wouldn't even be able to land an arrow within twenty feet of the target, much less hit a bullseye. If necessary, it would prove to be a very interesting tiebreaker.

When it was time to begin, all of the onlookers were seated on the grass, off to the sides of both Yvonne and Sir Rackley. A silver coin was flipped, which determined that Sir Rackley would go first in rounds one and three, with Yvonne going first in round two. Sir Rackley stepped up to the line with his first arrow, as he prepared to shoot for the Prince Agis grapefruit. He pulled the arrow back tight, standing motionless for two minutes. When the wind died down to nothing and every muscle in his body felt just right, he fired away. It was not the perfect shot he was looking for. The crowd gasped, realizing he hit the Prince Agis grapefruit above the nose, instead of directly into the nose. Sir Rackley tossed his bow away in disgust, disappointed he allowed his nerves to get the better of him in this shot. Now it was up to Yvonne. If she could control her nerves, this would be a relatively easy shot for her and an easy round to win. She calmly picked up her bow, pulled an arrow back, and let it go. It was a perfect shot, right through the nose of the Prince Agis likeness. Yvonne smiled, as everyone applauded her excellent shot.

The second round soon began, with Yvonne having to step back up and take another shot. In her whole life, she had never shot a flaming arrow, so this was going to truly test her. The arrow was lit and the wooden sparrows began moving across the field by way of the pulley system. Yvonne carefully aimed and fired. She thought it was another perfect shot, but it must have been slightly off, because even though she hit the middle sparrow, two sparrows caught on fire. She set down her bow, wondering if Sir Rackley would be able to avoid lighting two sparrows, which would give him the victory in this round. That was exactly what happened. Sir Rackley fired his shot, and only the middle sparrow caught on fire. Just like that, this competition was headed for the third round, the tiebreaker. Yvonne was glad that she would be going last, because it would put the pressure back on Sir Rackley. This time, Sir Rackley steadied his bow and arrow for over five minutes, staring far off into the distance at the standing target. When everything felt right to him, he finally fired the arrow. It looped up into the sky before sailing back down and landing on the target. Sir Rackley caught the edge of the bullseye, which was not a bad shot, but at the same time, possibly not good enough to win. The whole competition now rested on Yvonne's shoulders. She would win it, or lose it, with her last shot. And she was not about to let Sir Rackley win this one. She needed to win it, because she wanted to ask Sir Rackley to help her with the biggest problem in her life. Like Sir Rackley, she stood still for over five minutes, and then she let her arrow fly. Her shot also went briefly up into the air before heading back down towards the target. She hit the target, right on the edge of the bullseye, but on the opposite side of Sir Rackley's arrow. From this distance, it was too far away to declare a winner. Everyone stood up at once, running as fast as they could towards the target to find out who had won. When everyone gathered around, the winning arrow became evident, just barely. It was Sir Rackley's arrow. It was ever so slightly closer than Yvonne's was. Yvonne turned to him and congratulated him on winning the match. He held his hands up in the air, looking around at the crowd as they cheered his name. Yvonne was disappointed, but she was glad to see Sir Rackley enjoying his moment so much, because he was obviously very competitive.

When the celebration died down, Sir Rackley went over and thanked Yvonne for a great match. He told her, "You are a great archer, Yvonne. I think you would have beaten any native born Astorian, even royal archers, with the way you shot today."

"Thanks, Sir Rackley. You're very kind," she replied to him.

"Well, it looks like I get to choose your work assignment, since I won," he added.

"Yes, that was our deal. So, are you going to take me off the animal detail?" she asked.

"Actually, I'm going to keep you right where you are, because I can see how much you and the princess enjoy working together."

"Oh, you're so sweet, Sir Rackley. Thank you," Yvonne said.

"Wait, there's more. Even though I won, I am going to grant you what you wanted as your prize, if you had won. You told me that you wanted some help with something important to you. Let's sit down here, so you can tell me more."

"Really?" Yvonne said, with surprise. "You are such a nice person." After sitting down and gathering her thoughts, she explained, "You know my best friend Stefan. He's the one who has been giving me the grief. It's not anything specific he did. It has to do with my feelings for him. I have been in love with him for quite some time now, but he only views me as a friend. Over and over, I have tried dropping hints, but he never recognizes them for what they really are. I would like him to know that I truly love him, and that my feelings for him are genuine and deep. And if he would only give me the chance, I could make him the happiest boy in Astoria."

"Wow, I never could have imagined this would be the problem," Sir Rackley said. "So, what exactly do you want me to do?"

"Sir Rackley, I know you don't see him that often, but with the princess and I both here, I think it is likely he will come by sometime soon. When he does, or whenever the next time you see him is, all I ask is for you take him aside and explain to him how I feel about him. As you know, in our land it is not the custom for a girl to take the initiative with these things. It would seem very strange. That's why I need someone like you, who can convey my feelings and romantic interest."

"Of course I will do that for you, Yvonne," Sir Rackley said. "Hopefully, I will see him soon, so that I can try my very best to help you out. You are a lovely girl. I feel that it would be an honor to do this for you." Sir Rackley had more to say, but he noticed a commotion was going on over near the spot where he had been firing his arrows from. He stood up, shocked to see two rebel soldiers on his property, without permission. They were walking over towards the grapefruit targets. When they reached the spot, one of the rebel soldiers was so angry about seeing the face of Prince Agis with an arrow through it that he pulled out his sword and slashed the grapefruit in half. Sir Rackley left Yvonne and jogged over to where the rebel soldiers were, fearing for the safety of the princess.

Sir Rackley decided the best tactic in dealing with the unwelcome visitors would be to take a strong-handed approach with them. "Hey, you two!" he shouted at the rebels. "What do you think you're doing? You're not welcome on my property." The two rebels turned around to confront him. Seeing that he was unarmed, the rebel who had withdrawn his sword put it back away.

"We are welcome anywhere in Astoria," one of the rebels said. "The entire land is the property of Prince Agis."

The other rebel gave Sir Rackley an angry stare, then added, "And it appears that you, and those who work for you, don't have the proper respect for Prince Agis. What is the meaning of these arrows sticking through a picture of his face? Are you threatening to bring him harm?" Sir Rackley wasn't sure what to say to this, but he had to explain things the best he could. He was also hoping to delay the rebel soldiers a little bit, while all of the workers, including the princess, left to get back to work.

"We meant no disrespect for Prince Agis. As you may be aware, I am not a citizen of Astoria. I am the son of a king. It is my father who rules the land of Limekiln, which shares Astoria's border. We were simply doing some target practice out here today."

Upon hearing this, one of the rebels argued a point. "Perhaps you were doing target practice in preparation for an assault on the castle. Or maybe you are planning an assassination attempt on the life of Prince Agis."

"Not at all," Sir Rackley said. "Nobody here has ever been involved in any type of fighting. It is not my concern who rules this land. What you have found today is simply the workers having a little fun, that's all."

"We will see about that," one of the rebels stated. "Before we leave, we are going to walk around and check out all of your workers, to make sure none of them are involved in anything which would threaten Prince Agis."

"As you wish," Sir Rackley said. "But please carry out your investigation quickly. I do not want my workers to be disturbed for any longer than it is necessary."

The two rebel soldiers began walking around the estate of Sir Rackley, carefully looking over every worker. They would stand and watch each person for a few minutes, before moving on. Near the end of their search, the two rebels came to the wild boars pen, where Princess Stasia and Yvonne were working. The peasant girls were carrying buckets of boar feed over to the fence and then pouring it through a small opening into food containers. The princess really fit the part of a peasant girl, being dirty, wearing worn out clothes, and working hard. One of the rebels walked over to get a closer look at her. From a distance, the rebel thought she looked a little familiar, but he couldn't figure out where he had previously seen the face of the dark haired girl. He decided to speak to her, saying, "Peasant girl, how long have you worked here?" Princess Stasia stopped working and looked up at him, starting to get nervous.

"I have worked here for the past year, sir," she replied to him. The rebel soldier decided to test her, upon hearing this. He ordered her to prove her statement, by going inside the wild boars pen and catching one of the boars with a rope. Yvonne gave the princess a rope, which she took with her, walking towards the gate. Stasia had no idea how she was going to catch one of the wild boars. She did her best to make a loop with the rope, opened the gate, and went inside. After she shut it behind her, she went chasing after one of the wild boars. Yvonne couldn't help laughing, as she watched the princess running through the mud, chasing after the boar. The boar was making all kinds of noise as it ran away. The princess threw the looped rope toward the boar's head, but it missed completely. The boar then changed direction and came running right at her. Stasia panicked and dove out of the way, to her side. She landed face down in the mud. Stasia lifted up her head, and she was completely covered, from the top of her head down to her neck, with dirty mud. She spit some mud out of her mouth that she had almost swallowed. The two rebels began laughing uncontrollably, seeing this. One of them fell down to his knees, almost crying at the sight. After they regained their composure, one of the rebels spoke to Stasia.

"Thanks for the entertainment, peasant girl. I guess our search of Sir Rackley's estate wasn't fruitless, after all." The two rebels turned around, as they headed off to leave Sir Rackley's country estate. The princess looked over at Yvonne, who had also been laughing. When Yvonne saw the princess glaring at her, she quickly stopped, and apologized for thinking it was funny.

During those same three weeks, Sebastian spent a lot of time getting to know his long lost family. He came over for more meals, brought gifts to his parents, and tried to get to know Stefan as well as he could.

On the same day of the archery contest between Sir Rackley and Yvonne, some time was set aside for special bonding between Sebastian and Stefan. They both took the day off from work so they could go fishing together. As they rode their horses towards the Lower Norwalk River, Sebastian felt great inside. He really cared about his family members and could see they cared about him. Stefan never turned down an offer from Sebastian, always being willing to do whatever he asked. As they arrived at the river, they both tied up their horses and carried their fishing sticks and handmade nets toward the water. They walked along the bank for a short distance until they found the perfect spot. As they began fishing, Sebastian had some things that he wanted to talk to his brother about. "Stefan, it is great to be here with you today, fishing," Sebastian said.

"It makes me happy, too," Stefan replied.

"You know, your parents, or I should say, our parents, have been treating me so well," Sebastian continued. "I have never felt so loved or valued in my entire life, even while my adopted father Robbins was raising me."

"Our parents truly care for you," Stefan explained. "They recognize that you are their son. Though they have not seen you for a long time, they never stopped loving you. And it is the same for me. Though you were kidnapped before I could even understand what happened, I've always reserved a special place in my heart, hoping this day would come. And now, you have filled that place, my brother." Although Stefan was still trying to build up trust in Sebastian, he meant what he said. He was not saying these things to try to use Sebastian's feelings to his advantage.

"Thank you, your thoughts really bring me happiness," Sebastian told him. "That reminds me, I have put together a special gift for our parents, back at the castle. I have loaded up a cart full of all kinds of fruits and vegetables. Perhaps, after work tomorrow, you could pull it home with you, behind your horse." Taking something out of his pocket, Sebastian handed it to Stefan and continued. "You will need this written authorization to take the cart of produce off the castle grounds. Show it to the rebel soldiers on the way out, and you won't have any problems." Sebastian then began talking to Stefan about another subject, the castle prison. "Stefan, it is great that we are able to work together in running the prison. I am going to need your help, though, because I have been overextending myself, lately. Would you mind taking on a heavier work load at the castle prison?"

"I would be happy to, my brother," Stefan replied, as he pulled a fish out of the water that he caught.

"That's great to hear, and just in time. Tomorrow night is Prince Agis' celebration feast for all of the rebels, on the castle grounds. I would like to spend some time with my comrades, enjoying some wine and alcohol. If you think you could handle it, I would like to entrust you with the watch of the king and queen for a few hours. What do you say?" Stefan was caught by surprise, hearing this. He didn't realize how quickly he had won the complete confidence of Sebastian. And, hearing that there was going to be a rebel celebration involving alcohol, this sounded like it would be the perfect opportunity to get the king and queen out of the prison and off the castle grounds. If he was going to do this, he would have to do it tomorrow night.

"Sure, I will do whatever you need," Stefan told him. As the two continued fishing, Stefan tried to figure out a plan. At the same time, he tried to figure out how he would ever get the courage to betray his own brother, somebody who openly showed such affection for him. It was not going to be easy. In fact, betraying Sebastian would probably be even harder for him than helping the king and queen escape from the prison.

The next evening, Sebastian was reviewing some last minute details with Stefan, before he left for Prince Agis' celebration feast. "There shouldn't be a whole lot for you to do tonight," Sebastian told Stefan. "We will still have our two rebel soldiers posted outside of the prison, at the top of the stairway. So, you don't have to worry about anybody who does not belong getting in here. If you have any problems, run outside and ask one of them to give you a hand. Go ahead and feed the prisoners dinner, according to their usual schedule. I will check in with you in about two hours. Well, that's it. Thank you for doing this Stefan. You've been so good to me."

"It's no problem," Stefan said. With that, Sebastian left him there alone, going outside to join in the celebration. On the castle grounds, Prince Agis had arranged for a massive feast and party. All of the rebel soldiers were out on the grounds, with their friends and supporters.

The lamp torches were lit, all across the grounds, and music was being played by a group of conscripted musicians. It was a festive atmosphere, unlike any other that Sebastian had ever seen. Sebastian saw Robbins talking with a few rebels, so he went over to visit with him.

"Sebastian, my son," Robbins said, when he saw him. "I haven't talked to you this week. How have you been?"

"Please don't call me your son, anymore," Sebastian said. "We both know the truth about the matter. And while I appreciate how you have been mostly good to me, while raising me, it doesn't change what was done fifteen years ago."

"Sebastian, this is no time to be holding petty grudges," Robbins responded. "Tonight is a beautiful, moonlit night, the grandest this land has ever seen. Come, let's get some wine." Sebastian followed Robbins, saying nothing more, not wanting to ruin the mood of the night.

Fifteen minutes after Sebastian left, Stefan went into the prison interior. He first stopped and loaded up some food onto his push cart. It was for the sake of appearances, in case some unexpected rebel soldiers dropped by to see what he was doing. He pushed the cart all the way through the three locked doors, into the very back of the prison. Stopping outside of the king and queen's prison cell, Stefan was shaking. He was about to do something which there would be no going back from. And no matter what the final result was, Stefan would come out a loser in the end. If he was caught trying to help the king and queen escape, he would be thrown into prison with them. If he was successful, he would destroy Sebastian emotionally. Stefan knew that he would probably never be able to speak to Sebastian again. It was cruel, but there was nothing Stefan could do about it. He tried to focus on the bigger picture, that of helping the king and queen escape, which would enable them to figure out a way to take back the castle. There was nothing more to think about, so Stefan put the keys into the door and opened it, accepting full responsibility for whatever would happen next.

The king and queen were sitting on the ground inside, doing nothing. They barely took notice of Stefan as he pushed the cart of food inside. The king looked up only when Stefan closed the door most of the way behind him. Stefan turned to them, saying in a hushed voice, "King Charles and Queen Delphine, I am here to help you escape." Hearing his words, the king was energized and jumped up. He hurried over and took the queen's right hand, pulling her up to a standing position.

The king asked Stefan, "How are you going to help us escape? Are there not rebel soldiers on guard, everywhere?"

"Yes," Stefan answered, "but tonight is the best opportunity we will have in a long time. Prince Agis is throwing a huge party on the castle grounds to celebrate his greatness. Most of the rebels will probably be drinking vast amounts of alcohol, which we can use to our advantage. I can get us safely to the western part of the castle, into the clothing and laundering room, without encountering any rebels. And I can get us from the stables to the outside, I think. The only risky part is going to be getting from the laundering room to the stables."

"That's not a very far distance," the king remarked. "Even so, I would feel better if we had a little more help. Do you know where the royal knight Mathieu is being held?"

"Yes, I do," Stefan said. "He is being held at the end of this hallway. But, there is no way I can help more than two people escape. There simply isn't room in the hiding place I have set up."

"That's okay. Let's still get him," the king directed. "He will be able to help us get through the castle, and then he can take his chances on his own." Stefan led the king and queen out of their cell and down the hall to where Mathieu and the jailer Bailey were locked up. Stefan unlocked the door, leading all three inside. Mathieu's grim mood changed immediately upon seeing the king and queen come into his cell. Everything was explained to him, and he agreed to do his part to help them. Bailey was willing to come also, glad to be out of the prison and hoping to be of assistance.

After being told of the limited hiding spots, Mathieu told the king, "It is not my place to leave right now, anyhow. I would rather go visit with my family, if they are still here and I can get to them. Don't worry, I can find my own way off the castle grounds, if I really need to." Before leaving the prison interior, Mathieu wanted all of the cells to be locked back up, leaving the food cart in the room which had held the king and queen. That way, if anybody happened to walk by, nothing would look out of place. Stefan led the group past two locked doors and into the large hallway with the storage room and entrance to the secret tunnels. No rebel soldiers appeared on the way to the storage room, which was a big relief to Stefan. He pulled the planks off the wall in the storage room and lit two torches. Mathieu and the king each took one as they passed through the small opening into the tunnel. After everybody was inside, Stefan tried to block up the opening with the wooden planks. He wasn't able to do it perfectly, since he was inside, but he did the best he could. Stefan moved to the front again, leading the group straight through the passageways, making a few brief turns at junctions. Soon, the group reached the dead end at the clothing and laundering room.

Prince Agis was outside on the Castle Terrace at that very moment, giving a half-sober speech to the rebels and their supporters. Holding up a large glass of wine, Prince Agis built on what he had been saying. "So, my fellow rebel soldiers, this is our night. I have led us to victory and change, here in our land. The princess is probably hiding in a cave somewhere, even as I speak, living like an animal and drinking river water. Meanwhile, we drink wine!" Upon hearing this, the rebels all shouted and laughed, making fun of the princess.

Mathieu stepped forward, trying to see through the planks covering the wall. The room appeared to be dark, with nobody working inside. He put his ear up to the boards and listened for two minutes, before deciding it was clear. When pushing gently didn't get him anywhere, Mathieu used a little more force. Finally, one of the planks budged. There seemed to be something blocking the planks from pushing all the way out, like a piece of furniture. Mathieu asked Bailey for help, and they pushed as hard as they could on the loose plank. Slowly, the object that was propped up against the opening, pushed forward, causing the plank to fall to the ground. It made a fair bit of noise, so Mathieu and Bailey froze in place, listening once again. Nobody came, so they took two more planks off, enabling Mathieu to get out of the opening and into the room. A torch was passed out to him, and he could see that it was a sink that had been blocking their progress. Mathieu helped the other four out, and soon all were in the clothing and laundering room. They quickly covered the entrance hole back up and pushed the sink against the wall, to erase any evidence of how they had gotten inside. Spotting some rebel soldier uniforms hanging in the room, Mathieu and the jailer changed out of their prison clothing and put the uniforms on. "It's time to beat the rebels at their own game," Mathieu told the others, as he put on his new outfit. Inside the castle it was very quiet, but Mathieu could hear the faint sounds of music and voices, coming from outside of the castle. Mathieu decided it would be better to continue on without the torches, because they were too risky to use. The torches were extinguished, and Mathieu led everyone out into the hallway. The quickest way to get to the stables from here would be to cut through the Royal Gardens. So, Mathieu led them down several hallways and out one of the entrance doors, into the Royal Gardens. As the queen walked across the grass and past all of the flowers, she reflected back on all the memories that she had shared here, raising Princess Stasia. This was Stasia's favorite place to hang out when she was little, often times playing with her pet rabbit Mandy. As the group of five reached the halfway point of the Royal Gardens on their way to the other open door, they received a shock. Two rebel soldiers were inside the hallway they were headed for and walked past the open door. They happened to glance through and see the group walking towards them. With abundant moonlight shining, the two rebels could see that the king and queen were among the group of people. Immediately, they withdrew their swords and charged through the door towards Mathieu, who was at the front.

Chapter Sixteen:

Reunited With Her Family

The king and queen almost turned to run for it when they saw the rebel soldiers charging them. Though their group outnumbered the approaching rebels by five to two, they had no weapons to defend themselves with. They would be no match for two trained sword fighters. Resisting their initial fear, everyone decided to follow the lead of Mathieu, to see how he would handle the situation.

Mathieu decided it was not a good idea to fight, so he tried to use the rebel soldier uniforms that he and Bailey were wearing to their advantage. Just before the rebels reached where they were standing, outside in the Royal Gardens, Mathieu spoke authoritatively, saying, "Halt! We have the situation completely under control here." The two rebel soldiers slowed down and looked at each other, trying to figure out what was going on. They could see that the king and queen were among the group of five, but they couldn't figure out what they were doing out of their prison cells. Also, they didn't recognize Mathieu and Bailey, who were dressed up as rebel soldiers. One of the genuine rebels decided to ask Mathieu to explain the situation.

"Why have you taken the king and queen out of their prison cell?" he asked Mathieu.

"Haven't you heard?" Mathieu replied. "Prince Agis ordered them to be brought out tonight, so he could publicly humiliate them in front of all of us and our supporters. It's going to be a great moment. I can't wait to see what he is going to do." Upon hearing this, the two rebel soldiers again exchanged glances. Finally, one of the rebels spoke up again, as he put away his sword.

"What a great idea! No, we had not heard about this, but obviously you couldn't have taken the king and queen out of their cells without the permission of Prince Agis. I don't know what we were thinking, charging out here with our swords drawn. You won't tell Prince Agis about this, will you?" Mathieu assured them both that he would not and told them that he appreciated their alertness on the job. The rebel soldier then thought of an idea, so he asked, "Could you wait here for a moment? I have an idea which will help us all get into the spirit of the night." Mathieu agreed to wait, wondering what kind of idea the rebel had, but also slightly worried that he was leaving to get help. A minute after he left, though, the rebel soldier reappeared at the door, carrying into the Royal Gardens a barrel of wine. When he was at the place where Mathieu was standing, he set the barrel down and loosened the top, using his sword. Watching the rebel closely, Mathieu's curiosity soon turned to anger as the rebel picked up the open barrel of wine and dumped it over the head of the king. The king was completely drenched with red wine, as it soaked into his hair, beard, and upper prison garments. The king displayed a lot of self-control, because he didn't say anything or retaliate in return. When he was done, the rebel and his fellow soldier both started laughing hysterically. Soon, Mathieu and Bailey joined in with them, pretending to laugh as hard as they could. After a few minutes, the two rebel soldiers finally left, laughing as they walked away, and turning back to mock the king and queen.

After they were gone, Mathieu turned to the king and apologized, saying, "Sorry, King Charles, we had no choice but to laugh along with them." The king put his right index finger on his face to wipe off some of the red wine. He then put his finger into his mouth, tasting it.

"Don't worry about it, Mathieu. It's actually nice to have a taste of wine after spending such a long time in prison, drinking only water. It's just a shame so much wine was wasted." The group was able to continue all the way out to the castle stables after that, without any more incidents. There weren't any rebel soldiers posted there, either, which surprised Mathieu.

When they were standing next to the stalls, Stefan explained the rest of his plan. His rebel boss in the castle prison had arranged for a cart of fruit and vegetables to be left at the stables, which was sitting in place, right where it was supposed to be. It was a large cart that needed to be pulled by a horse. His boss, Sebastian, had further given Stefan a written authorization to drive the cart off of the castle grounds, which meant he wouldn't be searched, even if he was stopped. The plan was to remove some of the produce, which would allow for the king and queen to hide at the bottom of the cart. When they were safely in there, the produce would be put back in the cart, filling it up as high as possible. Stefan would then pull the cart behind his horse, right past the rebels and away from the castle. Mathieu agreed that it was an excellent plan, seemingly flawless. Mathieu asked Stefan if he could pull the cart across the servants' bridge, which would be a lot easier and less noticeable. Stefan replied that the servants' bridge had been broken and rendered unusable, ever since the rebel takeover. As the other four began removing some of the fruits and vegetables, Stefan went to get a horse to pull the cart with. But he didn't get just any horse. He took out the white horse Isobel. Stefan knew he would be taking a slight chance in doing this, but if he managed to pull it off, he would win even more favor with Princess Stasia. It was a risk he was willing to take, especially knowing it would further anger Prince Agis when he found out about it. As Stefan walked Isobel out towards the cart, the king noticed what he was doing. "Are you sure that's a good idea, to take Isobel?" the king asked him.

"Yes, for several reasons," Stefan explained. "Isobel is a lot stronger than my own horse, which will be very important later. Also, I don't want Prince Agis to take out his anger on her, when he finds out you two are gone. And finally, it will be a further embarrassment to him."

"I can't argue with that," the king said, smiling at Stefan. Soon, the work was finished and the king and queen climbed into the cart, laying down on the bottom. After making sure to keep a small path clear to the sides for breathing space, a cloth tarp was thrown over them. Then, apples, oranges, pears, lemons, and many other fruits and vegetables were loaded back into the cart, until it was almost full.

"Are you okay in there?" Mathieu asked the king and queen.

"Yes, I am fine," the queen said.

"Me, too. Let's get out of here," the king added.

"All right then, have a safe trip. I will try my best to join you all at Sir Rackley's, after I visit with my family." Mathieu and Bailey said goodbye to Stefan, thanking him for all of his help, and turned to walk back into the castle, heading for the eastern side.

Stefan climbed up onto the back of Isobel, slowly urging the horse forward. The cart was attached to the extended saddle and it moved forward, following the horse smoothly. Instead of being frightened over the possibility of getting caught, Stefan was enjoying this. He had always wanted to ride Isobel, the prized possession of Princess Stasia. And now he was getting the chance. More than that, he was very close to getting off the castle grounds and reuniting the princess with her family and her horse. Stefan rode Isobel through the opened stables gate and started to cross the great lawn. There were pockets of rebel soldiers standing, sitting, and lying around everywhere. Some of them were passed out, obviously from overdrinking alcohol. A few of the rebel soldiers looked at him as he drove the cart by, but they didn't say anything. He made it all the way to the entrance gate of the castle before a rebel soldier finally stopped him. "Stop right there, peasant boy," the rebel directed him. "Where do you think you're going with all of this fruit?" Stefan explained to the rebel that he was taking the fruit to family members of Sebastian's, who lived outside of the castle. He handed the rebel the written authorization which Sebastian had given him. The rebel looked at it and took it over to another rebel who was standing nearby. They both consulted for a minute, before waving Stefan through. He was now free to cross the main drawbridge and exit the castle grounds. When he was halfway across, one of the rebels ran back up to him, to ask a question. "Is this not the horse that was owned by the princess?" he wanted to know.

Stefan didn't waste a moment, he was prepared for this question. "Yes, it was. But Prince Agis has ordered this horse to be taken to the village of Norwalk, to be auctioned off to the highest bidder next week." The rebel let Stefan go, not questioning him any further. As Stefan crossed the rest of the drawbridge and began riding a little faster across the main dirt road to Norwalk, he knew it. He knew that he was in the clear, having accomplished an unthinkable feat for a peasant boy. Stefan had helped King Charles, Queen Delphine, and Isobel the horse, escape from the castle grounds. Even more, he had perhaps opened the way for Mathieu and Bailey to also escape. It was going to be a long night of riding through the forest, but when they reached Sir Rackley's country estate, he would make the princess the happiest girl in the world. At the same time, this would all come at a high price. He would gravely hurt his brother Sebastian, causing tremendous pain and suffering to be brought upon him. Stefan was bothered by that thought, as he rounded a bend in the road, finally out of view of the castle. He stopped Isobel there and disconnected the cart from the horse. Using his hands and arms, he began scooping as many fruits and vegetables out of the cart as he could. It wasn't long before the dirt road was covered with produce, and the king and queen were able to climb out of their hiding spots.

"Now I see why you wanted to bring Isobel," the king said to Stefan. "There are three of us and only one horse. Isobel is strong, but we can't make her carry all three of us, all night. We will ride her for an hour or so, into the forest. Then, you and I should take turns running alongside Isobel."

"Sure, that will be fine," Stefan said. "A few weeks ago, I followed the princess into this forest for an hour, towards Sir Rackley's estate. But the weather conditions were bad and I turned back after a while. Can you navigate your way through here?"

Looking up at the sky, the king replied, "I should be able to lead us directly there, with this bright, moonlit night." All three climbed on Isobel, no doubt causing the horse some discomfort, as they headed off into the forest.

After seeing off Stefan, the king, and the queen, Mathieu and Bailey made their way through the castle. They only encountered one rebel soldier as they passed through The Gateway into the eastern side of the castle. He didn't question them, seeing that they were dressed in rebel uniforms and had beards like many of the rebels. Mathieu soon knocked at the old door to his room, hoping his wife and daughter would be inside. Nobody answered, so he knocked again. He started to walk away, but turned back when he heard the door slowly open. It was Madison, looking out at him, nervously. She almost closed the door in his face as he ran back towards her, but stopped when she realized it was her father dressed in a rebel uniform. When he reached the door, she jumped into his arms, hugging him. He carried her inside and closed the door behind them, locking it. Soon, Mathieu's wife came into the entrance area to see what was going on. She was so happy to see Mathieu that she went over and made it a group hug. After a few minutes, Mathieu explained to them everything that had happened. He told them that he could only risk staying for one hour, before he needed to leave.

"But, father, I just got you back. I don't want you to leave me," Madison pleaded with him, tears forming in her eyes.

"I know, and I'm sorry," he said to her. "But this is the first place the rebels will come looking when they realize I have escaped from prison. You will need to convince them that you haven't heard from me, telling them that I did not stop by here tonight. The king and queen have also escaped. I need to join them at our meeting point, so we can all make preparations to take back the castle."

"Do you really think that is possible?" Mathieu's wife asked him.

"Not only do I think it's possible, I think it will become a reality," Mathieu assured her. "The entire royal family will be gathered together at our meeting point, hopefully along with some royal guards. It won't be easy, but if we can get the will of the people behind us, we will have success." After the hour was up, Mathieu asked his family if they knew where Delia was living.

"Why, she's here in this side of the castle," Madison told him. "She moved out of the western side a few days after the overthrow, into a room a few doors down from us. Prince Agis is having her teach our class, which now is made up of mostly rebel youths." Mathieu said goodbye to his family, which was a difficult moment for all of them. But, it had to be this way, at least for now. After closing the door, Mathieu stopped at Delia's room and knocked.

Delia opened up her door, trying to figure out who was standing there. She realized it was Mathieu and came out to give him a hug. "How in the world did you escape from the prison?" Delia asked him.

"I have no time to explain now, but know this. The king and queen have also escaped. They are on their way to meet up with the princess, to organize a revolution. We will all return here as soon as we can figure out a way to take back the castle. Please watch over my daughter Madison for me. I spent the last few weeks in prison, doing nothing but thinking and worrying about her."

"You have my word. I will watch over her with my life," Delia promised him. Mathieu then left to meet up with Bailey.

Mathieu and Bailey both walked back to the stables, still wearing their rebel soldier uniforms. They again didn't have a problem getting there, encountering only the same lone soldier from before. Quickly, they took out two horses and started riding them off towards the castle entrance. By now, more and more rebels were crashed out, asleep on the ground. Mathieu and Bailey made it all the way to the entrance gate, where they spotted someone who made them really nervous. General Robbins was talking with the two soldiers on duty, discussing a matter with them. Mathieu tried to look down as he was riding by, knowing that if Robbins spotted him, it would be all over. Robbins knew the face of both Mathieu and Bailey, having visited them several times in prison to interrogate them. They were almost past Robbins before he glanced up and recognized them. "What is going on here?" Robbins exclaimed. "Somebody, stop them! They have escaped from the prison!" Robbins started yelling very loud, getting the attention of all the rebel soldiers in the area, and even the rebel soldiers who were manning the lookout towers. But, Mathieu and Bailey were on horseback, giving them a distinct advantage. They just finishing crossing the drawbridge, when tragedy struck. Out of nowhere, a rebel soldier jumped toward Bailey, pulling him down off his horse. He must have been outside of the castle walls when he heard Robbins screaming. The two rolled in the dirt before coming to a stop, with the rebel soldier holding him down in place. Mathieu saw this and turned back to try to help the jailer. Suddenly, he felt a sharp pain in his lower leg. Looking down, he saw that an arrow had been fired into his leg, probably from one of the lookout towers. Before anything worse happened, Mathieu turned his horse back around and rode away from the castle as fast as he possibly could. There was nothing more he could do to help Bailey, without seriously jeopardizing his own life. When he was far enough away, Mathieu looked back to see Bailey being taken into custody. He didn't watch for long, because he knew that rebel soldiers on horseback were likely to be chasing after him. He rode off in the opposite direction that Stefan had, taking the direct route to Sir Rackley's estate. After a while, he dared to stop for a minute. With intense pain rushing through his entire body, Mathieu pulled the arrow out of his leg, throwing it into the bushes. He was bleeding, which wasn't good, because it would leave a trail for the rebels to follow later. But he needed to keep riding, so he could get to Sir Rackley's and have his wounds treated. Two hours later, he could go no further. With his leg constantly being shaken by the galloping, the bleeding wouldn't stop. After he crossed a bridge over a small stream, he directed his horse off the main road and into some brush. He tied it up there and put his leg into the cold water. After washing out the wound, Mathieu tried to bind it by tearing off strips of cloth from his uniform and wrapping them around his leg. Finally, he laid down next to the water and immediately fell asleep.

After Bailey was taken into custody, he was knocked around by some of the rebel soldiers, who were trying to get him to talk. As soon as word reached Prince Agis of the incident, he hurried over to the main entrance to investigate. Sebastian had been celebrating with him, so he followed right behind. When Prince Agis and Sebastian arrived there, a horrible fear and realization started to come over Sebastian. He recognized the jailer at once, realizing he must have escaped from the castle prison. But that wouldn't have been possible without either Stefan's help, or if somebody had hurt Stefan to break the jailer out. Robbins looked at them both, clearly agitated, and said, "I have terrible news, Prince Agis. We captured this prisoner trying to get away, but Mathieu escaped by horseback. One of our rebel soldiers hit him with an arrow, but I doubt his wounds are life threatening." Hearing this absolutely enraged Prince Agis, causing him to scream out in anger. When his thoughts became clearer, he looked at Sebastian and demanded an explanation.

"Sebastian, I am holding you personally accountable for this," Prince Agis said to him. "It was your responsibility to watch over the prisoners and manage the staff. You better have a good explanation as to why you were with me, and not on duty." Sebastian thought about his options. At this point, there's wasn't much he could do or say.

"Prince Agis, my master," he said, "I don't know how those two prisoners could have broken out. There was a trustworthy worker watching all of the prisoners. Something must have happened to him. Perhaps some royal guards snuck onto the castle grounds while we were celebrating and overpowered him and the two guards who were stationed out front."

"Whatever happened, your life and career are on the line here," Prince Agis said, making the consequences clear. "If anybody else is missing from their prison cells, like say, the king and queen, you will take their place in prison, for the rest of your days." Sebastian shuddered when he heard this and looked over at Robbins. Robbins glared back at him, not giving him any visible support. The three walked over towards the castle prison, while several rebel soldiers led the jailer back to his prison cell, behind them. Two rebel soldiers were still on guard at the top of the stairs. They reported to Prince Agis that nobody had walked past them, either into or out of the prison, during the entire night. Sebastian started to get a sinking feeling regarding what probably happened.

Walking down the stairs and into the prison, the place felt like it was vacant. Stefan was nowhere to be found. Sebastian lit a torch and used his keys to open the locked doors, leading the group through the hallways into the prison interior. The moment of truth was fast approaching, with Sebastian's fate resting behind the locked cell door of the king and queen. Turning his keys to open it, Prince Agis, Sebastian, and Robbins went inside. Nobody was in there. All that was inside was a food cart, which revealed what had happened. Prince Agis turned to Sebastian, digging his hands into Sebastian's shoulders. Prince Agis pushed him back hard against the prison wall, almost knocking him unconscious. "Your life is over, young man," Prince Agis shouted in his face, with spit flying everywhere. "You were given one simple assignment, keep the prisoners in the prison. But you couldn't do it. You wanted to come outside and celebrate, passing your responsibility off to a worker who was obviously loyal to King Charles." Prince Agis took Sebastian's keys and threw him onto the ground, before turning to walk out of the prison cell.

As Robbins started to follow him out, he told Sebastian, "Son, you brought this upon yourself. There's nothing I can do for you." The door was locked behind them, leaving Sebastian alone and in the dark.

In a matter of minutes, Sebastian went from being one of the top rebel soldiers, probably nearing the rank of general, to becoming a lifetime prisoner, at best. He was completely devastated by the series of events that had happened. The worst thing about it all was how he was utterly betrayed by his own brother Stefan. Sebastian trusted Stefan with all that was dear to him, but Stefan ended up using his feelings against him. Obviously, Stefan was lying to him all along, pretending to care for him. Stefan only wanted to build up enough confidence and trust so he could use it to his advantage. And what of Sebastian's parents? They were no doubt guilty as well, playing along the whole time, but not really caring for Sebastian. Sebastian didn't know how he was going to be able to continue living, knowing how badly his family had mistreated and hurt him. He did know one thing, though. He never wanted to see any of them, ever again. If he did, he would show them that he could be mean and inflict pain, as well. Sebastian hated them, all of them.

When Prince Agis and Robbins walked back outside, they again questioned the two rebel soldiers who were guarding the entrance. Both soldiers promised they did not leave their posts all night and had not seen anybody pass. Prince Agis didn't believe them, feeling certain they must have left their posts to get some wine. He ordered them to be taken into custody and placed in prison. They were screaming denials the whole way into the prison, but Prince Agis didn't want to hear it. They were pathetic excuses for rebel soldiers, and they were going to rot in prison for leaving their assigned places.

As the night turned into morning, the sun began rising over the hills, east of Sir Rackley's estate. The princess and Yvonne were walking off towards the gated area where the sheep were kept. One of the other workers was going to teach them how to remove wool from the sheep today. At Sir Rackley's estate, shearing was done twice per year: once in the spring, and once in the fall. The ewes and lambs that he owned

254

grew thick coats, which allowed for it. Also important was the moderate winter weather which this low elevation provided for every year. Princess Stasia was not looking forward to doing this. She asked Yvonne, "Aren't we going to hurt them by doing this? And what if I slip with the knife?"

Yvonne laughed, as she replied, "No, it doesn't hurt them at all, as long as you keep control of your blade. It's just like when we get our hair cut shorter. It doesn't hurt us at all."

"Okay, but I think I will watch and learn for a while," the princess added. They soon came up to the gated area and walked inside, where the worker had already started. Princess Stasia had learned to do a lot of things with her hands lately, but this was one she didn't care to be involved with.

When they were in the midst of doing their job, the princess looked over and spotted somebody running down the hill towards them, extremely fast. It was Sir Rackley, looking very excited. The princess grabbed Yvonne by the hand and pulled her out of the sheep pen, worried that rebel soldiers had arrived to once again search the place. Sir Rackley finally arrived at where they were standing, out of breath. He managed to say, "I have wonderful news, princess. Your parents are here." The princess screamed out with joy and started crying immediately. She could not believe what Sir Rackley just said. She didn't know how this was possible, but she followed Sir Rackley back up the hill, towards the estate house. It was true. She could see them now. They were standing next to her horse Isobel, and Stefan was there also. She ran up to them and hugged both of them at the same time. Yvonne caught up with her, and she went over to hug Stefan, overjoyed to see him. Stefan and Yvonne looked on happily as the princess was reunited with her family. After about ten minutes, the princess finally could speak. She told her parents, "Mother and father, I thought this day would never come. You are really here, standing next to me. Tell me, how did you ever get out of the castle prison and away from Prince Agis?"

King Charles looked over at Stefan, saying to his daughter, "You have your friend over there to thank for it. He was the one who made all of this possible. If it wasn't for him, we would still be locked up in prison, serving out our life sentences."

Princess Stasia let go of her parents and walked over to where Stefan and Yvonne were standing. She gave Stefan a long hug, and kissed him on the cheek. While she still had her arms wrapped around him, she said, "I cannot believe you were able to do this for me. You even were kind enough to bring back my horse with you. Thank you so, so much. I can never repay you for this unbelievable thing you have done. We will talk more later, after I have spent some time with my parents." The princess then asked everybody to meet back inside of Sir Rackley's estate house in one hour, to discuss things further. She walked off with her parents, wanting to spend some time alone with them. Stefan could hear them telling her about Mathieu's planned escape as they were walking away. When they asked her if Mathieu had arrived, she said that he had not, as of yet.

Stefan and Yvonne also walked off to spend some time together. Yvonne was both happy and relieved to see Stefan, as she had been worrying about him working at the castle with the rebels. "Tell me, Stefan," she asked, "how did you manage to get the king and queen out of there?"

"The best way to explain it," he answered, "is to say that I betrayed my brother."

"Your brother? Do you mean that literally?"

"Yes, Yvonne. I guess I have a lot to tell you about. It has only been a few weeks, but much has happened." Stefan went on to share the entire story with her. He told her about Sebastian turning out to be his long lost brother Lolek, about his expanded oversight at the castle prison, and ultimately, of his betrayal of Sebastian.

"What do you think will happen to him?" Yvonne wanted to know.

"I don't have any idea, but I fear for the worst. And I feel terrible about what I have done. There was just no other way to do it. In some ways, my actions are similar to what Prince Agis did to King Charles."

"Well, I understand how you feel, Stefan," Yvonne said, putting her arm across his shoulder. "And I am here to support you, if there is anything I can do for you. I am so pleased to see you. I don't want to ever lose you." Stefan looked over at Yvonne when she said this, thanking her. For the first time ever, the thought crossed his mind that she perhaps viewed him as more than just a friend. A moment later, he dismissed it, elated to be with his best friend.

Mathieu woke up, after having slept for the entire night on the bank of the river. He sat up on the ground, trying to figure out where he was. As he felt the pain coming from his leg, everything came back to him. He was riding away from the castle toward Sir Rackley's estate, when his wound kept getting worse. The constant shaking of the ride wouldn't allow the blood to clot, to stop the bleeding. Finally, he stopped and washed his leg off in the water of the stream, but passed out from a combination of pain and fatigue. Mathieu was relieved that no rebel soldiers followed him, because if they had, surely they would have found him by now. After untying his horse, he pulled himself back up onto it, riding away toward Sir Rackley's. When he reached Sir Rackley's, the servants hesitated to open the entrance gate for him, not wanting him to ride through. They saw the rebel clothing he was wearing, and although he tried to assure them that he was not a rebel soldier, they didn't believe him. Sir Rackley came down a few minutes later. He recognized Mathieu and ordered the gates to be opened for him. Sir Rackley told him that the king and queen had only arrived a few minutes earlier and were off visiting with the princess. He brought Mathieu inside and had one of his servants start working on his injury. "That was a close one," Sir Rackley said, as he looked at the wound. "If that arrow hit you a few feet higher, it probably would have killed you."

"I know it, believe me," Mathieu said. "It's a good thing I didn't make my wife a widow last night. I can't even bear the thought of her and Madison having to live without me."

About an hour later, everybody was together inside Sir Rackley's estate house, sitting around a lunch table. Mathieu and the king wanted to start discussing their strategy for taking back the castle, but the princess asked them politely to stop. "Please, I appreciate there is a lot of planning to do, but could we have this one meal together, without speaking of our problems? I promise that after lunch we can spend the rest of the day talking strategy if you would like, and planning out what we are going to do." All at the table agreed this was a good idea, so they spent the next hour enjoying a large meal, which Mathieu, King Charles, and Queen Delphine had not been able to have for many weeks, being locked up in prison. Stefan and Yvonne were also invited to the lunch feast, which they really appreciated. Everybody spent the time catching up, sharing the things they had been doing for the past few weeks. The princess told them all about her new job, pretending she was poor and working as a peasant girl. She even related to them the story about chasing the wild boar around, which caused hearty laughter at the table. Sir Rackley and Yvonne shared the story of their archery contest, which came down to the final shot. The king complimented Yvonne on almost being able to beat Sir Rackley. The king, queen, and Mathieu didn't share too much about their time in prison, not wanting to dampen the spirit of the princess, seeing how happy she was right now.

After lunch was finished, Princess Stasia asked for everybody to meet back in thirty minutes, to begin discussing plans to take back the castle. Not wanting to bring it up during the meal, Stefan asked Mathieu about Bailey's fate. "I have some bad news, Stefan," Mathieu told him. "Bailey was taken back into custody. I barely escaped with my life. I was shot with an arrow, right here." Mathieu pulled up the clean trousers he was now wearing, revealing a bandage covering a bad wound. "That's why it took me until this morning to get here," Mathieu added, "because I fell asleep by a stream last night. The pain was too much for my body, I guess."

Princess Stasia turned her attention to Stefan, saying, "Do you think we could have some time alone?"

"Of course, princess. That would be really nice," Stefan answered. The two walked away, headed outside, as Yvonne looked on. She couldn't help feeling a little jealous, seeing them together. The princess was the one girl who Stefan felt such great affection and love for. Even though it bothered Yvonne slightly, she was happy for Stefan. The princess obviously was very grateful for what he had done in rescuing her parents from the prison. She probably wanted to express her heartfelt thanks in person. Yvonne continued watching them until they walked out the back door, out of sight. She hoped that the princess would not reveal to him some of the personal things Yvonne confided in her. Yvonne was counting on Sir Rackley to do that, instead.

Princess Stasia and Stefan walked across the field, where the archery contest had taken place. The princess asked him, "Did you know that your friend Yvonne was so good at archery?"

"Yes, I have always known that," he replied. "She used to always make me go shooting with her. I think she never tired of beating me." They both laughed, thinking about this. When they arrived at the edge of the grass, they sat down in the shade of some trees to talk further.

"Stefan, like I said earlier, it is unbelievable that you were able to do this for me. When I sent you away with my request a few weeks back, I never dreamed you would show up one day with my parents. And I still can't get over the fact that you brought Isobel to me and helped Mathieu escape."

"Princess, it was truly an honor to do these things for you, to show my support and love for you," Stefan said.

"Thank you, my dear friend. You probably haven't forgotten that I made a promise to you, when I first sent you away," the princess told him.

"I haven't forgotten, princess. But I don't expect anything in return for what I have done. I did it for you, which already brings me great happiness."

"Please, Stefan, let me fulfill my promise to you. Otherwise, I will feel awful inside, as though I only take from you and never give anything back. Search your heart and tell me, what is it that you would like? I am willing to give you anything, as I told you before."

"If you must know, princess, then I will tell you," Stefan said, after hesitating. "It doesn't matter what I'm about to say, because you are engaged. The truth is, I have been in love with you for a long time. My one and only wish has always been to marry you. There is nothing else in this world that I want, only you."

Section 3

Happily Ever After

Forever it would be a night for the ages
To be remembered in the history pages
As they felt love and they shared laughter
Being together happily ever after

Chapter Seventeen:

Word Spread Through the Land

Despite being made aware of Stefan's feelings, the princess never expected this to be his request. She sat there silently for a few minutes, letting his words sink in. This was a complete surprise to her. She could tell that Stefan was nervously waiting to hear what she would say, as he looked down at his hands, playing with his fingers. Princess Stasia was not exactly sure how to reply, finally realizing she needed more time than just a few minutes to decide on a course of action. "Stefan, I am sorry for my silence. You kind of caught me by surprise."

"No, I am sorry, princess," Stefan said. "I shouldn't have revealed my feelings to you. It's not my place to speak that way to somebody who is engaged."

"Well, Stefan, while you were gone, Sir Rackley and I agreed to call off our engagement. But that does not mean I can just marry you, nor do I have the desire to marry anybody right now. There are more important matters to attend to in the land, as you are well aware. Let me ask you one thing regarding what you told me. Are you sure that I am the girl you really want in your heart? Might there be another?"

"Princess, there is no other," Stefan replied. "I am totally in love with you."

"I see," the princess said. "What I have promised you, I cannot take back. I asked you to risk your life for me and do the impossible, and you did it. If this is your one wish, to have my hand in marriage, then I will try my best to grant it, but at the appropriate time." The princess wanted to tell Stefan how Yvonne felt about him, but out of respect for

Yvonne's request, she didn't. She simply tried to guide Stefan to the answer, but Yvonne was right. Stefan could never see past the princess long enough to notice that Yvonne truly loved him. So, Princess Stasia acquiesced, realizing she had made a promise to the boy. The princess moved over closer to Stefan, wrapping her arms around him from behind, holding him. It was the best romantic gesture she could display towards him, and probably the only one for some time, in view of the revolution which would soon be organized. The two sat together under the trees, Stefan enjoying every second of it, until it was time to meet up with the others, back inside the estate house of Sir Rackley.

As they gathered around the table once again, Princess Stasia wanted to know what the wisest options were for taking back the castle. She asked King Charles and Mathieu to take the lead in this discussion. Mathieu began by outlining the first step in the whole process. "We need to organize a revolution. If we can gain the support of most of the citizens of Astoria, the rebels will be unable to deny the will of the people. All of us here today can have an important part in doing this. In two weeks time, we should be able to reach all of the people, in all of the villages. We should be able to spread the word all through the land. Princess, your biggest supporters in Astoria are the poor, lower class people. I recommend that we send Stefan and Yvonne as your representatives to them. Stefan is well known to poor people everywhere, being the person who you used to represent them at your coronation ceremony. Meanwhile, King Charles and Queen Delphine could focus on reaching the middle and upper class people, such as the wealthy landowners and noblemen. When King Charles was in power, he was able to build up fine relations with them for many years. Being one of the royal knights, I could first travel to Glaston to round up all of the royal guards who have been staying there at the guard station. Then, I could have all of the royal guards spread out throughout the countryside, to gather all of the other guards, trained archers, and sword fighters they can find. I would be able to join them in the search." When Mathieu was finished speaking, Sir Rackley raised his hand, having something important to ask.

"Mathieu, do you have an assignment I could do? I don't want to sit here idly at my estate. I want to be out there helping." Mathieu wasn't sure what to suggest, but the king thought of a great idea.

"I've got it, Sir Rackley," the king said. "If you are so inclined, why don't you and Princess Stasia travel to your homeland, to pay a visit to your parents? Explain the whole situation to them. If they wish to help us, the best thing they can do is send in some members of their army, perhaps even a few of their catapults and battering rams. We could also use a temporary bridge, to cross over the moat." Sir Rackley looked at Princess Stasia, to see what she thought of the suggestion.

"There is one thing you should know, father," the princess said to the king. "In view of the rebel overthrow, Sir Rackley and I are no longer engaged. That may have a bearing on whether or not his parents are willing to provide us with assistance."

"Well, it is still worth asking for," the king replied. "Sir Rackley's father and I have been close friends for many years, and I don't think he would cherish spending the rest of his life with Prince Agis in power right next to his border." King Charles next highlighted the key to ultimate success. "We need to capture Prince Agis, first and foremost. If you cut off the head, the rest will fall. He will be well protected, and we will need to get through the castle walls to reach him. But somehow we need to get him alone, away from the others."

"How can we do that, though, because the castle walls will be heavily guarded?" the queen asked.

"It will have to be by sheer numbers," Mathieu answered. "As we go out to all of the villages, we must instruct everybody to meet in two central locations, exactly two weeks from today. We will have one group meet in Glaston and one group meet at the Astorian Eagle Monument. Then, we will march on the castle from two different directions, completely surrounding it by four o'clock that evening. From there, we must find a way to either break down the walls, break down the entrance gate, or find another way inside. Stefan, regarding those secret tunnels you took us through, do any of them lead outside of the castle walls?"

"I'm sorry, Mathieu, but I didn't have enough time to determine that," Stefan answered.

"Well, we will have to find another way in, then," Mathieu said. "Somehow, someway, we will get inside. When we do, I will make it my personal mission to track down Prince Agis, wherever he is hiding out."

"What if he is hiding in the western half of the castle or the castle keep?" the queen asked. "That part of the castle can be sealed up tight, so nobody can gain entrance."

"We can figure that out later, and trust me, we will," Mathieu answered. "For now, let's focus on reaching out to the entire land for help. Princess, any thoughts on this course of action which has been suggested?" The princess pushed her chair out, standing up at the table. She looked at each person and began speaking.

"Stefan, Yvonne, Mathieu, Sir Rackley, mother, and father, these next two weeks will be critical to our success. We all have a part to do, so let us work day and night to organize this revolution. Our goal is to have every single citizen who opposes the rebels marching on the castle with us. As far as what to do when we get there, well, that will fall into place later. I am sending my love with each of you. Tell every person who you see that I need them, that their presence and voice are important to me, and that they forever have my gratitude for their help. If I don't see any of you again until we are outside of the castle walls, let me say thank you. Chadwick's betrayal has sent Astoria into its darkest period in history, but with your help, a bright future lies ahead." Everyone at the table applauded as the princess finished speaking. The princess walked around the table, hugging each person, knowing there was a lot of work to do for the next two weeks. A short time later, they shared one more meal together, before departing to fulfill their assignments.

Earlier that afternoon, General Robbins had been dispatched with three rebel soldiers to try to find out where Mathieu went when he escaped. Prince Agis felt it was important to try to track Mathieu down, if it was at all possible. Robbins found that Mathieu's trail was surprisingly easy to follow. Every once in a while, the group would spot drops of blood, which were obviously left by Mathieu's wound the night before. A couple hours into their search, they crossed a bridge over a small stream, when Robbins ordered that the group come to a stop. Pointing into the brush, Robbins said, "Look over there. It seems like somebody took their horse off the road. Let's go check it out."

The group rode through the brush, soon spotting some horse droppings near a small tree. "This is the place the person must have stopped. It looks like there was a horse tied up here," Robbins said. Robbins and the three rebel soldiers dismounted their horses and looked around. It soon became apparent they had found the spot where Mathieu slept the night before. There was a larger amount of dried blood than they had seen anywhere else.

"It's obvious the prisoner slept here last night," one of the rebel soldiers said. "But where do you think he went from here?"

"I think I have a pretty good idea," Robbins answered. "There are two likely places. Sir Rackley's estate is not far from here and the village of Glaston is also close by. I wouldn't be surprised if Sir Rackley was working against us. And I've heard reports of royal guards gathering in Glaston, staying at the guard station there. Either way, we need to get back to the castle and report these possibilities to Prince Agis." The group returned to the main road, heading back the way they came.

The next morning, Sebastian was awoken early as his prison cell door was opened. An older man was thrown inside to the ground, before the cell door was locked up again. The older man sat up, his eyes trying to adjust to the near total darkness. It was nearly impossible to see anything in most of these cells. The only light which came through was a very small amount of candlelight through the key hole, from the hallway outside. The old man thought he was alone, until he heard a voice from behind him. "Who are you?" Sebastian asked him.

"Wow, you gave me a scare," the old man said. "My name is Nathaniel and I guess I'm your new cell mate."

"Did Prince Agis send you in here to try to get more information out of me?" Sebastian asked. "Because if he did, you can tell him that I don't know anything else. I've told him everything." The old man laughed at hearing this.

"No, no, Prince Agis didn't send me here to talk to you," Nathaniel replied. "He sent me here because I refused to do something for him. You see, I'm one of the castle musicians who has worked here for a long time. I've played flute for many years for both Princess Stasia and the former leader, King Charles. Two nights ago, I was called in by one of the rebel soldiers to perform for Prince Agis at his celebration. I refused, because my loyalty is with the princess. I guess my refusal was reported to Prince Agis at breakfast this morning, because two rebel soldiers barged into my room and brought me here. They said that Prince Agis had sentenced me to six months imprisonment for refusing to obey orders."

Though Sebastian could not see his face, he realized that the old man's voice sounded very familiar. As the man kept talking, Sebastian thought he figured out who his cell mate was. So he asked him a question. "Nathaniel, let me ask you something. In your time working here at the castle, have you ever caught somebody trying to steal a musical instrument?"

"That's an odd question," Nathaniel answered. "Let me think. Yes, there have been a few times I have caught people trying to steal instruments. Most of the time it was badly trained children."

"What about at the games? Have you ever caught somebody stealing something at the games?"

"Funny you should mention that, because there was one thief who I caught several years ago, trying to steal a prized flute. I felt pity for the young man, though, and couldn't bring myself to report him to a royal guard. In the end, I gave him a wooden piccolo as a gift." Sebastian's suspicions were right. This old man was the kind musician who he had met many years ago.

"Nathaniel, I am that boy," Sebastian said to him. "I am one of the rebel soldiers who overthrew the castle, helping Prince Agis to get into power. Around five years ago, I came here to the castle on another mission, and you caught me trying to steal the flute. I've been looking for you since we took over the castle, but this is the last place I expected to run into you."

The old man sighed at hearing this, not saying anything for a couple of minutes. Finally, he told Sebastian, "I must say, I often wondered what happened to you after that day. But it disappoints me to know you were involved in something which has hurt the princess and the royal family so badly. You obviously continued to be involved in stealing and dishonesty, despite the life lesson I tried to give you that day."

"Nathaniel, your kindness that day did have an impact on my life. You have to understand, though, that I was raised by the rebels. They kidnapped me when I was really young, so all I have ever known is the way of life they taught me."

"If you're with the rebels, what are you doing in here?" Nathaniel wanted to know.

"The one time I trusted somebody who was not a rebel, he betrayed me," Sebastian answered. "The result was that a royal knight, the king, and the queen all escaped from prison. His treachery has cost me gravely, as I will probably spend many years or even the rest of my life in this prison. I hate the person who did this to me and I better not ever see his face again." Sebastian was getting angry, as he was forced to recount the evil things that Stefan had done to him. The old man reflected on this, allowing five minutes to go by before speaking again.

"I understand your pain, my young friend," he finally said. "To be betrayed by somebody who you trust is something which can never be forgotten. I'm sure the princess feels the same way, being that it was her own uncle who betrayed her to seize power for himself. But you should not hate the person who did this to you. His actions probably were not a reflection of how he felt about you, but rather, how he felt about Prince Agis. He did the same thing that probably every loyal citizen of Astoria would have done in the same circumstances. He took advantage of an opportunity to help the royal family. That being said, it sounds like you have been hurt a great deal and I am sorry." Sebastian didn't say anything more to the old man. He could see that Nathaniel had a point. Yet Sebastian would never forgive Stefan for his actions.

Stefan and Yvonne spent the previous evening visiting the poor neighborhoods of Glaston. They were each given a horse by Sir Rackley, which they rode to Glaston, a short distance away. Sir Rackley also gave them a letter, affixed with his seal, to verify they were speaking in behalf of the princess, in case anyone doubted it. Not entirely sure of how to spread the word through the entire village, Stefan and Yvonne began by knocking on doors of one of the streets. The first few people who answered, listened closely to what they said and agreed to help the princess. After an hour went by, Stefan and Yvonne had only managed to talk to five households. "This is taking much too long, Stefan," Yvonne said to him. "If we keep going at this pace, we're going to spend our entire two weeks here in Glaston. There has to be a faster way to get this done."

"I have an idea," Stefan said, as they approached the next door. Stefan knocked and soon a middle aged peasant man answered the door.

"Good evening," he said. "What can I do for you folks?"

"We are here in behalf of Princess Stasia," Stefan answered, as he handed the letter from Sir Rackley to him. "She has sent us here to ask for your help to retake the castle. She wants you to know that each person's voice and presence in helping her is very important to her and greatly appreciated." The peasant man looked down and studied the letter for a minute. He wasn't a perfect reader, but he understood the general sense of what was being conveyed in the letter.

"How can I help?" the peasant man asked, as he looked up and handed the letter back to Stefan.

"We are organizing a revolution to march on the castle, exactly two weeks from today. One of the two meeting points will be here in Glaston on that morning. If you wish to help, what we really need is your time this evening. If you could gather up all of your friends and family members, we need to inform every poor person in Glaston of Princess Stasia's plan. Perhaps we could get a large number of people to assist us tonight in spreading the word, so that we could reach the entire population of peasants. If we can reach everybody tonight, then my friend Yvonne and I could move on to the next village. We have to cover all of the larger villages in Astoria, so we only have about one day to reach each village."

"If you give me about thirty minutes, I'm sure that I could find at least fifty people who would be willing to spread the word tonight," the peasant man said.

"That would be wonderful. Thank you so much," Yvonne told him. True to the man's word, Stefan and Yvonne came back to his house about thirty minutes later, and there was a large crowd gathered outside of his house. Yvonne counted nearly one hundred people, not the fifty that the man had promised. As everyone gathered around Stefan and Yvonne, Stefan explained to them every detail of the revolution that the princess needed their help with. When he was done speaking, Stefan found that not only were they willing to help, they were excited to be able to have a part in helping the princess. These people absolutely loved Princess Stasia and would do anything necessary to help her reclaim the throne. Soon, everybody spread out into Glaston, knocking on doors and gathering support. Around midnight, when Stefan and Yvonne were preparing to leave, the poor areas in the village of Glaston were bustling with excitement. The people assured Stefan and Yvonne that they would continue gathering up every last person they could find in the village, as well as any weapons which could be made or found, in preparation for the march on the castle in two weeks. It was only Stefan and Yvonne's first stop, but it was a major success.

Because their next stop was in their home village of Norwalk, Stefan and Yvonne rode their horses for most of the night to get there. Finally arriving at daybreak, Stefan and Yvonne each went to their own homes to get some rest. Around noon, Stefan woke up and went into the kitchen to fix some lunch. His parents were in the front room, waiting for him. "Stefan, we haven't seen you for a few days. We were starting to get worried," Shaylene said to him, as she set down her knitting instruments.

"Hello, mother and father," Stefan greeted them. "There was nothing to worry about. A lot has happened in the last few days. I helped King Charles and Queen Delphine escape from the castle prison and took them to Princess Stasia. A revolution is being organized, even as we speak. Yvonne and I have been asked to go to all of the villages in Astoria to inform the poor people and gather support. Today, we're going to cover Norwalk, and we will need your help."

"Of course, Stefan," Martin said to him. "We will do whatever we can. And how is Sebastian doing?" Stefan's heart sank as he heard the question. Stefan had been so busy that he did not have time to think lately about what he had done to Sebastian. But his father's question caused a flood of terrible thoughts to rush through Stefan's head.

"I have some bad news, mother and father," Stefan began explaining. "The only way I could help the king and queen escape was by betraying the trust of Sebastian, my brother. He assigned me to watch over the king and queen, and I took advantage of the opportunity to get them out of the castle prison. My actions have no doubt caused Sebastian a lot of pain, because he probably took what I did personally. But trust me, there was no other way. It was something I had to do. The worst part is that he probably had to face the wrath of Prince Agis, as well." Martin and Shaylene looked at each other, shocked at this revelation. Finally, Shaylene spoke up, with a frown on her face.

"That is terrible, because Sebastian has been through so much tragedy in his life. I really wish there had been some other way to do this, without hurting him. I hope he is going to be okay."

"Perhaps we could go to the castle and visit him," Martin offered.

"I'm not sure if that would be a good idea," Stefan said. "There is a good chance you both could get thrown in prison, or that he could be in prison himself."

"Stefan, your father is right," Shaylene interjected. "I know there are risks, but we have to let Sebastian know that we love him." Realizing it was pointless to try to stop them, Stefan didn't argue the point any further.

"But, we will not go until tomorrow or the next day," Martin added. "Right now, we have to help you organize the revolution here in Norwalk."

Yvonne woke up late that morning, too. Ever since she accepted the job at Sir Rackley's estate, she had been waking up very early each day. Thus, she enjoyed sleeping in and was glad Lady Ruth did not wake her up. It was something else that woke her up this morning, the scent of fresh baking that filled the house. Around the same time Stefan woke up, Yvonne woke up from a dream she was having about sweet cakes. She soon realized why sweet cakes had been in her dream, because her whole room smelled like them. Yvonne climbed out of bed and walked downstairs, still wearing her clothing from last night. Lady Ruth was sitting at the table, eating some watermelon and a piece of sweet cake. "Good morning, Yvonne," Lady Ruth said to her.

"Hello, Lady Ruth," the sleepy girl responded.

"You just missed it. There was a starling bird chasing a squirrel out in the back. I have been watching them through the window. By the way, you didn't sleep in those clothes last night, did you?" Lady Ruth asked, with a look of concern on her face. Yvonne looked down at what she was wearing, realizing she had been too tired last night to change her clothes. Before explaining, she sat down and put several sweet cakes on her plate, and began eating.

"I am afraid so," Yvonne confessed, "but we have more important things to worry about today. Stefan and I need to reach all of the lower class citizens of Norwalk, to inform them of Princess Stasia's revolution."

"Yvonne, I would prefer it if you didn't get involved in any kind of a revolution. That sounds much too dangerous. Don't you remember what happened the last time we were both at the castle? Prince Agis threatened to burn down our home."

"Don't worry, Lady Ruth, this is not going to be a small thing. The princess is asking all of the people in Astoria to gather together and march on the castle, thirteen days from now. I'm sure that the royal guards, royal knights, and royal archers will take the lead in fighting. We just have to get the word out and show our support, by being there."

"All right, I guess that sounds reasonable," Lady Ruth said. "By the way, how are things going between you and Stefan?" Yvonne stopped eating and looked at Lady Ruth. This was the last question she wanted to deal with right now. Yvonne glared at her, causing Lady Ruth to back off, saying, "Sorry, I only wanted to know if there was anything I could do to help. It seemed like you two were getting pretty close during Princess Stasia's speech, but maybe I was wrong." Yvonne didn't say anything, but started thinking about Stefan once again. Yvonne figured that Sir Rackley did not have time to talk with Stefan before everybody went their separate ways. It was really too bad, because Yvonne was counting on him. Now, Yvonne either needed to wait until Sir Rackley had the time, or talk to Stefan herself. She decided that she would wait a little longer, to see if Sir Rackley would help. After breakfast, Yvonne rode her horse over to Stefan's house, and with the help of Martin and Shaylene, they began the process of reaching all of the peasants in Norwalk.

The royal knight Mathieu had gone directly from Sir Rackley's estate to Glaston, as Stefan and Yvonne had. But, while Stefan and Yvonne were visiting the poorer areas of the village, Mathieu went to only one place, the royal guard station. When he arrived there, he was surprised to see a small army of royal guards out front. They quickly recognized who he was and gave him one of the spare uniforms from inside to put on. Once he was back in the appropriate outfit, Mathieu asked all of the royal guards inside and outside to gather together. He split them into three groups, the royal guards, the royal knights, and the royal archers. Once that was done, he took a count. There were four royal archers, two royal knights, and thirty-seven royal guards. Mathieu was impressed. This was a great start to the forces they would need to build up for an attack on the castle. Mathieu soon spoke to everyone who was gathered around. "Greetings, everyone. I have not spoken to many of you since the overthrow of the castle. That night, I was tricked and placed behind bars in the castle prison. Chadwick deceived all of us, pretending to be a supporter of Princess Stasia and the royal family, while he was working against them the whole time. As you are all aware, Chadwick has seized the throne and declared himself the new ruler, now desiring to be known as Prince Agis. The princess has sent me here to you today, to ask you to join her in retaking the castle from the rebels. For the next two weeks, we will travel around the countryside, seeking to gather our forces. Then, we will split into two groups. Half of you will be sent back here to Glaston, to lead an army of citizens from this part of the land toward the castle. The other half of you will meet up with another army of citizens at the Astorian Eagle Monument, on the road to Sorensen and Langston. We will all converge upon the castle at the same time, with the hope of restoring Princess Stasia to power. While the common people will be arming themselves with whatever weapons they have, the responsibility for most of the fighting will rest on our shoulders. I will not mislead you. Many of us here today will probably end up losing our lives. But we cannot allow our fellow citizens, our children, and the royal family to remain under the control of Prince Agis. He must be defeated, at all costs. Can I count on all of you to support Princess Stasia in this attack?" As soon as Mathieu asked this question, all who were present shouted their agreement. Mathieu went on to lay out some of the finer details and instructed that all weapons be gathered up and taken with them. A few hours later, the royal guards who had been posted at lookout points outside of the city were also brought back to assist. The next morning, the royal guards, royal knights, and royal archers all marched together toward the next village to look for more of their forces, determined to help the princess.

King Charles and Queen Delphine traveled to the village of Carson Lake to start their efforts. They chose Carson Lake because it was one of the richest communities that existed in all of Astoria. Carson Lake gained its wealth from a diamond mine in the surrounding hills. There was only a small community of peasants there, who worked in the mine and provided labor for the upper class. Other than that, it was entirely comprised of wealthy landowners, noblemen and noblewomen, and dignitaries. The village wrapped all the way around Carson Lake, with large homes everywhere, along with several parks. When the king and queen arrived there, they were surprised to find that there was a group of about twenty people standing guard on the main road leading into the village. The group of people were heavily armed, with swords, lances, and bows. After the king and queen identified themselves, they were allowed to pass through. The group of armed people had been privately hired by the residents of Carson Lake to keep the rebels out of their village. The king realized this was probably the only village in Astoria which could afford to do something like that to provide protection.

Soon, King Charles and Queen Delphine were meeting with the village statesman, Lord Reed. A grand meal was spread out on an outdoor terrace, overlooking the lake. Respecting the appropriate customs, the king and queen did not immediately begin discussing the revolution or the help which was needed. Instead, they visited with the statesman and discussed how things were going at Carson Lake. An hour later, when they finished the meal, Lord Reed signaled it was time to discuss the important matters by stating, "You probably noticed we have hired a small army to protect our prestigious lifestyle and homes from the rebels."

"We did meet them," King Charles said. "And I would like to compliment you on planning ahead so brilliantly. The people of Carson Lake have done well, despite the turmoil the rebels have brought on the region and my family."

"It is true that we are safe for the time being," Lord Reed continued, "but this is only a short term solution. I imagine that you are visiting us today to offer us a better, more long term solution to the threat posed by the rebels."

"The fact is," the king explained, "we need your help. The princess needs your help. Princess Stasia is organizing a revolution that needs the assistance of every citizen in Astoria, both rich and poor. She has chosen a day in which she would like all of us to march on the castle. This will put tremendous pressure on Prince Agis and the rebels, leading to their downfall."

"What can we do to help her?" the statesman wanted to know.

"While the queen and I are here, we would like to visit with all of the influential citizens of Carson Lake, to explain what the princess has planned. Hopefully, all of them will agree to have a part in helping us. With your great financial resources, perhaps you could purchase swords and other weapons that could be used. Most of the fighting will be done by our royal guards, but it is important for as many of us to be armed as possible, to send a message to the rebels. On the given day, all of the citizens of Carson Lake can meet up in Glaston, where others will be waiting. Then, everyone can march together, meeting up with another large group which will be coming from the other direction, with the goal of completely surrounding the castle."

"It is a very well thought out plan," Lord Reed acknowledged. "I am sure you will find unanimous support from the affluent citizens of Carson Lake. Although some of them were initially opposed to Princess Stasia's reforms, the changes she made ended up working out very well for everybody here. And even if they had not, we would still do everything in our power to help her."

"Thank you very much," the queen said upon hearing this. "You will always have our gratitude and the gratitude of our daughter." The king and queen spent the rest of the day visiting upper class citizens all around Carson Lake, before retiring for the night at the mansion of a nobleman. The next day they moved on to another village, repeating their efforts, with similar success.

Back at the castle, the day after General Robbins had tracked Mathieu to his resting spot by the stream, Prince Agis was holding a meeting with him. Robbins wanted to know if he should take a group of rebel soldiers out to either Glaston or Sir Rackley's estate to try to recapture Mathieu.

"No, that's not a good idea," Prince Agis told him. "For now, we are going to have to let Mathieu enjoy his freedom. If we start spreading out our forces by sending rebel soldiers out on missions into the land, we will be lowering our defense capability here at the castle. I have heard of the royal guards gathering in Glaston, but they will be dealt with later."

"But, isn't it dangerous to have Mathieu, the king, the queen, and the princess all out on the loose?" Robbins wanted to know. "For all we know, they could turn people in the land against us."

"I have thought about that very possibility and agree with you that it is likely," Prince Agis said. "I have served at this castle for virtually my entire adult life, so I know how strongly it is built. It will be nearly impossible for any group of royal guards or untrained citizens that they can round up to break through our entrance gate or walls. Even if they should somehow manage that, the western half of the castle and the castle keep cannot be penetrated. I will remain in power. It will be impossible to overthrow me. I appreciate your concern with these things, Robbins. You are a loyal follower, unlike that pathetic excuse for a rebel soldier, Sebastian. But, let them make the first move. Whatever it is, we will quickly crush them once and for all."

Following a three day journey, during which they did not have the time or energy to talk about personal matters, Princess Stasia and Sir Rackley arrived at the palace of Sir Rackley's parents, King Dominic and Queen Bronagh. Princess Stasia had never been here before, so as she rode Isobel, she was looking around at everything, admiring the beauty. The road to the palace was paved with thin cut stones. Rowan and Aspen trees lined the sides of the road, with large fields of grass spreading out in both directions. After a short time, Stasia and Rackley were inside, visiting with his parents. They explained the entire story of the rebel takeover, Princess Stasia's journey into exile, and the eventual escape of King Charles and Queen Delphine. The princess then shared every detail of the planned revolution that would be marching on the castle in less than two weeks. King Dominic and Queen Bronagh asked

Stasia and Rackley to leave the room for a short time, while they consulted together about what to do. Fifteen minutes later, Stasia and Rackley were invited back inside. Sir Rackley's father smiled as he announced, "We are going to send half of our army with you, to help you defeat the rebels and return to power. The rebels will be unable to stand against our combined forces." Hearing this, Princess Stasia and Sir Rackley turned to each other and shared a long hug. The princess started to shed a few tears, happy but sad at the same time. Sir Rackley and his parents were doing this out of the kindness of their hearts, and also because of their love for her. Princess Stasia had long realized that Sir Rackley was in love with her. And although she had never revealed it to anyone, and long denied the truth of it to herself, she realized at that moment that she had some feelings for Sir Rackley. However, because of Stefan's request which involved her promise to him, the princess felt it was only fair to let everyone in the room know the truth.

"Before you make your final decision," the princess told Sir Rackley's parents, "there is something you should know. Sir Rackley and I are no longer engaged, and there is somebody else who I intend to marry."

Chapter Eighteen:

Millions of Commoners United

Hearing those words, Sir Rackley felt completely bewildered. He had obviously missed some kind of important development, which must have taken place between Princess Stasia's arrival at his estate and now. Only a few weeks ago, he was engaged to the girl he had grown up loving. And now, she was to be married to somebody else. Although this rattled him, Sir Rackley's love for the princess would not allow him to turn his back on her now. He realized that he needed to speak up fast, before his parents changed their mind about sending help. He told his parents, "Father and mother, what Princess Stasia has told you is true. We are no longer engaged to be married." The princess was wiping away her tears, listening to Sir Rackley speak. When he finished saying this, she turned her head over to the king to see what he would say.

"Rackley, my son, we were not aware of this development. In view of this, I am not sure if would be right for us to risk the lives of our citizens to help Princess Stasia."

Cutting him off, Sir Rackley disagreed, "Father, it is the right thing to do. Please do not penalize the princess for something I have done. I have fallen in love with somebody else, so I have set the princess free from our engagement." Princess Stasia looked at Sir Rackley, confused as to why he was lying to his parents. Then, the reason struck her. He was doing this out of his love for her, knowing that if he didn't, his father would not send help. Tears started flowing down the face of the princess once again as she thought about this. She had genuine feelings for Sir Rackley. There was no doubt about it anymore. Sir Rackley continued reasoning with his father, saying, "We must help the royal family of Astoria, father. For if we do not, Prince Agis will remain in power, spreading fear into our land. As he gains more power, he may even consider attacking Limekiln.

The king realized that Sir Rackley was right, so he looked over at his wife. She nodded her head in agreement, knowing what he was thinking. Finally, the king made his decision. "Let it be just as you have asked, Rackley. We will send half of our army with you on the appointed day. But I want you both to think long and hard about what you are doing. By marrying somebody else, other than each other, it is going to undo all of the work King Charles and I have done during the past fifteen years. Your union in marriage would have guaranteed peace between our people for a lifetime to come. I ask you both to reconsider."

"Thank you, father. We will take your words under careful consideration," Sir Rackley replied. With that, he took Princess Stasia by the hand, leading her out of the room.

A few minutes later, Princess Stasia and Sir Rackley were walking towards his room, because he wanted to show her something. Sir Rackley had a large room with its own small library, and portions of the walls were covered with paintings. Sir Rackley led the princess over to one painting in particular. It was a painting of the princess standing with her horse Isobel, feeding the horse an apple. The princess was surprised to see it on Sir Rackley's wall. "How did you get this?" she asked him.

"Don't worry," he replied. "I didn't take the painting that was hanging in the Grand Ballroom. I loved this painting so much that I tracked down the artist who originally made it and asked him to paint me an exact replica. Even though I don't live here anymore, anytime I come home to visit, seeing this painting of you always brings me comfort." Sir Rackley stepped in front of the painting, looking directly into Princess Stasia's eyes. "Stasia, you must know how much I love you. Everything I have done in my life for the past five years has been with you in mind. I thought you loved me, too. So how is it you are now engaged to somebody else?" Hearing these words hurt the princess a great deal. She knew how much Sir Rackley cared about her, but hearing him express it directly to her was hard to take. Especially in view of what she now had to tell him.

"Rackley, I know you love me. Time and time again you have proven that to me by your actions. And I am going to tell you something I never have said before. As I have grown up over the past few years, our arranged marriage has been constantly on my mind. Marrying you was never something that I personally desired, yet I was willing to go through with it for the sake of our two lands. Recently, though, I have felt a change inside. I have felt love for you growing in my heart. At this very moment, of all of the people I have ever met, if I had to choose one person to marry, it would be you."

"Then what is the problem, princess? We both desire the same thing, to be with each other. Once you are back in power, there will be nothing holding us back." Princess Stasia looked away as Sir Rackley said this to her. She wished what he said was true. But there was something holding them back, so she told him about it.

"Please understand what I am about to tell you, and try to look at things from my perspective. In regards to my life, I never put myself or my personal feelings ahead of others. A few weeks back, I made a promise to the peasant boy Stefan, who helped me escape from the castle when Prince Agis took over. I told him that if he helped my father and mother escape from prison, I would grant him one wish, anything he wanted. As you know, Stefan risked his life for me once again and reunited me with my family. When I asked him what his one wish was, he told me that he wished to have my hand in marriage. Although Yvonne had informed me that Stefan had romantic feelings for me, I never could have imagined he would ask this of me. And though my only interest in him is that of a dear friend, I felt compelled to grant his wish, as you and I were no longer engaged."

"This is a lot to take in at once," Sir Rackley said. "In fact, this is unbelievable."

"From my perspective, this is how I see it," the princess continued. "My first duty is to my own land and citizens. Without Stefan's help, I would probably have been captured by Prince Agis and be sitting in prison. And without his help, I definitely would not have my parents free, and we wouldn't be organizing this revolution. With these things in mind, how could I even dare consider denying his one wish? It simply is not within my character to do something like that. He is the sole reason I have a chance to return to power in Astoria." Sir Rackley sat down in a chair, as he continued taking all of these things into his mind and heart. Finally, he looked up at the princess and spoke.

"My dear Stasia, I cannot disagree with your reasoning. Stefan is well deserving of being the person who marries you. Please understand, though, that this will hurt me a great deal. I love you so much and probably always will. The strange thing about all of this is that Yvonne asked me after our archery contest if I would talk to Stefan for her. I guess that while Stefan has feelings for you, Yvonne has feelings for him. I never had a chance to talk to Stefan, but now I wish that I had."

"I am sure you will get your chance, Rackley. Let's drop this matter for now and return to it later. Perhaps Stefan will realize in time that Yvonne would be a better match for him, or perhaps not. Whatever happens, I deeply appreciate your standing by me. It is an act of great love."

Just under two weeks later, the morning finally arrived for the march on the castle. At the Astorian Eagle Monument, a large crowd gathered. Although the actual number was far less, it seemed as if millions of commoners, wealthy landowners, noblemen, and other citizens had united in support. The efforts of Stefan and Yvonne, along with the king and queen, were a tremendous success. There were so many people that the villages and towns throughout Astoria must have been nearly empty. While some of the older people came without weapons, many of the younger ones were armed with anything they could find. Their makeshift weapons included swords, bows and arrows, and homemade clubs. The army Sir Rackley brought with him was similarly numerous, but also well trained and well armed. Sir Rackley and Princess Stasia made their way through the crowds to the monument, where King Charles, Queen Delphine, Anton the bird expert, and his trained eagle J-Bird were waiting. "Greetings, father," the princess said. "It looks like everybody has done their part, because there are more people here than I ever would have expected."

"Hello, my daughter. Hello, Sir Rackley," the king replied. "You are right, this is an amazing turnout. Delphine and I had wonderful success as we traveled throughout the land. And from the look of things, it appears Stefan and Yvonne did just as well. Mathieu has placed the trusted royal guard Reginald in charge of our forces, while he will be personally leading the group out of Glaston. Reginald wants us all to leave here in about twenty minutes, so we can meet outside of the castle at exactly four o'clock in the afternoon."

"That sounds good, King Charles," Sir Rackley said. "I will go and inform my commanding officers that they will be taking their orders from Reginald, from here on out. My father has sent with our army some useful machinery and weapons. We have six wooden catapults and two counterweight trebuchets. We also have a pontoon bridge and several battering rams, to help us get through the castle entrance gate. I have sent advance word to Mathieu that we will have these weapons available for use, if he so desires." With that, Sir Rackley rode off to talk with his commanding officers, and a short time later, the people began marching toward the castle.

On the other side of Astoria, another mass of people were gathered outside the village of Glaston. Among them were Stefan, Yvonne, Martin, Shaylene, and Lady Ruth. Martin and Shaylene had hoped to visit Sebastian at the castle, while Stefan and Yvonne were traveling around the countryside. But it didn't work out. When Martin and Shaylene showed up, asking to speak with him, they were turned away at the drawbridge. It brought them sadness, but at least they tried their best to see their son. The royal knight Mathieu was currently speaking to all who were assembled. He was standing on top of a mobile siege tower, allowing his voice to carry as far as possible. As the people cheered their support after his every sentence, Mathieu shared some final instructions. "Remember, everyone, we are all in this together. Our first goal is to surround the entire castle, which will hopefully create panic in the rebels. Then, our archers will try to take down any rebel soldiers who are standing in the lookout towers or on the battlements. Next, we will try to get inside the castle walls in one of two ways. First of all, we will try to fill in part of the moat, which will allow our siege towers to be pushed close to the wall. If that fails, our second option is to use the catapults, pontoon bridge, and battering rams, which I have been told are being brought by Sir Rackley and his army. Once the castle wall is down, let me remind all of you of something which is very important. Before you rush into the castle grounds, first allow the royal guards and the Limekiln army troops to go inside. We will take the lead in fighting and defeating the rebel forces. But, we will not be successful without your support. Live or die today, please stand by the princess."

Shortly thereafter, the hundreds of royal guards and tens of thousands of citizens began marching towards the castle. Stefan, Yvonne, and their families all walked together. Yvonne brought her old set of bow and arrows, while Stefan somehow came into possession of an antique sword. "Are you sure you know how to use that?" Yvonne asked him.

"Actually, I've never used it before. But how hard can it be to swing a sword?" Stefan asked, laughing slightly.

"Just promise me you'll be careful with it," Yvonne pleaded. "We've come too far to lose our lives today over foolish actions. Let the royal guards do the fighting."

"Don't worry, I don't plan on actually attacking somebody with this. But what about you? Are you planning on shooting some of those arrows at rebel soldiers?"

"I certainly hope not," Yvonne said. "But if the opportunity to make a difference presents itself, I will not hesitate. After all, I may be Yvonne, humble sixteen-year-old peasant girl from the lower class of Norwalk. But I am also known as the second greatest archer in the entire land."

"Whatever you do, just stay close to me," Stefan insisted. "I don't want to see anything happen to you. Do you understand me?"

"Stefan, you're starting to sound like Lady Ruth now. I'm glad to know you care about me so much. But if you want me to fully listen to you, you need to take the next step."

"The next step?" was all that Stefan could ask in response, not understanding what she meant. Yvonne had spoken without really thinking. So when she realized what she said, her eyes opened wide and she covered her mouth with her hand. She then dropped behind to talk to Lady Ruth for a few minutes, leaving Stefan to try to figure out the meaning of what he heard.

The rebel soldiers who were in the lookout towers were the first to spot the two simultaneous approaching masses of people, coming from opposite directions. Prince Agis and General Robbins were informed, and they quickly went up to stand on one of the battlements to see what was going on. There was no doubt, for as far as the eye could see, two great armies were approaching. "Where could the princess have come up with such a large army?" General Robbins wondered, fear evident in his voice. "We will be no match for them."

Prince Agis looked over at Robbins, wanting to hit him. "How dare you imply that I am not smart enough to defeat anything the princess brings upon us. Look around, we are the ones who are inside the castle, they are the ones who are outside. In all of its history, these castle walls have never been breached by invading forces. Mark my words, it will not happen for the first time today."

"But what if it does, my master?" Robbins wanted to know. "It's not that I doubt your leadership abilities, but if these approaching armies find a way to break through our defenses, we will be trapped in the western part of the castle and the castle keep. That's not a good way to continue ruling the land."

"Let me worry about that," Prince Agis said, getting angrier by the second. "Just see to it that my orders are carried out. I want half of our rebel soldiers posted along the battlements of the castle, armed with bows and arrows. Put the best of our archers in the lookout towers and give them longbows with flaming arrows to shoot. Pull the drawbridge up immediately and close the metal portcullis at the entrance gate. Arm the rest of our rebel soldiers with swords and shields, in case the wall does get broken through." Robbins turned to walk away and carry out his orders, but Prince Agis stopped him, wanting to add something else. "And Robbins, keep ten of our best sword fighters inside the western part of the castle. In case something unexpected happens, meet me inside of there, and we will seal off the western part of the castle."

"Right away, sir," Robbins said, as he walked away. Robbins was surprised to hear Prince Agis give him the last set of instructions. Prince Agis seemed so confident, even getting upset with Robbins for even considering a backup plan. But then, Prince Agis seemed to change his mind, something which had rarely happened before. For that to happen, it meant Prince Agis felt some of the same fearful thoughts Robbins was now experiencing.

As the two massive groups of Astorian citizens reached the castle, the royal guards in charge instructed everybody to keep a safe distance between them and the castle walls. Within about fifteen minutes, the entire castle was surrounded by thousands and thousands of people. The one hundred or so rebel soldiers who were standing on the battlements which wrapped around the upper castle wall, stood in place, waiting for a chance to fire arrows upon anybody who came too close. As all of the Astorian people kept their distance, they began shouting and singing songs, trying to intimidate the rebel soldiers in the castle. Mathieu soon met up with Reginald so they could plan their next move. Mathieu first told him, "Excellent job, my friend. We both arrived here at the exact same time. It couldn't have been executed better."

"Thank you," Reginald said. "The hard part was holding the people back. Everybody was anxious to get here and do their part. So, what do we do next? We can't rush the castle walls, because there are rebel archers posted all over. I don't think we were expecting so many of them."

"Yes, you are right. I was hoping we could begin filling in the moat, but that's way too dangerous right now. Let's send in the catapults and counterweight trebuchets to try to break the wall down from a safe distance."

It took a little while, but the Limekiln army eventually wheeled the wooden catapults and trebuchets into place at the front of the castle. The trebuchets, which were similar in make to catapults, only more advanced, were covered with animal hides to prevent them from being burned up by flaming arrows. Each of the two trebuchets were manned by twenty-five men, who would work together to pull on the twelve ropes attached to the hurling arm at the same time. Among the projectiles available to be fired were two-hundred pound stones, burning logs, and even beehives. Beehives were one of the most popular weapons of war to use in the surrounding lands. If several beehives could be sent over a castle wall by a catapult or trebuchet, it would result in a brood of angry bees being released when the hive smashed into the ground. It was especially effective if a beehive landed on a castle battlement. Burning logs also served a good purpose, as they would be loaded on right before it was time to fire the projectiles. Because only one or two shots could be fired per hour, every shot needed to count.

General Robbins walked up to one of the lookout towers to make sure the archers were ready. He watched as the catapults and trebuchets were pulled into place. They were now being loaded with projectiles. Robbins asked one of the rebel archers, "What is the range of your longbow? It looks like those machines are quite a distance away from the castle wall."

"We can easily shoot that distance," one of the rebel archers answered. "The problem is, we don't have a lot of longbows here in the castle."

"Well, use whatever you have, and I want you to light some flaming arrows. Target those machines and try to destroy them. I want you to aim for the upper parts of the machines. Up high it will be hard to extinguish a fire once it has started, even if they have buckets of water down below." After giving these instructions, Robbins moved over to the other guard tower to tell the rebels there the same thing. A few minutes later, a cascade of flaming arrows was sailing through the air toward the catapults and trebuchets. Several hit their targets, and two of the catapults started burning up. Two flaming arrows also hit one of the trebuchets, but the fire was stopped by the animal hides which covered it, as well as by buckets of water which were thrown on the flames. Right after that, the first round of projectiles were launched. Several large stones crashed into the top of the castle wall, smashing through it, causing the wall to crumble back into the castle grounds. Part of the central battlement was destroyed, ruining the ability to walk across it from one side to the other. And one beehive landed on the great lawn, near several rebel soldiers. As soon as it crashed into the ground, a large brood of angry bees swarmed up into the air, immediately attacking the rebel soldiers. With a swarm of bees surrounding them, causing great pain, the rebel soldiers ran off in different directions. After things calmed down for a few minutes, the rebel archers fired some more flaming arrows with their longbows. Again, the flaming arrows failed to ignite the trebuchets. But, two more of the catapults were set on fire, soon being engulfed in flames.

Mathieu looked at Reginald and said, "This is not going very well. That was an effective first shot, but it is going to be some time before we can take another one. By then, we will have lost all of our catapults and maybe even our trebuchets. Any ideas?"

Reginald thought about it, and offered a solution. "We need to get some more buckets of water over here as soon as possible. More importantly, we need to take out those rebel archers in the lookout towers. It seems they have a limited number of longbows, otherwise everybody would be using them right now. It is going to be very dangerous, but we have to send in some of our royal archers." Mathieu agreed, and ordered that the royal archers be dispatched to the land below the front two lookout towers. About ten royal archers went forward on each side, holding shields in front of them. Before they could get too close, they came under heavy fire. The royal archers backed up a little bit and returned fire, shooting arrows in the direction of the lookout towers and the battlements. Even though they were still too far out of range to take all of the rebel archers out, at least they were engaging them in battle, which prevented them from firing any more flaming arrows towards the machines. The battle raged for a while, but it was going poorly until reinforcements came in from the Limekiln army. A short time after they started helping, the rebel archers were overwhelmed and defeated.

However, there was one particularly elusive rebel archer, who continued firing flaming arrows from the right side guard tower. One of his shots hit another catapult while it was being loaded. Despite efforts to stop the flames, the catapult was consumed in an inferno, rendering it useless. The rebel archer kept avoiding the mass of flying arrows that was coming his way, always ducking down at just the right time. He continued lighting flaming arrows, firing them with his longbow, and then getting back down below the merlon. Soon, he took another successful shot, this time lighting one of the two trebuchets on fire. The flaming arrow had pierced the animal hides, landing squarely in a piece of wood near the top and out of reach. Seeing this, Mathieu shouted toward Reginald, "We have to stop that rebel archer! We are down to our last catapult and last trebuchet."

"There is nothing more we can do," Reginald responded. "Many of our archers are already down. The archers we have left are continuing to fire up towards his position, without success."

"Perhaps I can help," said a voice from behind Mathieu. He turned back to see Anton the bird expert standing behind him, with his trained Astorian eagle sitting on his arm. Mathieu was badly in need of a solution, so he listened to Anton's suggestion. Anton explained, "My eagle J-Bird is very intelligent. I can instruct him to fly over to that guard tower where the rebel archer is standing and have him attack."

"You really think that could work?" Mathieu asked.

"There is some risk to the eagle, as he could be hit by a flying arrow. But if I am right, the rebels will be taken by such surprise that the eagle will complete its mission before the rebels even know what has happened." Mathieu agreed to give Anton's idea a chance, as he was out of other options.

Pointing his arm toward the guard tower, Anton ordered the eagle, "J-Bird, go seek out prey. Fly!" The eagle immediately flew up into the air, taking a flight path in the direction of the guard tower. Several rebel soldiers who were standing on the battlement saw the eagle but did not view it as a threat. They assumed it was just another eagle that happened to be flying by the castle, although at the wrong time. As the eagle speedily approached the guard tower, it stretched out its talons. Right then, the rebel archer stood up to fire another flaming arrow. The rebel archer was caught by surprise at seeing the eagle closing in on him. The astonishment of the moment caused the rebel to drop his longbow and flaming arrow over the edge. The eagle attacked the rebel archer in his face, sinking its talons into his forehead. As the rebel tried to fight back with his hands, the eagle let go and flew up into the air a few feet. The rebel began swinging his hands wildly into the air, jumping up to try to hit the eagle. After landing back on his feet, the rebel tripped and fell over the edge of the guard tower. A few seconds later, a splash was heard. The rebel soldier landed in the moat below the castle walls. As the rebel tried desperately to get out of the moat, the Astorian eagle flew back and landed on Anton's arm. Mathieu was amazed at what he had witnessed and so was the vast crowd of people who were watching. Cheering broke out everywhere, as the people realized this had turned the tide in the battle.

Soon, another round of projectiles were fired from the remaining catapult and trebuchet. Two large boulders smashed into the wall, destroying more of it. A burning log landed on a large stash of arrows, causing them to catch on fire. But, the biggest hit came from the two beehives, which landed directly on opposite sides of the remaining battlements. Angry bees emerged as the hives were crushed, attacking the rebel soldiers in large swarms. Several of the rebel soldiers fell over the wall, landing in the castle moat. The rest of the rebel soldiers either jumped off the battlement onto the great lawn below as they were panicking, or ran for the stairways as they tried to escape the bees. Seeing the battlements and lookout towers now cleared, Mathieu ordered that the siege tower, pontoon bridge, and battering rams be brought forward. The pontoon bridge was a temporary bridge which could be moved quickly into place. Crowds of people watched as the pontoon bridge was brought forward by a large number of troops from the Limekiln army. It was carefully placed over the moat. One of the commanding officers of the Limekiln army asked Mathieu if he wanted them to start filling in the moat, so the siege tower could be used. Mathieu told him to hold off for the moment, while they tried the pontoon bridge and battering rams. After the bridge was placed across the moat, one of the battering rams was carefully brought across it, coming to rest right in front of the castle entrance gate and metal portcullis. The battering ram held a massive tree supported by ropes, which had been stripped clear of branches and bark. On both ends of the tree, metal coverings provided extra strength and power. The Limekiln army members began swinging the giant metal-tipped timber forward and back. It began picking up a lot of speed and smashed into the entrance gate, putting a severe dent into it.

On the other side of the gate and portcullis, frightened rebel soldiers could see that the battering ram was soon going to break through, allowing those who surrounded the castle to gain entrance. Prince Agis came up to them, reminding them that they needed to stand their ground and fight. The rebel soldiers didn't have much of a choice, because there was nowhere for them to go. More rebel soldiers arrived from other parts of the castle, all with their swords drawn, prepared for the battle ahead. After he gave his instructions, Prince Agis turned and headed towards the western part of the castle. General Robbins was waiting for him at the main entrance, and the two of them went inside. The ten well-trained sword fighters who Prince Agis had requested were in there waiting for them. Prince Agis ordered that the entire western part of the castle be locked down and sealed off. He told Robbins that the rebel soldiers outside would hold off Princess Stasia's army for as long as they could, but in the end, they would be defeated, because there were too many people. Prince Agis' last play would be to keep all of the royal guards out of the western part of the castle and ultimately take safety in the castle keep, if necessary. The ten rebel soldiers worked hard to secure everything for the next thirty minutes, making access into the western part of the castle impossible. When they were finished, Prince Agis ordered them to wait in the castle keep, where several years worth of supplies had been stashed. Prince Agis wanted General Robbins to stay with him in the main part of the castle, to keep an eye on what was going on outside. The two of them watched the battle from an upstairs vantage point.

Meanwhile, the battering ram continued to do heavy damage to the castle entrance gate. After about thirty minutes, the moving timber finally broke through to the other side. The Limekiln army repositioned the battering ram slightly and started swinging it again. It wasn't long before more of the gate broke, flying backwards into the castle grounds. The hole was now big enough for two people to go through at once. The battering ram was pulled back and royal guards joined the Limekiln army troops in flooding through. Rebel soldiers were there to greet them with resistance on the other side. Sword fighting broke out everywhere as the rebel soldiers tried their very best to stand their ground. But more people kept coming through the opening, causing them to quickly get outnumbered. There were casualties on both sides. Mathieu and Reginald came through the entrance opening, stepping off to the side to observe the fight and decide what to do next. Once all of the army troops and royal guards had come through, armed citizens started coming inside. The rebel soldiers were getting overwhelmed by the sheer number of people. About fifteen minutes later, Mathieu saw somebody familiar come through the entrance opening. "Stefan! Over here!" Mathieu shouted towards him. Stefan had his sword drawn, expecting to get involved in fighting, but was relieved to see he wasn't needed for that. Stefan and Yvonne walked over to where Mathieu and Reginald were standing.

"Mathieu, you have done it. You have got us back inside the castle grounds," Stefan said to him.

"No, we have all done it," Mathieu replied. "Could you two please stick with me? I may need your help down in the castle prison, to lock up any captured rebel soldiers." Stefan and Yvonne agreed to stay with him. They were glad to be staying away from the fighting, keeping a safe distance. Stefan and Yvonne watched everything in awe, amazed at how full the castle grounds were already getting.

When the rebel soldiers had suffered a great number of casualties, those who were left threw down their swords and surrendered, bringing an end to the fighting for the time being. They were quickly taken into custody by those around them. Everyone in the crowd who made it onto the castle grounds cheered at seeing this. Princess Stasia, Sir Rackley, King Charles, and Queen Delphine now came through the small entrance opening and walked over to where Mathieu was standing. "Hello, princess," Mathieu said when he saw her.

"Mathieu, it looks like we control this area. Have we already won?" the princess asked.

"Not yet," Mathieu cautioned. "We have taken control of the entire castle grounds, but I have not seen any sign of Prince Agis yet. My guess is that he has holed up inside the safety of the western part of the castle. You should know that we have lost many of our royal guards already. They fought valiantly in your behalf."

"Their sacrifice will be remembered for all time in the Royal History Pages," the princess said. "Let us hope we do not lose any more of them tonight."

"It will take a long siege to break through into the western part of the castle and castle keep, if that is what is necessary. Don't forget, the castle keep is designed so that nobody can ever get inside, once it has been closed up."

"I have an idea," Stefan said, speaking up. Everyone turned to look at him, surprised that somebody with such limited experience in combat had a suggestion. "Tell me if I'm wrong, but what if we use the secret passageway in the castle prison to gain access to the western part of the castle. Wouldn't that work and catch whoever is inside by surprise?" Mathieu was impressed upon hearing this, feeling kind of surprised he did not think of the idea himself.

"You know what, Stefan," Mathieu told him. "I think you may have solved our biggest problem. It is possible that the rebels discovered how we escaped from the castle prison. If they did, they probably sealed up the tunnel, or left it open to set a trap for us. But if they didn't, it could save us weeks or months of trying to break through into the western part of the castle and the castle keep." Everyone around took turns commending Stefan on his idea, after Mathieu finished speaking.

An hour later, the castle grounds were completely filled with royal guards, Limekiln army troops, and brave citizens. Mathieu and Stefan were taking about twenty captured rebel soldiers down into the castle prison. Yvonne stayed behind with Princess Stasia and Sir Rackley. When they walked down the stairs to the entrance of the prison, Mathieu went inside first, along with six royal guards. They were prepared to fight, but it wasn't necessary. The castle prison was deserted, as the rebel soldiers stationed there had gone outside to join in the battle. Stefan came inside and looked over the charts on the front counter. He could see which prison cells were currently holding royal guards and loyal citizens that the rebels had jailed. Stefan took a spare set of keys from one of the closets and led Mathieu, the royal guards, and the group of prisoners down the hallway. They decided the easiest way to handle this would be to release the royal guards who had been imprisoned, and put rebel soldiers back in their place. This exchange continued until all of the rebel soldiers were placed in prison cells. As Stefan was double checking his chart, one of the names jumped out at him. It was Sebastian, who was imprisoned with a castle musician named Nathaniel. "Are there any more royal guards we need to let out?" Mathieu asked Stefan.

"No, Mathieu, we have released them all," Stefan answered. "However, there is one more person I would like to release. It is my brother. He was a rebel soldier but I believe he will support us."

"I don't know if that's such a good idea right now," Mathieu said. "It might be better to consider doing that later."

"Please, Mathieu, this is very important to me," Stefan pleaded.

"All right, but let's make it quick. I want to get into those tunnels so we can take down Prince Agis. That is our highest priority right now." Stefan led Mathieu and the royal guards down to Sebastian's cell and unlocked it. As it swung open, Stefan, Mathieu, and a royal guard who was holding a torch stepped inside. The moment that Sebastian saw Stefan's face, he jumped up from his sitting position and charged him. He reached Stefan and pushed him hard into the prison cell wall, knocking the wind out of his chest. As Stefan slumped to the ground, he could hear the rage in Sebastian's voice.

"I hate you, brother. I hate you!" Sebastian was saying to him.

Chapter Nineteen:

A Night for the Ages

Prince Agis and General Robbins could see that the rebel forces outside had been completely defeated from their lookout point upstairs. In frustration, Prince Agis took out his sword and smashed it into a table close to where he was standing. He told Robbins to keep an eye on things, while he went downstairs to the throne room. Prince Agis walked downstairs and entered the throne room, furious over seeing his forces beaten. The golden crown was sitting on the throne. Prince Agis picked it up and put it on his head. Then he sat down on the throne and closed his eyes, trying to calm down. He had been in power for over a month, yet it was all coming to an end so fast. Prince Agis had expected to remain in power for the rest of his life. But that seemed to be a very remote possibility now. Everything was going fine until a couple of weeks ago, when King Charles and Queen Delphine escaped from the castle prison. Somehow, they had helped Princess Stasia organize an army, which had marched on the castle and broken through the castle walls in a matter of hours. Prince Agis tried to shut all of these thoughts out of his mind, reminding himself that he was still the ruler of Astoria as he sat on the throne, wearing the golden crown.

When Sebastian attacked Stefan in the castle prison, everyone was caught by surprise. Mathieu reacted a moment later by pulling Sebastian away from Stefan and slamming him hard to the ground. Stefan slowly stood back up, struggling to breathe normally. After he finally caught his breath, he looked at Sebastian and tried to explain things to him. He said, "Sebastian, please do not hate me. I am sorry I had to betray your trust in order to help the king and queen escape. Believe me, I never wanted to hurt you, and those things I said to you about caring for you were all true."

"Liar!" Sebastian shouted back at him. "You used me to get what you wanted and then left me here to pay the price of your actions."

"There was no other way to help the king and queen, Sebastian. If I had come to you and explained what I was going to do, you would never have allowed it. My first loyalty, beyond anything else, is to the princess and the royal family. Even if it had been our parents, or my best friend Yvonne who had to suffer in some way, I still would have done whatever was necessary to help the princess. And because of this, the princess has now recaptured the castle grounds. Royal guards are in complete control of everything outside."

"That's impossible. I don't believe you," Sebastian said. "How did you and your friends get in here, anyway?"

"What I am telling you is true, my brother. Please, promise me that you will leave the castle grounds in peace, and we will set you free. Although you were not aware of it and are angry about it, you actually helped this revolution take place. Obviously Prince Agis does not care for you anymore, otherwise he would not have put you in prison. I am sure the princess would forgive your involvement with rebel activities in the past, in view of everything which has happened." As Stefan finished speaking, the castle musician named Nathaniel had something to say. He had been watching and listening to the exchange take place between Stefan and Sebastian.

Nathaniel said, "Sebastian, you and I have come to know each other these past two weeks. Please, accept Stefan's offer and start a new life, one with honesty and truth. Leave the rebels behind and forgive your family members. Life is too short to carry grudges and hatred with you along the way."

After a minute went by, Sebastian finally said, "So be it. I will accept your offer. But that doesn't change the fact that I never want to see you again." Mathieu released his grip on Sebastian and allowed him to walk out of his prison cell, leaving everyone behind. It wasn't Mathieu's preference to let him go, but he understood that Stefan had played a key role in taking back the castle, so he allowed him this consideration.

When Sebastian was gone, Mathieu wanted to head into the tunnels. Soon, Mathieu, Stefan, and six royal guards were all in the storage room climbing through the small opening into the passageway.

When they arrived at the end of the tunnel, they found that the entrance into the clothing and laundering room had not been sealed up. They were able to push the boards and sink away once again to gain entrance. Mathieu went out first, to be sure everything was clear. Nobody was around, so he helped Stefan and the six royal guards out of the opening. When everybody was gathered inside the room, Mathieu gave his instructions. He wanted Stefan to wait there, where he would be safe. The six royal guards were instructed to head over to the castle keep, to find out if it had been shut tight. If it was still open, the six royal guards were to seize control of it, doing whatever was necessary. Mathieu was going to walk quietly through the western part of the castle, looking to either open up one of the doors to the outside, or find Prince Agis and take him into custody.

As Sebastian emerged from the underground prison, he was still upset, but glad to be free. He realized that he would be able to blend in with the crowds, because he was not wearing clothing which would identify him as a rebel. He was still wearing the clothes he had worn to the feast thrown by Prince Agis, which were dirty but not conspicuous. Sebastian surveyed the scene on the castle grounds and found that what Stefan told him was true. The grounds were now completely controlled by royal guards. The surprising part to Sebastian was that there were common people mixed in with the royal guards, even outnumbering them. The common people had brought weapons of their own, evidently intent on doing their part to help defeat the rebels. Sebastian began walking towards the castle entrance gate, planning on disappearing forever. He wanted to leave Astoria and the bad memories held there behind, to start a new life somewhere else. As he came to the entrance gate, Sebastian was surprised to see that the gate was not open, but it was broken through in two different areas. People were continuing to climb through the openings to get onto the castle grounds. He watched the people coming through for a few minutes, fascinated by all of this. Suddenly, a familiar voice spoke to him from behind, saying, "Sebastian, is that you?" Sebastian turned to look and of all people, it was his mother Shaylene.

"Sebastian, my son, it is really you." Shaylene's eyes were forming tears as she stepped forward to try to embrace Sebastian. She wanted to give him a hug and tell him how much she loved him. But as she approached him, he stepped back. He was just as upset with his parents as he was with Stefan.

"Mother, I don't want to see you anymore. You and father betrayed me, the same as my brother did. I am going to leave Astoria and never come back."

"Please, Sebastian, give us a chance," Shaylene pleaded. "We didn't know Stefan was going to help the king and queen escape behind your back. We tried to come to the castle to explain this to you after we found out, but we were turned away at the drawbridge. We love you." Sebastian tried to remain tough, not wanting to show any emotion. He did not want to grant forgiveness to those who had betrayed him.

"Well, I don't love you, I don't love my father, and I don't love my brother. This is the last time you will ever see me. I do not want to be a part of your lives. For all I care, you can spend the rest of your days thinking about what you have done to me." Sebastian turned and walked away, not leaving the castle, but heading off in the opposite direction. He needed to be alone for a while to stabilize himself emotionally. Sebastian also wanted to wait until there were less people crowded around the entrance, before he would leave. Martin had watched the conversation take place between Shaylene and Sebastian with great sadness. When Sebastian walked away, he took Shaylene into his arms to allow her to cry. It was one of the saddest moments of Martin's life, but there was nothing he could do to change Sebastian's feelings.

Delia was sitting in her room in the eastern part of the castle, when she heard an excited voice coming from the hallway. Somebody was running through, knocking on every door as he went by. The person was shouting out about the rebels being overthrown. Delia opened her door and looked out. The man was nearly to the end of the hallway, so she called to him, asking what the commotion was all about. "Haven't you heard?" he asked. "The rebels are no longer in power, and the princess has control of the castle grounds!" The man turned and left, continuing to shout as he disappeared from her sight. This was a totally unexpected development, one which Delia found hard to believe. Just in case, she walked over and knocked on the door of Mathieu's family. Madison opened up and came out into the hallway to talk with Delia.

"Hello, Delia. My mother is not feeling well today, or I would invite you inside."

"That's all right," Delia said. "I was wondering if you wanted to go outside with me to take a walk. A man just ran down the hallway, shouting and claiming that the princess has retaken the castle."

"Yeah, I heard him, but he sounded like a crazy person," Madison replied. "Do you really think it is possible?"

"It is worth checking out to see for ourselves. Even if he was making it up, at least you and I could get some fresh air outside."

"Okay, I will go with you," Madison said. "But let me get something warmer to wear, because it must be starting to get dark outside."

Delia and Madison walked out of the doors of the eastern part of the castle and found that everything the man said was true. As the sunlight was fading, they could see there was a mass of people on the castle grounds. Nearby, a castle worker was starting to light the lamp torches. Delia and Madison walked past him, looking for the princess or anybody they might recognize. It was hard, because there were so many people. After a short time, they saw a large number of royal guards gathered in one area, so they headed over in that direction. Behind the royal guards, Delia and Madison spotted them. There was the princess, the king, the queen, and Sir Rackley. When the princess saw them walking over, she ran over to greet them. She gave Delia and Madison each a hug, being thrilled to see them. "Aunt Delia and Madison, you are both okay!" the princess said with an excited voice. "I have been worried about you."

"And we've been worried about you," Delia told her. "I never thought this day would come, but here you are at the castle again. Do you have any idea where Mathieu is?"

"Yes, he was here, but he left a little while ago," the princess answered. "He went with Stefan to take a secret tunnel into the western part of the castle to try to apprehend Prince Agis."

"Please, Princess Stasia, tell me where I can find this tunnel," Delia asked. "I may be able to help talk Prince Agis into surrendering. I fear that if I am not there, Prince Agis may end up fighting back and being killed."

"I can take you to this tunnel," the king said, as he walked up. "I have been through this tunnel before and I know the way. Like you, I don't want to see Chadwick have to die. He has done terrible things to all of us, but I still care for him. Maybe we both can convince him to surrender instead of fighting to his death." Before anyone could object, King Charles and Delia headed off for the castle prison. They both were intent on saving Prince Agis, before he did something which would cost him his life. Being in such a hurry, they forgot to ask some royal guards to come with them. Princess Stasia understood what they needed to do, so she put her arm around Madison and talked to her for a while. As King Charles and Delia came closer to the prison, Sebastian was sitting nearby and he saw them walk past. He overheard the name of Prince Agis mentioned, which sparked his curiosity. Seeing they were headed for the castle prison and wanting to know what had become of Prince Agis, Sebastian stood up, deciding to follow them from a distance. About twenty seconds after King Charles and Delia walked into the castle prison, Sebastian opened the door slowly, following them inside.

Mathieu had been searching around the western part of the castle for some time, not encountering anybody. But when he walked into the throne room, he saw Prince Agis. Prince Agis was wearing a golden crown while he was sitting on the throne in quiet meditation, with his head bowed and his eyes closed. The rebel leader did not notice that Mathieu had walked into the room. Mathieu looked around and didn't see any other rebel soldiers, so he spoke up as he took out his sword. Mathieu said, "Prince Agis, your days on the throne of Astoria have come to an end." Prince Agis immediately opened his eyes, shocked to see Mathieu. He did not immediately get up from his throne, but spoke back to him.

"Well, if it isn't my long lost friend Mathieu," Prince Agis said.

"We are not friends, Prince Agis," Mathieu replied. "I once respected you, but that was a long time ago."

"You always were jealous of the fact that I was the Chief Royal Knight," Prince Agis added. "You even had to go around me to get the princess to promote you from being an ordinary royal guard to a royal knight."

"I was never jealous of you," Mathieu argued. "But I didn't think you did a very good job in protecting the princess, always disappearing on trips for weeks at a time. Now we all know why you were gone, you traitor. I am here to take you into custody."

"Never!" Prince Agis shouted. He rose up from the throne and threw the golden crown off his head, onto the ground. Next he pulled out his sword and moved in the direction of Mathieu. Mathieu met him halfway and the two began sword fighting in the middle of the throne room.

Prince Agis swung his sword straight down from over his head, making the first move. Mathieu went into a defensive mode and held his sword horizontally, blocking the attack. Prince Agis swung his sword in several other directions, trying to hit Mathieu. Mathieu continued blocking, using all of his strength to ward off the blows. The two were evenly matched, both being well-trained sword fighters, perhaps the best in the land. Prince Agis swung wildly, causing Mathieu to jump back out of the way. The edge of Prince Agis' sword landed in one of the wooden chairs, briefly getting stuck. Mathieu saw this and charged forward, looking to take advantage of the mistake. Prince Agis saw him coming and stopped trying to pull his sword out for a moment. He stuck his foot out and kicked Mathieu as hard as he could in the stomach, causing him to fall backwards onto the ground. Prince Agis then used both of his hands, pulling back as hard as he could, finally getting his sword loose. As both fighters regained their positions, they continued battling it out, exchanging sword blows. Mathieu seemed to gain the advantage, as Prince Agis was slowly backing up in defense. Not realizing he had gotten to the stairs leading up to where the throne was, Prince Agis tripped over them and fell backwards. Mathieu's eyes lit up, figuring he was about to win the battle. He lifted his sword and drove it downwards, hoping to end this fight. Just before the edge of Mathieu's sword pierced through him, Prince Agis moved out of the way, leaving his sword behind. Mathieu swung his sword with such power that the vibrations caused when his sword hit the stairs caused him to let go of his sword. Both fighters no longer were holding their swords. Prince Agis leapt up and lunged toward Mathieu, tackling him to the ground. They rolled around, exchanging punches and blows. Prince Agis took the upper hand and started choking Mathieu by the neck. Mathieu could feel his consciousness starting to fade and realized he needed to do something fast. He couldn't reach his sword because it was too far away, but there was something else nearby. He picked it up with his left hand and could feel that it was the golden crown. With every last bit of strength, Mathieu slammed the golden crown over the head of Prince Agis, causing him to break his stranglehold on Mathieu. Prince Agis winced in pain, putting his hand to his head and staggering back. Mathieu was still catching his breath, so he stood up and went to pick up his sword. Before he could get there, Prince Agis charged him once again. Mathieu saw him coming and ducked out of the way, just as Prince Agis lunged at him. Prince Agis' momentum carried him past Mathieu and caused him to smash into a chair, breaking it into pieces. Mathieu picked up his sword, now being the only person who was holding one.

"This is the end, Prince Agis. The fight is over and you have been defeated," Mathieu said to him. "Give up now and your life will be spared." Prince Agis decided to talk to him, trying to buy a little bit of time. As Mathieu walked towards him, Prince Agis backed up, keeping a block of chairs in between the two of them. He finally came up with an idea which he decided to try.

"Please, Mathieu, show mercy to me. I am unarmed. I surrender!" Prince Agis dropped down on his knees, making it appear as if he was giving up. Mathieu saw this and walked around the chairs over to him, still holding his sword out. At the same time, Prince Agis reached into his clothing and pulled out a hidden poniard. A poniard is almost like a miniature sword, although it is not as long. It is slightly bigger than a dagger and has a very sharp edge. When Mathieu arrived at where Prince Agis was kneeling down, he ordered him to get up. Prince Agis listened to him and rose from his position on his knees. However, as he was standing up, Prince Agis made his move. In one very quick motion, Prince Agis stuck his poniard into Mathieu's side. The pain hit Mathieu at once, causing him to drop his sword and fall onto the ground, lying on his back. Prince Agis left him there and went to retrieve his sword. When he had his sword, he walked back over to where Mathieu was lying, as blood was coming from his wound.

"You should have known better than to challenge me," Prince Agis said to him. "It will be the last mistake you ever make." Assuming that Mathieu was now dying, Prince Agis left him there and headed off to another part of the castle, picking up the golden crown before he left. After a few minutes, Mathieu pulled the poniard out of his side and threw it to the ground. The poniard had somehow missed Mathieu's internal organs, only cutting through his skin and tissue. Mathieu picked up his sword and limped off to one of the nearby private changing rooms, with blood dripping from his side. When he went inside, he used whatever he could find to dress the wound and wrap it up. Not willing to give up, Mathieu was soon once again limping through the western half of the castle, looking for Prince Agis.

The six royal guards who had been dispatched to the castle keep arrived outside of the lower door. They were surprised to find it still open. Inside, they could hear the voices of quite a few rebel soldiers talking. The royal guards listened in to the conversation. One of the rebels said, "Where do you think Prince Agis and General Robbins are? They should have been here by now."

"Don't worry about it. It is none of our business," another rebel answered.

"Well, I sure hope they come quickly, because we need to get this place sealed up so we will be safe from the royal guards," another added.

At hearing this, the six royal guards huddled outside the door and whispered a plan that they came up with. Shouting with a loud voice, one of the royal guards said, "Soldiers, come out here quick! Prince Agis needs your help!" Reacting without thinking, the rebel soldiers ended their conversation and rushed out the door. They didn't even bother to draw their swords. As soon as they came out, the royal guards attacked them, quickly subduing all ten of them. None of the royal guards were hurt in the fight, as the element of surprise worked well.

The ten rebel soldiers were tied up and separated from one another, also having their weapons taken away. Two of the royal guards then went inside the castle keep and confirmed that there were no more rebel soldiers inside. The royal guards now controlled the castle keep, and they waited patiently in front of it, to see if Prince Agis or General Robbins showed up.

Around that time, Stefan was still waiting in the clothing and laundering room of the castle. He heard voices coming from the tunnel he had come out of and saw an approaching torch light getting brighter. Worried it might be rebels, he backed into a corner, hiding behind a small table. Just in case, he took his antique sword out of the scabbard he was wearing, ready to use it if necessary. He was relieved to see it was King Charles who came out of the small opening in the wall, with Delia emerging right behind him. Stefan put his antique sword away and came out of his hiding spot, giving the two of them a brief scare. The three talked for a short time, with Stefan explaining that he had been asked to wait here, where it was safe. Not wanting to stay there by himself any longer, Stefan asked if he could go with the king and Delia. They agreed, glad to have somebody else with them. Soon, they were walking through the hallways of the western part of the castle, searching for either Mathieu or Prince Agis.

After looking for a short time, Mathieu finally found Prince Agis. Mathieu walked up to him for the second time, without Prince Agis being aware that he was in the room. This time, Prince Agis was standing in the Grand Ballroom, staring at a painting on the wall. It was the painting of Prince Agis with his parents and his brother Charles, when they were all much younger. Prince Agis was studying the painting for some unknown reason. Mathieu figured that perhaps Prince Agis was finally feeling some remorse for what he had done. This thought was shattered, though, as Prince Agis took his sword and swung it as hard as he could into the painting, severing it right down the middle. "I guess you don't have any love for your family," Mathieu said from behind him. Prince Agis turned around, surprised to see Mathieu still alive and in the same room as him. He was furious at the interruption and let Mathieu know it.

"You should have stayed away from me, if you wanted to live," Prince Agis told him. "I am not going to make the same mistake twice. This time I will make sure you are dead." Prince Agis then charged towards him, prepared to continue the fight. Although he had been injured and was in pain, Mathieu didn't feel it anymore as he clashed swords with Prince Agis. The Grand Ballroom had been cleared of all chairs, leaving only the wooden dance floor for them to stand on. There was no place to run and no place to hide. One of the two would win this fight, and one would lose. Prince Agis attacked with all of his power, swinging his sword in every direction. Mathieu fell back into a defensive mode, blocking the shots the best he could. As Prince Agis was having trouble breaking through his defenses, he tried to think of another way to fool Mathieu. He couldn't come up with anything, being that the Grand Ballroom was nearly empty. Soon, the momentum changed and Prince Agis was the one who was backing up. Mathieu unleashed a fury of sword blows. Prince Agis was having trouble holding him off, barely being able to hold onto his sword as he blocked blow after blow. Just then, King Charles, Delia, and Stefan came into the Grand Ballroom, immediately seeing the fight. Mathieu heard their voices, but would not allow himself to be distracted, which would have given Prince Agis the advantage.

Delia was calling to him, pleading, "Please don't kill him, Mathieu. I love him." Mathieu didn't want to kill him, but he also didn't want to be fooled once again. In the throne room, showing Prince Agis mercy had almost resulted in Mathieu's death. The two continued fighting, as Prince Agis backed up all the way to the stairs leading up to the stage in the Grand Ballroom. He slowly backed up the stairs, still warding off sword blows from Mathieu. Then, suddenly, Prince Agis tripped once again, as he did earlier in the throne room. When he had first arrived in the Grand Ballroom, Prince Agis sat down for a few minutes on the stairway, setting the golden crown next to him. As he tripped, Prince Agis looked down in horror to see that it was the golden crown he had tripped over. With one swift motion, Prince Agis dropped his sword and gravity caused him to fall forward, towards Mathieu. Before Mathieu even knew what happened, Prince Agis' body was pierced by Mathieu's outstretched sword. The weight of Prince Agis caused them both to fall onto the ground below. Prince Agis was on top of Mathieu, but lying motionless. Mathieu pushed him away and stood up, backing away from the scene. King Charles and Delia rushed forward and knelt down by Prince Agis. They could see it in his eyes, but to be sure, King Charles felt his neck. There was no pulse. Realizing what had happened, the king looked at Delia and shook his head.

"I'm sorry, but he's dead," the king said to her.

"No! My Chadwick, my husband," Delia said back, as she started crying. She placed her head down on his heart and rested there, letting the tears flow out. Mathieu left Delia and King Charles, knowing there was nothing he could do to change what transpired. He moved to the other end of the Grand Ballroom, where Stefan was standing. Stefan could not believe he had witnessed the death of Prince Agis. Although he knew that Prince Agis was an evil person, Stefan took no joy in watching him die. He realized that Mathieu didn't mean to kill Prince Agis, but his death resulted from tripping over the golden crown. In some ways, it was a fitting end to the unlawful reign of Prince Agis. It was just too bad that it had to be this way. Mathieu came back to where Stefan was and asked him to watch over King Charles and Delia.

"Despite this fierce battle I have been in, I have more to do. I need to go check on the six royal guards who were sent to the castle keep, to see if they need any help. I will be back here as soon as I can." Mathieu took one more look back at Delia, feeling sympathy for her, before leaving the Grand Ballroom and heading for the castle keep.

Sebastian had trailed King Charles and Delia all the way through the tunnels, following behind them in the darkness. When they went out of the opening in the wall and into the clothing and laundering room, Sebastian waited behind. He listened to them talking to Stefan in the room. When all three were gone, he climbed out of the opening and continued following from a safe distance. When they eventually walked into the Grand Ballroom, Sebastian slowly crept up to the door and looked inside. The first thing he saw was Prince Agis trip over the golden crown and fall onto Mathieu's sword. Somehow, Sebastian resisted the urge to scream out. He backed away from the entrance and moved over by the wall to sit down in the shadows. It was a good thing he did, because a few minutes later Mathieu walked out of the room. Mathieu didn't notice Sebastian sitting there, as he seemed to be focused on going somewhere else. Sebastian could see that Mathieu was now walking in obvious pain, with part of his clothing soaked in blood. He was carrying his sword, which he must have removed from Prince Agis' body after the accidental death. When Mathieu had been gone for a few minutes, Sebastian stood up from where he was sitting and walked boldly into the Grand Ballroom.

Stefan walked over to look at the painting which was destroyed before the fight. He heard Sebastian call out to him as he walked into the Grand Ballroom. Stefan turned to face him, feeling afraid because Sebastian looked like he was angry. King Charles and Delia looked up from the other side of the room, watching to see what would happen. Stefan took out his antique sword, not wanting to use it against Sebastian, but realizing he may have to defend himself. Sebastian was unarmed and soon spoke up, revealing his intentions. "Stefan, my brother," Sebastian called out, "I am not here to hurt you. I know Prince Agis is dead. Many other terrible things have already happened on this day. I only want to talk to you before I leave Astoria." Sebastian didn't get a chance to finish what he was saying, because General Robbins entered the Grand Ballroom through the side door. Robbins looked around, surveying what had transpired. He could see King Charles and Delia over by the fallen Prince Agis, who was clearly dead.

"What happened here tonight?" Robbins asked Sebastian. Sebastian stopped walking towards Stefan and turned his head, looking at Robbins. Sebastian decided to give him a suggestion.

"Robbins, put down your sword and turn yourself in," Sebastian said. "The rebels have lost today, Prince Agis has been defeated, and you are going to prison."

"You talk as if you are on their side," Robbins replied, with disbelief in his voice. "You are my son. You are with me. Come, let us take King Charles into custody." Hearing this answer made Sebastian very resentful. It had been Robbins who had taken his life away from him, by kidnapping him when he was but a mere one-year-old child. Robbins forced him to be raised as a rebel, taking him away from the loving home which would have been provided by his real family.

"Don't you ever call me your son again!" Sebastian screamed across the room at him. "You destroyed my life and the lives of many others. When Prince Agis threw me into prison, because my brother here helped the king and queen escape, you did not care at all. But my brother cared and my real parents cared. They wanted to come and see me."

"You needed to pay the price for your own stupid mistake, my son. That is all in the past. Let us leave it there. I don't care if you help me or not, but I am going to take King Charles back into custody." Robbins turned and started walking across the wooden floor towards King Charles, with his sword out. King Charles saw the sword of Prince Agis lying nearby, but decided not to pick it up. He felt that more fighting would only result in more death.

Sebastian turned to Stefan and said, "Give me your sword. I have to stop him." Stefan didn't hesitate, giving his antique sword over to Sebastian. Now holding the sword, Sebastian charged across the room, wanting to attack Robbins from behind. Robbins could hear him coming, so he turned around to face off against his adopted son. The two began sword fighting, as the king and Delia backed away from the area.

Sebastian was younger and stronger than Robbins. Yet, his advantage was offset by the fact that he was using a much weaker sword. Sebastian swung the antique sword hard, but it almost bounced back at him when it hit the sword of Robbins. Robbins realized that he had the upper hand in the fight and began using the power of his sword to push Sebastian back. Sebastian was forced to go into defensive mode. He backed around in a circle, soon standing near the body of Prince Agis. "Because of your stupidity, my son, you are going to end up just like him," Robbins told Sebastian. Sebastian spotted the sword of Prince Agis lying nearby and realized he needed to get it. In a surprise move, Sebastian threw the antique sword he was holding right at Robbins, almost using it like a lance. Robbins warded off the incoming projectile with his own sword, causing the antique sword to fall to the ground. But in that short time, Sebastian moved over and picked up the sword of Prince Agis. Sebastian charged Robbins, energized by having a more useful weapon. This time, it was Robbins who went on the defensive, being driven back. Stefan was watching the fight, wishing there was something he could do to help his brother. He came halfway across the ballroom, but stayed a safe distance away. As their swords continued clashing, Robbins was driven back, down onto his knees. He still was fighting off Sebastian's blows, but knew he couldn't win this fight. The victory was sealed when Sebastian knocked away the sword of Robbins, out of his hands. Sebastian didn't stop with that, as he drove his sword into the upper leg of Robbins, not wanting to kill him, but wanting to make it clear that the fight was over. Robbins screamed in pain, as the sword went into his leg and then was pulled back out. He rolled over on his side, holding the wounded area with both hands. Sebastian picked up the other two swords on the ground and walked back over to where Stefan was standing.

"It is finally over, my brother," Sebastian told him. "The last rebel has been defeated." At the other end of the room, Mathieu and four of the six royal guards walked into the Grand Ballroom. Stefan and Sebastian looked over as they came in. Mathieu started to ask what had occurred, but then saw Robbins start to sit up near the bottom of the stage. As Stefan and Sebastian were looking at Mathieu, he pointed behind them, saying with urgency, "Look out, he has a dagger!" Stefan and Sebastian turned around and saw Robbins holding a dagger in his hand, which was stretched out behind his back. He was ready to throw it.

"Your brother caused all of this to happen, Sebastian. And now I am going to make him pay for what he has done to all of us!" The moment he finished speaking these words, Robbins hurled the dagger through the air, with all of the strength he had left in his body. Time seemed to slow down as the dagger left his hand and began flying through the air, directly at Stefan. Sebastian did not have time to think, he only had time to react. Using his instincts, Sebastian dropped the swords and jumped to his side, intending to come between Stefan and the flying dagger. That is exactly what happened. The moment Sebastian moved in front of Stefan, with his feet still off the ground, the dagger struck him, digging deep into his chest. Sebastian fell to the ground in front of Stefan, with pain cascading through every part of his body. Several royal guards rushed past Stefan and Sebastian, taking

Robbins into custody. But the damage was done, Sebastian was dying. As he was lying there on the ground, Stefan looked down at him, tears streaming from his face.

"Don't die on me, Sebastian. Please don't die," Stefan pleaded. With life fading from Sebastian's body quickly, he looked up at his brother.

"Please, brother, don't cry for me," Sebastian said. "I want you to know that I love you. Will you do something for me?"

"Anything, brother," Stefan said through his tears.

"Will you please tell our mother and father that I did not mean the things I said to them today? I love them and wish I could have spent more time with them. At least I was able to save your life tonight. Please remember me." Sebastian could barely get the last few words out of his mouth as his head slumped back to the ground. Much as Delia had done earlier, Stefan rested his head on Sebastian's lifeless body, absolutely devastated to lose him.

Chapter Twenty:

A Hero's Welcome

One week later the land was returning to normal. All of the remaining rebels had been placed in prison, and the last remnants of their presence had been removed from the castle. It was a time of great happiness for Princess Stasia and her family, while it was a time of grief for Stefan and his family. A few days ago, Martin and Shaylene buried their youngest son Lolek, who was also known as Sebastian. Stefan was thinking back on that day as he was waking up, still lying in his bed. Sebastian had sacrificed his own life so Stefan could continue living. When Robbins hurled that dagger towards Stefan, Sebastian reacted instantly, without any hesitation. Stefan moved his hand up to his neck and felt the two necklaces which were now around his neck. Each of them held a brasta wood pendant. After Sebastian died, Stefan removed Sebastian's necklace and intended to wear it around his own neck for the rest of his life. Wearing both necklaces together would serve as a constant reminder to Stefan of his brother's love and great sacrifice on that night. After thinking for some time, Stefan finally found enough willpower to get out of bed. He heard his mother call him and went into the front room to have breakfast with his parents.

"Good morning, Stefan," his father Martin said to him. "You must be excited about your special day today." Shaylene walked into the room with two plates of food, greeting Stefan as she set them down. She went back into the kitchen to pick up her own plate, and they all sat down at the table to eat.

"Yes, father, I am really excited about today," Stefan finally responded. "But I only wish Sebastian was here to share it with me."

"We all wish that could be true," Shaylene said, as everyone began eating. Early this afternoon, there was to be a special event at the royal castle. Stefan was going to be rewarded for how he had helped the royal family. As the princess returned to power, one thing was very clear to everyone who knew what happened. It was the courage and loyalty of Stefan which opened the way for the rebels to be overthrown and for Princess Stasia to take back her rightful place at the castle. Without the things he had done, Prince Agis would still be the leader, and the princess, the king, and the queen would all probably be locked up in prison. Stefan didn't really know what to expect from the special event, but he would try his best to focus on the positive things, like being in the presence of the princess. He didn't want his grief to ruin the day or the happiness of others.

Across the village of Norwalk, Lady Ruth and Yvonne were busy in the kitchen, cooking together. Usually Lady Ruth let her servants do all of the work, but this morning she wanted to teach Yvonne how to make a special soup that her own mother had taught her. "Okay, now let's add a touch of salt to the pot and that should do it," Lady Ruth said. Yvonne added a little salt and Lady Ruth stood there, stirring the mixture together. "We will have the servants watch this while we go to the castle, a few hours from now. It should be ready to eat tonight for dinner."

"I am glad you are coming with me today, Lady Ruth," Yvonne said.

"I wouldn't miss this for the world. It makes me so proud to know that you and Stefan helped the princess. And now she wants to honor you both."

"It will mean a lot to me, but it would mean even more if Stefan cared about me. Lady Ruth, I can't go on like this anymore, loving him but not having my love returned. It's killing me inside." Lady Ruth walked over and put her right arm on Yvonne's shoulder, trying to comfort her. It hurt Lady Ruth to see Yvonne feeling downcast, when today was supposed to be a special day for her. As the two were standing in the kitchen, there was a knock at the front door. The servants didn't answer it, as they must have been either out back or upstairs working. Soon, there was another knock.

"I will get it, Lady Ruth. You stay with the soup," Yvonne said, walking through the house to the front door. Yvonne opened the door and saw two people, a man and a woman, standing on the porch. "Good morning, folks," Yvonne greeted them. "What can I do for you today?" The man and woman looked at Yvonne without saying anything and then looked at each other. Suddenly, the woman started wiping away tears from her eyes and reached out to hug Yvonne. Yvonne stepped forward, allowing the woman to wrap her arms around her. It was then that it hit her. Yvonne realized who the man and woman were and it caused her to start crying. Standing on Lady Ruth's front porch were Yvonne's birth mother and father. Yvonne had not seen them in ten years. After searching for them at Princess Stasia's feast for the poor, Yvonne had finally given up on the thought that she would ever see them again. But here they were, still alive and back in Yvonne's life. Yvonne couldn't say anything, she just stood there in her mother's arms, both of them now crying. Yvonne's father walked over and put his arms around both of them. Lady Ruth soon walked through the house to see what was going on. When Lady Ruth saw the three of them together, she wasn't sure what to make of it.

"Yvonne, is everything okay?" Lady Ruth asked. Yvonne turned back and looked at Lady Ruth, her eyes red from the tears.

"Lady Ruth, my mother and father have come back for me," was all that Yvonne could manage to say. A few minutes later, Lady Ruth finally convinced all three of them to come inside the house and sit down in the front room, with Yvonne sitting in between her mother and father, who were named Pierre and Ashmina.

"Forgive me for asking, but where have you two been these past ten years?" Lady Ruth wanted to know.

"We have been living on one of the border villages, working day and night, almost like slaves," Pierre said.

"We had no choice," Ashmina added. "Many years ago, right before I dropped Yvonne off on your doorstep, the rebels took away from us all of our money and valuable property. Because of this, we were unable to pay the debts we owed to others and our small mud flat home was taken away from us. We were forced to do ten years of hard labor as compensation."

"That is so terrible, mother and father," Yvonne said.

After allowing their words to sink in, Lady Ruth further asked them, "Why were you targeted by the rebels?"

"It was because we refused to pay their unlawful tax," Pierre answered. "Back then, all of the poor people in Norwalk were required to pay two silver coins per month to the Order of Rebels. We needed the money for food, so we refused for several months in a row. One night, we paid the price for our refusal. Three rebel soldiers showed up at our home and ransacked it, taking all the money they found, along with anything that was valuable."

"How I have wished for many years that we had paid their tax," Ashmina said. "Maybe then things would have turned out differently."

"To be honest," Pierre added, "we have been in town for the past week, struggling to find the courage to come here. We participated in the revolution and the march on the castle which took place. After the princess reclaimed the castle, we stopped here in Norwalk for the first time since we left ten years ago. Because of our mistakes, we didn't feel that we had the right to be a part of Yvonne's life again."

"It's true," Ashmina said. "But we finally realized that we couldn't leave without at least seeing our daughter one last time."

Yvonne was still crying as she listened to her parents' explanation of things. She finally told her parents, "That's my decision to make, and I want you both to be part of my life."

Lady Ruth, Yvonne, and Yvonne's parents continued talking for a while. Before they knew it, several hours went by and it was nearly time for Yvonne to leave for the castle. She asked her parents to stay for the special ceremony and they agreed, planning to ride over to the castle with Lady Ruth. They were so proud of Yvonne, once they learned of her involvement in helping Princess Stasia reclaim the throne. Yvonne's parents also invited Yvonne to move back with them to the border village where they were living, if she wanted to. Lady Ruth wasn't thrilled about the idea, but realized it was Yvonne's decision to make, so she didn't want to interfere. Yvonne promised them that she would think about it and let them know later in the day. When

Yvonne was ready she went outside to wait for Stefan. It was only a few minutes before he rode up on his horse. They were going to ride to the castle together, like old times, meeting up with their parents later. "Hello, Yvonne. Are you ready for our special day?" Stefan asked.

"I sure am!" Yvonne answered, as she walked her horse outside of the gate and climbed up on it. "Let's go. This is going to be so much fun." The two rode their horses out of Norwalk, in the direction of the royal castle. When they were getting close to the castle grounds, they slowed down to have a brief conversation. "Stefan, I have to tell you what happened this morning. My birth parents unexpectedly showed up at my front door."

"Are you serious, Yvonne?" Stefan asked. "That is amazing. I know you have been hoping for that moment for years. And what a day for it to happen on."

"No kidding, it is a great coincidence. I am delighted that they are coming to our special event today." Yvonne thought for a few moments and then she added something she wanted Stefan to know. "Stefan, my parents have invited me to move back with them to the border village where they have been living for the past ten years."

"Well, you're not thinking of going, are you? I couldn't imagine what life would be like without you in Norwalk."

"Actually, I think I am going to accept their offer," Yvonne said. "I would like to spend some time with them and I am ready for a change."

"You are ready for a change?" Stefan asked in disbelief. "That doesn't sound like the Yvonne I know. Please don't leave Norwalk, Yvonne. Is there anything I can say to you to change your mind?"

"Oh, Stefan, if there was you would have already figured it out by now," Yvonne answered. Stefan thought about her words as the two crossed the drawbridge, entering the castle grounds at the main gate. They put their horses away in the peasant stables and walked together to the western castle entrance. This afternoon's ceremony was going to be held in the throne room, which was much smaller than the Grand Ballroom, but even more meaningful and special of a place. As they walked up the stairs, Sir Rackley was waiting for them out front.

"Hello, Stefan and Yvonne," he greeted them. After they returned his greeting, Sir Rackley asked, "Stefan, might I have a word with you before you go inside?" Stefan agreed, and Yvonne looked at Sir Rackley with a twinkle in her eyes, smiling at him. Yvonne knew what Sir

Rackley was going to talk to Stefan about, which made her feel good inside. Yvonne continued walking into the entrance room of the castle, while Sir Rackley and Stefan headed back down the stairs to visit for a few minutes.

Putting his left arm across Stefan's shoulder as they walked across the great lawn, Sir Rackley said, "Stefan, I want you to know that I appreciate all you have done. In my whole life I have never met anybody as courageous as you. I'm sure you've heard that a lot lately and you certainly deserve it."

"Thank you, Sir Rackley," Stefan said. They continued walking for another minute, as Sir Rackley gathered his thoughts. Finally, they stopped walking and sat down on the lawn. Sir Rackley looked at Stefan with a serious expression on his face.

"Stefan, there are two things I actually wanted to talk to you about, before we go inside. I don't mean to burden you with thoughts, right before your special ceremony. But these are two things I feel it is important for you to know about."

"Sure, Sir Rackley. Please, tell me what is on your mind."

"I guess the first thing I should start with involves a conversation Yvonne and I had a few weeks ago, right after our archery contest. As you know, I defeated her in a very close match. Afterward, Yvonne and I sat down and talked about something dear to her heart. Or, I should say, *somebody* dear to her heart. That person is you, Stefan." Sir Rackley paused, waiting to see what Stefan's response would be.

"Yvonne is dear to my heart as well. She is my best friend," Stefan said.

"Stefan, you're not getting the point," Sir Rackley continued. "She likes you more than just as a friend. She is in love with you and has been for quite some time. She told me that she has been dropping you hints, trying to let you know. But you never seem to catch on to what she is actually saying. Think back on your time with her during the past year, does anything come back to your mind?" Stefan looked down, closing his eyes to reflect back. This was the last thing he ever expected Sir Rackley to want to talk to him about. But, Sir Rackley was right, many things regarding Yvonne's behavior of late showed evidence of romantic feelings. And not only her behavior, even the things that she had been saying to Stefan. Now Stefan realized why she was so willing to leave Norwalk and move to another part of Astoria. Her bottled up feelings were probably causing her a lot of grief. Finally, Stefan looked up at Sir Rackley and spoke.

He said, "I can see now that you are right. I guess I was too wrapped up in my feelings and interest for Princess Stasia, which blinded me to Yvonne's feelings."

Sir Rackley nodded his head and continued, "You and Yvonne really need to have a heart to heart talk. She seems to be really hurting inside. I can still remember one sentence that she said to me, word for word. She said: 'If he would just give me the chance, I could make him the happiest boy in Astoria.' That girl loves you, Stefan."

"Thank you for telling me about this, Sir Rackley. I have a lot of thinking to do. You said there was a second thing you wanted to talk to me about?"

"Yes, Stefan, there is," Sir Rackley said. He gathered his thoughts, because telling Stefan what he wanted to say next was a hard thing to do. "The second matter has to do with Princess Stasia. I think that the truth is, you and I both feel the same way about her. We are both in love with her. As you know, the princess and I were engaged for many years, before the rebel overthrow took place. At that time, the princess called off our engagement due to the uncertainty of what would happen next in Astoria. When we went to my homeland to gather support for the assault on the castle, Princess Stasia and I had a chance to talk. She informed me of her new intention to marry you, to fulfill your one wish in life. Stefan, please know I am not here to try to change your mind about wanting to marry the princess. If she chooses you, it will hurt me to lose her, but I do feel you are well deserving of the honor of marrying her. As we continued talking, she confessed something to me which I feel you have the right to know about."

"What did she tell you?" Stefan wanted to know.

"She told me that of all the people she had met in her life, I would be the person she would choose to marry. Even so, she said she was willing to set her personal feelings aside and marry you, because you are a dear friend and are the main reason she had a chance to gain back the throne. That's it, Stefan. That is all I wanted to tell you." Sir Rackley finished speaking and stood up, offering his hand to Stefan. Stefan accepted it and was pulled up to a standing position, next to him. The two walked back together, with Stefan deep in thought. As they came close to the castle entrance once again, Stefan had one more thing to say.

"Thank you, Sir Rackley, for everything," he said. "I really appreciate you sharing these things with me."

Inside the throne room were all of the people who had played an important part in helping restore the princess to power. The new Chief Royal Knight, Mathieu, was standing up on the stage watching over everything. His assistant Reginald, who had been promoted from royal guard to royal knight, was standing next to him. Princess Stasia was sitting on her throne to the right of them, once again wearing the golden crown. On the other side of her was a tall perch, on which sat an Astorian eagle named J-Bird. J-Bird looked out at all of the people, enjoying the attention as he occasionally stretched his wings. Behind all of them, several castle musicians were playing a song called 'The Queen's Intermezzo'. Among the musicians was Nathaniel, who was playing his bronze flute. Below the stage, the king and queen were visiting with Lord Reed, the village statesman of Carson Lake, thanking him for his support. Delia was talking with Anton, the bird expert. She said, "I still am amazed at hearing how J-Bird took out that rebel soldier who was in the guard tower."

"I knew he could do it," Anton bragged. "I only feared for his safety, with arrows flying through the sky everywhere." Anton paused briefly, then expressed his condolences. "Delia, I am sorry to hear about your husband Chadwick."

"Thank you, Anton," she replied. "Although Chadwick and I had been distant for quite some time, I still felt love for him. It really hurt a great deal to lose him. I suppose, if he had survived, that the pain I would have felt long term would have even been greater. The only future Chadwick had before him was a lifetime prison sentence or exile out of Astoria."

"That is very true. You know, it is probably bad timing, but I wanted to extend an invitation to you," Anton added. "I understand if you're not up for it right now, so feel free to tell me if you think it is too much. I wanted to invite you to come with me next week to the mountains of Sorensen, just beyond the village of the same name.

There is a lake up there where an Astorian eagle pair has been nesting. According to my field researchers, one of the eggs is supposed to hatch next week. Just imagine, we might be able to witness the birth of a new eaglet. And I would love to spend some time with you, to get to know you better." Delia's face beamed as she heard Anton's final sentence. She had been through a lot, but wanted to go with him.

"I would be happy to accept your invitation," she told him. "Some time away might do me good, to help me clear my mind. But promise you'll keep me company up there."

"Don't worry, you will have a great time," Anton promised.

The rest of the throne room was filled with other important people and visitors. A few minutes before the ceremony was going to begin, Lady Ruth came in with Pierre and Ashmina, Yvonne's parents. Martin and Shaylene were right behind them. Alana and Madison, two of Princess Stasia's closest friends growing up, also walked in. Soon, everybody took their seats and the music stopped playing. As the room quieted down, the princess stood up and started speaking to everybody. "Thank you all for coming here to the royal castle this afternoon," she began. "Only a week has gone by, yet our wounds are already beginning to heal from the treachery of Prince Agis and the rebels. My thanks goes out to all of you here today, for without you, Prince Agis' rule may have lasted a lifetime. While I deeply appreciate the role all of you had in bringing me back to power, I thought today that we would especially honor two of Astoria's finest citizens, my dear friends Stefan and Yvonne. Please, won't you both join me up here on the stage?" Stefan and Yvonne stood up, walked onto the stage, and turned around, one standing on each side of the princess. As they did this, everyone in the room applauded. Stefan and Yvonne were both embarrassed over being given so much attention. Yvonne's face started to turn red, as she was blushing. The princess then invited Sir Rackley up to the stage. He was carrying something with him, but Stefan and Yvonne couldn't see what it was, because it was covered with a red cloth. Sir Rackley walked up on the stage and turned around to look at everybody, holding the mysterious object.

The princess continued, "It is my pleasure to now reward you both for how you have helped us. To start with, Sir Rackley has a surprise for both of you to share, which has been generously donated by the village of Carson Lake. Sir Rackley, if you will do the honors, please." Hearing his cue, Sir Rackley lifted up the red cloth, revealing a golden plate. The crowd looking on gasped in awe when they saw what was sitting on the plate. Sparkling colors filled the room as light reflected off a mound of Carson Lake diamonds. Stefan and Yvonne's eyes opened as wide as they could possibly get at seeing the treasure. They looked at each other and smiled, knowing what this meant. The pile of Carson Lake diamonds which was being given to them was enough to make them both rich. The best thing about this was that both Stefan's parents and Yvonne's birth parents could now be lifted out of poverty. Stefan and Yvonne both immediately started thinking about how they could use their newfound wealth to help others. The princess continued speaking, saying, "Stefan and Yvonne, you will never have to struggle to make ends meet again, because these diamonds are worth a fortune. Let us all thank the village of Carson Lake for providing such a wonderful reward." Everyone in the throne room applauded loudly, appreciating what the citizens of Carson Lake had done. Lord Reed, the statesman of Carson Lake, was smiling, proud of his village for giving such a generous donation. When the applause finished, Sir Rackley backed up and stood next to Mathieu, setting the golden plate of diamonds on a small table.

The princess then said, "Stefan and Yvonne, there is more. As the second part of your reward, I have good news for both of you. Mathieu, would you please bring forward their invitations?" Mathieu stepped forward, holding two folded pieces of paper in his hands. He handed the papers to Princess Stasia and went back to stand next to Sir Rackley. Unfolding the pieces of paper, Princess Stasia read the first one out loud. "This invitation is addressed to Yvonne. It reads: 'Yvonne of Norwalk, you are hereby invited to move into the royal castle of Astoria. If you accept, you will receive a large, private room which you may live in for as long as you wish. Further, you are invited to serve the princess as a royal archer. After being trained, you will be assigned to the prestigious post of one of the royal castle lookout towers. Sincerely, the royal family.' Here you go, Yvonne." The princess reached out and handed the invitation to Yvonne, who accepted it and thanked the princess. Princess Stasia asked her to say a few words to those who were assembled. Yvonne looked out at the audience. She could see her birth parents sitting next to Lady Ruth. It brought her great joy to see them together, not rivals for her affection, but sharers of it.

"My dear friends and family," Yvonne said. "It gives me great pleasure to accept this invitation from the princess. Thank all of you for the kindness you have shown towards me today. Many of you don't know this, but this morning I was reunited with my birth parents for the first time in ten years." Speaking in their direction, Yvonne told them, "I love you both." Then, looking at Lady Ruth, who was sitting next to them, she added, "And Lady Ruth, you have been a wonderful mother to me during these past ten years. By taking me in, you saved my life when I was but a little girl. I hope that I have grown up to make you proud and that I will continue to do so, as I serve the princess here at the castle as one of her royal archers." Next, Yvonne turned to Stefan and said, "And to my best friend Stefan, I guess you should know that I won't be leaving today, as I was considering earlier. There is no way I could turn down this offer from the princess. I want you to know, Stefan, one more thing. Being a part of your life has been the best thing that ever happened to me. I love you and would do anything to prove that to you." That was all she could say. After that, Yvonne looked down as everyone in the room applauded.

"Stefan, I also have an invitation for you," the princess continued. "Let me open it up and read it to you. It states: 'Stefan of Norwalk, you are hereby invited to move into the royal castle of Astoria. If you accept, you will receive a large, private room which you may live in for as long as you wish. Further, you are invited to serve the princess as her representative to the people. This is a new position which will require you to meet with citizens from Astoria who come to visit the royal castle. When the princess is unable or unavailable to see visitors, it will be your assignment to represent her and speak in her behalf. Sincerely, the royal family.' This is for you, Stefan." Princess Stasia handed the invitation to Stefan, who gladly accepted it from her. However, the princess did not ask Stefan to speak, as she had asked Yvonne to speak. She moved over right next to Stefan and continued talking. "All of you here today know of the courage and love that Stefan has showed in my behalf during this ordeal. Along with Yvonne's help, Stefan rescued me from the royal castle on the night of the rebel takeover. He saved me by making me jump into the moat which surrounds our castle. We swam to the other side just in time, escaping from both the crocodiles and the rebels. Then, he used his wisdom to help my father, my mother, and Mathieu escape from the castle prison. Finally, along with Yvonne's help once again, Stefan went out to all of the poor people in the land and gathered up support for the revolution. With these things in mind, I would like to now grant the one wish Stefan has always had. I promised him that I would give him anything his heart desired in return for his help. Of all of the things he could have chosen, there is only one thing he wished to have." Stefan's heart started racing when he heard this. He realized that in front of everyone, the princess was going to ask for his hand, offering to be his wife. She was willing to marry and love him like no one else could. And, indeed, this was the one thing Stefan always dreamed of having. During the past five years, the princess was all that he had thought about. He thought about her while he was working, spoke about her to others, and dreamed about her while he was sleeping.

The princess turned to look him in the eyes and pulled a small golden ring out of her pocket. Stefan was right, the princess was about to ask him to marry her, in front of all the people who mattered to her. Once she asked him, there would be no going back. He would not be able to turn down her proposal once she spoke in front of all the people. Stefan looked at the princess, and then looked over at Yvonne. Yvonne's eyes were tearing up, probably because she realized what was happening. Stefan thought back to his brief conversation with Sir Rackley. Stefan could feel a battle waging in his heart, knowing he needed to make a decision fast. He had to choose between Princess Stasia and Yvonne. Would he choose the princess, who was the girl of his dreams, or Yvonne, who was the one who truly loved him? The princess began speaking again. "Stefan, I have one question I would like to ask you now, in front of all these witnesses today." Stefan could not wait any longer. He cut the princess short, before she could ask the question.

"My dearest princess," Stefan said to her, "before you ask that question, I have a few things I would like to say. First, I will be happy to accept your offer to be your personal representative to the people. It would give me great pleasure to serve you in that capacity. Second, I would like Sir Rackley to come over here for a moment." Sir Rackley was caught by surprise as he heard Stefan's request, but he walked over to stand next to Stefan and Princess Stasia. Stefan continued, saying, "It is clear to me that the two of you are in love with each other. If you are both willing, I would like to see you get engaged once again and be married, at the soonest time possible. It will be a great blessing to the people of both lands, and I know it will bring you both much happiness." Stefan finished speaking and looked at them both, to see what their reaction would be. In a rare showing of public emotion, the princess started crying and wrapped her arms around Sir Rackley. They held each other for several minutes, while those in the audience applauded their approval.

When she regained control of her emotions, the princess looked over at Stefan and whispered the words "thank you" to him. She then looked out at the audience and spoke to everybody, as she held hands with Sir Rackley. "My dear people, Stefan is right. I am in love with Sir Rackley and wish to spend my life with him, as his wife." The people applauded yet again, as many in the audience developed tears along with the princess. None in the audience, except for Yvonne, figured out that the princess was originally going to ask Stefan to marry her. Those who spotted the golden ring assumed she was going to ask Stefan to be the best man at her wedding with Sir Rackley.

Stefan had something else to say, as he was not yet finished. He asked the princess if he could say more and she approved. "Our wonderful princess told you all that I have a wish. Indeed, there is one wish that I have, which is clearer in my mind today than it has ever been before." Walking over to where Yvonne was standing, Stefan looked deep into her eyes. She stared back at him. As Stefan dropped down to one of his knees, he maintained eye contact with Yvonne. The expression on her face gradually changed to a smile, as she realized what he was about to do. Stefan spoke to her, saying, "Yvonne, my most dear friend. I do have one wish, and I hope you will grant it to me today. I am in love with you." Using a twist on the words Sir Rackley told him earlier, Stefan next said, "It is my desire to make you the happiest girl in Astoria. Earlier you said that you wanted to prove your love to me. That is not necessary, for your love has already been proven time and again. However, I would like to prove my love for you, once and for all time. Yvonne, will you marry me?" When Stefan asked her that question, Yvonne's face lit up with the largest smile she had ever displayed. Like everyone else, she was crying. Through her tears, she managed to say, "Yes, Stefan, I will marry you." Stefan stood up and they embraced for a few minutes, while applause in the audience erupted once again. Finally, both couples moved over to stand next to each other, in front of the throne. Yvonne and Stefan were standing together, holding hands. And Princess Stasia and Sir Rackley were standing together, holding hands. For all four people involved, it proved to be the best moment of their lives. That was how the ceremony ended, after which, everybody started conversing with each other.

Sir Rackley soon walked up to Stefan, saying, "Thank you for what you did today."

"No, thank you," Stefan said. "You opened up my eyes to something I should have seen and realized a long time ago. I wish you and the princess a lifetime of happiness together. I am really happy that I get to continue working here at the castle, to support you both."

The princess walked over and added, "You are one of a kind, Stefan. Thank you for allowing me to have some of my own happiness."

Everyone congratulated the two newly engaged couples. Surrounding the princess and Sir Rackley were King Charles, Queen Delphine, Mathieu, Reginald, Delia, Anton, Alana, Madison, and many other well wishers. With Stefan and Yvonne were Martin, Shaylene, Lady Ruth, Pierre, Ashmina, and others who knew them. As their lives were forever intertwined, arrangements were made to hold a double wedding, with both couples getting married on the same day, exactly one week from now. The wedding ceremony would be held in the

Grand Ballroom, with the reception on the Castle Terrace and festivities throughout all the castle grounds.

Later that day, the two new couples took some time to be alone. Princess Stasia and Sir Rackley went by horseback to the waterfall near the royal castle. They rode together on Princess Stasia's white horse Isobel. When they arrived at the waterfall, they tied up Isobel and walked together towards the falls. Water was cascading down, spraying mist everywhere. "This is such a beautiful place, my dear," the princess said to Sir Rackley.

"That may be true," Sir Rackley said, "but it's not as beautiful as you." The princess smiled at him, appreciating the compliment. Mist began soaking their hair and clothes, but they didn't mind. Sir Rackley wrapped his arms around the shoulders of the princess, while the princess wrapped her arms around Sir Rackley's waist. They then shared a kiss lasting for several minutes. Or it could have been longer, because time stood still for the two people in love.

Stefan and Yvonne went back to Norwalk, after asking Mathieu to keep their reward of Carson Lake diamonds locked up safe at the castle. On the ride back, they talked about their wedding, which was only one week away. Instead of both receiving a large room to live in at the royal castle, now they would only need one. They couldn't wait to start their new life together. Right now they were on their way to Norwalk Lake, to go swimming for old times' sake. Stefan had taken a rose from the ceremony at the royal castle and brought it with him. He asked Yvonne if they could make one stop along the way. She agreed, and found out that the stop was at the cemetery. After they tied up their horses, Stefan held Yvonne's hand, leading her up the small hill to the grave sites. They walked over to Sebastian's marker. Stefan took the rose out of his pocket and placed it there, still holding Yvonne's hand. He spoke to the marker, saying, "Sebastian, I wish you could have been here to share this moment with us. I will never forget you, for as long as I live. I love you, brother." Before he was swallowed up with sadness, Stefan turned to Yvonne and said, "Thank you, I needed to do this. Now let's go swimming." The two walked back down the hill and rode their horses out to the pristine water of Norwalk Lake.

Soon they were in the water, swimming and splashing each other. After a few minutes, Stefan and Yvonne came up close to one another. They swam together a short ways back to shore, where they could touch the ground with their feet. Then, they wrapped their arms around each other and kissed. The kiss lasted for a long time, as Stefan and Yvonne were in the same spot as the sun started going down. They didn't even notice how cold the water was, or how chilly the air was outside. They only noticed each other. With love in their hearts, happily ever after was what was in store. And so it ended as a tale of love, timelessly told.

About the Author

Steve Alfred Hall, Jr. was born in Greenbrae, California on November 2, 1974. He has spent most of his life residing in Marin and Sonoma counties, north of San Francisco. Steve has two brothers and two sisters– James, Lowell, Annie, and Tiffany. Through his school years, Steve developed a love for creative writing. Eventually, this translated into writing poetry, lyrics for songs, and journals. It was the compliments received for journals and travelogues which Steve wrote that ultimately pushed this book forward. Additionally, his good friend Anthony, who is also an excellent writer, encouraged Steve to finish the book despite the great sacrifice it would take. Steve's personal interests include visiting Death Valley, playing tennis, horseback riding, backpacking, playing guitar, songwriting, and traveling the world.

The story of the book "A Young Princess" dates back to March of 2002, when Steve began outlining the initial story through songwriting. Steve was a part of the locally known music group Wagon Band, who have produced five independent albums. At that time, he wrote a song called "One Majestic Night". During the next fifteen months he wrote two more songs, entitled "A Young Princess" and "Happily Ever After". When these were completed and released, a three song trilogy was formed, telling the story of a young peasant boy and a royal princess. In October of 2004, Steve began writing out chapter treatments for a book to expand the story to epic proportions. Three years later, the book was finally completed. Assisting with editing were Anthony Gordon and Barbara Nelson. In case you were wondering, Steve has two sequels in mind. The first covers the events in between chapters five and six, when the main characters move from being twelve years old to sixteen years old. There is a great story in that time frame, covering the lives of everyone over a four year period. That book would be entitled "Majestic Times", if it was ever written. The second covers the events after the end of chapter twenty, a true sequel. However, the writing of this book in your hands has been a long road which Steve might never travel again. No matter what, the journey to the end will never be forgotten.

About the Editor

This story was edited by Mr. Hall's friend and literary advisor, Anthony C. Gordon.

Anthony Gordon was born and raised in the town of Sonoma, California. His mother and both of his grandmothers inculcated in him a love of reading; and, not surprisingly, a love of writing quickly blossomed also. He began writing when he was only a boy, writing a story and then drawing an illustration to accompany it.

In Anthony's pre-teens and teens, his preferred literary medium was the novel. He didn't restrict himself to only one genre, but wrote fantasy, mystery and adventure. However, while he loved to begin a new novel, he always found it difficult to finish it before the next great idea came along. So, while his literary abilities and skill as a writer developed considerably through this period, he had little to show for it except for several unfinished novels.

In Anthony's mid-20's, however, he discovered quite by accident a medium completely new to him: short stories. Anthony quickly realized that the short story was his ideal medium. He now found himself having quite a few short stories to his credit, including his "Jack Pike" detective series, his two "Arctic Adventure" stories, his time-travel science fiction adventure, and others. Perhaps Anthony's finest work is his short story, "The Princess Who Never Laughed," a dramatic parody of the fairy tale with the same name, featuring an unnamed time traveler who interviews the melancholy princess.

In 2001, Anthony met Steve and became the keyboard player for his band, Wagon Band. This introduced Anthony to songwriting and poetry, allowing him to write "The Invisible Man", "Find Me", "Comedy Club", "Somehow, Wednesday", and others. Anthony continues to enjoy writing both poetry and short stories. Today Anthony lives in the town of Glen Ellen, California, and continues to pursue his love of writing.

After Steve asked Anthony to help him with the editing, he also asked him if Anthony wanted to be a character in the story. Humorously, Anthony replied that he wanted to be a legendary hero who dies tragically right after confessing his love for Princess Stasia.

A day or so later, Anthony decided to help Steve out with developing this character by writing a short story as though it were an excerpt from the book. However, this was before Anthony understood the development of the plot and the characters, so the person and situation Anthony wrote about was never used in the book. But Steve and Anthony both liked the short sub-story that Anthony wrote, and they thought it should be included at the end of the book for the entertainment of the reader.

So, please enjoy the exploits of . . . The Scarlet Saber!

The Scarlet Saber

A short story by Anthony Gordon based on the characters from "A Young Princess"

At last. They had won! Stefan and Stasia watched as the last of the rebel forces were driven off by King Charles' loyal soldiers and the peasants who banded together to fight at their side. King Charles and Queen Delphine stood behind them and shared a feeling of overwhelming relief and swelling gratitude to Stefan for all he had done for them. And then, suddenly, all appeared lost. A band of over twenty rebels appeared out of nowhere! They attacked with a frenzy, with an unparalleled desperation that marked the final, last-ditch effort. It was all or nothing now; there was no going back. These men did not have a battle plan, they did not have a retreat contingency. They flung themselves into battle as do men who do not expect to live. The rebels rushed in upon Stefan, and Stasia, and her parents. The corps of loyal peasants was mainly concentrated near the drawbridge or outside the castle battling the few remaining rebels who hadn't been able to escape. The king's soldiers were chasing and routing those who were running away. And there were only Stefan and Stasia and the aged king and queen against over twenty armed and desperate men. "No," the queen whispered, "Please, not my little girl."

"Back, you scoundrels!" a strange voice rang out. Suddenly, a dashing figure of a man leapt down in the path of the sweeping rebels, catching not only our four heroes but also the twenty rebels completely off guard. "Take thee back to the Hades which spawned you, knaves, and come no more into this haven of peace and justice!"

Stasia gasped. Stefan pointed. "Look! It's him! It's really him! The *Scarlet Saber*!"

"Yes, my friends, it is I, and you have no more to fear from these scalawags! Haha! En guard, wretch!" The Scarlet Saber lived up to his name, wearing a scarlet mask, a wide-brimmed black hat with a long, scarlet plume, and a flowing scarlet cape. His saber, also legendary, seemed to fly through the air almost independent of the hand which held it – blocking, feinting, thrusting, slashing, all so quickly and smoothly that it seemed as though the sword was dancing in air. The Scarlet Saber bounded from here to there; he would be in a spot for a moment, but when his enemy's sword came down, somehow he would seem to vanish, only to appear somewhere else. He moved with the speed and fluid grace of a jaguar, with the cunning of a serpent, with the strength of a bull, with the courage of a lion. He was nothing short of the legend told about the man: The Scarlet Saber.

Seven rebels fell wounded in stunningly quick succession. The others saw they were no match for this mythical-hero-turned-man. As the cowards they were, they turned tail and ran, not even looking back to see if their fallen comrades still lived. "Run, scoundrels!" The Scarlet Saber shouted after them. "Run as far as your cowardly legs will take you! But The Scarlet Saber will always remember your lawless deeds!"

"The Scarlet Saber," Stasia breathed his name with awe. At hearing his name, their savior turned. "We owe you our lives, my dear sir. As the new ruler of Astoria, I bestow upon you the thanks and gratitude of an entire nation and people. And as a very grateful princess, I promise you any reward you may name. Please, tell me how we may repay the courage and gallantry you have shown today."

"Would that I could have the one reward which can truly please and delight me, my fair princess," The Scarlet Saber breathed as a man does who comes close to that which he loves best. "How many times have I been this near you and been afraid to touch? How many times have I spoken words to you, and yet not those truly in my heart? There is one reward, and only one, which would make me a whole and happy man this day, Princess. Say unto me that your heart is mine and my heart is thine."

Princess Stasia stared at the man with a numbed shock that reached her very core. This man *knew* her? *The Scarlet Saber was someone she knew?* "Who are you?" she whispered. Slowly, deliberately, The Scarlet

332

Saber reached a gloved hand up to his head, lifted off his hat, and tossed it to the ground. Then his hand grasped the mask which had inspired hope, which had excited dread, which had begun a legend. He grasped the mask and lifted it . . . lifted it off his face. And to the ground.

And Stasia let out an audible gasp as her hands flew to her mouth and her eyes grew to great round circles. He was none other than . . . "Duke Anton of Gourdain?!" Reality and fantasy swirled around in Stasia's mind, colors and lines and motions for a moment blurred and merged into one, and she felt Stefan's reassuring hand on her shoulder; it wasn't until then that she realized how close she had come to falling down faint. She tried to speak, but she was somehow breathless and no sound would come out. "Duke Anton? Y . . you are the Scarlet Saber?"

"I am." He spoke gravely. "As a soldier, I showed extraordinary skill, but had no stomach for generals with no concern for their men and kings with no sympathy for their people. But I heard your cry of love for your people, great and small. I, too, felt the injustice of the peasantry, and I, too, wanted to come to their aid. When you chose to side with them, I chose to side with you; and every act you carried out, every step you took since then made me admire you more and more. And, finally, I knew admiration was not the end of the yearnings of my heart. I loved you. Yet, as brave as I am in combat, I am thrice the coward in love. I could not tell you. I longed, I yearned to be your love, to earn your love, to feel your love . . . but I could not tell you.

"Then you were kidnapped, and I threw myself into finding you, saving you. When I heard that you had been saved, I was full of contradictions: I was enormously relieved, because you were safe; and yet, I was enraged, because you had been saved by another. I swore then that I would not rest until I became your champion.

"I know that you are betrothed to another; and yet, as noble a man as he is, I also know you do not love him." He stood closely to her now, looking earnestly into her eyes and speaking out of a heart that was full to overflowing. "I present myself to you as a loving and devoted suitor. I lay my heart at your feet. I am yours, my Princess, to do with as you wish. Please, let my heart rest next to your heart, and my love will be yours for the rest of our days."

Princess Stasia looked up at the legend of the man who had just professed his love for her with a tear in her eyes. It was a tear of sympathy, for in her heart she knew she could not tell him what he wanted to hear. She wanted to look away, and yet she could not. To tell a man of his caliber something like this, she owed him no less than to look him in the eye. "My dear Anton . . ." she began slowly. "My dear friend. I . . . would like nothing more than to see you happy, with a woman who loves you with all the noble and beautiful heart and mind that a man like you deserves. But," she sniffed now, as a tear rolled down her cheek, "but I fear I can never be that woman. I am so terribly sorry, my dear Anton, but . . ." quickly, without even meaning to, her eyes stole a glance at Stefan, "but my heart belongs to another."

Anton drew back. It was a crushing blow to the noble man. He closed his eyes to block out the sudden onslaught of tears; he gritted his teeth and clenched his fists and did everything he could to keep the raging pain and mournful sorrow storming through his heart from spilling out. His hopes were dashed, his spirit was done for. He was a man who lived for one thing only . . . and that one thing was once and for all time gone out of the world. And he also wished he could go out of the world. Because the world no longer had anything for him. He yearned now only to be done with it all. He opened his eyes again and gazed at her, the object of his devotion. He knew that he would for all time give a love that would never be returned. It was the life that not even the lowliest of the most pitiful wretches deserved. And yet it was his lot. He needed to tell her . . . he needed to say . . . that he would forever . . .

He looked at her. He opened his mouth, a mouth suddenly dry and tongue-tied. "I . . . will . . . always . . . "Ahhhh!!!!" The Scarlet Saber cried out in agony as an arrow pierced the heart which only a moment ago contained only nobility and love. Behind him, one of the king's royal archers had spotted him and mistaken him for an enemy. He realized only too late the death-dealing mistake he had made. Duke Anton, The Scarlet Saber, fell to his knees. He looked dumbly down to the arrow shaft which now protruded from his chest, then back up to Stasia. His strength left him, and he fell backward, still staring up at

Princess Stasia, who gaped down at him with horror and despair. His eyes never left her as he whispered his three last words, "I. . . will. . . always. . ." His life fled from him, and Duke Anton of Gourdain, The Scarlet Saber, was no more. Stasia threw herself into Stefan's arms and wept bitterly. The princess had met many wonderful people in her short life. She could have asked for no finer parents. She had made loyal friends, met humble yet good-hearted peasants, courageous and true noblemen and . . . well, there was no lack of fine and good words to describe the young, lionhearted Stefan.

And yet, The Scarlet Saber . . . here was a man who could exist only in legend, with the wonderful qualities which, combined, could only be found in His Word. And now he was gone. And, in her heart of hearts, she knew that the cause of the destruction of this fine, noble man was nothing more than his selfless love for her. And that was the most terrible, most tragic thing that Stasia had ever heard in her life. She continued to weep on Stefan's sympathetic shoulder for some time.